The Last Heir

BY

Shannon McDermott

Cover design by Meghan McDermott

Published by SALT Christian Press
2131 W. Republic Rd. #177
Springfield, MO 65807

Dedication

To my brothers and sisters—Michael and his wife Stephanie, John, Meghan, William, Kathleen, Keenan, Heather, Bridget, Kelly, Josiah, and Isaac

Also to my parents, who gave me, among other priceless things, eleven siblings

Foreword

I hope you enjoy *The Last Heir* as much as I did. *The Last Heir* is very well written. The story is filled with suspense, intrigue, and unexpected twists and turns in the plot. And Shannon's characters are real people, who must also navigate courtship, marriage, and children issues while the fate of the Empire is being determined. *The Last Heir* is simply a great read. But what separates this book from most science fiction is that it reflects a Christian world view. I wouldn't characterize this as a wholly Christian story in the way *Pilgrim's Progress* is a Christian story. Rather, I would say *The Last Heir* is more in the spirit of C.S. Lewis' fiction. *The Last Heir* does have some "Christian" dialogue, but it is lightly sprinkled throughout the book. I think what will most excite Christians, however, is that difficult moral issues are being determined from a Christian point of view. And *The Last Heir* is missing explicit violence, sexual immorality, profanity, and support of issues, philosophies, and religious beliefs that are hostile to Christian sensibilities. Christians won't have to put blinders on and ignore the garbage in order to enjoy this great story.

I know that some of our brethren would find fault with fiction generally and science fiction particularly as unspiritual. I believe, however, that creative imagination is a gift of God and is only possible because we were created in the image of God. The fact that unbelievers dominate the creative arts and use them to promote all manner of wickedness doesn't make the creative arts inherently sinful. That would be akin to banning food because so many are guilty of gluttony, or banning tools because people use them to build murder weapons. No, the creative arts – music, books, movies, etc. – can be just as powerful a force for good as for evil. It just depends who is telling the story. I, for one, am glad that Shannon is telling this story. - **James McDermott**

Book I

Since the founding of the Empire

Year 688

CHAPTER

I

* * * * * * * * * * * * * * * *

TELNARIA, the City of the Emperors, was quiet, and it was dark. The lights set to illuminate the Palace, the monuments, all the city's great buildings—all such lights were dark this evening. The black-crepe cloth was hung throughout Telnaria and the people had darkened their houses. The standards were lowered over the city, and every fourth hour a doleful refrain sounded.

It was the second time in five years that Telnaria had clothed itself in mourning for the death of an emperor.

At the Royal Palace, a man stood on a narrow balcony, the Palace dark behind him. His hands rested on the parapet and he was gazing out. He could barely see as dusk faded into night, but his imagination carried him to the Great Plaza, which spread out before the Court of Justice. On the Court's terrace, before the crowded plaza, every new emperor had stood and taken the oaths of his office. Kinlol knew every step of the ceremony, the minutiae, the old, exalting words. He could guide his imagination through it.

But today the thought of it brought him no comfort, no pleasure. It only reminded him of the Empire's troubles—and the Empire's troubles were his own. The emperor had been young and strong and no one had expected his death. Kinlol's own surprise had faded, usurped by a growing heaviness. This was more than a tragedy. It was a crisis.

The faint hissing of an opening door came from behind, and

light from inside the Palace. It hissed again and the light vanished. A man joined Kinlol at the parapet. He didn't need to look to know that it was Gawin Gaelin.

"Well?"

It was a single word, spoken low, though there was no reason for it. "We must take counsel," Kinlol answered. There was no reply, so Kinlol continued, "The Empire needs an emperor."

"It has one."

"In no practical sense."

Gaelin went on, as if unhearing. "Alexander Cyneric Alheenan the Fifth, son of Emperor Judah, descended in straight line from Alexander the Mighty."

"Fine names, but only names, Gaelin. The child is seven years old. He cannot rule."

Gaelin sighed and leaned against the parapet, head bowed. He said nothing.

Kinlol was disturbed. His friend's posture implied defeat, or at least weariness, and he did not like that.

After a moment, Gaelin spoke softly. "Must we talk of this, tonight of all nights? We buried the emperor just today. The Empire won't crumble—"

"We have already waited too long," Kinlol interrupted. "Already people are turning away from the emperor's death and looking towards the future. They are beginning to wonder who will rule. We must have an answer. We must let no one take advantage of the situation."

Gaelin sighed. "Who can we put on the throne? Alexander is a child; he can't rule. And there is no other heir—no one who can assume the throne until Alexander is ready. That is the only provision the law has made for this eventuality."

"No man knows the law like I do," Kinlol answered. "And rare is the scholar who knows our history as well. I know that law and precedent have failed. And don't you see that that is exactly the point?" Kinlol looked at Gaelin and felt his impatience rising. This lethargic sorrow was unacceptable in any official, even if his wife was the emperor's sister. Kinlol considered this no time for softness and spoke his next words deliberately, "That is why weakness and indecisiveness are the last things we need."

Gaelin straightened up, not liking Kinlol's words or tone. He looked in his direction, but he could barely see him. "Is that a rebuke, Kinlol?"

"No, Gaelin," Kinlol answered coolly. "A reminder. We have no time for dallying."

"I await your brilliant ideas with bated breath."

"Sarcasm."

"The blindingly obvious," Gaelin shot back. "If you have anything worth saying, say it. Otherwise I'll rejoin my wife."

"Very well, Gaelin." Kinlol paused, and when he spoke again it was in a much different voice. "As Chief of Justice I am an expert in the law—in all its precedents and particulars, in its history, traditions, and foundations."

"Impressive litany—to say nothing of long," Gaelin muttered. He knew Kinlol didn't deserve it, but he was still irritated with the man and was in no mood for one of his little Council speeches.

Kinlol went on, ignoring him. "Alexander is emperor, as the law decrees. The law has no regulation or precedent for transferring his authority to any outside the Royal Family. In fact, the Ancient Code forbids that the emperorship be reduced, or taken from the line of Alheenan, till it or the Empire itself perishes."

Gaelin stared out at the city, and it was nearly swallowed in darkness. "And so you are saying," he said slowly, "that we shouldn't appoint a regent."

"Cannot, by the Ancient Code."

"So Alexander is emperor, and the Empire will be managed by the Council of Chiefs—"

"As always."

"But always the emperor has managed *them*. Alexander cannot, and if he does not rule the Council—"

Kinlol's voice was calm, businesslike. "We will rule the Empire."

"Is that legal?"

"It is not illegal."

"Is it wise?"

"It is shrewd, Gaelin, very shrewd. This way we can care for the Empire and protect Alexander until he rules. They will both be safe in our hands. Don't you realize how dangerous it would be to appoint a regent? And that's our only other option! A regent would take the emperorship—when would he give it back? If he wasn't willing, how could we make him? No one can fight against the power of the emperorship."

"What sort of man do you think we'd choose?" Gaelin demanded.

Kinlol half-shrugged, unperturbed by his incredulity. "It hardly matters. The regent would rule for years—ten at least. That's long enough for any man to learn to love power—love it more than anything."

"You have so little faith."

"Experience and history teach me to have little in humanity." Then Kinlol turned—not exactly congenial, but certainly comradely. "Gaelin, we have served the Empire and our emperor together for years. And now—now still, now more than ever—it is our duty to serve them. We must retain the emperorship for the house of Alheenan."

"Kinlol, no matter which course we take, the house of Alheenan will be deprived of the emperorship. Neither the Council nor the regent would take the title emperor, but under both the house of Alheenan will lose all its power."

"The difference, Gaelin, is in whose hands the power will be."

"Yours." The statement was almost an accusation.

"Exactly."

Gaelin drew a breath and let it out slowly. "So little faith in humanity," he said. "So much in yourself." His voice was soft. He felt the irony of it, and he felt he should feel angry. But his thoughts were churning and he had no time for anger. "I wish, Kinlol," he said after a long pause, "that I could say you were wrong."

"And you can't?"

"I don't know yet."

"You will—"

Kinlol's question was broken by a soft hiss, and the balcony was suddenly flooded with light. Gaelin stood a moment, letting his eyes adjust to the light, and then turned towards the open door. A man stood there, bowing slightly.

It took Gaelin a minute, especially with the light shining behind him, but he recognized the man: The commander of the Emperor's Guard.

Kinlol was quicker in turning than Gaelin and quicker to speak. "What is it, Colonel?"

"By your leave," the colonel said, "let us move inside. I have a message." He walked through the door and stepped to the side, letting the other two pass him, and then the door closed.

"Yes?" Gaelin asked.

"I have a message for Emperor Alexander."

"Who sent that child a message?" Kinlol demanded—but beneath his gruffness there was the same flicker of uneasiness that Gaelin felt.

The colonel studied both their faces and lifted his right hand, giving the men a good look at his compad. Kinlol supposed he was going to read off the message, but then he held out the compad to him.

Kinlol accepted it, and found its screen blank. He looked over at the colonel, and—increasingly disturbed at how this was proceeding—Kinlol touched a key. Immediately an image appeared —the seal of the Assembly, seven pillars and one bright star ...

Kinlol looked up quickly, his eyes shooting to the colonel. "Where did you get this?"

The colonel looked at him, his expression inscrutable. "A delegate came to the Palace and delivered it—a leader from the delegation of Norphatt. The Assembly"—his voice took on a note of declaration—"begs permission from Emperor Alexander to convene."

The old formulation was not so much a request as a notification. Kinlol lowered the compad, knowing now exactly what had been programmed into it. He looked at Gaelin; Gaelin raised his eyebrows, his expression asking him what he had expected. Kinlol looked away again, his brow furrowing, his eyes growing thoughtful.

The colonel stood in silence, watching them both.

It was not a large room and it seemed smaller yet, filled with a long oval table surrounded by broad-backed chairs. Elymas Vonran, Premier of the Assembly and chair of this meeting, sat at the head of the table. Leading men of the Assembly ringed the table, serious and ready for their business. Their chosen spokesman entered the room, returning from the Palace, and their eyes fixed on him as he made his way to the table and sat down.

He did not look around, but looked straight at Vonran. Vonran raised his eyebrows. The man nodded slightly and then, shifting his gaze to include his other colleagues, said to them, "I went to the Royal Palace. I said I had a message for Emperor Alexander that was to be received by the commander of the Emperor's Guard—not any servant. Colonel—" He stopped, grasping.

Vonran knew the colonel's name, but he did not supply it. One of the other delegates said it. "Kereth."

"Colonel Kereth," the spokesman continued, "came out to me and took the message."

"That is all?" asked Vonran.

"That is all."

Silence. Garin Dorjan spoke the question that hung in it. "But we don't know what he will do with it."

"That question needs no Solomon," said Vonran. "He cannot keep it to himself, and he knows that telling the child is inadequate. He will share it. Whomever he chooses—any official, any servant of the emperor, even the Lady Mareah—our message will soon be known to the Chiefs."

"If it isn't already," said the delegate from Norphatt. "Some of them were at the Palace when I arrived."

"Will the Council oppose us?" asked Nemin Ziphernan. A

new delegate in his mid-thirties, he was the youngest man in the room. Vonran hadn't invited Ziphernan; his name had not been so much as mentioned when this meeting was planned. But though he was surprised, and less than pleased, when Ziphernan arrived, Vonran said nothing of it. The potential benefits from doing so were quite outweighed by the potential harm from offending Ziphernan and whatever delegate he had wrangled an invitation from.

Now Vonran glanced at the younger man as he answered his question. “The Council is only men—only eight men. Chief Kinlol has the senior position on the Council. He will oppose us—and the other Chiefs will follow him.” Vonran turned to Dorjan. “Garin, how many provinces have responded to the notifications we sent?”

“Most of them. They will be sending their delegations to Telnaria as soon as possible. The provinces we have not received confirmation from are Lithia, Siym, Anarett, Verz, Charim, and—” Dorjan sighed and finished, “And Regial.”

Regial had one of the largest delegations, for it was very populous, if also very poor. It was on the outskirts of the Empire, sharing a border with Far Vothnia and cutting a long, lonely line across Unknown Space. There was no province further from Telnaria; the journey would be longer for their delegation than for any other.

And it was a well-known fact that if Regial didn't consider one of the Assembly's special sessions worth their time, they wouldn't send anybody at all.

“Regial is unpredictable,” someone said.

The leader of the delegation of Tremain, Colten Shevyn, spoke up. “Between the delegates who are already in Telnaria and the ones who will be arriving, we should make quorum within three days.”

There was a flurry of response to that. “What shall be our first order of business?”

“Hold forums—”

“We must make an official declaration—”

“But even if we have quorum—”

Vonran held up both hands to stop the voices. When he had

silence, he said, “All these are necessary questions. By all means keep them in mind. Think, consult, debate. But don't stake anything on false assumptions.” All eyes were on Vonran, and he paused to let the tension build. After a moment he continued, “Even if we make quorum, it's no certainty that we can begin our business.”

“Why not?” demanded Shevyn.

“The Council will oppose us, Shevyn. Never make plans without taking into account your opponents.”

“What can the Council do to stop us?” demanded Ziphernan. “It is the law that the Assembly can conduct its business when it achieves quorum.”

“It is not the law that the Assembly can make decisions about the emperorship,” Vonran answered.

“There is nothing in the law at all about our current situation,” Dorjan pointed out. “The Council has as much—or as little—authority as we.”

“And that, my friends,” announced Vonran, “is the sum of the situation. The Council and the Assembly will decide the ruling of the Empire, without either the law or the emperor.”

It was well after midnight when Elymas Vonran finally stood on the steps of his Telnarian home. It was a warm night and the stars were out, brighter over darkened Telnaria than they had been for years. But the delegates' meeting had kept Vonran late and he did not linger to enjoy the night; he barely noticed it. Shifting his compads from one hand to the other, he keyed the security pad—discreetly positioned to one side of the front doors, close to the jamb—and then stood, palm extended, while a light swept his hand. The doors swung open and he slipped in quietly.

Vonran knew some men who had their servants stay up, or the house kept lit, until their return, even if it was closer to dawn than sunset. Vonran had never approved, and sometimes his disapproval bordered contempt. He set times in his house and he saw to it that they were kept. It was for his household's good running, and he didn't change them. Even when his work kept him late, his household still retired at the proper time. His wife was its only member who had ever waited up for him, and she was gone now. When Vonran stepped into the foyer he didn't bother to turn a light on; he was comfortable in the dark and he could move easily in it. He had lived in this house for thirteen years and he moved soundlessly in it, even in complete darkness. He crossed the foyer and climbed the circular staircase up to the second floor. There was another foyer at the top—a small one—and then a dimly lit hallway.

Vonran touched the light panel, increasing the light a little. Time to make his rounds. He was closest to Zelrynn's bedroom, but she was fourteen years old and no longer needed to be checked on every night. He crossed the hall to another room and stood in the doorway, trying to see by the faint light spilling in. He could make out Lydia tangled up in her blankets, and Vera— He leaned forward, straining his eyes, but after a moment gave up and walked, as quietly as he could, to the bed beyond Lydia's. Vera was there, sure enough —but it was wise to be sure. Vonran left and headed to another room —the smallest bedroom, right next to his own, where little Calanthra slept.

Dianthe and he had chosen that name for its beauty, but when, after months of waiting, they finally held their baby, it seemed too long—longer than the little girl who owned it. She had quickly become Cala to her family. Now, nearly four years later, they still called her by it.

Standing in Cala's doorway, Vonran again couldn't make out his daughter in the rumpled blankets. He came up to the bed and found it empty.

His heart beat faster, but he wasn't worried, not yet. Sometimes Cala got out of bed at night. She never went far: she was afraid of the dark, empty rooms. She either went to Zelrynn's bedroom, or, more likely—

Vonran hurried to his own room, turning the light on as he entered. And there on the bed, Cala was fast asleep.

Vonran stood and looked at her a minute, alone on the large bed. He felt, for the first time, a pang of guilt at not having come home that day. Ever since she was given her own bedroom Cala would sometimes pad to her parents' room, favorite doll hooked in one arm, and climb into the bed. Vonran had not had his wife's tolerance of the habit, despite its infrequency. But after Dianthe died Cala started coming into his room more often than she stayed in her own, and Vonran's patience had no limit. He had lost his wife and he hardly knew what to do for his girls, and if Cala could be comforted even a little, he was willing.

As the days turned to weeks and a year passed, Cala came less and less. Occasionally she still wandered into her father's room. And tonight he had been away.

Sighing inaudibly, Vonran put his compads on an end-table next to the bed. He leaned over and covered Cala properly. Then he pulled off his boots and went into the bathroom, coming out in a few minutes ready for bed. Vonran sat up on the bed and, picking up a compad, clicked it on and began to review the notes he had made that day. Most of them were about convening the Assembly and notifying the emperor, and that night's meeting. Settled business for the most part, nothing he needed to remember or do. Six provinces hadn't confirmed yet, but he expected to receive confirmations from five of them the next day or, at the very least, the day after.

Regial, though. That province was a different question. One of the delegates had called them unpredictable, but he didn't think they were. He didn't think anyone was. Everyone had their way, and if you understood it you could predict what they would do. But Regial's way was not Telnaria's way, and the affluent men of the Assembly were often at a loss how to deal with the free-minded provincials. For himself, Vonran intended to treat them in a way that didn't usually occur to his high-society colleagues. He would treat them as equals. In the morning he would call the prefect of Regial and the leader of their delegation.

Vonran came to a note near the end: *Ziphernan*. The young delegate obviously had plans for his place in the Assembly. It'd be worth it to keep an eye on him—and find out, if Vonran could, what friend or mentor had provided the invitation.

Vonran closed his eyes and leaned his head back against the wall and worked his final evaluation of the day. He had accomplished all that he had wanted as well as he had wanted, and he calculated what progress he had made towards his goal. It was good, but this was still very much the preliminaries. As hard as the work had been, he considered it only stretching his muscles. The real fight was still to come. He had to unite the Assembly and lead it to defeat Kinlol and the Council. That was the battle that would win him his spoils. Uniting the Assembly was a task in and of itself. He would have to undercut his political opponents, persuade the delegates and the leaders—it was like herding cats sometimes—dealing with their thousand different designs and motivations, to make his goal theirs and them a force that would follow him to win it.

One step, one day, Vonran reminded himself. One step, one day. He opened his eyes and looked over at Calanthra. Vonran stretched out a hand and rested it, lightly, on her hair. All his other daughters had hair dark like his own, but this one had her mother's honey blond hair and the same gray eyes. Vonran was still, his mind turning down old pathways, and a quiet, familiar pain crept back into his heart. After a moment he roused himself and lifted up Cala. When she didn't make a sound, he carried her to her room, laid her down and covered her. He leaned down and kissed her forehead. "Sleep well, Cala," he whispered, and returned to his own room. The night was slipping away. He had five hours before he needed to begin the next day and he wanted to get sleep while he could. Exhaustion bred error and weakness, and Elymas Vonran had no tolerance for either.

Colonel Adon Kereth, commander of the Emperor's Guard, was in his office, pecking restlessly at his computer. It was late—at the end of the third watch—and no one had asked or expected this of him. He could have gone home hours ago, but he remained in his office at the Palace's security center.

Kereth did not, in any definite way, want to be there. He couldn't sleep and even if this had been a normal night as far as businesses were concerned, he wouldn't have wanted to go into the city. And there was no one waiting for him at home. But there was nothing keeping him at the Palace, either. He had nothing to do; the past hour or so he had spent waiting for the morning's reports to come in. Before that he strolled through the Palace and its grounds, but his men—who knew that their commander should have been in bed, where most of them would heartily like to be themselves—had started looking at him strangely. So Kereth retreated to his office and looked for work that could hold his attention. He'd had little success, but it didn't matter, not that much. Boredom wasn't what was fueling his restlessness.

It was uneasiness. Kereth had met that delegate and heard his message—not particularly pleased by the haughty demand that was his summons, but he found overlooking insults to often be the better part of valor. He had retreated to an alcove off a broad corridor where he could stare at the compad and no one would see the commander of the Emperor's Guard looking befuddled. He looked at it, turning over his options in his mind. Obviously, he had to show it to someone; keeping it to himself had to violate some regulation or law. And as for showing it to the emperor—well, Kereth guessed this emperor would need help reading every other word. The long words favored for governmental formalities tended not to be in seven-year-olds' vocabularies.

Then he considered other people. The emperor's personal servants might be entrusted with such a message, but, honestly, what would any of them do with it? Exactly what the good commander was doing in the alcove. As for the empress—well, the Lady Mareah couldn't have done much herself, and Kereth much preferred not to bother her. And so, the emperor's officials. Kereth did believe that Chief Kinlol and General Gaelin were still in the Palace.

So he had delivered the Assembly's message to them, after an exasperating search. He didn't know why the two men were conversing out on the balcony in the dark, and he didn't care for the looks of it. Still, Kereth wasn't much disturbed by it. But the whole incident had left him with a sense of uneasiness that he couldn't shake. As the night wore on, it deepened to an almost awful presentiment.

XIX

And here the third watch found him, sitting in his office, waiting for the morning's reports to come in. He knew they came in overnight, but apparently it was still too early to be receiving most of them. He was beginning to consider this ridiculous, considering how late it was.

With an air of disgust, Kereth put his computer into lockdown and stood up. Time to take another walk. Soldiers were never hurt by having their commanders wander in unexpectedly, and he needed the activity.

Kereth strode through the halls, head high, military carriage flawless. He was walking through a part of the Palace sealed off from the public when he nearly collided with a man turning the corner. The man drew to a full stop and, without missing a beat, swept his hand up in a salute.

Kereth returned it. "I thought you were already off duty, Captain Dilv," he said, archly ignoring the fact that he himself had been off several hours.

"I am," Dilv replied, falling into step beside Kereth. "And now I'm going home. Just finished some busy work for the bureaucrats. Sent in my reports."

Kereth nodded, wondering if there were now reports waiting in his computer, wondering what Dilv would think if he knew how Kereth had been waiting for his busy work. Kereth turned his head and suddenly noticed two guards standing sentry next to—a tapestry? Kereth stopped and stared at them.

Dilv also stopped, looking at them, then him. "When the empress forbade any guards in the family's rooms, we blocked off all possible entrances."

"I know there's a reasonable explanation, but ..." He pointed to the tapestry. "An entrance?"

"Behind the tapestry, sir. Servants' stairwell."

Kereth shook his head. "That's near the kitchens."

"Well, the one they use now. This is the old one. It's a kind of leftover from before the major reconstruction of the Palace more than a hundred years back. That was when they expanded the Palace and created this security center. All this area we have now—it used to be the kitchens and other servants' rooms. That's why that stairwell's there—and now it leads up to unused bedchambers. In fact, in most of the modern plans of the Palace, it doesn't even show up."

"We should fix that," Kereth murmured, smarting over his own ignorance of it. How had he missed an entrance to the emperor's chambers?

"If the colonel orders it," Dilv said. The men walked in silence for a few minutes, and Kereth was almost startled when Dilv suddenly gestured. "I never expected to see the black-outs up again so soon."

Kereth looked over to the windows and the black covering that had been put in place over them. "No one expected the emperor to die." He glanced over at Dilv. The captain looked grave, almost troubled.

"What will happen now?" he asked.

Kereth thought of the stairwell they had just passed that led up to the Lady Mareah and her son, the young emperor. "The whole Empire is wondering that."

"And the great ones will decide."

For a moment Gaelin and Kinlol stood before Kereth's eyes. "Aye."

"And we?"

"We have our duty, Captain," Kereth replied, letting a note of sternness creep into his voice.

"I am a soldier, Colonel," Dilv answered. "I know my duty and I do it. But there will be change, sir." Captain Dilv brought up his hand in salute. "By your leave, sir. My wife is expecting me."

Kereth returned the salute, watched the man turn smartly and march out. His gaze was drawn to the covered windows in the outer wall. Unexpected. And now the great ones must sort the matter out.

Well, he was no great one, no wise man. But he knew this: The Assembly and the Council were getting ready for a fight. He'd seen it in the delegate—he was like a man delivering a challenge. He'd seen it in Gaelin and Kinlol when he gave them the message. He didn't know who would win, or what it would mean if either one won. But Kereth could smell the fight coming, and Dilv was right: There would be change.

And Kereth knew then that it didn't matter, not to him. As commander of the Emperor's Guard he'd been given a charge and he had sworn before God to keep it. His duty was to protect the emperor, and that never would change. Whatever happened now and whatever followed, he would stand by his emperor to protect and serve him.

Kereth drew himself up to attention, hardly aware that he was doing it. “Long live the emperor,” he said aloud in the empty corridor. “Hail to Alexander the Fifth.”

CHAPTER

II

* * * * * * * * * * * * * * * * *

IT was said of the first emperor, Alexander Alheenan, that he had a terrible temper kept under stern control. Loss of that control was rare and spectacular. One contemporary of the great man wrote that Alexander the Mighty defeated the Augustii, but to the end of his days he struggled to master himself.

Centuries had passed, but there was still fire in the Alheenan blood. Emperor Issach—who reigned only fifty years ago—had a legendary temper. The stories of it were still told in Telnaria. Among the most infamous were the times when Emperor Issach, in a rage, fired subordinates and when he was calm again—either repenting or forgetting what he'd done—acted as if nothing had happened. Telnarian lore held out (though how accurately was a matter for the historians) that one Chief was thrown off the Council three times in the same afternoon. It was said that during Emperor Issach's rages sparrows did not dare to fly, and after them they could eat from his hand.

The next emperor, Rikon, plumbed neither the heights nor the depths of his father's mercurial temperament. He experienced neither Issach's fierce anger nor the sympathy and even gentleness he was capable of in his better moments. Rikon was willful, obstinate, and proud. He stored up his anger in grudges and long memories.

These were the immediate predecessors of Judah Zebulun III, in the emperorship and in ancestry. If genetics did not decree, at least it suggested that Emperor Judah would follow as another able, difficult ruler, with anger either hot and brief or cold and enduring. Able Judah had been, but of such a controlled and gentle temper that few guessed, until experience showed, that he quietly held something of his father's resolute strength.

Kinlol had pondered these things through the morning, with remote regret. The Empire had lost years of wise rule when the emperor died, and now the Empire had entered into uncertainty. Kinlol disliked uncertainty; he intuitively saw in it the seeds of both weakness and disorder.

To Kinlol, action was not called for; it was vital. The Council of Chiefs was meeting that morning and Kinlol had arranged a brief (he had promised) meeting with the empress beforehand. He thought it would be appropriate to speak with Mareah, considering how much the following events would concern her son. But more than that he had an instinct that meeting the empress was a wise preface to his efforts against the Assembly. His reason could not prove the instinct false, and so he went.

A servant led him into a parlor and asked him to wait. And Kinlol did, his mind turning to Emperor Judah's marriage. He had watched it come about with great interest ten years before.

The unmarried heir to the throne was always the most eligible man in the Empire, but Judah had been even more so than usual. In everything he recommended himself, in personality and character and even in the small things that so pleased women—looks and charming ways. The whole Empire watched intently for the woman who would be their next empress and the mother of their future emperor. Telnarian society watched anxiously, because they expected her to be chosen from among their own. They all thought the heir would marry soon, as they knew (who did not?) that Emperor Rikon wanted his son to marry early.

But Judah did not marry early. He didn't even marry at the usual age. Considering he had the finest women of his own nation (and of several other nations, if he'd ask) to choose from, this inability to find a wife was strange, and becoming insulting and therefore, intolerable.

The wrong impression, the Empire's higher class assured each other, should not be drawn. They were not like those people in Cythe or Regial, who married mostly in their teens or early twenties and were puzzled and skeptical of delay. No, they were tolerant of late marriages. They understood that people—and especially men—might spend a few years in gainful pursuits before settling down to married life. But Judah was a special case. He was the heir to the throne, he had no brothers and his father had no brothers; it was his duty to marry and produce heirs for the house of Alheenan. And he was not like the other young men who must establish themselves. He had all the wealth and all the position—and the greatest prospects—anyone could desire. And, well, what of his father?

Yes, what of Emperor Rikon? That was the point that concerned Kinlol. Rikon dealt no gentler with his son than with anyone else. As his son, his subject and his heir, Rikon was even more domineering with Judah. And so it was greatly interesting to Kinlol that Judah managed to resist his father's will. One year after another passed, and as the festivities for Judah's twenty-eighth birthday commenced, Telnaria gathered to loudly wish him many happy returns and whisper to one another, "Twenty-eight and still not married."

Perhaps it was coincidental, perhaps not, that at this time Judah departed from Telnaria, though he didn't go far. Outside the city were the farms—the maize-fields they were called in Telnaria, though fruits and vegetables were grown there also. The Royal Family bought all its produce from one man, and Judah went to visit him. When Judah came there was already a family staying at the house. Its head was one of the host's closest friends, and a considerably less successful man. Mareah was his oldest daughter.

Kinlol didn't know—and did not consider it his business to know—why Judah rejected all the refined, educated beauties and gave his heart to a sweet, simple, pretty girl from the maize-fields. He was not a romantic, and he considered all notions of destined or inevitable love unfortunate nonsense. But there it was, and Kinlol knew that Emperor Rikon would not be pleased. He would attempt to change his son's mind, or at least his decision, and Judah would resist. Kinlol did not miss his guess. Rikon and Judah did quarrel, but so discreetly that nothing certain ever escaped into general knowledge except the result. Judah and Mareah were married before his twenty-ninth birthday.

The whole affair had interested Kinlol as a way of judging the man he expected to serve as his emperor. He now wished he had spent more time studying Mareah. He would be dealing with her often from this time until Alexander reached the age of majority. That would be ten years—ten years of dealing with a woman he didn't know about her only child, beginning this day. Kinlol did not feel prepared.

As he thought this, he glanced up and saw Mareah Alheenan standing in the doorway. Kinlol came to his feet and bowed. "My Lady."

"Chief Kinlol," she returned, her voice carefully detached. She didn't smile, nor did she look as if she were going to for the length of their meeting.

Kinlol didn't expect her to. He chiefly hoped she wouldn't cry.

Mareah came and sat down opposite him. She had schooled her face into a calm expression that hid much. But Kinlol noticed the tenseness of her hands as they lay clasped together in her lap, and no one could miss the sorrow that hooded her mild gray eyes.

Kinlol sat also and, mustering his tact, began, "Lady Mareah, I have expressed my condolences to you already, for what little they are worth. I have come to speak with you of something else—your son." Kinlol paused, but Mareah sat like a statue. So Kinlol continued, filling the silence. "You know that he is emperor, but he is not old enough to govern the nation. He will become able to assume his duties, and until that time comes the Council is able ..."

If you were to trace the Council of Chiefs to its oldest roots, you would find those dug further back in time than the Empire itself. You would come to the Great War, when war sprawled across the galaxy and Alexander the Mighty led thirty-three protectorates against the

Augustii of Vothnia. He had many followers and allies, and led a vast army, but his closest circle was no more than a dozen select men. After victory was theirs and they had moved from waging war to building a nation, Alexander formalized his chief officials and advisors into part of the government, calling the group the Emperor's Council. The formalization would continue, and in due time it was fully transformed from the unofficial coterie of its origin. In the beginning positions were added to the Council because there were men to fill them; soon men were added to the Council because there were positions to be filled. And so the Council became an institution.

The Council was changed over the years. It was not until the reign of Alexander II, the great-grandson of Alexander the Mighty, that its final structure was achieved. The number of men was reduced to eight, and their titles were uniformed to the same pattern, the name of Chief. In time the Council itself came to be called the Council of Chiefs, which gave it an air of autonomy it did not actually possess.

And still Alexander the Mighty had managed to give his descendants what he had had. For all the changes the Council was remarkably true in character to those first twelve men. The Chiefs were all powerful men, with authority throughout the Empire. But their power was derivative and their authority came from the emperor. He had complete authority over the Council, to remove and appoint whomever he pleased. If a man wished to have any independence the Assembly was his place, not the Council. The Chiefs were chosen to be wise in counsel, competent in discharging the emperor's business, trustworthy, and intensely loyal.

Another thing that was unchanged was the eclectic duties of the Chiefs. Only five of them were truly administrative—the commander-in-chief of the military, the Chief of Intelligence, the Chief of Commerce, the Chief of the Treasury, and the Chief of State. The Chief of the Provinces was a kind of liaison between the emperor and the prefects. The Chief of Justice and the Chief Counselor were the emperor's most esteemed advisors.

The Chief Counselor's sphere was unlimited, and so, in theory, was that of the Chief of Justice. But it was his special trust to advise the emperor on all matters of law and justice, and those chosen for the position were presumed to be experts in the law. Chief of Justice was often considered to be the most honored position on the Council, and Gerog Kinlol had only enhanced its reputation. He had long been the most powerful Chief on the Council, a voice that spoke close in the ears of Emperor Rikon and Emperor Judah Zebulun. Now that no emperor was listening to him, his power was diminished, and he knew it. But Kinlol was still confident of his ability to lead the Council to do what needed to be done. The Chiefs would not challenge him, at least not now. The commander-in-chief, Fionn Dheval, probably wanted to, but he would never do it alone.

Kinlol did not dislike Fionn Dheval, however low his opinion of him was. He considered Dheval to be, at best, a merely competent maintainer of the status quo; he lacked not only vision, but adaptability. If something terrible happened and everything changed, then, when he was needed most, Dheval would fail.

Kinlol had advised Emperor Judah to replace him. He had explained Dheval's failings; he had suggested to the emperor's imagination the Empire being struck with the worst calamity of all—full war with Vothnia. Even Emperor Judah wasn't untroubled by the thought of Dheval, hand on the helm, in such perilous waters. But he still didn't remove Dheval. If war with Vothnia was a terrible prospect, it was also an unlikely one. The strength of the two nations was just on the balance, and everyone knew that a war would devastate winner and loser both.

Still, if the fear grew faint, it never entirely disappeared. For, like their strength, their enmity also was on the balance. The Empire and Vothnia were both proud and unyielding with each other. And the Vothnians were haunted by a specter of the glory so long destroyed, a dream of the shattered kingdom. And the Empire, ruled by the dynasty of Alexander the Mighty, lived beside them and prospered.

Kinlol had appealed to this risk and fear, but he didn't end there. He also spun out the advantages of a change. Kinlol presented several candidates, but most of them he gave only enough praise to convince Emperor Judah that they were better men than Dheval. It was Gawin Gaelin he wanted to become commander-in-chief. He was a superior leader and strategist, and he was respected by all the military and had standing in Telnaria. And he was a Gaelin, and that was nothing small; the Gaelin clan was strong and united, and they had intermarried with the Royal Family. Gawin Gaelin's marriage to the emperor's older sister, Layne, was only the most recent example.

Somehow, Dheval learned or guessed Kinlol's campaign to have him removed, and he never spoke a word to Kinlol he didn't have to. Kinlol was aware of Dheval's animosity, and he did not resent it or consider it unfounded. And it did not give him pause.

But for the first time it was something to be taken into account. Fionn Dheval might repay Kinlol's attempts to undermine him with Emperor Judah by attempting to undermine Kinlol with the Chiefs. Kinlol would watch for any sign from Dheval, beginning with that morning's Council meeting.

That was the Council's first meeting since Emperor Judah died, and the Chiefs gathered grimly. The seriousness could be felt in that room, and became almost a law of conduct for those who came there. The Chiefs greeted each other without smiles, and conferred together in low voices until the meeting was called to order.

That duty was Kinlol's; as the Chief of Justice he presided over Council meetings in the emperor's absence. He opened with a brief speech that was in part stating the obvious, mostly politesse, and then moved the Council to business: "As you have all learned, the Assembly has declared a special session. They are convening as soon as quorum is achieved."

"What will they do?" asked Dheval.

"All that they can. They want control over the situation," said Kinlol. It was an obvious answer, and therefore good as a first, small test of Dheval.

He passed. Showing no irritation, Dheval said mildly, "I know. But how will they do it?"

Kinlol noted the reaction and replied, "We can't know for certain. Probably they don't, not yet. But I believe they will try to appoint a regent."

At that Kavin Gyas, the Chief Counselor, rapped the table

softly with his knuckles, staring past Kinlol to the wall. He said nothing.

Kavin Gyas couldn't hide it when he was thinking, not for all the Empire. The rapping and the stare always gave him away. But Kinlol never could tell what or how much he knew, so he continued, “If they appointed a regent, he would have complete authority over the Council. All the power would go out of our hands.”

“And out of theirs,” said Trey Uman, Chief of the Treasury.

All eyes turned to him, but Gyas' fairly shot. Kinlol sat right across from him, but took only quick notice. His attention also was drawn to Uman, and he frowned. “What do you mean?”

Uman was in no hurry to give his answer. He looked at Kinlol musingly. His eyes were cloudy blue, his features marked by a youthfulness that belied the shocks of white scattered through his blond hair. “Don't you see it? We would lose control, but so would they. It would go from our hands to theirs to the regent's.”

“The Assembly would appoint him.”

“And there their power would end. A regent is as uncontrollable as an emperor.”

Kinlol had not considered this, but still ... “Then tell me,” he said, sweeping the table with a stern gaze that encompassed all seven Chiefs. “If they will not appoint a regent, then what will they do? They do not want us ruling the Empire!”

The silence that followed this challenge spoke in Kinlol's favor. Perhaps that was why Dheval broke it. “What about Elymas Vonran?” he asked. “He is the Premier of the Assembly. Everyone knows that he wanted this session. What does he want?”

There was a murmur of acknowledged ignorance around the table, and Kinlol had to join in. “Elymas Vonran is deep,” he said. “He can keep his own counsel and his own purposes. I don't know what's in his mind.”

“I know what's in Colten Shevyn's,” said Chief Gyas.

And now we have it. Kinlol turned to Gyas. “The head of the delegation from Tremain,” he said, his even voice concealing his interest. “What does he want?”

“No regent,” Gyas said. “He wants a council made, or a

commission, with members appointed by both the Assembly and the Council. As Shevyn envisions it, the Council and the Assembly will carry out their duties, with this commission supervising in place of the emperor."

"The emperor?" Trey Uman rubbed his neck. "A corporate regent instead of an individual?"

"No," said Gyas. "Not quite like that. I think he envisions the commission as—passive. A remote superintendent, not an active leader. The main function, I suppose, is to maintain unity between the Council and the Assembly—and have a mechanism in place should an emperor's decision be absolutely needed."

Kinlol's first, faint reaction was pleasure at the thought that perhaps the Assembly would not be fighting for a regent after all. This was overwhelmed by pure appall. "Rule by a commission! Rule by a committee! A regent might be dangerous, but at least he could be competent!"

"Perhaps we should hear your ideas," suggested Chief of Intelligence David Ithran.

That was a popular sentiment. "What would you have instead?" asked Uman. "The regent?"

"And why not?" challenged Dheval. "A regent—"

"Would not be safe," Kinlol cut in. "We can't give the emperorship to anyone—not while a son of Alheenan's dynasty still lives. How could we get it back? We have a duty to the house of Alheenan."

"We also have a duty to the Empire," said Kavin Gyas.

Dheval nodded to Gyas as if he'd found an ally. "We must think of both."

"I do think of both," said Kinlol. Of all the arts of speech, brevity was the hardest for Kinlol to master; he had more well-crafted sentences to follow his protestation, but Dheval took back the floor.

"We know how you have thought of Alheenan's dynasty," he said. "But what of the Empire? You would leave it leaderless. That is to say, in chaos, in anarchy, in disarray."

Through a supreme effort, Kinlol did not interrupt this

offensive litany. He did see Gyas' thoughtful expression, and knew by the others' look that some of them were edging towards agreement. Dheval paused, maybe for flair, but Kinlol had no respect for the man's rhetorical efforts. He seized the silence, his voice even and masterful: "Chaos, Dheval? Disarray? Anarchy? You deal with reality, Chief Dheval. Don't substitute it with abstracts.

"Is there a man at this table who is not tending to his work? What in the Empire is going to anarchy? Are the taxes not collected? Do the prefects no longer govern? Are the people rioting? Chief Dheval, the Council would know if there is rebellion among the officers or enlisted men."

Trusting that his point was made, Kinlol fixed the Chiefs with a stern gaze. "We are the stewards of the Empire. We can manage its affairs. The Assembly will deal with us and we will deal with them. Together we can conduct all the Empire's business. When Emperor Alexander reaches his majority, he will take the throne left empty for him.

"What else have we heard? Subjugate the whole Empire to a committee? *That* would be anarchy. What then? Put a regent on Emperor Alexander's throne? The Ancient Code forbids that, and all prudence is against it."

Gyas sharply rapped the table. "I don't know, Chief Kinlol, that the Ancient Code forbids it."

"He is right about the danger, though," said Uman. "What if we gave the emperorship to another man and he wouldn't yield to Alexander? We couldn't get it back for him—except through war."

That solemn truth brought a moment of silence to the table. Uman lifted his eyes to Kinlol, then moved them to the other Chiefs. "Committees are good for developing ideas—or killing them. I wouldn't leave one in charge of a confectioners' booth—let alone a nation."

No one looked about to argue, so Kinlol said, "All the Chiefs know my proposal. I set it before them, and I request the judgment of the Council." Kinlol stopped there. He let a few moments of silence pass, to allow the Chiefs time to think, and then Kinlol said, "Let the Chiefs pronounce their judgment." And then—because there was a order in which the Chiefs pronounced—he said, "I am in favor."

"I see the flaws all too well," Gyas said, "but I have heard nothing better. I am in favor."

Dheval hesitated a long moment. "I abstain from judgment," he said at last.

And, one by one, the Chiefs spoke:

"I favor the proposal."

"I am in favor."

"I favor it."

"I favor it."

"I am in favor."

"Seven in favor and one abstaining," said Kinlol. "The Council's policy is set."

"Now what?" asked Dheval, sounding a little suspicious.

Before Kinlol could launch his careful reply, Uman spoke. "Our policy, Dheval, is that everything remain as it is at this moment. The only thing we have to do is make sure no one else does anything. We have to wait. We can't stop the Assembly until they do something."

Uman had a habit of such colloquial excursions, and he delivered them with an undercurrent of merriness Kinlol distrusted. He tried to restore seriousness to the discussion: "You prepare for the battle long before it is joined. Prepare weapons, cultivate allies—"

"Of whom are you thinking?" Gyas interrupted to inquire.

Respect—and annoyance—flickered through Kinlol as he turned to Gyas. He was aware of all eyes locking on both of them. "Of General Gawin Gaelin. He is respected by the military and all the Empire, and he has standing in Telnaria. His support is valuable. I wish to have him as an ally. If the Chiefs are not agreeable, I would hear their concerns."

No one took up the opportunity, but that is not to say that no one wanted to. Dheval looked at Kinlol—long, silently, and darkly.

Vonran's days began early. He had already been awake and at his work for two and more hours before his family had their breakfast.

After the meal, Vonran kissed his daughters good-bye and promised to be home for dinner. He was leaving for the Hall of Assembly, and he did not expect a busy day.

The Hall was deep into the city. It was a notable building, and in Telnaria that was not an easy thing. The Empire's capital city was filled with the buildings where the nation's most powerful men conducted their business, with monuments, memorials, mansions, and the Royal Palace looking out over all. Architects rivaled in designing buildings of magnificence and originality. In all this, the Hall drew attention at least. It was enormous and, in an eccentricity, actually shaped like a hall. Two-thirds of the building was given over to the Assembly Room, and the rest of it to the delegates' use. When the space had become insufficient, they had built a complex to the north of the hall, connecting the two by an enclosed colonnade and an underground passageway. It was not efficient, but it had the virtue of preserving the Hall's structural integrity.

That was like Telnaria. Vonran knew it as well as any native, although he himself was not one. His native city was Traelys, on Vaz in the Lorda Province. It was not the place where he'd been born or raised. That he had left long ago, without looking back. Traelys was where he had settled as a young man first starting out; he made it his own, his home. Traelys was to the Empire's economy what Telnaria was to its government: It was the capital.

And it was ruled by a different ethos. The very architecture of the cities was different. Telnaria had borrowed much from the architecture of the ancient pagan cities, as they had borrowed other things. Traelys was a modern city, built of synthesized metal and not stone. There the buildings soared into the sky and their long spirals pierced the clouds, sharpening to a lethal, invisible point. It made for different skylines, and both were forged in Vonran's memory.

Telnaria's power was built on covenants their ancestors had entered into, an enshrined constitution. Traelys owed its power to the living, not the dead. Its power was in meeting the shifting needs and desires of billions of people. Vonran had spent his first years of adulthood in apprenticeship of that art, and he had taken it with him when he moved into the profession of politics. True, delegates were not popularly elected. They were appointed by the legislatures of their provinces—and legislators were popularly elected. Many a legislator had risen and fallen because of a delegate. Vonran had learned—far better than most of his colleagues—the value in appealing to the people. While he didn't neglect the men who appointed him, he was more concerned with the people. He cultivated their favor with active courting and lasting vigilance. It mattered less what the legislators thought, when the people were on his side. Lorda's legislature gave him his position, and the people's favor gave him independence.

When Vonran arrived at the Hall, he found it mostly empty. He stood alone in the anteroom, letting his gaze travel along the carved entranceways, the off-white marble floor mottled with blue-gray, and each province's commemorative seal hanging on the cool, pale brown walls. He envisioned the anteroom as it would soon be, filled with hurrying people, the murmur of their voices and movements. Vonran crossed over to the lifts—his office was in the Hall itself, because of his position—and found one waiting, empty. It stopped on the second floor to pick up a peevish-looking secretary and a bright young aide, who greeted Vonran by name. He returned the wishes for a good morning; the secretary said nothing and Vonran returned that, too. They got off at the next floor; Vonran went on to the fourth. He strode down the hall, soon espying a small knot of men near an open door. It was a regular occurrence, in and out of session, but there was no intensity to these men now. They were standing and talking in the easy informality that reigned until the Assembly convened. Vonran slowed as he came to them—Garin Dorjan, Colten Shevyn, Nemin Ziphernan, and Theseus Declan.

Theseus Declan, one hundred and one, was the oldest man in the Assembly, and one of the most respected. He was venerable in his old age, and his mind was still keen. No emperor had lasted as long, no delegate had known the Assembly without him, and he was almost an institution in himself. Declan enjoyed a deep and widespread affection, though not all the delegates who felt so knew it. But many did, for it was not only the enduring, comfortable familiarity of Declan that inspired affection. He was well-liked also because he was kind, unpretentious, respected the divine image in every man, and harbored no ambitions beyond what he already had.

Vonran at least fully understood his sentiments regarding the old man, and they were not exactly like those most commonly felt. He respected Declan's age and experience, but even more his skill in dealing with others. Declan always gave an impression of opposing policy rather than people, so that even those he had opposed again and again were rarely inspired to enmity. Vonran, not easy to surprise, was surprised anew at how a man in Declan's position could give so little offense to others' pride and so little threat to their ambition. Not least of all, Vonran trusted Declan, personally as well as professionally, and that, too, did not come easily to him.

As Vonran came near the four men, Garin Dorjan stepped forward and met him, drawing him a little to the side of the other three.

"Verz and Charim have sent their confirmations," he said in a low voice. "I am told to expect Anarett's any time now. All are moving along ... except Regial."

"I thought as much." Vonran also kept his voice down. They were standing near the other men, and it was quiet in the halls. "I have had my staff arrange calls with Regial's prefect and the leader of their delegation. I will do what I can. And the delegates in Telnaria ... "

"Many didn't come to the Hall today. But some did." Dorjan gestured behind him, and Vonran glanced at the men.

"Anything interesting?"

Dorjan shook his head. "Nothing worth reporting."

Vonran took another glance, noticing that Declan was listening more than talking, and Shevyn and Ziphernan were standing closer to each other than either was to Declan. "Do they get along?" he asked. "I mean, the two."

"Shevyn and Ziphernan? Oh, famously, Elymas, famously."

Vonran added Shevyn to a mental list of Ziphernan's possible mentors. Then, sharing a look with Dorjan, he turned towards the men, Dorjan following his lead. They spoke cordially together for a few minutes, and then Vonran excused himself.

He went to his office, where his first order of business was to speak with Regial's prefect and lead delegate. He brought all his persuasive powers to bear, but with what effect he couldn't tell. Later he learned that the Council was meeting that same morning, but no word came from it. Vonran was not surprised. He expected the Chiefs to act, but he did not expect them to be hasty.

The hours passed and work lagged. A few hours after noon Vonran took out his compad—the special one—and activated it. It was programmed to launch his file immediately after it had been activated and the password entered. He was writing when his intercom came alive: "Delegate Shevyn requesting an interview, sir."

"Granted. Send him in." Vonran didn't really listen to his secretary's acknowledgment as he put the compad into sleeper mode and slid it into a drawer. He rose as the door opened and greeted Shevyn. Shevyn answered very properly and both men were seated.

"Our situation is urgent," Shevyn began, "and I believe we should move to resolve this trouble as quickly as possible. We can begin seeking a resolution even before the Assembly convenes. The delegates will reach consensus faster if they have already begun to propose and consider ideas."

"Doubtless that's all true," said Vonran. "But haven't they already begun?"

"Informally, they have. I believe we should carry on the process officially. If you would issue an executive order authorizing a forum, we could begin immediately."

"It is unusual to begin the forums before the Assembly has convened."

"But not unheard-of. It has been done before—and on things less weighty than the ruling of the Empire."

"So it has," Vonran agreed. It had been done—sometimes for the sake of speedy action, a few times as a political weapon. He considered for a long moment and then turned back to Shevyn. "Your point," he said, "is well-made. But for the time too few delegates have gathered to hold forums. However, I will keep your recommendation in mind. If, as things develop, it seems a good idea, I will act on it."

XXXVII

Shevyn pondered this and nodded. “That is reasonable.” He rose. “Thank you for your consideration and your time.”

“It is my pleasure,” Vonran responded. He watched Shevyn go, and as the door shut he took his compad from the drawer. He had only gotten so far as to write “Shevyn” when his secretary's voice cut in again: “Delegate Declan, sir.”

“Send him in.” Vonran tilted the compad, looking at the face of its screen with a twinge of disappointment, then put it away as he had with Shevyn's arrival.

Theseus Declan came in, wearing a friendly expression. “Are you occupied, Elymas?”

“I'm not busy,” Vonran answered.

Declan nodded. “It is slow—but not for long. In a few days we will have quorum and this quiet building will be swarming. People and bustle and hurry and much too much noise.” Then Declan laughed. “Nemin Ziphernan is anxious for it to begin. But he is young, and I am old, and I am no longer impatient for the calm to end and the storm to begin.” Declan regarded Vonran thoughtfully, as if gauging his own eagerness. “It will be an important session. Even I, who have been in the Assembly sixty years, would call it so. We are entering history.”

“I know.”

“You are not excited?”

“Are you?” Vonran parried.

“Ah, Elymas, at my age excitement is a threat to my health. The doctors advise against it. But you are not old; you should not be tired.”

“I,” Vonran said, “am not quite old, but I am not quite young, either. Why should I share Nemin Ziphernan's anxiousness?”

“You *are* young,” reprimanded Declan. “If you think you are not it's only because you are ignorant of old age. *I* am old. I know.”

Vonran looked at Declan, amused. “Might it be, Theseus, that your perspective is skewed? You are old enough to be my father.”

“That is not quite true,” Declan answered. “I am old enough to be your grandfather. I have great-grandchildren the age of your own children. You are young."

Vonran laughed. "I concede. I won't argue."

Declan took the concession in the good humor it had been given. He smiled and shook his head, and changed the subject. "I was wondering, Elymas, if you would come over to my house for dinner tonight."

Vonran shook his head. "I promised my girls I would be home tonight. But you could come over and have dinner with us—you and your wife."

"My wife is in Carsyt. I was intending to join her there after the emperor's funeral, but now that the Assembly is convening ... " He shrugged. "But I would be glad to come—if you don't mind."

"If I did, I wouldn't have asked." Vonran quickly collected what he needed from his office and they went to his home. It was a large house, built broadly and handsomely, of a fine and enduring gray stone. It was by no means a palace, and the grounds were more impressive than the house itself. It was not that there was anything exotic or unusually fine about that very fine land. But it was extensive, and cut off from the rest of the city by a tall wall that ringed the whole estate. In a city—and especially Telnaria—land was an expensive commodity. To anyone who knew this, cutting out a large parcel of land in the middle of Telnaria and then contentedly planting flowers gave a definite—and to no politician unwanted—impression.

Both men disembarked from their hovcars in front of the house, and began to go up the stairs as the drivers swung the hovcars around. But Vonran stopped abruptly, catching a faint noise. He listened closely, and this time he heard it again and was certain: a little girl's laugh. He looked over at Declan and motioned to him to follow.

Retracing his way down the steps, Vonran led Declan around the house and onto the lawn. The grass grew thick and green, and ahead, beginning at the back of the house, was a stone wall. They had already passed the first, looming wall, and this waist-high one was probably aesthetic in purpose. Agvihn bush-trees of the finest breed were planted near it; Declan had never seen the dark green leaves so deep and vibrant.

They came to a gate which was about broad enough for two to walk through abreast. Vonran quietly slipped the handsomely wrought latch, and the gate opened with remarkable quietness. Vonran shut and latched the gate again after both men had gone through, and they went forward. They were so close now that even Declan's old ears could clearly hear the sounds of children playing. The Agvihn bush-trees grew close together, and their many, leafy boughs obscured the lawn beyond. But soon they had come to the trees and could see Vonran's four daughters playing near a tall fountain.

There Vonran came to a stop, apparently content to watch. Declan stopped also, but after watching the children for a few moments he looked at Vonran—a long and careful look. Then he spoke. “Elymas, I have been curious, since the session was called ...” Declan let that sentence trail to its end, and Vonran looked at him, but without shifting his posture; he barely turned his head. Declan met his eyes. “Elymas, what do you want?”

Vonran's gaze returned to his daughters. “Want?” he repeated.

“From the Assembly. What do you wish us to do?”

Vonran looked back at Declan, but his expression was inscrutable. “The best thing.”

Declan began to speak and stopped. Then he nodded, slowly. “What do you believe that is?”

“Whatever will provide the Empire with the leadership it needs. The child cannot even begin to learn how to rule; someone must.”

“Or someones.”

“What do you mean by that?”

“Haven't you heard?” Declan's voice was odd, as if his question was about half-rhetorical.

“Do I seem to have?” Vonran asked, more sharply than he had intended.

“Obviously not.” Declan clasped his hands together, as if meditating on some thought. “Elymas, Colten Shevyn wants the

Assembly and the Council of Chiefs to appoint a commission in the emperor's place."

Vonran said nothing. He was looking towards his daughters but no longer really watching them. His mind had flown to his other world; it was taking this information, sizing it up, fitting it in. So Shevyn had hatched some ingenuous—though not necessarily wise —idea, sprung it on Telnaria and then came into Vonran's office to ask for forums to advance it. He probably guessed that the idea hadn't reached Vonran's ears yet; doubtless he also guessed that Vonran wouldn't like it. Typical of Shevyn.

Vonran grasped all this quickly, and it cost him only a short pause before asking, "Is there much support in the Assembly?"

"I can't say. No one has had time to think yet, and many haven't even heard. What do you think?"

"It sounds impractical," Vonran muttered. "A commission?"

"It intrigues me—and makes me leery," Declan said. "But we may hear nothing better."

"I doubt that."

"So you are not in favor?"

Vonran shook his head. "I think not."

"What do you want?"

Want. Again. Irritation surged through Vonran, and he didn't know whether it was at Declan for pressing the point or at himself for not having already decided when and how to reveal his desires. It was as easy for Vonran to deflect a question as it was to answer it, but now he didn't know which he wanted to do. He looked back at his girls, buying himself that second to grasp for the wisest response. "Impractical, did I not say of Shevyn's commission?" Vonran allowed a short pause, for Declan to nod and himself to order his next words. "If *practical* is to be our watchword, we would appoint a regent. An empire without an emperor is a very awkward thing."

"Well said," praised Declan. "And I agree. But there are other ideas. And many motivations."

A feeling of discomfort suddenly came over Vonran, and he knew without looking that Declan was gazing at him intently. The old man was insightful, could draw the truth from a man's soul like water from a deep well. But what disquieted Vonran was that, somehow, Declan's steady gaze could make him also peer into his own soul. And so it occurred to him to consider his motivations, and not only wonder what Declan thought or guessed of them.

Vonran turned his gaze back to Declan—and suddenly caught sight of Cala leaning far over the fountain's basin, stretching out a small hand into the cascading water. She looked on the verge of pitching in headfirst, and while the water was not very deep, the stone floor of the basin was very, very hard.

“Cala!” he yelled. “Get down!”

The shout startled the girls, who hadn't even known that he was home. It startled Declan, who was quite focused on another matter. Even Vonran hadn't been expecting it; it was pure parental reflex.

Zelrynn moved quickly to retrieve Cala from the fountain, but Vera and Lydia paid attention to their father rather than their little sister. Vonran left the trees' shadows to go to them, his discussion with Declan effectively ended.

No opportunity came to revive it. While they were still with the girls dinner was called, and shortly after they finished Declan announced that he must be going. Vonran had the summons sent to his driver and then walked with Declan to the door. They didn't speak, and Vonran wondered if Declan was planning to return to the evening's earlier topic. Declan halted in the foyer, looking around it and to the staircase before and the rooms flanking it. But he continued without comment. They stepped outside and Declan looked behind and upward, getting a very limited view of the house's front. “It's a fine house, Elymas,” he said. “It stood empty so many years before you and Dianthe moved in. I used to wonder why. I was surprised when I learned you had bought it, Elymas. Of course, I barely knew you then, but you were still a new delegate ... ”

Vonran nodded, to show that he understood and Declan didn't have to finish the sentence. Declan's hovcar drew up before the house. Declan was shivering a little in the cold wind, and when he saw the vehicle he nodded to Vonran. “A fair night to you, Elymas,” he said. “And God's favor on your family.”

XLII

"A fair night to you also," returned Vonran. He watched Declan leave and then turned back to his home. He stopped as soon as he crossed over the threshold, looking around. Declan didn't know why the house had stood empty all those years, but he did. After all, the owner for all that time had been his father-in-law.

Gazing around the foyer, Vonran's mind stepped back into another time, when he had first stood there with his father-in-law, his wife, and his only child, a little girl just beginning to walk. He and Dianthe looked around, trying to see into the darkened rooms and up the stairs, while Garis Sejen extolled the house's qualities. The memory of it was vague but quickly grew sharp, as if the words were traveling to Vonran from thirteen years before.

And Vonran remembered the pause and all its expectancy, and then the tone, so immensely pleased, as his father-in-law went on ...

"It's yours, Dianthe. You and Elymas and Zelrynn and the little ones to follow."

"Father!"

Dianthe's voice was startled and a little reproving, but Vonran said nothing. He had learned one thing about his father-in-law: Dianthe dealt with him like no one else could. And he had learned one thing about life: hasty reactions were often uninformed reactions, which were often bad reactions.

"Now what's wrong? You and Elymas have been looking for a house; this one is the best in Telnaria—not for holding banquets, maybe, but for raising children. You said it yourself about the grounds—a place for children to play. Now, with these little ones ..."

"I know. It is true. But Elymas hasn't said he wants it, and even if he does, we can pay for this house."

"You will not. It's a gift, little girl. Can't a father give his daughter a gift?"

"When it's a house!"

"Dianthe, I haven't even given you your inheritance—and here you are, a grown, married woman! Can't I give you something?"

"Father, I didn't want the inheritance. I said I would never

take it. Oh, Father, you know I did; you know why."

"I do. And now you have him." Garis Sejen thrust a thick, brown finger towards his son-in-law. "So now you can take it."

"Father, I said I wouldn't accept the inheritance and I will not. I gave my word."

"Then keep it. This isn't your inheritance. It's a gift—and for my grandchildren, too."

Vonran drifted away from the conversation, after Zelrynn who was toddling towards the stairway. He felt a sympathy with his father-in-law. Dianthe was his only daughter, the child of his old age, and he adored her. And this man, at one time the wealthiest man in the Empire, expressed his love in giving. Often it was very extravagant giving, but he didn't know it. He thought of it only as giving his daughter things that she would enjoy, only as making her happy. He wanted—it was a deep and unfailing desire—to do both.

And well Vonran understood, for, like Garis Sejen, Dianthe was the apple of his eye ...

"Father?"

For a moment, the voice was Dianthe's and it was Zelrynn's, too, and then Vonran was back in the present. He blinked quickly twice, feeling an unusual wetness in his eyes, and turned to Zelrynn. "Yes?"

"Is Delegate Declan gone?"

"Yes."

Zelrynn looked curiously up at her father. "Will you be busy now?"

Vonran nodded, looking at his daughter thoughtfully. She was an intelligent girl, and at fourteen was beginning to let go of childhood. She knew what was going on. Maybe she was his only child who did. Lydia and Cala were too young. Did Vera understand? "I will be very busy for a while, Zelrynn. But I am not tonight. Come. Let's go to your sisters."

"You're the first to arrive, Kinlol," said Trey Uman, by way of greeting. "I hadn't expected anyone yet."

Kinlol nodded, and wondered if that was why Uman was not wearing shoes. This meeting had been Kinlol's idea; he had proposed to Uman that they meet together with Gawin Gaelin—knowing even as he did so that Kavin Gyas, too, would come. The friendship between Gyas and Uman made it inevitable.

Kinlol looked around the living room. "Will we be meeting in here?"

"I was planning on the patio. The weather is finally pleasant and nature is in full bloom. The flowers are even better than last year ... Have you seen the epiphyllum?"

Kinlol allowed that he had not.

"They are our newest experiment. I wasn't sure how well they would do—look, I mean—but it's turning out well. Annora has claimed the victory in another debate."

Annora was Uman's wife of thirty years and more, and Uman did not mind announcing his loss to her in this question of landscaping. Kinlol nodded politely to Uman's comment and hoped the others would arrive and save him from further discussion of flowers. Or rather, further commentary. Kinlol had nothing intelligent to say on flowers or landscaping, and had hardly even a compliment to give.

Fortunately for him, Kavin Gyas arrived then. Not bothering with the most perfunctory greetings, Gyas, smiling broadly, said, "I would like to announce the arrival of another Gyas. My grandson was born early this morning."

"Congratulations," said Kinlol.

"Don't think," said Uman to Kinlol, "that we are the first to know. He probably told the servant who let him in. Annora and I were dining with him and his wife in a restaurant when they got word of their granddaughter's birth, and he told the server." Uman turned back to Gyas. "All right. Let's have the name, weight, length—everything. And he knows it, too." This last was another aside to Kinlol.

Kinlol stood there, but he tuned out the conversation. This was somcthing he had gotten used to. He had watched his friends and the men he knew marry and have children; over the years this passed to their children marrying, and they became grandfathers. Kinlol stood apart, never married and childless. He had filled his life with other things.

Gawin Gaelin arrived a few minutes into Uman's and Gyas' conversation, and the round of greetings and news was repeated. Finally Uman led his guests out to what he called the patio. A fine brownstone pavement adjoined the back of Uman's home; it was not very broad as patios went, and it was not roofed. It was, however, terraced, for the house had been built on a ridge. A balustrade lined the patio, with a flight of broad steps leading down to the lawn and the gardens.

One of the tables had been set for the sort of meal that was eaten with small plates and no utensils. As his guests settled around the table, Uman poured the drinks and began the conversation. “It has been three days since the Council met,” he said. “Since then, Elymas Vonran has issued an executive order that permits the delegates to hold forums before the Assembly's convening—today, in fact, they begin. The leaders in the Assembly and of the delegations are meeting this afternoon, and this morning the Assembly announced it will convene tomorrow. And while the Assembly has done all this, the Council achieved ... nothing.” Uman illustrated this with a gesture that sent dark liquid sloshing from the cup in his right hand. “Which is why we are here, is it not, Kinlol?”

“It is,” Kinlol said. “The Council must act—but I can't call the Chiefs together without anything to put before them.”

“It is a matter of strategy,” asserted Gaelin. “And the first question is, what is the objective?”

“You know,” said Kinlol.

“Then you won't disagree with my summary,” said Gaelin, a little irritated at Kinlol's lack of cooperation. “To wit: To keep the Assembly from wresting control of the Empire from the Council. Even more simply, to keep the state of affairs static.”

“And the Assembly is meeting with the precise intention of changing it,” said Gyas.

“That,” Gaelin said, “is why I call it an 'objective'. Now, if that is our objective, what is the best way of achieving it?”

"We must thwart the Assembly," said Kinlol. "But if the Assembly changes anything, it will be by instituting a new power in the Empire—a regent or Shevyn's commission. That is what we have to prevent."

"The Council could challenge the legality of the Assembly's actions," said Gaelin, looking at Gyas and especially Kinlol.

"Better yet," said Uman, "we could rally the people against them. The delegates are not like us. They have to fear the legislators, and the legislators have to fear the people. If the people do not want them to change anything ..."

"Can they be so convinced of the merits of the Council ruling the Empire?" Gyas asked—and not without a satiric edge.

"They don't need to love it, Kavin," said Uman. "They need to feel secure in it. They need to know that all will be well if ... " He trailed off, as if his own words had started something in his mind.

"Well?" asked Kinlol, a little puzzled and a little eager. "How can we convince them of that?"

"Maybe it wouldn't be effective to tell them," said Uman, staring hard at nothing and speaking a little distantly. "Maybe we could show them ... That is what we have that the Assembly does not!"

The puzzlement could be heard in the silence. Uman looked impatiently from face to face. "Do you not see it? The regency, the commission—ideas, merely ideas. The Council as caretaker—that is reality. It is what is happening right now. The emperor is dead and buried, and the Empire—"

"Still runs," finished Gaelin. "That's magnificent."

"So our proposal has been tested and found true—thus far," said Gyas. "But it has not been far at all."

"The Assembly does nothing quickly," said Kinlol.

"True," said Uman. "And as more and more time passes, and it slowly dawns on everyone that we have no crisis ... Why such radical change?"

"Is there any way to get more time?" asked Gaelin.

"We could turn obstructionist," said Gyas, but he spoke as if the word tasted bad.

“It isn't always bad,” said Gaelin.

“At any rate,” Uman said, “what can we do? The Assembly convenes tomorrow. Other than contesting their proposals—which we would do anyway, happy side benefit or not, as the Chiefs agreed—other than that, what can we do?”

Kinlol's mind was turning furiously, and he spoke with uncharacteristic slowness. “The Assembly has not convened. We may be able to keep them from it yet.”

“How?” demanded Gyas.

“They have quorum,” said Uman.

“But is it enough?”

“It always has been,” said Gyas sarcastically.

“Do you know your government's history no better than that? Only once before has an assembly of representatives met to determine the governing of the Empire. That was the Great Council, when they ratified the Code and made Alexander the Mighty emperor, and his heirs ever after.”

“The Assembly is not establishing a government,” Uman pointed out.

“They're establishing a new governing authority, at least,” said Kinlol. “And they are much closer to the Great Council than to their normal sessions—with their inter-provincial squabbling. For those sessions, quorum is sufficient. For the Great Council, they waited two fortnight past the set time of beginning, waiting for all to arrive.”

“It may be true,” said Gyas, doubtfully. “But—”

“I will call the Council together at once,” continued Kinlol. “We must agree and send them a message in the name of the whole Council. And we must be quick!” Kinlol got up from the table and left in a hurry, Uman and Gaelin following after.

Gyas was alone in the calm that followed their hasty departure from the patio. He picked up his cup and took a long drink. It was a good cordial—blackberry, his favorite—and he savored its taste and its smooth way down his throat. His contemplative gaze drifted to the sky in the distance, and the trees that stood up straight into it.

XLVIII

It was not at all uncommon for the leaders of the Assembly to meet together apart from the rest of the delegates. In most times there was a certain level of cheerfulness to the meetings, owing in part to their lesser degree of formality, and even more to their exclusivity. All who attended knew they had a seat of power.

Elymas Vonran held the highest seat, that of Premier of the Assembly. He was young as political leaders went, but no one despised or resented that; it seemed a negligible point. There was something about him that surpassed the years, and age was not a measurement. He was a striking man, in more ways than one. He was tall, and though his eyes were black and his hair was quite a dark brown, his skin was unusually fair. By all measures he was a handsome man, and by no measure the most handsome in the Assembly. But his looks were of the kind that bears age graciously, refined by maturity and unmarred by gray hairs.

But it was more than this, and more than the charm that was his natural gift, and whose uses he had so well learned. There was something commanding in his demeanor, and deep in his eyes there was an intensity, a still burning. No one who ever met him doubted that he was a man of considerable will and intelligence.

Elymas Vonran presided over the leaders at their meeting, and it was a happy, necessary, thoroughly predictable affair, until the end.

That was when they had their first sign of the surprise about to be visited on them—the entrance of one of the Assembly's auxiliaries. The young man made his way to Vonran, attracting the looks of men wondering if he had a good enough reason to enter their gathering. "Premier Vonran," he said, "the Council of Chiefs has sent a message for the whole Assembly. They requested that I tell you that it is urgent and deserves your immediate consideration. They also want me to relay your reply, or at least your estimate of when you will have one." There was, in this last sentence, a sudden, slight trace of doubt.

Vonran nodded and held out a hand. The young man placed

a compad in it, and Vonran dismissed him. “We will call you when we have an answer for the Council.” Vonran read the message, unhurried despite the eyes on him and the complete silence that had fallen. He looked up, his face calm and unreadable, and handed the compad to Garin Dorjan, who sat beside him. “You can all study the message for yourselves, but simply put, the Council wants—no, insists—that the Assembly does not convene tomorrow.” An angry murmur swept down the table, but Vonran spoke over it. “They want us to wait until all the delegates have arrived.”

“Why?”

“What right is it of theirs?”

“What—”

Vonran's impatience with the rising voices and mounting wave of questions—useless, all of them, since no one waited for a reply—was immediate. He thrust both hands outward, and made it a commanding gesture.

They obeyed. There was quiet again, and Vonran spoke. “The Council believes that we should wait. There is some talk of a precedent. But there is no law and they cannot compel us. No one can. It is our decision only: Will we defer convening?”

“Why should we?”

Vonran glanced at the delegate who asked this, but it garnered approval from many of the others.

“If the Council wants us to defer, it must strengthen their position somehow,” said Colten Shevyn.

“*If* they want us to defer,” said Dorjan. “It could be that they want us to fight with them about deferring.”

“It takes two for a fight, and the Council doesn't qualify. What would they do? Send a sternly worded memo?” scoffed Shevyn.

“An endless stream of memos that we can't ignore might be problematic.”

“Only irritating, Dorjan,” said Shevyn. “Don't grasp at straws. You don't have to defend your comment.”

Dorjan only looked at him, perhaps grasping now for a sufficiently insulting comeback. Declan spoke up. “How would the

Assembly deferring strengthen their position? Maybe it's an honest concern."

There was a brief silence at this suggestion; then the delegates were recovered enough to dissent.

"Maybe the Council wants to establish their legitimacy," said Shevyn. "Insert themselves into the Assembly's internal affairs. If we accede we legitimize their interference. It's a test run of the debate they truly want to be in. If we let them interfere now we'll only strengthen them against us when they want to interfere with our business. The Assembly will not have a forum or a meeting that we won't be getting Kinlol's legal opinion on afterward."

"That's logical," said one.

"Guesswork," said another.

Vonran let that debate run until it began going in circles. Finally he interrupted. "Gentleman, here is something you should consider." Vonran turned to Dorjan. "Garin, read that part of the message about the precedent."

Dorjan found the place and read, "No precedent can be found for the Assembly undertaking such proceedings as you now are, in passing decrees for the Empire not according to law, but by *fiat*. The Ancient Code has not conferred this executive and judicial privilege upon the Assembly, nor has it permitted the Assembly to institute new governing authorities over the entire Empire, not by *fiat* or even law. However, once a representative body met to consider and rule on such questions, and institute governing authorities for the Empire. This was the Great Council, held ... "

Vonran made a shooing motion with one hand. "Skip the history lesson."

Dorjan skipped it. " ... In the end, they waited two fortnight for all the representatives to appear, pursuant to the consensus of all, that to conduct their business without full representation of the people would undermine their legitimacy.

"The Council harbors a similar concern here, that the Assembly's proceedings on this matter would have no legitimacy if not undertaken with all the people of the Empire represented. According to the historical precedent, to prudence and to good sense, it is the contention of the Council of Chiefs that the Assembly should not convene or hold forums until all the people are fully, equally represented."

There was silence; some were thinking, but most couldn't see the point and didn't want to admit it. "Well?" asked Shevyn at last. "Did you have a remark on all that?"

"I've made it," Vonran answered. "You should consider it, all of you. Those are their reasons for demanding what they do."

Declan repeated his earlier point, talking a little slowly. "Their concerns may well be legitimate. I see their point."

"Maybe, Theseus," one of his colleagues answered. "Probably they are legitimate. But what other motivations do they have?"

"Say it plainly," said Shevyn. "Where's their self-interest in those demands?"

That started the discussion off again, and it promptly returned to the circles it had been running. But not for long. Shevyn ended it, raising his voice over the others'. "Listen to me. Whatever they hope to gain by this, we all agree they hope to gain *something*. Somehow delaying the Assembly's convening helps them. Does it even matter how? Will we give them any aid? No! We must be strong if we are to win—strong from the very beginning, strong from the first battle. We must not capitulate to the Council."

Agreement rose up from all around the table. Shevyn turned to Vonran, triumph only half-concealed glittering his eyes. "You have our advice."

Vonran had stoically heard the arguing voices suddenly unite in consensus, and he nodded briefly and wordlessly to Shevyn. "Summon in the aide," he said, to no one in particular.

The aide was summoned, and he came before Vonran. "Give the Council our reply," Vonran said, his voice alone in the silence. "We have considered their assertions ... and we agree." The silence wasn't broken, but it was suddenly transformed. Vonran felt it as he went on, "The Assembly will not convene until all our delegates have arrived. Relay this message to them at once."

The aide bowed and left, and there was brittle silence.

Colten Shevyn stood up. He stood up slowly and spoke in a quiet voice heavy with anger. "Perhaps you can tell us why you did that."

Vonran raised one eyebrow. "The decision was mine, not yours."

That was undeniably true, but it only fanned the delegates' anger and rubbed salt into their wounded pride. Another delegate stood. "But we would like," he said, "to know why."

Vonran knew his colleagues had power in their own right; he knew that they could be dangerous foes and treacherous subordinates. Their anger was on the verge of mutinous. But Vonran leaned back in his chair and surveyed their faces with intolerable calm, and his coolness held all their anger in scorn.

The delegates granted Vonran their silence as they waited for him to speak, but their patience felt predatory, ready to leap. Finally Vonran spoke. "I never took Kinlol for such a fool, and the rest of you disappoint me also."

This was no explanation, and far from complimentary, but the delegates were too bewildered to offer an immediate response.

They didn't have time for anything more. Vonran's own anger suddenly flared, and he stood up, fixing all the men at the table with a hard gaze. "Have you lost all your shrewdness? Do you have no subtlety left at all?

"Don't you understand? Victory goes to the one who wins the last battle, not the first. What do you gain if you win a battle but lose the war? But you want so badly to win this one tussle with the Council that you have forgotten everything else. You have forgotten where victory lies. You have forgotten the war."

Vonran's anger cooled as quickly as it sprang up, but he was still stern as he went on, "You have no strategy. You have forgotten that you can lose to your own gain.

"So it is here. The Council found our great weakness. We have no right to create a new institution, no right to issue decrees by *fiat.* The most we can say is that we operate without the law because there is no law to direct us. Kinlol could have challenged us for going beyond the law, and the struggle between the Council and the

Assembly could have gone even to the courts.

"But even the very wise can be very foolish, and so Kinlol said that we lack legitimacy—without full representation. And if this Assembly is illegitimate without it, then it is legitimate with it. So the Council has said."

Vonran stopped, looking at his colleagues. "Do you see now? Without realizing what they were doing, the Council has sanctioned our right to *fiat* and to create a ruling authority over the Empire. I don't know what they hoped to gain by delaying us. But I am willing to gamble that it is not as great as what we are gaining."

The pause stretched long. "That is shrewd," said Dorjan, at last. "You are right."

"And so was the Council."

"What?" demanded Shevyn.

Vonran looked at him. "The Council was right. The Assembly should not make a decision like this without all the people being represented."

"I never heard that objection from *you*."

"Why should I have made it? You were never going to get that far—not without everyone present."

"And how," inquired Shevyn, "did you come by that prophecy?"

"It was no prophecy. I never intended to let you go so far as to vote."

"Even the Premier doesn't have the power to stop a vote."

"But I have other powers, and I know how to use them." Vonran turned to the rest of the delegates. "We will have a few days' wait at least, as the Regial delegation has not even left Regial and we cannot conduct our business without them. If any of you has any concerns or advice, I would be glad to hear them. You may contact me at my home—as that is where I am going, as soon as I issue the moratorium on the forums and the convention. This meeting is dismissed." Vonran stepped between his chair and Dorjan's and circled past the table. He didn't look back until he had nearly reached the door, and then he turned around to all the men watching him and said, "And a fair day to you all." And so Vonran was gone.

LIV

Shevyn sat down slowly and looked around at the others, to find them doing the same. It seemed like something should be said, but no one could think what it was.

"They are fine girls," said Declan.

"What?" asked Dorjan, for all the delegates.

Declan nodded towards the door. "His children. They are fine girls, every one of them—lovely like their mother was."

They stared at him. Dorjan shrugged. "That's true. It has nothing to do with anything we were talking about, but it's true."

Declan explained, "He said he was going home, to his girls. They need him more, now that their mother is gone."

Shevyn shook his head. "You live in a different world, Declan, and sometimes I think it is a better one. But one thing I do know."

"What is that?"

"It is well that Elymas Vonran's mind works so well, because it works alone." And there was bitterness in his voice.

CHAPTER

III

* * * * * * * * * * * * * * * *

THE Assembly's opening ceremony did not manage to be short enough. That was Elymas Vonran's opinion.

Of course, he had to endure it. As Premier of the Assembly, he had to participate. And so he did, convincingly pretending that it was not the tedious affair it was. After it was through, it was time for the part he really did like.

Vonran had arranged to give a speech directly after the Assembly's opening. If the numbers Garin Dorjan had given him were right, billions from all over the Empire were watching. It sent a tremor, a small and pleasant thrill, through him.

Vonran had written his speech carefully. He had even dressed carefully, choosing a dark tunic with a pattern woven into the collar and cuffs, and slashed across the chest. The thread looked like silver, but the discerning eye could tell that it was platted azor. It was expensive enough to impress those who cared for such things, plain enough not to offend those who did not. Vonran expected both to watch his speech, and he meant to bring them all to his side.

After the ceremony was over, Vonran climbed the steps of the podium. It was so high it was almost bizarre—like a small tower—but it allowed a speaker to address everyone in the Hall. The podium was at the front of the Hall, not far from the presiding officer's rostrum. It was reserved for occasions such as this; the delegates most often spoke and debated from the floor.

Vonran took his place and swept his eyes over the delegates seated in the Hall. There were galleries descending down to the floor, each projecting further than the one before. Shevyn was seated high up with the delegation of Tremain and Vonran looked up and saw him. He wondered if his imagination or the lights deceived him, but he thought Shevyn's eyes glittered as he looked down at him.

No matter. Vonran knew Shevyn was watching him with eyes like an eagle's—Shevyn, and other men, too, not least among them Gerog Kinlol.

And what Vonran felt then was not anger or even hostility, but something that was almost joy. *Here's to you,* he thought to Shevyn. *And here's to all the other eagles. I wouldn't ask for lesser opponents.*

They made the battle all the more challenging, victory all the sweeter. Vonran was ready to join the battle with them, and he would with this very speech. Standing at the podium, he felt on him the eyes of the delegates and the people, and the eyes of the eagles. And he began, "Delegates and fellow citizens, we are gathered here today in the wake of a tragedy that has left the Empire leaderless. And so I address not only the Assembly, not only the Council of Chiefs and the officials, but all the people of the Empire ... "

The Chiefs, along with Gawin Gaelin, had gathered to watch Vonran's speech. Gaelin was hosting the men at his home, and they were physically comfortable, even if their mental state was more tense. After opening, Vonran reviewed their present situation. His words on the late emperor were moving, his summation of their situation eloquent and persuasive. He went on to the Assembly's special session, and a general feeling of depression spread through the Chiefs' gathering.

"We were fools," said Trey Uman.

"We were hasty," corrected Kinlol.

"We were fools to be hasty," Uman said. "Why didn't we think more carefully? Why weren't we more skeptical?" The words were no sooner out of his mouth than he looked sharply at Kavin

Gyas.

Gyas was gracious enough to say nothing, but he did rap his chair's wooden armrest twice. Several of the Chiefs became irritated guessing what had gone through his mind.

They grew quiet, listening to Vonran again. “And so,” he was saying, “the Council of Chiefs and the Assembly agreed on this course, and now we are all gathered. Assured of the unity between these two bodies, we go forward together ... ”

“At least we got our foot in,” said Gyas.

“It is known as salvaging disaster,” said Uman.

“Listen,” said Kinlol.

“Our task is clear,” Vonran continued. “We must provide leadership for the Empire. Until Alexander can arise to take his own, someone must fulfill his duty, and go in and out before the people ... ”

The gathering seemed to take in a collective breath. “We have it,” said Uman. “He wants a regent.”

“Just as I said,” said Kinlol. He turned to Dheval. “Once you asked me, Dheval, what Elymas Vonran wanted. Now we know. Now everyone knows.”

One man stood up at the table. He held a small device, the remote by which he was controlling the holo-projector. It was projecting a three-dimensional floor plan of the Palace. A green circle was in the image, crossing through the blue lines of the Palace. “And that,” he said, “is our review of the last security perimeter. It is difficult because it is fluid, always moving with the emperor. But we have found it secure.”

Adon Kereth nodded to his subordinate. “Thank you, Major,” he said. “And the old servants' stairwell?”

“Sir, we closed and sealed the doors and then we disabled the circuitry. After that, we set up a bookcase at the exit into the emperor's chambers, and built a false wall over the entrance in the command center. That should do it, sir. Even if anyone should break through, they would find the doors inoperable.”

"Very good," Kereth said. "Anything else?"

"Yes, sir," a captain spoke up. "Will there be any changes from the review you ordered?"

"I haven't decided on any," Kereth answered. "Anyone else?" Nobody spoke. "Dismissed."

The officers stirred and began to collect their compads. "I had thought," the major said as he closed down the holo-projector, "that the Assembly might do something by now."

"They've been in session less than a week," said Kereth.

"I know. And still—you know what they said. This Assembly was going to be like the Great Council. The Chiefs and the delegates had agreed. All would be settled. They would resolve the crisis!" He shook his head. "They're doing nothing, and life goes on."

"They've been holding those forums and debating the matter. They're deciding, Daven. Have you ever tried to get a thousand men to move quickly?"

"Certainly. I sent them all deployment notifications."

"All right. Have you ever tried to make a thousand politicians move quickly?" Kereth amended.

"No, but you said 'men'."

"Aren't politicians human?"

"It's a theory, anyway."

"They did make a great noise over their convening," inserted Dilv. "My parents in Neven watched Vonran's speech—and so did everyone they know."

"I heard the same from my brother in Byzal," said another officer.

Kereth strode out of the room, the officers' voices fading behind. But one—a lieutenant—followed. "Sir," he said, hurrying to catch up. "Sir, I wanted to talk about the schedule."

"Yes?" Kereth asked, not breaking stride.

"Sir, I was told I would be off-duty Friday. But now I'm on."

"You heard the announcement of the changes, Carlon. There is an unexpected increase in activity that day. We need more security and so we are calling you back."

"What about Lieutenant Miyl?"

"He is on special assignment."

"The evaluation."

Kereth stopped and turned at Carlon's tone. "And if so?"

"Sir, it isn't urgent. He could take my post, no harm done. It's very important for me to be off-duty."

"Why? Your wedding day?"

"No, sir, the anniversary of it. Colonel, you've had us working harder lately and I haven't had the time to be the husband I ought to be." Kereth went completely still, and Carlon didn't notice. "Sir," he continued, "I need to give this day to my wife. She's been very good to me and she deserves it. I have my duty to her, too."

Kereth's discomfort with Carlon's words turned to a sour feeling, burgeoning guilt and regret, and the loneliness he had tried to hide from himself. "Your duty to your country is first," Kereth responded with a harshness that surprised himself. Scrambling for a recovery, he went on, "Lieutenant, our work is important. I work as hard as any man and probably hardest of all. I allow nothing to supersede the carrying out of my duty. Do you know what that means?"

The lieutenant looked at him, slightly perplexed, like a schoolboy called to answer a question that had not been in the lesson. "Sir?"

"You are in the military, Lieutenant. I expect a devotion appropriate to your calling. You should have known going in that there would be sacrifices for you and your whole family."

"I know, but, sir ... one day?"

Kereth looked at him wordlessly for a long minute. "You are dismissed, Lieutenant."

"Yes, sir." Carlon saluted and hurried away.

Kereth turned away, but the episode was unpleasant to him and he sighed a little. He walked through the command center, into the Palace proper. He was in the outer corridors, near the entrance to the gardens, when he saw the Lady Mareah and her son, accompanied by a guard. The time for wearing widow's reeds had passed, but she still dressed plainly, even by her standards.

Kereth stopped, and so did Mareah. She stood a short distance from him, her right hand on her son's shoulder.

Kereth bowed. "Hail, Empress," he greeted her. "And hail, Emperor," he added, kneeling to be at eye-level with Alexander.

The child, his liege, looked at him with a kind of solemn puzzlement, as if he were deciphering Kereth's words. Kereth looked at him, his serious gray eyes, only a moment before glancing up at Mareah. Her left hand had come to Alexander's other shoulder, and Kereth was surprised by the disapproval he saw in her eyes. He stood up, and Mareah nodded to him, polite but not warm. "Good day, Colonel."

"Good day, Lady Mareah," he answered.

Mareah guided Alexander onward and they walked past Kereth, the guard following in their wake. Kereth watched them go, puzzled. *What did I do*? he wondered, and walked on. He returned to his office and settled behind his desk, calm and feeling like a man who had failed. His emotions were still and his mind was clear, and after a little thought he keyed a frequency into his comm. "Major Daven?"

"Yes, sir."

"I want you to re-order the guards' schedule for Friday. Lieutenant Carlon had that day free originally and I want him to have it again."

"Have you re-evaluated the security needs?"

"No. Keep security as tight as planned. And if you can't spare one man ... there's Lieutenant Miyl. You can take him off that CR evaluation for a day. It isn't urgent."

"Yes, sir."

"Thank you, Major." Kereth switched off the comm.

"Some of the delegates still want more forums, Elymas," Garin Dorjan said.

Vonran glanced at him. "We have had a week of forums," he said mildly.

"Many think it's not enough."

"Yes," Vonran acknowledged, hardly even trying to keep his apathy from bleeding into his voice. "A speedy decision is important: We must strike while the iron is hot. But it's not an argument worth making, not when we are on our way to the meeting of the leaders."

Dorjan sighed. "No, not now. But I have had to make it again and again— None of the leaders are entering this fray. A mild 'It might be better to wait' is the most any of them will say in favor of delay. They will not argue their own point of view. But the other delegates! They keep coming to me, stopping me in the halls, calling me!"

Vonran's lips twitched, but he succeeded in keeping his amusement off his face. "I, too, have had to deal with them. They do not want a resolution so soon."

Dorjan shook his head. "No, they don't. And that Nemin Ziphernan! For being so new he should be more silent!"

"Indeed." Vonran took his compad off his desk and made his way to the door, Dorjan following. The two men took a lift for the floor beneath, and they went through the halls and came to a large, long room. There was a large table in its center, shaped like a rectangle with its corners cut off. Vonran took his seat in the middle of the table, and Dorjan sat beside him. He spotted Theseus Declan and leaned over to Vonran, speaking low even though no one was near them. "It's good you persuaded him, Elymas. He has been persuading others, and they have all been arguing for a regent in the forums, convincing other delegates and advocating the regency to their prefects and legislators."

Vonran thought of the other half of the clinch, how their work in the media had been turning popular opinion in their favor. That put pressure on the legislatures to support a regent also, and the legislatures in turn put pressure on the delegates. Vonran never assumed victory; he moved and watched carefully. But things seemed to be going the right way.

Seemed. Nothing was done until it was done. As Vonran looked towards the room's entrance, he saw Colten Shevyn enter the room. He looked at Vonran and their eyes met, but only briefly. Shevyn turned away and went to greet the other men.

Vonran felt Dorjan's gaze and looked over at him. "No more proxies," he murmured to him. Dorjan looked as if he understood.

Vonran watched the rest of the men filter in, trying to tamp down his impatience to begin. The meeting of the leaders was the beginning of the end of debating in the Assembly; everyone knew to expect the vote within days. In addition to the delegation heads, there were the other leaders in the Assembly—caucus and party leaders and the elders. Declan was an elder, and the exemplar of the elders; they were wise and respected men who had achieved no formal position of leadership. They were chosen by vote, and there were not many of them. It was an irrevocable privilege, and that limited the number of men who were given it. But the delegates enjoyed elevating men to become elders; it was like laymen sending a few of their own into a conference of theologians.

When everyone was gathered at the table, Vonran called the meeting to order. He rose and addressed them, "Gentlemen, leaders of the Assembly, we are gathered today to debate the matter currently before the Assembly. For seven days now it has been in the forums, and everyone has said what they wished. Now may we come to a resolution. And as you seek it, gentlemen, I ask you to remember that you are here not only in your own right, but also in the place of your provinces and fellow delegates. They have the right to demand an accounting.

"As you all know, the matter before us is how the Empire should proceed in the face of Emperor Judah's death and his son's incapacity. The delegates have debated two proposals. One"—Vonran turned towards Shevyn—"has been proposed by the head of the delegation of Tremain, Colten Shevyn. If you would sum up your proposal for us, Shevyn, we would be pleased to begin." Vonran sat down, having thrown the conversation to Shevyn like a brick with no warning.

Shevyn caught it. Rising to his feet, he explained, "I proposed a commission, with members appointed by the Council of Chiefs and the Assembly. This commission would maintain harmony between the Assembly and the Council. Should the need for an emperor become absolute, it would also provide a mechanism by which the two bodies may settle the matter." Shevyn took his seat again and turned to Vonran. "Now perhaps you, Premier Vonran, may explain your view."

Shevyn probably enjoyed turning the question back on him, but Vonran had steeled himself for harder things than that. He smiled at Shevyn and didn't bother to rise. "It needs no explanation. I advocate a regent—nothing so new or complicated as a reigning commission."

"If the commission is more complicated, it is because it shares the duties and powers, rather than concentrating them all in one man."

"It pleased the founders of this nation to concentrate it all in one man." Vonran turned to the rest of the men. "And what has pleased the delegates and the provinces?" he asked.

"As for what has pleased the provinces," one of the delegation heads said, "I have been consulting with the prefect and legislators of my province. But no final decision has been reached, and I hold those discussions in confidence."

Other delegates nodded at his words. Vonran knew that they were either undecided, or they hadn't brought their legislatures to their own point of view. The delegates were required to consult with their province's prefect and legislature, but they voted as they pleased. And yet they were not entirely free, for they were appointed by the legislatures. It was a complex relationship, fed on tensions between the delegates' freedom and their dependency, the power of the legislators to appoint and the shrewdness of delegates who understood their own advantages.

Vonran looked around to see if anyone would speak. The leader of the delegation of Teari—whom Vonran had always respected, even though he often didn't like him—spoke up. "The legislature of Teari is divided, and I am not surprised. There is wisdom and peril on both sides."

"The question, then," Vonran said, "is which side has the greater wisdom or peril."

"To be sure," Theseus Declan said. "And I find them both to be on the same side. A single man can rule far better than a commission, but if he is not a good man, how much worse he would be!"

"Then it is incumbent on us to choose him wisely," Vonran answered.

"That is what Norphatt desires—a good regent," said a delegation head.

"I, too, am in agreement," said Declan.

One man—the leader of the Builders Party, of which Vonran was nominally a member—was looking around the table, at the men's faces. Finally he turned to Vonran. "Premier Vonran," he said, "you favor a regent. All of the delegates have heard you speak of it. But not often. You have presided at some of the forums, but you have debated little. But now, Premier, state your case to us and defend it. Are you not a leader among us?"

All eyes were on Vonran, and he was struck by their intentness. Vonran's gaze landed on Shevyn, and then he understood. These were all politicians, practical men who chose their battles. They were keen to discern who had power, and now they wanted to know. The Assembly was divided between two ideas, and they wanted to see the leader of each side go against the other. They wanted to know which was the stronger, which would come out the better man.

And, whoever he was, they would feel a powerful urge to join him. All politicians had an almost overwhelming instinct to side with the stronger, even those who did not succumb. It was a weakness and a strength, wise in its time and short-sighted in its way. It had been an obstacle and a help to Vonran in the past. And now, whether he approved or not, he was faced with it again. So he would have to make it a help.

"I thank you for the invitation to make my case to you," Vonran said. "I will be brief, gentlemen. I have no need to be long. I will speak to the peril of it, and the prudence. First, for the peril: You feel it is great, but think! Do you see how much we are at the mercy of fate, being ruled by those who gain the throne by ancestry? We don't choose our emperors, but we will choose our regent, and we know his time is limited. We face much less danger here than we will on the day of Alexander's coronation.

"For the prudence: My friends, this is plain and clear before you. Our government is centered around an emperor; without him, we have no leader. Who here would have a body without a head? Who would have an empire without an emperor? If we cannot have an emperor, we must have a regent."

" 'Must' is a strong word, Premier," Shevyn said. "Do you see no other alternative?"

Well, the delegates wanted a confrontation. A confrontation Vonran would give them. He turned to Shevyn and asked, "Such as your commission?"

"Yes," said Shevyn. "Such as that."

"I do not say it has no merits. But it is not our system of government, and it would not be wise to have the Council and the Assembly assuming the emperorship."

"You mischaracterize my proposal, Premier."

Vonran raised an eyebrow. "And how is that?"

"The commission would ensure harmony between the Council and the Assembly. If there were a matter beyond their spheres, it would be settled through the commission. I do not intend the commission to *rule*."

"A passive emperor is still the emperor. A passive commission reigning in the emperor's place still reigns." Vonran turned his gaze from Shevyn to all the men at the table. "We have lost an emperor. We will have a substitute to stand in his place. The only question is: Which will we put on the throne—a man, or a committee?"

Vonran didn't even look at Shevyn; he looked at all the other delegates, judging their expressions to see if they accepted his wisdom.

And, as he had said, it was plain and clear before them.

Kinlol looked down at the summary of the Assembly's law, and he hated it. It was just what he had expected, just what he had feared, and he hated it.

Kinlol looked back up at Elymas Vonran and thrust the compad to him. "I knew all this."

Vonran nodded, accepting the compad with more grace than Kinlol had given it. It was easier to be gracious when you were winning.

The two men were outside the Palace, walking along a stone path. Vonran had suggested that they, as leaders of the Council and the Assembly, meet for a few minutes before the other Chiefs and the Assembly's representatives did. Kinlol accepted, though Vonran's graciousness in making the suggestion—like his graciousness in agreeing to the meeting with the Council and its location at the Palace—irritated him. The Assembly was ready to vote, and they expected the law authorizing the establishment of a regent to pass. Kinlol doubted the Council's opposition would have any effect at all. But he didn't tell that to Vonran as they walked.

"The Assembly," Vonran said, "has agreed to this meeting to hear the Council's view on the proposed law. We have no agenda beyond that. Has the Council any other issues it will raise?"

"No," Kinlol said. "It, too, is focused solely on this law. And there will be eleven men, besides yourself?"

"Yes."

"And you will preside over them, to have an orderly and relevant discussion?"

"As you will preside over the Chiefs, Chief Kinlol."

"Indeed." Kinlol looked ahead; an offshoot of the path traveled to the Palace and led the way to a door. "Come, Premier. Let's go inside. It's nearly time." Kinlol led the way into the Palace, to one of the council rooms at the officials' disposal. It was empty, and the two men stood beside each other at the table. Then the door slid open, and Trey Uman stepped in. As he greeted Vonran, Kinlol crossed over to the other side of the table, sitting in the middle. Uman soon joined him.

The rest of the men gathered quickly, dividing themselves onto each side of the table, Kinlol with his Chiefs facing Vonran with his delegates. Kinlol began by offering a politic statement he did not enjoy delivering, and then he said, "The Council has considered the very course you have now proposed. And we have seen one great danger—that the regent you appoint, having gained the power of the emperorship, may refuse to relinquish it. The Empire would then likely descend into civil war. Even if it does not —if the usurper is not opposed—it would do great destruction to our law and our honor."

"We have also considered that danger," Vonran answered. "But we have concluded that it is not so great as to outweigh the wisdom of a regency."

"We must choose wisely, Chief Kinlol," Garin Dorjan added. "You may trust that we will be careful."

Trey Uman responded to that, but Kinlol knew it was pointless. He let the conversation go for a few minutes, and then he intervened. "Premier," he said, looking at Vonran, "there is a strange oversight in the law you have proposed. It has not set the time at which the regent will step down."

"Is it not in the language of the law that the regent shall yield to Alexander when he is ready to rule?"

"It is. But I believe we should name a time." Kinlol nodded at his fellow Chiefs. "You have heard us express our concerns. You have acknowledged that you share them. It would allay our fears to know that there is a set time at which the regent would be compelled to yield."

Colten Shevyn spoke before Vonran could. "And what time do you have in mind?" he asked.

"The day after Alexander reaches his majority."

Vonran registered a response—at least as much of a response as he ever did. He raised his head and looked at Kinlol, and the light glinted off his eyes. "He would be only seventeen."

Kinlol nodded. "Young to bear the emperorship, I know. But still an adult. Do we have cause to withhold the emperorship from the son of the emperor, once he is a man?"

"I would have the emperorship in the hands of a wiser, more experienced man," Vonran said.

"As would I," said Theseus Declan. "But the law places it in the hands of the son of the emperor, whether he is a young man or not, whether he is wise or foolish. We must yield to the law."

There was assent on both sides of the table. Vonran's expression revealed nothing to Kinlol, and neither did his voice. "I will have language providing that written and submitted to the proper committee. Once it passes through there, the Assembly will vote on its inclusion."

Kinlol bowed his head. "That is all we expect." And it was, unfortunately, the most he could hope to get.

The meeting had no real purpose after that. Kinlol—and, he could tell, Vonran—saw it. Kinlol announced that all the Council's advice had been presented, and Vonran took leave for himself and all the delegates. The Chiefs rose from their seats, but it was their territory if it was anyone's, and the delegates were quicker to leave.

Kinlol crossed to the other side of the room, moving in the general direction of the door. He watched for an opportunity, and surely enough it came. Some of the delegates had already left, and others were following—Colten Shevyn among them. He started to pass by Kinlol, who stepped forward. "I had guessed you would be among Vonran's delegates," he said.

Shevyn looked at Kinlol, stepping closer, out of the way of those passing towards the door. "I believe I can take that as a compliment, Chief Kinlol."

"So you can," Kinlol assured him. "I heard of your proposed commission, Shevyn. An innovative idea—though I see the Assembly did not accept it."

"Enough of them didn't," Shevyn answered. "But you would not have approved, Kinlol. Any more than you approve of the regent."

"So we have both lost," Kinlol declared. "And we know who it is who has won."

Shevyn said nothing, gave no indication he knew who Kinlol was speaking about. His expression was guarded but not hostile, and he waited for Kinlol to go on.

"Elymas Vonran has achieved the regency he desired." Kinlol paused, and his expression turned serious. "Speak honestly, Shevyn. Do you have any doubt that Vonran intends the regent to be himself?"

Shevyn's expression only barely hardened. "We have not come so far, Chief Kinlol. If you will excuse me, I must be going." He turned and strode out. No delegates now remained, and the Chiefs stood together in silence. Slowly they disbanded, returning to tend to their usual business.

True to his word, Vonran had the language written and submitted to the committee for revisions. That afternoon they assembled to consider it. Vonran had, at the beginning of the session, declared it urgent, and he put the Assembly under constraints so that it could not recess or consider any other issue until the matter before them was resolved. The committee members, therefore, had nothing to do other than consider the proposed language. That evening they approved it, and sent notice to Vonran.

Vonran had his staffers draw up a summary of the amendment and its history. Once he approved it, the summary and a copy of the language were sent to every delegate. Vonran officially put the amendment before the Assembly, and a copy of it was placed on the presiding officer's desk.

By then it was after dinnertime, yet the delegates debated the amendment hours into the night. The Council of Chiefs sent a memorandum explaining and advocating the amendment, and that stirred the delegates up all the more. So the delegates stayed late that night, and gathered again early the next morning. That night they called for a vote, and the amendment was added to the proposed law.

But their night's work was not over. Vonran called on the Assembly to vote on the amended law, and they did. It passed and a regency was established for the next ten years.

The delegates abandoned the Hall—tired for the most part, but buoyed with a sense of the significance of what they had just done. But, even as his colleagues streamed home, Colten Shevyn remained.

He was not a happy man. At this point, it was not really the death of his commission that bothered him. He had fought for the amendment—not that he had any enthusiasm for it, but he intuited that Vonran didn't like it and that was enough. What he wondered was why Vonran hadn't fought against it. Shevyn had come up with two reasons: Either Vonran didn't consider success likely enough, or he had perceived that if you wanted to become regent, you should not be seen fighting to make the regent's rule unlimited.

Shevyn thought it was the latter. Because he had no doubt at all that Vonran intended the regent to be himself.

He couldn't admit that to Kinlol. Shevyn couldn't tell him that his words had crystallized an unease, a suspicion that had lurked beneath Shevyn's thoughts. Shevyn was certain of Vonran's ambition, and it deeply bothered him. It didn't fade with time; it grew.

And, walking down a wide, deserted corridor, passing ornate doorways to dark rooms, he could stand it no more. Shevyn stopped abruptly, spun around, and marched to Vonran's office. It was the dead of night and he was likely to be gone, but that didn't stop Shevyn. In his mood, he might follow the man home.

Shevyn found Vonran's secretary gone, but he tried to enter Vonran's office anyway. The doors slid open to reveal a dark room, and Shevyn went in, too hurried to be surprised. He called for the lights and looked around. The room was empty, and in the far corner he spotted a discreet door—a nice study was adjacent to the premier's office.

Shevyn made for the door. It was hinged, and Shevyn gripped the gilded doorknob and threw the door open. He strode in—to darkness.

Shevyn came to a stop, finally calm enough to think. The rooms were dark; Vonran was gone; it was curious that the unoccupied rooms weren't locked; he wouldn't follow Vonran home; probably. He began to turn to the door, and a voice came out of the shadows: "A man of your rank may easily make an appointment."

Shevyn jumped in an all-too literal way; his heels actually left the floor. Then he despised himself, because of course he recognized Vonran's voice. Shevyn turned towards the left side of the room, beyond the door. It was all darkness there; Shevyn was standing in the little light that spilled into the study. “Why are you in the dark?” he asked.

“I think I have more of a right to ask why you are here.”

That was true. Shevyn wasn't about to say so. “May we talk in the light?” Shevyn expected Vonran to turn on the overhead lights, but he didn't speak. Shevyn could sense movement in the darkness, then there was light in the room.

But not enough. Vonran had turned on a lamp. It was on an end table beside the easy chair Vonran sat in. “You may speak now,” he said. “And you may sit, if you desire.”

Shevyn stood near a chair; he pulled it closer to Vonran and sat. “The law has passed.”

Vonran met Shevyn's eyes with his insufferable calm. “I know.”

“Now we have to appoint a regent.”

Vonran raised his hands in front of himself and pressed his fingertips together. His fingers were long and his skin was fair, but there was strength in those hands. “I know,” he said, with a mildness only a fool would take for weakness.

Shevyn was burning with anger, but he didn't speak quickly. “Tell me, Vonran,” he said when he trusted his voice and words. “Don't you want to be regent? From the very beginning, hasn't that been in your mind?”

Shevyn had half-hoped Vonran would be disturbed by the direct question. He wasn't. He looked at Shevyn long and intently, and though he seemed tired his eyes had not lost their intensity. At last he spoke. “Let us dispense with politics, you and I. Let us forget we ever learned to speak neither truth nor lies. Above all, let us dispense with false modesty.

“Lesser men than we have been emperor. But because of our ancestry, we are disqualified from the prize. Now we have a chance to sit on that high seat—only for a few years, but even that is glory beyond anything we might have dreamed.

“Is it not so, Shevyn? I desire that high seat; I know I can discharge its duties as well as any man. Do you condemn me?”

Shevyn stared at Vonran, who met his eyes unwaveringly.

And no lie, no politic answer would come to Shevyn's lips. He couldn't speak any objection to Vonran's words. A few hours ago—even in private—he would have guarded himself against admission of such truths, but the world seemed different now. The light the lamp threw didn't travel far, and the men were surrounded by shadows, overhung by darkness. They were alone in an edifice—and there is no place so lonely as one made for humanity and then deserted by it. In the middle of the darkness and emptiness, pretense and guile fell away, and only the truth remained.

There was a long silence. Finally Shevyn rose to his feet and left without a word.

In the wake of Shevyn's departure Vonran sat alone again, with his quiet thoughts. It had been a strange visit, like he'd never had before. But now was not the time to think about it. Now it was time for Vonran to go home. He'd been putting it off too long. He had soothed his conscience earlier with reminders that his children were already asleep anyway, but he knew he ought to be home. It was an act of will to go; Vonran so wanted to tell Dianthe that he had won so far and he was glad, but she wouldn't be there. There was no one at home for him to tell anything to. But there were his daughters.

When Vonran arrived home he went upstairs and checked on Cala first. He was relieved to find her safe in bed, and went on to the room that Vera and Lydia still shared. He had considered giving Vera her own room and moving Cala in with Lydia—it might do Cala good to share a room, but the other girls probably wouldn't like it. They were only two years apart and had always been close. All three girls could share a room for a few years. Of course, there was no bedroom big enough, but that was easy to solve. He would call in an architect and have him ...

Vonran let the thought go. It could be the problem of another day. Tonight he would only check on his girls and then go to bed. It was a late night, after many late nights, and he was tired, and not only in body.

Vera and Lydia were sound asleep. Vonran looked at each

one, standing between their beds. Zelrynn took after him, and Cala after Dianthe, but in the middle two there was a fair mix of them both. Dianthe was already in Vonran's thoughts and he could see her in his daughters' faces, and that, likely, was the reason he thought of it.

Vonran knelt down by Lydia's bed, resting a hand lightly on her head. He tried to pray, but the words didn't come as easily to him as they once had. Dianthe and he used to pray regularly for the children. It was easy then, but that changed, and Vonran knew when.

In the wake of Dianthe's death, Vonran had tried turning to God in prayer, and it left him feeling cold. He felt like he was standing outside a house, shuttered and bolted against him, and he came to wonder if the reason it seemed so silent was that it was empty.

He stopped praying for himself, though he occasionally prayed for his children. He didn't know why. Maybe it was because he hoped that even if God wasn't concerned with him, He might care about the girls. But then—how much could He? He had left them motherless. Perhaps it was all merely for Dianthe, since the ritual of prayer had meant so much to her. Or maybe it was some last scrap of faith, turning him insensibly back.

Vonran didn't know. He hadn't realized how much his faith had depended on Dianthe's until he lost her. Then he learned. He had built his house on sand and it collapsed. And yet, maybe, beneath the sand, there was rock, or at least a place where a true foundation could be laid. He never swept the sand away to find out. He had no heart for such a laborious task, no heart to knock on the bolted door.

No heart, hardly, to pray anymore. He hardly knew what to ask, even for his daughters, from One who had stood aside when Dianthe died, and their happiness with her.

Vonran stood on his feet and quietly left the room, closing the door behind him.

“And now, the first order of business,” Kinlol announced to the Chiefs. “How many men will we recommend to the Assembly? Shall we make up a list, or recommend only one man?"

"For me," said Gyas, "the answer would depend largely on how many men I think are truly qualified to be regent."

"As a matter of strategy ... " Kinlol began.

"Oh, strategy, strategy," interrupted Trey Uman. "What has all our brilliant strategy gotten us? Everything Vonran wanted on a silver platter."

"Not everything," Kinlol said. "I don't believe he wanted that term limit."

"Probably not. I don't care much. Let's go back and consider what Gyas said. Who's qualified to be regent?"

"Well, we can't recommend anyone on the Council," Gyas said.

"I guarantee the Assembly is going to nominate a delegate," Kinlol said.

"I don't doubt it. But I believe we should all stay on the Council, to ensure that it will remain an undivided advocate for Alexander until he becomes emperor. We are all loyal to Emperor Judah and to his son. And is there any one among us with a serious desire to become emperor? I at least have never envied the task."

The Chiefs looked around at each other, watching their colleagues' reactions, waiting to see who would deny or not deny such ambition. No one spoke.

Chief of Intelligence David Ithran cleared his throat in the awkward silence. "We are Chiefs," he said.

Kinlol glanced at him and then the other Chiefs. "My friends," he said, "you know that I have not lacked ambition. But I never wanted to be the emperor, only to serve him."

"So then," said Uman. "Whom shall we consider? Are there any prefects you would vest with the duty?"

There was a moment of silence. "Alec Niktos is an impressive man," said one of the Chiefs.

"And Armana is a large province," said Kinlol. "Populous as well."

"Of course, the largest and most populous province is Regial," said Uman. "Therefore I propose we nominate Yorik

Bemus. For laughs alone it would be worth it."

"Be serious," said Dheval, with a crossness Kinlol suspected he'd arrived with.

"One can't always be serious," Uman replied. "It would be unpatriotic. How could we destroy an industry so large as entertainment?" Dheval didn't reply; he just kept looking cross.

"I have found Lorda's new prefect to be an effective leader," said Gyas.

"Too new," said Uman. "Little tested."

"Elymas Vonran probably runs circles around him," Kinlol added. "But the prefects—though they are often fine leaders and executives—have no experience with national issues. How many of them understand Telnaria? How many have friends or allies here to help them as they learn?"

"Well, what of those in Telnaria?" Uman asked. "Besides the Chiefs, what other leaders can we turn to?"

"The generals," Kinlol said. "And of them I find Gawin Gaelin the most impressive. He is a leader of men. He knows Telnaria. He has many friends and allies here. He is married to Layne, Emperor Judah's older sister. Alexander is his nephew, and his children are Alexander's blood cousins. He would be competent, as well as safe."

There was a pause. "I agree," said Uman. "We should recommend him, at least. Is there anyone else to consider? What about the Assembly?"

"Theseus Declan is the best man there," said Gyas, "but too old. Garin Dorjan—he is not too great a leader. I wouldn't recommend Colten Shevyn." Gyas stopped and looked around at the other Chiefs, and when none of them spoke his expression became a little angry. "I'll say it. What none of you want to, I will. What of Elymas Vonran for regent? He is a master politician, a man others look to to lead. He would be at least as competent a ruler as any we have mentioned. He is the Premier of the Assembly, and few have his stature."

"We don't need to recommend him," Kinlol answered. "Mark my words, he will recommend himself."

"And whom will we recommend?"

Kinlol looked around the table. "Whom does the Council approve?"

"These are the men the Council approved." Dorjan scanned the list before handing the compad to Vonran. "You're not on it."

Vonran read the names. "Gawin Gaelin and Alec Niktos. Not bad."

Dorjan glanced around the corridor to see if anyone they were passing had heard. He noticed nothing. "Are you sure you want to preside over this meeting? You will not be allowed to nominate anyone."

"That is fine."

"What if your choice is not nominated?"

Vonran's choice was himself. If no one else would even nominate him, it wasn't likely they would choose him. And if he was nominated, it would be better if it was done by someone other than himself. "I trust the delegates will nominate all good candidates," Vonran assured Dorjan.

The two men walked together only a short distance before parting in different directions, going to separate entrances to the Hall. Vonran entered near the front and took his seat up in the presiding officer's chair. The officer's desk was one piece with its rostrum, and a compad was laying on it. Vonran picked the compad up and reviewed its contents briefly, to make sure he was fully apprised of everything before the Assembly.

He was. Vonran laid the compad down and turned to his computer. There was a computer screen in the surface of the desk, and one operated the computer by touching it; there were no keys or buttons at all. The computer was networked with all the delegates' stations. "Station" was a misnomer in the opinion of many, for something that was little more than a panel. Each delegate had his own station by his seat, with a biological sensory program that allowed only him to use it. The delegates cast their votes through this machine, and registered in the roll-call through it.

The roll-call was what Vonran was looking up. He checked the number, and even as he looked it went up. It was ten minutes until the Assembly was scheduled to start.

Vonran leaned back in his chair and waited. When the ten minutes had elapsed he called the session to order and addressed the delegates, his words amplified so that they all heard him: "The business before the Assembly today is to appoint a regent. The Council of Chiefs has recommended two men: The prefect of Armana, Alec Niktos, and General Gawin Gaelin. They are men whose reputations are known to you all. The Council has found them fitting. Do you—or does another man recommend himself to you above these?"

And so the debate began. Vonran presided and, in what was considered good form, did not enter it. After a while there was a lull, and Theseus Declan immediately stood up. Vonran recognized him, and he nodded to him, and then turned to his colleagues. Declan motioned with his hand and began, "Friends and colleagues, we have considered the Council's recommendations and other men have been nominated. They have all been prefects and generals and officials of the Empire—but now I propose to you a man from our own midst. You have already approved him as a leader, for you have made him your premier—Elymas Vonran."

All eyes turned to Vonran; he kept his eyes on Declan. But before Declan could continue—if he intended to continue—Shevyn stood up and did not wait to be recognized. "Your nomination is noted, Declan. Does the premier accept it? And will he argue on his behalf?"

"I will answer your questions, Shevyn," Vonran said, "but since I preside I will speak only shortly. I would be honored to serve as regent over this great nation, and I would willingly accept the position—should you choose to grant it to me. I will not argue on my behalf; I have been among you more than fifteen years. You have known me, how I have acted among you, and how I have led. You may judge for yourselves whether I am worthy."

A silence fell on the chamber. Finally a delegate stood up. "I second the nomination," he said.

Another man stood. “I second the nomination.”

And then another stood and proclaimed the same, and another and another ...

The news came to Kinlol late that night. *Elymas Vonran has been appointed regent.* It spread throughout all the Empire like wildfire. *Elymas Vonran has become regent, Elymas Vonran is regent ...*

He was not surprised. The amendment to limit the regent's term was merely cutting losses; the nomination of Alec Niktos and Gawin Gaelin was a try without hope—but it was his duty to try. And now—now Kinlol continued his work, his task of keeping for Alexander what was his own. The first and best strategy had failed; Kinlol was devising his second, and the strategy after that.

Gerog Kinlol was not a stubborn man in all ways; he saw the world changing and he prepared. He prepared for the ten-year emperor.

CHAPTER

IV

* * * * * * * * * * * * * * * *

ADON Kereth, as commander of the Emperor's Guard, occupied a unique position in the Empire's military. A general had been assigned to him as a superior officer, but they had little contact and Kereth carried out his duties with significant autonomy. But even he, sometimes, was required to go to his superior officer. Kereth had come upon just such a time, and so he left the Palace for the Avidon—the headquarters of the entire military. Typical of Telnaria's most prestigious buildings, the Avidon was huge. Atypically, it was ugly.

At least Kereth had always thought so. Humility suggested he call it one man's opinion; frankness forbade it, because it really was ugly. The heavy masonry, the weathered granite, the huge square columns—maybe it had all aged badly, and in the beginning was not so offensive to the human eye. Maybe. Kereth placed no confidence in the idea. Militaries had often been renowned, but never for a sense of aesthetics.

In the Avidon Kereth reported to his superior, a second-tier general. After they were through with the routine matters, Kereth said, "General Ikron, I told you there was something I wanted to discuss with you today. It concerns Regent Vonran. I believe he should receive full protection."

"We have concluded the same," Ikron said. "General Avvon has already been tasked with creating a guard."

If Kereth remembered correctly, Avvon was a fourth-tier general. "General, I think the Emperor's Guard should be given the job. We are already an existing command; we have developed structure, methods, and procedure. We have men with experience and knowledge.

"Additionally, sir, I'm sure you will understand my concerns at having security teams always in the Palace but not under my command. You know, sir, the troubles that arise when all the forces in an area are not unified under one commander."

"You haven't given me the impression, Colonel, that you have resources equal to taking on such a task."

"Allocate them to me, sir. I will manage it. The Palace is already fully under our control. We will have to assign guards to the regent—"

"I don't think you understand the situation," Ikron interrupted. "You would have to guard the regent's house as well. He is not moving to the Palace. He is commuting."

Kereth let out a short, involuntary laugh. "It will never last." Ikron continued to stare at him. "Sir," Kereth said, "allocate the proper resources, and I will create a division of the Guard to handle this task."

"That would complicate your command, Colonel. It would mean a great deal of work for you."

"I am capable, sir."

"I would not want your family life to suffer."

If Ikron knew anything about his family life he wouldn't have said that. Or maybe he did, and the comment was a low blow rather than an ignorant brush-off. Kereth couldn't tell. He managed to mostly quell his instinctive sarcasm, saying only, "Is that a no, then, sir?"

"Yes."

"Very well, sir. But I maintain that Regent Vonran will move to the Palace, and I request in advance that when he does, you will put his protection beneath my authority."

"You would then have a more compelling case, Colonel."

Kereth stood and saluted. Receiving the general's salute in

return, he turned and left. When he returned to the Palace's command center, Major Daven came to meet him. "Vonran arrived just a few minutes ago. There was a major with him."

Kereth thought he knew what to make of that. "Probably Avvon's pet officer."

"What?"

"Avvon's creating the Regent's Guard. My name," Kereth added. "The major may be the officer he intends to put in charge. He's certainly been assigned to protect Vonran. Didn't he tell you?"

"No. All he told me was that his rank was equal to mine and he was under orders from a general."

"Why didn't you ask him what his orders were?"

"I did. That was his answer."

"Let's go have a talk with the good major."

"This way." Daven led the way to the Ambassadors Room—a receiving room for foreign visitors—and the two men stepped in. Elymas Vonran stood at the front of the room, opposite a prominent judge of the high courts. A handful of men from the Council and the Assembly, and General Gaelin, looked on. Kereth's eyes searched out a man in a major's uniform, standing against the wall. He glanced at Daven, who nodded.

But this was no time or place for a scene. Kereth took a place at the back of the room, and Daven joined him. They stood, discreetly watching as the judge administered the oath, then said something Kereth couldn't hear. And then it was over. The quiet men disbanded; the conferring of power was complete.

Kereth did not make history, but he saw it and he read it. He knew that the turning points—the great events—often came without fanfare, without even a word in passing.

As the officials began to leave, Kereth made for the major, Daven at his heels. The man was beginning to leave himself, but he wasn't quick enough and his way was blocked. The major looked Kereth and Daven up and down and then tried to bypass them.

Kereth stepped in his way. "May we have a moment, Major?"

"I must follow the regent."

"Oh?"

"I have my orders."

"Truly?"

The major looked at Kereth. "Colonel, these are *orders*. The regent must be protected at all times."

"He is very protected here in the Palace. If it worries you so, Daven can follow him. After all, he has been doing such work much longer than you, and he is of equal rank." Kereth let that sink in, and then said, "But I am not. I am of superior rank, and I am in command here. I demand an explanation of your business and orders."

The major's expression was hard. "I am protecting the regent by General Avvon's orders. You can't countermand them, and you can't keep me from obeying them. If you tried you could bring down bad consequences on yourself."

It was not a good thing to say. Kereth's hand jerked, but he held it still. "There is something I would like you to understand, Major. A certain fact, generally kept from the public, is that the Palace is a military installation. If you knew the sort of defenses the Palace has, you would understand that's not only a technicality. I am in command of this installation, and my superior is General Ikron. Neither you—nor General Avvon—has the authority to interfere with my command. Is that well understood?"

"I hear," the Major said shortly. "Is that all, Colonel?" As soon as Kereth nodded, he passed around the men and was on his way.

"Avvon outranks you," Daven reminded Kereth.

"And Ikron outranks him."

"So he'll support us against Avvon's intrusion?"

"Maybe. I've had no guarantee from him." Kereth turned away and strode out of the room. He began to pass by Chief Kinlol in the corridor, but the man lifted a hand and said, "Colonel Kereth."

Kereth stopped and turned to him. "Yes?"

"I have heard that you ordered a review of the Guard."

"Yes."

"Are you worried?"

Kereth regarded the Chief, annoyed by the questioning and

feeling as if he'd already been annoyed quite enough for one day. “Chief Kinlol, it is my business to be worried.”

Kinlol nodded and smiled. “Very good.”

Even that was a little annoying. Kereth inclined his head and marched on.

Vonran arrived at the Palace in the morning to take his oath. The oath had been proposed by Kinlol—a modified version of the emperor's oath, and a badly modified one at that. Vonran didn't squabble over it—or over the judge and location Kinlol proposed.

It was a short and plain ceremony, with only witnesses from the Council, the Assembly, and the military in attendance. Vonran took the oath, the judge congratulated him and admonished him to serve well. And it was done. Vonran was regent.

He didn't know quite what to do, but he knew the Ambassadors Room was not where he was to do it. Vonran joined the exodus out, but before he reached the door a voice called to him, “Regent!” Vonran turned and saw Trey Uman approaching him. “Congratulations on your appointment,” Uman said, “and my best wishes. Chief Kinlol—” Uman glanced over at Kinlol. He was standing a few feet away, but paying no attention. His gaze was focused on something across the room. Vonran looked that way and saw two men in military uniforms approaching each other—

Uman's voice brought his attention back: “—discussed it. The second floor has wholly been given over to the Lady Mareah and Emperor Alexander. However, all the emperor's rooms on the first floor have been given to you—except the Judgment Hall.”

Vonran nodded. That was reasonable, and he had no use for the throne room anyway. “And my staff?”

“They will have offices to use as well,” Uman assured him. “Come, I will show you your office.”

Vonran followed him out. Uman led him to a large office that was impressive without being gaudy. Vonran had been there before, meeting with Emperor Judah. He walked up to the desk and stopped by one of the visitor's chairs. He suddenly felt that Uman was going to sit down in the other chair, and after a few minutes Emperor Judah was going to walk in, and they would stand ...

Vonran looked around the office, the solid reality of the colors and the furniture, and the sunlight laying across the floor beneath the window—but the vision lingered just beyond it. His new life was overtaking his old reality, and the two brushed for just a moment in passing. Vonran let go of the old, reached for the new, reminded himself that this was his office now and there was no emperor to walk in. He would not have to rise ... would they rise for him?

Suddenly it came crashing down on Vonran that he was not alone, and he looked quickly at Uman. Uman was watching him, his head slightly cocked, his eyes bright.

He understood. Vonran knew that then, and he was surprised by it. For just a moment they looked at each other, and then a harsh buzzing sounded in the room. Vonran looked around; Uman didn't. "Someone to see you," he explained. He stopped, but something had come to him, and after a moment he went on, "We always wondered why it didn't bother him. I cringed every time I heard it. But the emperor never minded at all ... " Uman trailed off, looking a little distant and a little sad. Then he snapped back. "Do you wonder who your first visitor is?"

"Enter," Vonran commanded, by way of reply.

Theseus Declan did. He came to a stop, looking between the two men. "I didn't mean to intrude ... "

"I was on my way out," Uman said. He looked at Vonran and bowed his head. "My best wishes to you again." He strode out, and as the door closed behind him Vonran turned to Declan.

"I came here to congratulate you," Declan said.

Vonran smiled. "Thank you. And thank you for nominating me. It was an expression of esteem I value."

"I knew you wanted it, and I knew you were worthy. Elymas, I know you will do well. You have much to be proud of. Only remember—remember, Elymas—that you have much to be humble about also. God has given you many good gifts, but they are only gifts. We are only creatures, and we all have one Creator."

Vonran listened and wondered what the point of all this was. It may have shown in his face, because Declan went on, "Beware of pride, Elymas. It goes before destruction."

Ah. A warning. Pride was ... destructive. Vonran took note and dismissed it from mind. He smiled at Declan. "Are you worried so soon? I have been regent ten minutes—and that ceremony was nothing to go to my head."

Declan didn't allow himself to be drawn into Vonran's good humor. He looked at Vonran solemnly. "I have been worried from the very beginning."

Vonran's smile faded away and he looked at Declan in perplexity. "Then why ... ?"

"There was a best solution, but not a perfect one."

Vonran turned away, anger bubbling up inside him at hearing Kinlol's doubts coming from Declan's lips. Was this what they all thought of him?

Behind Vonran Declan sighed. "I'm sorry, Elymas. I don't want to take away your joy, but you should be on your guard. You must be ... careful."

Vonran didn't respond or turn back. After a long moment he felt Declan's hand rest gently on his shoulder. "I will leave you to your work. Do good, and God go with you." And he left, his footsteps lost beyond the closing of the door.

Vonran was alone in the emperor's office—his office—for the first time. He slowly turned around and went and sat at the desk. He leaned back in the chair and looked at the room from this new perspective. It felt good, and restored some of his happiness. Trying to retake all of it, Vonran put his whole conversation with Declan out of mind and began his work—an emperor's work.

In another part of the Palace the Chiefs met together. And they were not happy.

They completed their business, but no one left, and Kinlol did not dismiss them. "It seems," Trey Uman said, "that we ought to say something."

LXXXVI

Javor Khiv, Chief of the Provinces, turned off his compad. “I knew you weren't listening to my report.”

“No, I mean something about Vonran taking power this morning.”

“What's to say?” Khiv asked. “We lost. He's regent. It's over.”

“And now we live in a changed Empire,” Kinlol said. “At our next meeting, we won't be alone.”

“What do you mean?” Dheval asked.

“Vonran will probably be joining us.”

“Is that necessary?” Uman asked.

“A regent is a temporary emperor. Every emperor meets with the Council. It is an essential part of ruling the Empire.”

“It is necessary.” Uman sighed. “He's been regent two hours and already I'm not liking it.”

“We can't change anything,” Gyas said—warned, maybe. “For ten years, this is the way it is.”

“It's what happens at the end of those ten years that concerns me,” Kinlol said.

“We know,” Ithran said. “And what can we do? We are not autonomous. We serve at the pleasure—and under the authority—of the emperor.”

“Vonran rules us,” said Uman—and he said it as if the words were bitter in his mouth.

They were bitter to Kinlol. “You are right—both of you. The Council cannot oppose Vonran as it did before he became regent. He is over us now.”

The other Chiefs stared at him. “You give up the battle?” Gyas asked.

Kinlol wasn't about to, but he was not going to explain his new method at a Council meeting. “How can the Council fight? Vonran is regent by law, and until he violates the law, we must abide by his rule. I do not approve of the law; I do not like the situation. You all know that. But I will not tear the government apart. Vonran has done no harm ... yet.”

No one disagreed, and there was a brief silence. “It's

strange," Uman said. "I feel as if we are at the end of something."

"We are," Kinlol said. "We are at the end of our battle against Vonran."

Uman looked at him, long and intently, but he said nothing. "And you have nothing to say?" Ithran asked. "No 'Farewell' or 'Well-fought'?"

"I'll not say good-bye, Ithran," Kinlol answered. "We will serve Vonran together—and we will serve Alexander, too. We must keep him and his rule always before us—all these ten years. But for the second ... " Kinlol was not a man given to praising others, but he could give his fellow Chiefs this, " ... the Council did all it could, and I thank the Chiefs for giving their best." Kinlol allowed them a moment of silence, and then said, "The Council is dismissed."

The Chiefs rose and began to leave. Uman intercepted Kinlol and drew him to the side. "A word, Kinlol," he said.

Kinlol lifted his eyebrows. "Yes?"

"I want to know what plot is brewing in your mind now. I know you well, Kinlol; the Council may have ended its battle against Vonran, but you have not."

"You do know me, Uman. I am still fighting for Alexander—and if that means opposing any move of Vonran's, I will be ready."

"What are you doing?"

"Do you want to be included?"

Uman was silent a moment, in thought. "The Council will not be fighting with us."

"Until Vonran breaks the law, the Council cannot plot against him."

"But a Chief—or Chiefs—can. So you must think. Have you exchanged open opposition for a conspiracy?"

Kinlol considered that. "You might say so. But it is a loyal conspiracy; it is a conspiracy to hand power over to Emperor Alexander—forcibly, if necessary."

"I pray God that it is not necessary." Uman thought a long minute, then glanced around the now-empty room. "I will have part in your conspiracy, Kinlol. For Alexander. Not against Vonran—not unless he refuses to yield to Alexander."

Kinlol smiled. "So be it. I am glad to have you. We will not be alone, Uman. We must soon meet with Gawin Gaelin."

"And Kavin Gyas," Uman said. Kinlol raised an eyebrow, and Uman held his gaze. "You bring your friends, I bring my own."

Kinlol almost smiled, nodded. "So be it."

The intercom buzzed loudly, and Kereth was really too busy for it. He kept on typing, and when it buzzed again he answered distractedly, "Colonel Kereth."

"Colonel," Major Daven's voice came, "I took a message from General Ikron for you."

Kereth stopped typing then. "Ikron? Aren't you at the CC?"

"Yes, sir."

"Why did he call the CC instead of my office?" Kereth wondered—aloud, before he thought better.

"I don't know, sir. I offered to transfer the call, but he only wanted me to take a message."

"What is it, Major?"

"He wants you to come over for after-dinner drinks, sir."

"Come over ... ?"

"To his house, sir."

Kereth pondered that. "Thank you, Major." He switched off the intercom and sat back in his chair, puzzled. He and Ikron had never socialized before. Even their professional relationship, though it worked, was not particularly comfortable. Maybe that was the reason Ikron called the command center; he didn't want to answer any questions. It gave Kereth a bad feeling, but he would go anyway. Though it sounded like a social invitation, Kereth had a clear idea his professional life would suffer if he didn't comply.

That evening Kereth had dinner at a restaurant, for no other reason than he was tired of ordering into his office and didn't want to go home. Afterward he went to the general's house. The general's wife let him in and led him to a lounge. There General Ikron and General Avvon sat together, drinks in hand.

Kereth came to a halt, but only for a second. He strode in, faced Ikron, and brought his hand up in a very sharp salute.

"At ease, Colonel," Ikron said, not saluting in return. "None of us are on duty. Avvon and I aren't even in uniform."

Kereth considered saying that he was, but that was self-evident. "Yes, sir," he said, lowering his hand.

"Sit down, Kereth. What can I get for you?"

Kereth glanced at the generals' cups and guessed what strong drinks they were drinking. He considered asking for berry juice, had enough consideration for Ikron—and his own career—to modify the request. "An ale, sir. Takari root ale." Ikron hesitated just a beat, continued on. Kereth noted where Ikron had been sitting and took a seat as far away from the generals as he could without being rude—or obvious. Ikron came and gave him a clear glass cup without a handle, filled with dark liquid. Kereth had always used a large mug; he wondered if this was the high-class way of drinking ale. "Thank you, General," he said. "You have a nice home. I've never been here before."

If Ikron thought that comment was pointed beneath its innocuous irrelevancy, he didn't let on. "Thank you, Colonel. Now you must be wondering why I invited you here tonight—"

"Yes, sir," Kereth interrupted, and immediately regretted his tone. It was, maybe, just a little too enthusiastic.

Ikron ignored it. "I thought, Colonel Kereth, that you and General Avvon should become acquainted."

"Why? I mean, sir, you have shown no interest in facilitating friendships for me."

"Quite true." Ikron nodded to Avvon. "You are going to be working together closely to ensure harmony between your commands. You should work smoothly."

"Major Skarti informed me of your discussion," Avvon said. "I think you should know, Colonel, that I have no intention of interfering with your command. But my orders make it necessary for my men to work within it."

Ikron nodded. "So you must work together, to see that both of you carry out your duties without hindering the other."

Kereth sat listening, looking between the two men, and he had a bad, bad feeling. His raised cup was still full, and finally he took a drink of the ale. Too sweet. “General, I brought up this problem ... ”

“And we have agreed, Kereth,” Ikron interrupted. “That is why I have invited you two. Things must be clear from the very beginning, so there will be no conflict.”

“Yes,” said Avvon. “If any issue should arise with how my men conduct themselves in the Palace, I will be available to you at any time.”

The bad feeling turned to anger. Kereth couldn't say thank you; sarcasm wouldn't just bleed into the remark, it would overflow. “I will take advantage of your offer whenever I find it necessary.” Kereth looked down at his ale and suddenly wished he had asked for something he could throw down and be done with, so he could be done with the whole meeting. He looked at Ikron. “And you, sir?”

The general's eyebrows went up. “Me, Colonel?”

“Where are you in this arrangement?”

Ikron smiled. “I'm not. At least, I hope not to be. You are both adults—mature, intelligent men—and soldiers of the emperor. You should not need me to referee you.”

“So, Colonel,” Avvon interjected, “how long have you commanded the Emperor's Guard?”

“Four years.”

“That's quite a while. Do most commanders stay that long?”

“It's about right.” Kereth took a long drink, letting the ale flow down his throat.

“What were you doing before you were given command of the Guard?”

“I was earning deep-selection for general.” It wasn't really what Avvon had asked, but suddenly it seemed to Kereth to be a highly relevant answer. He placed his cup down on the table; he would leave without finishing it. Kereth stood to his feet. “By your leave, generals, I will be heading home. It isn't very late, but I am tired.” That was the truth, though Kereth hadn't realized it until it passed his lips. “Perhaps we could do this ... some other time.”

Kereth was certain they never would.

He let himself out. Kereth went home. He had a large apartment with spacious rooms. He was forty years old and he still saw no reason to own a house. He didn't need a yard; he certainly had no time to take care of one.

Kereth went first to his computer; the communications system, like everything else that could be controlled technologically, had been networked to it. He checked to see if anyone had tried to contact him from the Guard. It was habit; Kereth was not feeling attentive. He was angry; yes, angry, and it burned dully through his fatigue. He had warned of the danger of conflicting commands, and what solution had they come up with? To make him consult Avvon. That was the solution. That was the plan. Avvon's people would be scurrying through his facility and if he ever had a problem, he could just call Avvon.

Ikron's words ran through Kereth's mind again: *You should not need me to referee you.* It was all Ikron's way of excusing himself from the whole affair. He wasn't going to back Kereth up. It was Kereth alone against Avvon—a colonel against a general. Well, Avvon wasn't in Kereth's chain of command, and Kereth wasn't going to forget it. The Palace was his command and he wasn't going to lose his dominance to some fourth-tier general, even if his superior officer wouldn't help him. He knew his authority, and if they thought—

His fury finally outran his energy, and Kereth sighed and scrubbed his hand through his hair. He could maintain his hold if he fought, and he was good at fighting. He had the stomach for it, and most times he had the heart, too.

Not this time. It was running away from him, all of it was running away from him, and he couldn't summon the passion to run also. Kereth would not allow his authority to be compromised to make his superiors' stupid ideas work, but he didn't want to fight for it, either. Maybe, then, it was time to step aside.

I was earning deep-selection for general. But commanders of the Emperor's Guard were not generals. Worse yet, they were rarely made into generals. If Kereth was to become a general, it was best that he apply for a transfer to a conventional military command. He'd already been in the Guard too long. And was there any reason for him to continue? He had always wanted to go as high as first-tier general. And why not? He was as good as any of them. He was very good. He had proved it his whole career, had worked hard every day. He had paid his dues, by day and night.

Kereth suddenly became aware of the screen he was staring at. No messages to read, but he had one to write.

A small triangle at the upper-left corner of the screen caught his eye. It was a file he had never read and would not close. He knew what it was and had not yet chosen to make use of it. But now Kereth hesitated, his eyes fixed on that small triangle. The thought ran through his head ... and he dismissed it. This was a decision to be made alone, because he was alone. He had come to realize that he didn't like it, but that was okay. People who couldn't treat others right deserved to be alone.

Trey Uman seemed to regard the contents of his cup and then swirled them around. He looked around at the men with him and raised his cup. “A toast, gentlemen.” They—Gyas, Gaelin, and Kinlol—regarded him suspiciously. “Gentlemen, to defeat and a new battle!”

“I drink to a new battle,” said Gawin Gaelin, and drank from his cup.

Gyas also drank; Kinlol simply ignored the toast. “What truly disturbs me is that Vonran controls the military,” he said. “You are with us, Gaelin, but we must have more. We must bring another into this loyal subversion of ours.”

“Dheval?” Gyas asked.

“No. I don't trust him, and he doesn't like me. I'm thinking of Adon Kereth.”

Gyas' eyebrows shot up. “*Kereth*?”

“You know him,” Uman said. “Colonel, commands the Emperor's Guard. Sharp uniform, ramrod bearing, dark hair with a bit of white, huge chip on his shoulder.”

“I know who he is,” Gyas said. “But why him? He's only a

colonel."

"He commands the Emperor's Guard," said Kinlol.

"Which is small considering what generals command."

"It's more than size. Kereth is in charge of protecting Alexander; he operates with considerable autonomy; he knows all the strengths and weaknesses of the Palace. And ... " Kinlol paused and looked at the others. "He's strong. I think that in a fight he would be a fierce and unrelenting opponent."

"He scraps," Uman said.

"I can undercut half of that right now," Gaelin said.

"What?" Kinlol asked.

Gaelin looked at him and then the others. "Normally I wouldn't share this. But the child is my emperor, and he is my wife's flesh and blood, and so my own. I was at a meeting this morning with the High Command. Ikron—a second-tier general—brought a matter that had not been on the agenda. Last night Kereth put in a request for a transfer. As you know, the High Command is tasked with choosing the commander of the Emperor's Guard. Kereth's request will probably be granted."

"Probably?"

"The situation is complicated. On the one hand, he is a fine officer and has done very well. Choosing a new commander would not be an easy task. As a rule, only colonels are selected. Many military men—however good they are—are not very well suited to bodyguarding."

"And we demand excellence for the emperor," Kinlol said.

"Of course. Many officers don't want the job; they view it as a career-killer. For all its glory, the Guard is not a conventional military command and may hurt rather than help an officer's rise."

"The years spent in the wilderness ... " Gyas muttered.

Gaelin nodded. "Exactly. Kereth has been exceptional, and the High Command might normally be inclined to keep him a little longer. But there is another issue. As you know, the military has created a guard for Vonran. Kereth wanted to create a new division in the Guard and handle the task himself. He was overruled, and when a major of the new command arrived at the Palace, he asserted himself quite strongly.”

“Asserted ... ?” Uman spoke the rest of the question by waving his hands.

“Asserted his authority. None of Vonran's guards are under his command, but the Palace is. They are not under his authority, but they are operating within his command.”

“Sounds difficult,” said Gyas.

“It is ambiguous. There is room for conflict. It calls for both parties to be accommodating, even compliant ... Kereth will not be.”

“So he resigns,” Uman said. “It solves their problem. And they must add 'compliant' to their list of qualifications.”

“That's the most likely scenario.”

“What will happen to Kereth?” Kinlol asked.

“He will be newly assigned. Quite likely, in a few years, he will become a general.”

“Is he that good?” Kinlol asked.

“He is unusually good. He would be a fine general.”

A silence fell over the group. After a few moments Gaelin turned to Kinlol. “Now whom do you want?”

“Kereth.”

The other three looked at each other. “Let's think about Dheval,” said Gyas.

Kereth was hard at work when he heard his office door open. He looked up, ready to snap at whoever had entered without permission, and stopped.

Chief Kinlol stood there. Kereth sat back in his chair and looked at him. “May we talk, Colonel Kereth?” Kinlol asked.

“Yes.” Kereth gestured to a chair in front of the desk. “Sit down.” Kereth waited until Kinlol did, and then asked, “What do you want?”

Kinlol regarded him for a long moment. “A favor,” he said. “A big one.”

Kereth felt his eyebrows go up, and he wondered why Kinlol felt they were on terms to be asking each other for any sort of favor at all.

"Colonel," Kinlol said, "I have come to ask a great deal from you, so I will be entirely frank from the very start. I am a loyalist of the House of Alheenan. I am devoted to supporting and preserving the emperorship as the Ancient Code established it. It is my life's work. I failed to prevent the regency, and now I can only labor—with unceasing vigilance—to ensure that Alexander receives his own."

Kereth pushed away from his desk and went to stand by the window behind it. He gazed out, his back turned to Kinlol. Such personal testimonies discomfited him at the best of times; coming from a virtual stranger, they made him nervous.

Kinlol was not deterred. "Others have joined me in my quest. I want you to also."

It took a moment for Kereth to process that and believe it. He turned around. "Me?"

"You command the Emperor's Guard. You can protect Emperor Alexander until he takes the throne."

"Any commander of the Guard would do that." Kereth turned back to the window.

"If they could. I have it from General Gaelin himself that you are exceptional. Kereth, aside from the child's mother there is no one closer to him than you. You have great access, great proximity to the child and his mother—and that is power in its own right."

"Well, it's a power I'll soon lose. I have already requested a transfer." Kereth thought this a crushing blow and turned to Kinlol as he spoke it.

Kinlol wasn't fazed. He almost smiled. "I know. That's one of the reasons I'm trying to convince you to stay. The High Command will see to it that the next commander is more compliant than you."

"Someone's been talking out of school. So you want to have the commander of the Emperor's Guard in your alliance, and you want that commander to be me. You trust my ability. Do you trust my loyalty?"

"Of course."

"Why?"

"Kereth, for years we have stood in the corner of each other's eyes, lived at the edge of each other's lives. I don't know if you have taken my measure, but I have taken yours. You have been faithful; you have been devoted to your emperor and your task. And you are strong. I would have you at my side."

"At the emperor's side."

"Yes."

There was a moment of gentle silence. Then Kereth raised his voice. "Do you have any idea what you're asking me to do? Ten more years commanding the Emperor's Guard! It'll ruin my career—even if I don't get court-martialed for joining your merry little band! I could be a general! I'm a soldier! You want me to spend nearly fifteen years of my life being a *bodyguard*?" Kereth waved his hand vigorously. "No, no, don't answer that. I'll make this simple. I'm already leaving. The decision is made. The High Command is probably getting ready to transfer me right now."

"Withdraw your request."

"Brilliant. Now I can be a flip-flopper, too."

"Tell them you desire to continue serving your emperor in this way."

"I *don't*. Let someone else run the Guard. Why me?" Kereth waved his hand again. "Don't answer that. The new commander may be a bit of a—well, a bit of a milksop, but they're not going to choose an incompetent. Go bond with him—and his proximity, access, power."

"If it were that way, I wouldn't need any alliance at all."

Kereth jabbed his hand at Kinlol, ordering, "Explain that." He had been told that the gestures he was prone to make when worked up were aggressive. What he had not been told was why that was bad.

"It's not merely the protecting. You are in the Palace, you have forces under your command here. You know the Palace's defenses. You know where it cannot be infiltrated ... and where it can be. If Vonran tries to usurp the throne, someone may try to kill Alexander. Or we may have to kill Vonran. Either way, you would be vital."

Kereth stared at Kinlol. "You think it could get as bad as that?"

"It could get as bad as a civil war. In that case, Colonel, you would become a general."

"And you have a grand conspiracy to keep all of this from happening, and you want me in on it?"

"Yes."

Kereth turned back to the window. "The passion to run," he said softly.

"What?"

Kereth looked back at Kinlol. "Private comment. Sorry. Is Vonran so bad?"

"He is an ambitious man."

"So am I."

"He is a proud man."

"So am I. Though not too proud to admit it, and not enough of a fool to be pleased with it."

"He is alone in his cunning and desire."

Kereth absorbed that line. "Oh, that sounds good." But he was thinking seriously. "Without God, we all stand at the edge of a long descent, don't we?"

Kinlol looked at him with mild interest. "You believe in God, then?"

"Yes. I haven't been ... I have believed," Kereth repeated, turning away from the admission. He looked at Kinlol critically. "Why are you doing all this?"

"Duty, loyalty, honor."

"Even evil men can cover their actions with virtue."

Kinlol regarded Kereth, then slowly shook his head. "You want me to prove my sincerity? How? Have you ever been married?"

"I was. I am," Kereth amended quickly.

Kinlol gave no sign of noticing. "I have never been married. But I feel about the emperorship as a husband feels about the wife he loves—to protect, to cherish, to care for."

Kereth's throat was tight, as he suddenly felt sad. "Aye."

"You understand?"

Kereth nodded slowly. "Aye." He didn't look at Kinlol.

Kinlol waited a long minute, and then asked, "What's your decision?"

Kereth was about to ask for time to think about it, but what was he going to weigh? His selfish ambition against the good of his emperor and country? Kereth felt then that he couldn't; he'd sinned enough. "Yes," Kereth said.

Kinlol's voice registered surprise. "Yes?"

"Yes."

Kereth's den was decorated in dark colors, with low, strongly built furniture. It had a distinctly masculine feel; Kereth had saved it from the woman's touch quite deftly. The room would win few accolades from professional decorators, but he enjoyed it.

Kereth sat in his den that evening, a mug of Takari ale in one hand, and considered his day, his decision, his sanity. He had contacted Ikron, withdrawing his request, and now he found himself evaluating the risk of the regency. It seemed wrong to wish there was serious danger, but if there wasn't, then Kereth was a fool.

He felt like a fool. He had never thought to join the Chiefs in anything. They were fine men, maybe, and useful in their own right, but they were politicians; they fought with words and the cleverness to twist all things—laws, knowledge, reality—to their own ends. Kereth was a soldier, and he fought to kill with the honest weapons of war. He had never dreamed he would make common cause with the Chiefs; now he had joined a conspiracy of them. It was funny, in a way he couldn't put into words, and spending fifteen years running the Guard was flatly ridiculous. He could kick himself.

Kereth drank the ale, trying to remember what Kinlol had said and why it was so convincing at the time. For no good reason, a question came back to him. *Are you married?* And his answer also returned, *I was. I am.* A faint wash of shame swept over Kereth, and he said aloud in the empty room, "I am."

He was. Eighteen years this autumn. It didn't seem long, but the beginning felt very far away. They had been very young, just over twenty. He could still remember their hope, their eagerness in the newness of their love. They were ready for the future; they were ready for the world. They thought their love would conquer all, their joy would never fade.

Kereth couldn't name one moment when it had changed. It had changed in a series of moments and days, and in silences more than words. It had changed over the years. It had begun with Kereth: That he would admit. To put it simply, he fell in love with the military. He had been in the Academy when he and Susanne first met, and when he was finally done with the Academy's systematized tyranny, he was commissioned an officer. He assumed his authority and his responsibilities, and when he grew experienced enough to be at ease with them, he discovered how much he loved it. He pressed on, eager to rise, eager for this life he had chosen.

It made him less eager for other things. His mornings became earlier, his days more frequently ran long, and his work followed him home. And there was another thing. When they were first married they had been eager for children. None came, and Kereth's desire passed away with the years.

Susanne's didn't. If anything it grew stronger. They did nothing to prevent children, and Kereth never spoke of his shifting focus. But Susanne knew, just like he knew her desires. They continued, bound in marriage while their hearts turned to different things—Susanne's to the children she did not have, Kereth's to the career he so ardently pursued.

They both knew these things, but neither said anything about it for a long time. That changed one day, when Kereth was deep in his work at home, minding his own business and expecting nothing. Susanne came and sat by him and said nothing for a long time. That wasn't unusual. She spoke up quite suddenly, asked if it would be all right with him if she went to the doctor to see if something was wrong.

He knew immediately what she meant, and an unpleasant feeling spread through him. He told Susanne that he didn't care if she went, but he didn't want to know the diagnosis. He didn't tell her that he was not afraid to hear that the problem lay with her but that it didn't, because then it would be him. And though he didn't like himself even as he said it—though, when she said nothing and left, he felt himself lower than any human being since Judas betrayed his Master with a kiss—he never apologized. And that, too, was a shame he still carried in his soul.

They never talked about it again, but eventually Susanne began bringing up adoption. Kereth always responded that they would talk about it later, when he wasn't so tired, when he wasn't so busy, when they had more time ... Later never came, and in time Susanne stopped mentioning it. Like everything else between them, it became unspoken.

Even their separation was unspoken. Kereth came home late one evening, and the first thing Susanne asked him was whether he wanted to go see her parents, who were only a few hours' travel away. Kereth begged off with some excuse he had used a thousand times. It usually ended the matter.

Not this time. Susanne stood very still, and she held her head erect and said in a clear, quiet voice, "Then I'll go alone. I already made the arrangements for this evening. If you want to get in touch with me, I left all the information in an open file on the computer. Your dinner is ready for you in the kitchen."

Kereth watched her go and retrieve a travel case he hadn't noticed sitting against the wall. A horrible numbness spread through him, and he could barely find his voice to speak. "How long will you be gone?"

Susanne stopped and looked back at him. "I don't know." She held his eyes for a moment and then turned away.

And she left. Kereth stood unmoving in the lounge for a long time. Eventually he drifted to the kitchen.

It was a long, unpleasant night, and in the morning he went to the Palace again and immersed himself in work. That part of his life never changed, and over time Kereth stopped waking up in the night. The days turned to weeks and the weeks to months, and slowly—as he lay awake in the darkness, as he thought alone in his empty evenings, in a flash of thought as he looked up from his work—he came to understand. He put together the pieces of their past, and he knew how the years had passed for Susanne: the long days, the empty cradle, the waiting—waiting for her husband to come home, waiting for him to stop working and turn his heart to her desires, turn his heart to children ... So many days waiting had been the rule of the hours, and they went without a quarrel, without a raised voice, without a flash of anger. They ended as they had passed, with hardly a word in passing. Kereth supposed the years had grown too long.

He didn't blame Susanne. He knew he had failed far more than she had—had failed Susanne with his selfishness and his silence, had wronged her by abandoning his zeal to walk with God, by running after his ambition and not turning his heart to her or the children he might have had. And he had wronged her by letting her go.

Kereth unconsciously tipped his forgotten mug in his hand. It all came to him quietly and inexorably, like a wave sweeping towards the shore. He had failed so badly, worked so hard, lost his wife, and never had children—for what? A career he had just tossed into the incinerator. He had laid down the work and the ambition of more than fifteen years with a single word, and some part of his soul ached for the loss. But what surprised Kereth was that it was other things that tore such a gaping hole in their absence, things he was beginning to feel—like a slow dawn—might still be within his reach.

What surprised him was a sense of liberation, for he had not known he was chained.

The Siloan Plains were in the west, not far from the coast. They were far from the cities that dominated the continent further inland—and the jewel of them all, Telnaria, the City of the Emperors. Few people lived in the plains and, if they were not in the towns, lived far from each other. The land was endlessly flat, the distant horizon unbroken by trees.

It made an impression on Kereth. It always had. He had never grown used to it—to see for miles around, see—nothing. This was the place of Susanne's birth and upbringing, and he had never told her that where she saw wild freedom, he saw only soul-deadening monotony. It was windy on the day he arrived, and that, too, was how he remembered it.

The house was not, not quite. He stared at it, leaning against his hovcar, trying not to squint from the wind against his face. The large house looked older, more worn by the elements, and he didn't know if his memory was wrong or the years had truly been so hard on the old building. He hadn't been here in years.

It occurred to Kereth that that was another reason for his in-laws not to like him—not that they needed any reason beyond Susanne's unhappiness. But even when she was happy, they had never been fond of him. It might have been nice if Kereth had dropped in more often, but his relationship with his in-laws had always been best conducted at a distance. It was better if they did not meet. Meeting like this—as Kereth came to win Susanne back—was bound to be painfully awkward.

But Kereth was a soldier; he was trained to endure worse things. So he went onto the porch, to the door, and pressed his fingers against the caller's pad. Then he waited, trying not to be self-conscious of the fact that his image was being transmitted to inquisitive eyes wanting to know who was at the door. What expression was on his face? What expression should be? Penitence? Regret? Hope? Happiness at seeing Susanne?

Kereth looked down at his boots. He could see himself in their shine. He had rooted out of his closet a civilian outfit, but had been content to simply roll his trouser legs over his military boots. Kereth stood waiting, and as the time began to feel long he wondered if his father-in-law had decided to let him cool his heels. It was a tactic with little effect on Kereth. It had been used on him too many times in the military—and sometimes by men even more intimidating than his father-in-law.

The door opened, and Kereth lifted his head erect. Jakin Ahira, his father-in-law, looked at him, a long and critical gaze. Finally he said, "It's been a long time, Adon."

"Yes, it has. How are you?" Kereth had been married nearly eighteen years, and he still didn't know what to call his father-in-law.

He didn't know what he'd do in a pinch, but he had a feeling he'd call him "sir".

"I've been fine. And you?"

Kereth wondered if "fine" would be an offensive answer. "I've been ... healthy." A pause. "Thanks." They stood in silence, Kereth more than half waiting for Ahira to say something unkind. He was Susanne's father, after all.

"You came," Ahira said.

"Yes. Can I go in?"

"Why?"

Kereth considered that obvious. "So I can see my wife."

"Do you think she wants to see you?"

Kereth's heart sank. "She didn't tell me not to come."

"You gave her that choice?"

"Yes."

Ahira stepped back, allowing him space to pass. That was Kereth's invitation, and he took it. As soon as the door was closed, he asked, "Where is Susanne?"

"In her room."

"I'll go up to see her." Kereth allowed just enough assertiveness into his voice to make it clear this was a statement, not a request. Whatever had passed between them, Susanne was still his wife, and he didn't need Ahira's permission to be in her room.

Ahira only nodded, and Kereth headed off. He had not been allowed to pass time with Susanne in her room when they were courting, but he had a fairly certain idea of which room was hers. He went to the door and stopped. Then slowly, even gently, he lifted his hand and keyed the open-pad. The door wasn't locked; it slid open and Kereth walked softly in. He saw Susanne sitting on the bed, across the room. An open window was at the foot of the bed, and a breeze rustled through Susanne's dark hair.

She was beautiful. That was the thought that struck him still. "Do you ... " Kereth stopped, surprised at his voice—surprised to hear it, surprised at its hoarseness. "Do you mind if I sit?" he asked.

Susanne tilted her head to the chair by the writing desk. Kereth crossed over, drew it closer to the bed, and sat down. Susanne looked at him but said nothing. Kereth could tell she was leaving it to him to take the lead.

He didn't know what to say. He had played out their reunion in his mind, over and over, all the journey here. It all escaped him now. He had so much to say, and he didn't know where to begin. “Susanne,” he said, “I came because ... well, because we need to do something. So much has come between us. Even separated, it's still between us. We can't go on like this. Something needs to change.” Kereth watched Susanne for her reaction.

She didn't give it to him. She remained still, her expression unchanging, but it was the forced, guarded stillness born of a determination to let nothing show. After a moment Susanne asked, “Are you considering a divorce?”

Shock stole Kereth's voice, but he recovered it after a moment. “No. No, of course not.” And though his heart pounded with dread he asked, “Are you?”

“No.” But she looked away.

“Then why did you ask if I—”

Susanne shrugged a little. “I just thought you might.”

Her voice was soft and her words were not sharp, but they plunged into his heart. “It never even occurred to me. I love you. I want—I was hoping you would come home with me.”

Susanne stared at him, an expression disturbingly like disbelief coming onto her face. “For all these months I've been gone you haven't called or come or sent any message. You let me go without a word. Now, after seven months, you want me to come back. Was that how long it took you to miss me? Seven months?”

The words pierced their way into him, and he felt his shame again. “Oh, Susanne. I never wanted you to leave. I went numb. I didn't know what to do, what to say. I didn't understand what was happening.”

“And these months?”

Anger and hurt still mixed in Susanne's voice, but she was listening ... hoping, maybe? Kereth held her gaze, determined to tell her the truth, no matter what she asked. “There were a lot of reasons. I didn't know what to say. I didn't understand. I didn't know how to make things better, and I couldn't bring you back to your unhappiness. You wanted to be gone. I deserved to be alone."

"You could have told me any of that," Susanne said, but her tone was soft again.

"I could have. I should have. I didn't know how to. But I thought about it, Susanne. I tried to understand what changed—what had happened to us. We used to think the world was ours."

Susanne smiled. She remembered, too. But there was sadness in her eyes. "The world wasn't what I thought it would be."

"Or wanted, I suppose," Kereth said. "Like our marriage." Susanne looked down. "It's okay. I know. I wasn't the husband you wanted me to be—the husband you thought I would be. Worse, I wasn't the husband God wanted me to be to you. No man can love his wife like Christ loved the church, but I was often too caught up with myself to even try." Susanne looked at him, something in her expression changing. "Now," Kereth said, "it's my turn."

Susanne's eyebrows went up. "Turn?"

"To ask a question. Susanne, why did you leave?"

Susanne stood and walked around the bed, brushing past Kereth's knees to stand by the window. "It's hard to say, Adon. My life was the same day after day, year after year. Except that every day, every year, it seemed a little grayer, a little emptier. The time came when I just couldn't go on. So I came here."

Kereth nodded. "But what do you really want? It can't be this."

"No, it isn't." But what it was she didn't say.

Kereth didn't think it was because she didn't know. He stood and stepped so close to Susanne their bodies nearly touched. He laid a hand gently on her arm, just below her shoulder, to give reassurance. "Come on, Susanne," he said. "No more silence."

She didn't respond. Kereth waited, and finally Susanne spoke. "I want children. I want you—like it was in the beginning, when I knew you loved me. I want you to look at me like you did then."

Kereth nuzzled his face against Susanne's hair, and he was captured by a desire to take her into his arms. He didn't bow to it, not yet; there were things he had to say. “Susanne, I love you. I never stopped loving you. But I got so caught up in my ambition I lost sight of what mattered more. I drifted away from God, and I drifted away from you. Now I'm seeking you both again. I'm asking you to forgive me, Susanne, to give me a second chance. We'll talk about children; we'll decide what to do. But first we need to be committed to each other. We need to be ready to do this God's way, ready to do it like we promised.” Kereth paused. “What do you say, Susanne? Do you want to try again?”

A few heartbeats, long moments to Kereth. Then Susanne stirred. Kereth stepped back as she turned, tension racing through his blood. But there was a smile playing on Susanne's lips as she looked up at him, and she gave her answer: “I do.”

The words sank in and Kereth felt a smile spread over his face. And he took her into his arms.

Chapter

* * * * * * * * * * * * * * * * *

Alexander Cyneric Alheenan the Fifth, emperor and last heir of Alexander the Mighty, sat in the chair, kicking his heels. He had completed his lesson, and he was eager to be free.

His master was Gerog Kinlol, Chief of Justice and recent instigator of conspiracies. One might reasonably wonder why such a man would play the role of schoolmaster, even to a child like Alexander. It was an investment; it would pay off.

Kinlol reached down, took the book from in front of Alexander, and surveyed what he had read. He nodded. “Very good. You may go.” The child slid off the chair and scampered away. Kinlol went to the bookshelf and slid the book into its place. These paper-and-ink books were expensive and many of them were old, and on all of them the same smell lingered—the smell of a dry, preservative chemical.

Kinlol turned back, and saw Mareah Alheenan standing in the doorway. “He's not going to remember any of it,” she told him.

Long after Alexander forgot his lessons, he would remember that Kinlol had taught them to him. Kinlol nodded to Mareah's comment and turned back, taking up his compad. He could feel her eyes on him, and he knew she was still studying him, still evaluating his purposes and actions. He had only asked to teach Alexander the subjects that connected to his future duties, and Kinlol knew Mareah never would have permitted it if her husband hadn't trusted him.

Even now she remained wary. So Kinlol tried to be non-threatening; he tried to be approachable. Above all, he tried not to raise against himself the mother's love that could make the most sweet-tempered woman a tigress.

Kinlol turned back to Mareah and bowed. "By your leave, Lady, I will say good evening."

She raised her hand. "A moment. What did you have Alexander read?"

"The same book I showed you when I began. He read a simple history of Emperor Cyneric's war against the Vothnians. Not explicit, I assure you."

"Did you give him a lecture concerning the reading?"

"No, Lady."

She regarded him critically for a moment, then stepped away from the doorway. Kinlol took the hint and, bowing his head to her, left the Royal Family's living quarters. In the lift that carried him to the Palace's first floor, Kinlol pulled his carry-comm off his belt and checked the time. Colonel Kereth should be getting off duty shortly.

Kinlol was pleased. He had been surprised but glad when Mareah permitted him to teach Alexander so late in the day. It allowed him to meet with Kereth much more easily, and much more unobtrusively.

Kinlol wove an unhurried way towards the Judgment Hall on the west side of the Palace. There was a holding room in front of the Judgment Hall, for petitioners waiting to be led into the emperor's presence, and Kinlol went to it. The Emperor's Guard put all unused rooms under lock, but Kinlol hadn't reached his place in government without acquiring some security clearances.

Kinlol ran his fingers against the side of the door jamb, and a small square of wall slid away to reveal a security pad. Kinlol keyed his code in, and then held out his palm for the sensor sweep. The door drew open, and Kinlol stepped into the holding room. The lights were activated at his entrance, and he crossed the room—not to the great double doors leading into the Judgment Hall, but to a door in the side wall. He repeated the same procedure as before to open the door, and he walked out onto a verandah.

At the end of the verandah was a short flight of steps that led down to a patio. Near the steps were large square pillars, upholding the Palace. The pillars—like the steps and the floor of the verandah —were made of near-marble. It was a synthesized material, with the cool smoothness of marble but a different appearance. This was swirled purple, speckled with gold.

Kinlol made his way across the verandah to the alcoves built into the wall at one end. They were open, but this place was deserted without a ruling emperor, and there was no one to hear. Kinlol went into the nearest alcove and waited.

Kereth arrived shortly. He came into the alcove and stopped, leveling his gaze at Kinlol. "Here I am," he said. "Do we need passwords?"

Kinlol considered this difficult. "Don't you approve of our meeting?"

"I approve of our meeting. I've been *insisting* on our meeting. But why couldn't we have met like honest men?"

"Because we are conspirators."

Kereth appeared to dislike that, but he was apparently not able to combat it. "What's going on, Kinlol?"

"What do you mean?"

"What's going on? What are we doing? I ruined my career to help *you* save the Empire"—Kinlol wondered if he caught a note of sarcasm—"and I don't grumble. But I want to get to the saving. We've done nothing."

"We can do nothing until we plan, and we cannot plan until we are all together."

"I might have expected more urgency from you, Kinlol."

That dug a little under Kinlol's skin. "I'll ask you to remember, Kereth, that I wanted to meet within days of your joining, but you left Telnaria."

"I had more important business."

Kinlol looked straight at Kereth, and Kereth met his eyes, inviting him—daring him—to disagree. Kinlol didn't. He let it pass. "And then General Gaelin left. With two other generals and one of Dheval's deputies he's traveling along the Vothnian border, inspecting our defenses. He can't excuse himself."

"He's been gone four weeks."

"It's a long border." Kereth only looked at Kinlol, who went on. "What can he say? That he has an urgent meeting to conspire against the regent?"

Kereth hissed out a breath. "Stop it, Kinlol. Stop making it sound criminal. I'm not conspiring against the lawful regent; I'm protecting the lawful emperor—only."

"Take your own view," Kinlol said. "It's all the same in the end—if you're for Alexander. At any rate, Gaelin sent me a message. He is coming back. We will meet together in a few days."

"Where?"

"At my house. I'm the only one who lives alone."

Kereth looked at Kinlol, seeming to evaluate what he had just said. "I'm not sure this secretiveness is healthy."

"It is prudent."

"Was it prudent to wait until we could all meet in person?"

Kinlol shrugged. "It seemed best in every way." He eyed Kereth. "All this bothers you, doesn't it?"

"I'm a military man. I'm used to keeping secrets. Most of my work is classified now. I'm not used to slinking around for fear of my own government."

Kinlol sighed. "Neither am I, Kereth. Neither am I."

The Assembly had recessed four weeks ago, and the delegates had gone to their home provinces. Vonran, regent now, remained in Telnaria, and he was well-occupied. His days were filled with work. He was easing into his full authority, trying not to alarm government agencies and officials as he took control over them. He was beginning to make headway even in the Council of Chiefs. Kinlol was not blocking him; Kinlol was not doing much that he could see. It made him wonder what Kinlol was doing that he could not see. It was possible that the old fox had given up, but Vonran would wager little on the idea.

These things ran through Vonran's mind as he put the

computer in the emperor's—his—office into lockdown. Vonran gathered up his two compads and dismissed such thoughts. He was going home; it was time to turn his thoughts there. Vonran had already dispatched his security detail to get the vehicles ready for his departure, and he left also.

But not by the usual way. Vonran had discovered a back exit in the study adjacent to his office, and he left through that way. He was learning—and enjoying learning—the back ways and narrow halls of the Palace, its architectural oddities. He was familiarizing himself with the Palace; he was beginning to feel he was not a guest.

Vonran made his way through the narrow halls, coming to a door at the end of one. This door led to the verandah—put there, doubtless, so that the emperor did not have to go through the Judgment Hall's holding room. Into the security pad, Vonran entered the code that had been given him when he assumed the regency—he had already discovered, and not without pleasure, that it opened doors locked by the Guard. Vonran walked through the door—and stopped.

There was light ahead, spilling onto the verandah from one of the alcoves. Vonran frowned at the sight, puzzled. No one had any business here. Even the patrolling guards wouldn't linger. Now, servants might be sent to clean the place, but they were off-shift now, and the lights in any room would deactivate if it was empty long enough. Unless, of course, they had been set otherwise.

And while Vonran was trying to read the riddle, a solution came to him: Approach and find out. This he did, walking close to the wall and stepping softly. As he came near he heard voices, and then—the realization sent a tingling through his blood—he recognized one of them as belonging to Gerog Kinlol.

Curiosity did not so much overcome ethics as crowd them out. Vonran, without a thought otherwise, drew nearer until the voices became intelligible, and then, stepping against the wall, he eavesdropped.

"... the regent?" That was Kinlol.

Whatever he had said, it didn't please his companion. Vonran heard a hiss, then: "Stop it, Kinlol. Stop making it sound criminal."

Criminal?

That question—that thought—was overwhelmed by Vonran's next: He knew this voice, too; it was ... "I'm not conspiring against the lawful regent; I'm protecting the lawful emperor—only."

Adon Kereth, the colonel who commanded the Emperor's Guard. He wasn't conspiring ...

Kinlol's voice again: "Take your own view. It's all the same in the end—if you're for Alexander."

All the same ...

"At any rate, Gaelin sent me a message."

Gaelin?

"He is coming back. We will meet together in a few days."

"Where?"

Well, Kereth was conspiring a little.

"At my house. I'm the only one who lives alone."

There was a pause. Then Kereth's voice: "I'm not sure this secretiveness is healthy."

"It is prudent."

"Was it prudent to wait until we could all meet in person?"

At this point Vonran turned and began to go back. The conversation had the sound of dissolving into an argument, and at any rate they seemed to be making arrangements for another—wider—meeting. And Vonran couldn't be caught. He had already heard much, heard more than he could yet think over.

As Vonran reached the door and slipped out of the verandah, an old, half-forgotten proverb flashed into his mind: Kings' servants know kings' secrets. He added his own ending to the saying: It is because they walk in kings' corridors.

Vonran abandoned the back ways he had been learning for this night, and he walked in the main corridors. Outside, at the front of the Palace, his guards were waiting for him with the vehicles.

At home, he was just in time for dinner. Vonran sat with his daughters and ate the meal, but he was preoccupied throughout. When his daughters asked for permission to leave the table, he gave it automatically, not even remembering to see if they had eaten their dinners. When he himself was done—having hardly tasted his food

—he laid his fork down and stared into space, trying to assimilate this new reality. Kinlol, and Kereth—Kereth!—together with Gaelin —General Gaelin, obviously—were meeting together about, against, him ...

"Father?"

The voice brought him back to the dinner table from miles away, and he glanced at Zelrynn. "Yes?"

She hesitated, seeming unsure what to say. "Are you going to read to the little ones tonight?" she asked after a moment.

Vonran glanced around the table, fully realizing only now that three of his daughters were gone. "Do they want it?" he asked.

"I think so."

Vonran wanted to be left to himself to work through this new situation, but he was gone so much ... "Call your sisters to the lounge," he said. "Tell them to choose a book and bring it."

The book they brought to him was a large storybook, bountifully illustrated and written with elegant lettering. Its stories were like an old song to Vonran—stories of peasant girls who married princes, powerful men who were evil and common men who were brave, beautiful princesses and daring princes, dire peril and happily-ever-afters. Dianthe had bought this book when Zelrynn was little. When she had shown it to him, his first thought was that this was a rare failure of judgment for his wife, paying so much money for a book of fairy-tales—fairy-tales that were old when Vothnia was young. Dianthe told him that he could read to their children from it, that they would love the book of fairy-tale stories. She was right, and even Vonran came to see in the stories a kind of melody. It was another thing she saw that he didn't, another thing she taught him to see.

Vonran told the girls to choose a story, and as the younger ones paged through the book, hotly debating the question, he glanced over at Zelrynn. She was sitting alone on the couch at his right, withdrawing from the process in every sense of the word.

"This one."

Vonran turned his head at Lydia's voice, looking back towards his younger children. "This one," Lydia repeated. Vonran held his hands out to take the book. Cala clambered onto his lap, Lydia and Vera sat on each side of him, but Zelrynn didn't move closer to see the illustrations. She probably knew what they were already.

At the story's end, Vonran sent the girls to get ready for bed. He saw Zelrynn begin to rise, and he added, "And Vera, I want you to make sure Cala gets ready."

"Can we play afterward?" Lydia asked.

"You can play until I come up," Vonran answered. After the girls had gone, Vonran looked over at Zelrynn. "I don't want you to do everything while I'm gone. It's not good for you and it's not good for your sisters. Vera and Lydia are both old enough for some responsibility, and they should be given it. Now," he changed the subject, "was there any trouble while I was gone?"

"No."

"Are the girls minding you? Are they minding their tutors?"

Zelrynn nodded. "But we wish you were home more," she added.

"I know. I do, too. But with all the work that comes with the regency ... Zelrynn, there's one way I could be home more every day. But it would mean moving from this house."

"Moving where?"

"To the Palace. I would have to make an appeal to the empress, but she would probably grant our family some kind of accommodations at the Palace. But we would have to move from our home. And the Palace is a government building as much as a house. I would be able to be home for every meal, for all the time I now spend commuting, but I'm not sure it would be worth it."

Zelrynn seemed to consider all this. After a minute she said, "I would be fine with it."

Vonran nodded to the assurance, and wondered how the little ones would take it.

Later that night, after the girls were in bed, Vonran's mind turned again to the conversation he had overheard. Now he knew: Kinlol, Kereth, and Gaelin had formed an alliance to support Alexander. As far as Kereth was concerned, that was all it was, but

Kinlol considered it an alliance against Vonran himself.

Well, what would they do? What could they do? Did even they know? Was that the question they were meeting to answer? And would Vonran learn only too late? They would act in secret. They already were.

Kereth didn't like it. That Vonran made careful note of. It was a fracture in their alliance, though how serious a one only time would tell.

Vonran didn't know what would happen, what these men would do. He didn't know what he would do. But he knew one thing, beyond any doubt: Now he had to watch.

Mareah received the call that morning, from a woman on the Palace staff assigned to the Royal Family. The regent, she was told, wanted an appointment with her—that day, if possible. That morning was possible, but Mareah did not want to appear too available. She granted Regent Vonran an interview shortly after the noon meal.

When the time approached, Mareah sent Alexander off to play and went to the open, sunny parlor where she had been receiving visitors for years. Mareah walked around the room, glancing out through the windows, and wondering with mild curiosity what the regent wanted.

"My Lady." The voice surprised Mareah, and she turned to the door. An attendant stood there, Elymas Vonran behind her. "Regent Vonran."

Mareah nodded to the woman. "Thank you." The attendant withdrew, and Mareah turned to the regent. "Please, Regent Vonran, be seated." Mareah went and sat herself, and Vonran sat across from her. "How are you finding your new duties?" Mareah asked, using her proper tone.

"Quite well," the regent answered. "It is consuming work, as I'm sure you know. My only problem is that it keeps me from home so much. I still live in the city and I commute back and forth."

Mareah looked at the regent and suddenly guessed that none of this was merely conversation. "Yes?" she asked.

He looked faintly amused. “Are you asking for the point of this?”

It sounded rude put that way, but it was still true. “Yes,” Mareah confirmed.

“And so I will tell you. Lady, the emperor lives in the same building he works in; this has long been a custom of rulers. I have found it is more practical than I guessed. I am away from my daughters more than I like.”

Mareah saw his problem, and it made her a little nervous. “What can I do for you?” she asked.

“I would like to live in the Palace; I would like to have the guest wing as a home for me and my daughters.”

The guest wing was at the back of the Palace—separate enough to provide some measure of privacy. It was two stories and had a full range of rooms, though anyone who tried to make it a home would have an odd configuration at best. All things considered, it was as fine accommodations as Vonran could get—as, doubtless, he knew.

When Mareah said nothing, Vonran continued, “Lady, if you have use for it, I will seek something else. But if you do not, I ask that you give it over to me.”

It was a bold request, but the longer Mareah considered it, the more reasonable it seemed. She had no use for the guest wing; spare rooms abounded in the Royal Family's residence. And the regent could put it to good use; he could be home with his daughters more. That was especially important because he was now their only parent, being a widower ... Mareah looked at the regent and nodded. “You may have it,” she said. “I have no need of it.”

The regent smiled and bowed his head. “Thank you, Lady Mareah. This is a kindness I will remember. Now, may I inquire after the emperor?”

Mareah was adjusting to the fact that “the emperor” was now her son instead of her husband, but it still dispirited her. “He is well,” replied Mareah. She drew her leg closer to the couch and looked down, adjusting her skirt. She could feel the regent watching her, and when she looked up, there was a thoughtful expression on his face.

"Lady," he said, "you know of all the controversy that followed your husband's death over how the Empire should be ruled. Many did not want there to be a regent."

Mareah nodded. She knew of it, but she hadn't followed it closely; she didn't care much what they did.

"Do you share their concerns? They were for your son as well as the Empire."

"I hadn't noticed," Mareah said lightly. It was not really her son—her Alexander—any of them cared about; it was the emperor. It was always the Empire. "Regent Vonran, your ... ascension ... doesn't worry me."

He nodded. "I am glad to hear that. Chief Kinlol has been *very* concerned." He paused, as if choosing his next words carefully. But all he said was, "Who knows what he may do?"

Mareah certainly didn't, except for one thing ... "He has been teaching Alexander. That is all I know."

"That surprises me," said Vonran, who looked mainly intrigued. "I am sure you do not take offense, Lady Mareah. Your child is important, but the Chief of Justice has never been a tutor."

"He is now, but only of what he says concerns Alexander's future duties."

"I see. Well, if you ever need anything for yourself or your son—or if you have any concerns—please tell me. I will do what I can. Thank you again for allowing my family the guest wing, Lady Mareah. I bid you a fair day."

"The same to you," Mareah said as the regent rose. He bowed to her and left.

Mareah sat alone in the parlor, thinking the conversation over. The regent had been gracious, even friendly, and she wondered how sincere his offers were. She almost felt guilty of her skepticism, but she had not lived ten years in Telnaria without learning certain things. One of those was that everyone had—on the surface or beneath it—their own motives and own desires. She didn't know if Regent Vonran was generous or calculating, or a blending of both. She had the same doubts concerning Chief Kinlol.

Mareah's mind turned to Vonran's request, and the fact that

she had just renounced all claim on the Palace's guest wing for a decade. It was another twist in the situation. It also meant—this came to Mareah quite suddenly—that she would, in a way, have neighbors now.

This was interesting. That was what Kereth was telling himself. It was interesting.

He sat in Chief Kinlol's lounge with the nation's most prominent general and three of its Chiefs. They were much more important men than he was, and they did not all seem certain of him. Kereth had more than once caught a discreet, measuring look focused on him.

Kereth enjoyed it. He enjoyed watching these finely-dressed, well-groomed, clever, careful men caught between the clash of their curiosity and their good breeding. He accepted a drink from Kinlol and surveyed his fellow conspirators. This was fun already.

Kinlol began the meeting. "We are here to devise a strategy to protect Alexander and his rule over the Empire. Vonran legitimately rules for ten years. He may try to hold onto power after that, and that is what we must prevent if we can, and prepare for in case we can't."

"It will not be easy," Gawin Gaelin warned. Gaelin was a soldier, like Kereth, and a good one. Kereth respected him more than anyone else in the room. "Vonran is taking control of the government. Even the High Command feels it. If he attempts to usurp the throne, we will have all the power of the government to contend with. In other words, our strategy must be to overthrow an emperor."

That was easy. "Overthrowing an emperor is simple," Kereth said. "You kill him. There are two ways to go about that. One is to assassinate him. The other is to wage war." Kereth stopped, looking at each of the well-groomed, finely-dressed men. "What's your choice?"

Gaelin's eyes were dark with sober thought; Gyas and Uman looked at each other uneasily. Kinlol looked at Kereth steadily, and he didn't waver—not in one look, one flicker of the eye. “Assassination is more efficient—and less risky.”

Uman glanced at him. “I could keep a cleaner conscience by shooting a man to his face than stabbing him in the back.”

“Assassination is a filthy business,” Gaelin said. “But it is better that one man die than many.”

“Who can disagree?” Gyas answered. “But if that is your argument, we will not attempt an assassination until the only alternative is war.”

Gaelin nodded. “So be it.”

“That's all well and good,” Kereth said. “Make it a policy: If war is inevitable, we will assassinate Vonran—if we can.” He watched them absorb his point, and went on, “Assassination may not be to your liking. It will be less to your ability. Vonran will not steal an Empire and leave himself undefended. Already he has his own Guard. What will he have ten years from now, when he turns usurper?”

Uman looked at him—and Kereth knew he was being evaluated. “And do you have any recommendations as to what we should do, Colonel?”

“Yes, point of fact. Here is my advice: Prepare for war. If assassinating Vonran fails—and most such attempts do—you will be finished if you are not ready to stir up war.”

Uman continued to look at him. “You?” His voice was low, his tone pleasant, and his point very sharp.

“We,” Kereth corrected himself, and quickly moved on. Picking up his discourse, he said, “For war you need an army. Vonran has ours, and we cannot get another one. A military is a costly thing and impossible to hide. You cannot even make one in secret, because you could not get recruits. So one option is left to us,” he concluded. “To carve out from Vonran's army our own share.”

“Subvert the army?” Kavin Gyas asked.

“And be ready to take supplies and equipment,” Kereth said. “A difficult task, and not to be conducted under Vonran's nose.”

Trey Uman rubbed his face. “It sounds hard.”

"It is," Kereth affirmed.

"There is another way besides violence to unseat a ruler," Kinlol said. "That is to take away his people."

"And how would you achieve that?" Gyas inquired.

"I would have all the provinces declare for Alexander the day of his seventeenth birthday," Kinlol answered.

There was silence as the men considered this. "We would have to go to the provinces and build support," Uman said. "The legislatures and prefects would have to commit in some definite way. But if we could ... Vonran would be effectively renounced."

Kinlol nodded. "And Vonran could never object. Unlike the military, we could act in the open."

"Quite an advantage, isn't it?" Kereth commented, and did not mind when Kinlol shot a vexed look at him.

Gaelin was looking at them. He saw it, but Kereth could tell by his expression that he did not understand it. "We should explore both policies," he said. "We can pursue them at the same time."

This met with general agreement. Uman said, "And we must keep an eye on Vonran, to see what he does. We must watch."

"One thing I am curious about," Gyas said. "I have heard that you, Kinlol, have often been to the Palace these past few weeks."

Kereth nodded his agreement—actually his confirmation; he would know.

"I have begun tutoring Alexander," Kinlol said.

"Is Telnaria so short on teachers?" Uman asked.

"What begins now as history lessons will end in training the child to be emperor. Along with facts he will learn his heritage, what his ancestors were and what he must be. I will be his teacher, and he will listen to me."

Kereth thought that over and nodded. "After all," he said, "it would be very awkward if we tried to save his throne for him and he declined."

Gyas glanced at Kereth, amusement in his face. "True enough. Having joined Alexander's side, we must see to it that he joins ours."

"The path from teacher to mentor to advisor is not inevitable," Gaelin told Kinlol.

"I know. But Alexander must be trained, and he must learn to trust us, or Vonran may deceive him and steal from him by trickery."

"And what about his mother?" Kereth asked, half-rhetorically. He had an instinct that leaving the empress out of consideration would be a mistake.

He was met with silence, as if he had raised an irrelevant point and no one could intelligently respond to it. Kereth was fairly sure it would be wiser to say nothing more. He pressed the point anyway. "She is the child's mother."

"She cannot keep him from being what he is," Kinlol said. "She cannot keep him safe from the regent."

"She can keep you from teaching him."

"She has not," Kinlol pointed out.

This time Kereth yielded to wisdom, and shut up.

"I propose a division of labor," Gaelin said. "We have two policies to pursue—a political strategy and a military strategy. We have three politic men—three Chiefs. These three should devise and implement the political strategy. And the two military men"—Gaelin turned to Kereth—"shall devise and implement the military strategy."

Kereth looked at Gaelin, pleased to work with another soldier, pleased to have a military assignment. "It is to my liking and my ability, General," he said.

"I agree also," Kinlol said, and Uman and Gyas echoed him.

Gaelin nodded to them and smiled. "Now we must wrap this up, gentlemen. I have an appointment I cannot miss."

"Do we need a security clearance to know what it is?" Uman asked.

Gaelin glanced at him. "No, not at all," he said, an ironic smile twisting his lips. "I am going with Dheval and three other men to give Vonran a full account of our findings concerning the security of the Vothnian border."

Vonran had decided that what he enjoyed most about the regency was commanding the Empire's military and foreign policy. All he had done in the Assembly—resolutions, intra-provincial affairs, molding and approving trade agreements with foreign powers—paled next to this.

Fionn Dheval, commander-in-chief, his deputy, and three generals arrived in the afternoon to brief him on the security of the Vothnian border. Their investigation had been long, thorough, and on-site. It had also—Vonran had read the classified memorandum—been ordered by Emperor Judah. Citing vague concerns, he had instructed the generals to go to the border and inspect the defenses. He had also permitted them to take up to a month, noting that he expected a "careful inspection" to take a minimum of two weeks.

It was a warning, though not put in so many words, that a short investigation would raise his skepticism. Vonran had respected Emperor Judah, and he was intrigued by the care the emperor had taken in mandating the generals' mission. He had been worried. His worries were credible.

The generals and deputy presented their report, finding only minor faults and recommending only minor improvements for a great length of the border. Then they came to the border between Regial and Far Vothnia.

Dheval began tensing up as General Gaelin moved to that part of the review. He watched his subordinates, his face revealing nothing, but Vonran saw how stiffly he held himself. And Vonran saw why. After offering a bleak assessment of Vothnia's capabilities along the Regial border, General Gaelin offered a very similar assessment of the Empire's.

"So," Vonran said, "they are weak, but we are equally so?"

Gaelin considered that and nodded. "Yes. Vothnia could send a cloaked force to the Regial border and almost certainly break through before reinforcements arrived."

"Then the Empire is vulnerable to a Vothnian invasion."

"They could enter, Regent; I do not know how far they would get."

Vonran regarded Gaelin, and the thought that he had been

keeping back the whole briefing came to the forefront of his mind again: Here was the man who was conspiring against him.

Dheval spoke. "The situation is unacceptable to the military. There is great work to be done there. We are devising a proper defense of the Vothnian border, determining the extent of the work and the resources that are needed for it."

Vonran glanced at him, trying to re-fix his focus on the matter at hand. Dheval seemed to take the torpor of his response as a bad sign, and pressed on. "In all likelihood we will reassign the commander of the region."

Gaelin's conspiring was still in Vonran's mind, but he heard Dheval. And an idea flashed like lightning into his mind. "By all means, Chief Dheval, do it," Vonran said. "Bring in another commander, a known and respected general, to give this work weight. Appoint a man whose skill is beyond dispute, and who knows the work he will be required to do. If the borders are not secure, neither is the Empire." Vonran could have gone on, but he checked himself. It was too soon, too public, to reel Dheval further in. Vonran leaned back in his chair and glanced around the table. "Is there anything more, gentlemen?"

There was not. The meeting ended, and as the men rose and began to leave, Vonran turned to Dheval. "May I have a moment, Chief Dheval?" he asked.

Dheval nodded and, glancing at his subordinates, moved to join Vonran. Vonran drew him to the side of the room, out of the way and out of earshot. "The security of the border has deteriorated to a shameful degree," he said. This was not why he had drawn Dheval aside, but it helped to cloak his real purpose. "Emperor Judah was wise to be concerned. I want this to have the highest priority from you. And you must choose this general who will re-build our defenses wisely. As I said, he must know the work. Any of these three generals would qualify." Vonran let the three men become candidates in Dheval's mind and proceeded, walking a fine and careful line. "He must also have prestige. Of course, it would banish the general from Telnaria, forcing him to live and work in Regial ... " Regial, the lowest region in the Empire. Regial, farthest from the

Empire's shining cities, its pinnacles of wealth and power. Vonran waited a short moment, waited while the general on whom Dheval most wished such a fate rose in his eyes. Then he concluded, "But the loyal soldiers of the Empire will rise to their nation's need."

Dheval nodded to him, but he was distracted, suddenly preoccupied with a thought of his own. His head turned, his eyes sought out Gawin Gaelin, standing across the room in conversation with a fellow general.

And Vonran knew he had succeeded.

The chaos and work of moving can never be entirely overcome. Vonran mostly withdrew. By an established method, he mustered his household together and gave them instructions on the work. He then dismissed them and repaired to his study.

He had not long been at work when his comm panel came to life, flashing red, and its computer voice spoke: "*Caller attempting to establish contact.*"

"Identity?" Vonran asked.

There was a pause; then: "*Chief Fionn Dheval.*"

"Allow the call through," Vonran ordered.

"*Caller is attempting to engage visual setting.*"

"Fine." Vonran leaned back in his chair, away from his work, and fixed his eyes on the air above his desk. In a moment, a holograph appeared—a transmission of Chief Dheval.

Dheval bowed his head. "Regent Vonran, I have called you to make an inquiry concerning your protection."

"My protection?"

Dheval nodded. "Your protection, like the emperor's, is in the military's hands under the purview of the High Command. Now that you are moving into the Palace, we are considering merging your detail with the Emperor's Guard."

A week ago Vonran would have immediately agreed. Now he thought of Colonel Kereth, who commanded the Emperor's Guard and had joined forces with Kinlol. The plain wisdom of the matter was that he must not allow those men to be in such a position over him, but still he hesitated. He remembered Kereth arguing with Kinlol, saying that he was only protecting Alexander ... "I would prefer," Vonran said, "to have an independent guard, if it will have the skill and professionalism of the Emperor's Guard."

"It will," Dheval assured him. "There is another matter, Regent. I have chosen a general to fortify the Regial border."

"Whom?" Vonran asked, though he knew.

"Gawin Gaelin." His tone was measured, dispassionate. No one would guess he was exiling a subordinate who had been his rival.

Vonran knew, but he, too, had a part to play. He affected consideration a moment, then said, "A good choice. Go ahead."

Dheval bowed his head. "Thank you, Regent. A fair day to you."

"And you, Chief Dheval." Vonran could see Dheval shift—reaching forward, he could tell—and the holograph disappeared.

Vonran tilted his head back, considering, and what came into his mind was not so much a thought as an emotion: He was pleased. He had gotten Gaelin out of Telnaria, away from Kinlol, far from the drama and its players. In Regial Gaelin would fade from the scene, from memory, from prominence. And Vonran hadn't even sent him away. He hadn't even mentioned his name. He only had to nudge Dheval, and he knew what direction he would run in. Vonran heard the rumors of Telnaria, he had seen Dheval's bitter glances towards Gaelin when he overshadowed him, heard the hostile edge of a remark ...

Something niggled uncomfortably in Vonran's mind, a suggestion that carrying out his plan against Gaelin by appealing to a man's malice and bitterness was low, unseemly. Vonran returned to his work, dismissing the thought. He had dealt with a problem. It worked. It worked well.

Kereth stared at his compad. "So," he said, "we need the equivalent of twelve full-sized bases, complete with weapons, supplies, equipment, vehicles, and men. General, we can't subvert soldiers, we need to subvert *battalions*. And even if they all brought a piece of the army with them ... " Kereth shrugged, almost helplessly, looking at the figures on the screen. "None of them can take a facility with them. You can't hide a missile in your pocket or a vaporizer in your knapsack. Squadrons, cruisers, sensing equipment, communications equipment ... " Kereth broke off, suddenly wondering if he was being tiresome, and looked up at Gawin Gaelin.

The general nodded. "All true," he said. "And then there is the issue of gathering them all together. If we could seize a base ... "

"If it was in the right location, far from Vonran's military strength and in territory where the people follow Alexander ... " Kereth sighed and shook his head. "I barely know where to begin. How do two men go about creating a force loyal to Alexander from a military under Vonran's command?"

"A military whose every member swears allegiance to the emperor," Gaelin reminded him. "None of them have sworn allegiance to Vonran."

"Then is that where we begin—finding allies?"

"If we could sift them out," Gaelin said. "What we need is the space, the freedom to work, and we need to be there—on the bases, with the soldiers. We need to be able to touch what we need to have. Here in Telnaria we are too far away—and too near the power struggles. There are too many watching eyes."

Kereth thought about that. "What place should we be in? And how do we know the eyes wouldn't watch from a distance?"

Gaelin didn't answer. He looked off into the distance, his eyes unseeing. Finally he shook his head. "It is a hard question, Colonel. It is a hard task. But we have undertaken it, and we must work with all we have."

Kereth looked at him and then down at his compad, struck by the enormity of the task. "May God show us the way," he said. "Now. We need an army. We can't take it piecemeal. We can't fit a thousand small pieces together—but maybe we can fit a dozen." Kereth's mind was running with the idea now, and he began to talk faster. "If we could take it one regiment at a time ... "

"And how do you take a regiment?"

Kereth looked at Gaelin. "You take the leaders and the rest will follow. You take the officers and you have the enlisted men."

"Your theory, then, is that if we can subvert those who control the military—we will have the military?"

"Yes! But we still a need place to work, regiments where we can exert that kind of control ..."

A mechanical chirping interrupted Kereth. Gaelin pulled his carry-comm off his belt. "General Gaelin." He was silent, listening. "I understand. ... No, I have no objections. ... Very well."

Kereth spent the conversation looking at the darkly-painted wall of his den. He heard every word and curiosity sprang up in him, but he said nothing to Gaelin as he clipped his comm back onto his belt.

"Well, Colonel," Gaelin said, "I believe God has shown us the way."

"Over your comm?"

"That was Chief Dheval."

"A far cry, wouldn't you say?"

Gaelin ignored the comment. "I am taking a command in Regial. I have the task of fortifying the border."

There was a silence, and Kereth kept his eyes on the floor, working through the information. Then he slowly raised his gaze to Gaelin's face, and he saw his own thought reflected in his eyes.

Vonran stood in the lounge, and he heard running and faint voices from the floor above—his daughters exploring the guest wing, and having the time of their lives.

He hoped there was nothing valuable in a vulnerable position up there. Vonran looked around, sizing up the room, deciding its use. He had an eye out for a room he could make his study.

Vonran turned to walk out—and saw the Lady Mareah in the entranceway. "I hope I'm not intruding," she said. "I wanted to speak to you about this place. I've had the servants remove the dishes, linens, towels—I assumed you would bring your own. Now, about the furniture and the decorations. Do you want those?"

"Some. I haven't decided how much. I am keeping my house and think my family may go there on occasion, so I will still need some furniture there."

"Tell the Palace staff if there are things you want removed," Mareah told him. "They will put them in storage."

"Thank you, Lady Mareah. I had been thinking, Lady," Vonran changed the subject. "Perhaps we should begin meeting regularly." She tilted her head to one side, looking at him. Vonran explained, "You may find your position difficult. You are the empress, and the legal guardian of your son. But you have no power within the government, and hardly a voice, now that your husband is gone. You are in danger of becoming isolated. That is why I propose these meetings. I would ensure that you are not unheard and your son's interests are not neglected. As regent, I consider it nothing less than my duty."

Mareah thought, and nodded. "I agree, Regent. How often?"

"How often would you like? Once a week?"

Mareah nodded again. "Very well." She stopped, listening to the noise from the floor above. "Your daughters?" she asked.

"Yes. I told them they could look at the bedrooms and tell me which ones they wanted."

"When I told Alexander you were moving into the guest wing, he wanted to know if there would be any boys his own age. I told him I wished you had sons, but—" Mareah stopped at her own words, and her cheeks flushed.

Vonran laughed. "So have I," he assured her, and kept to himself this thought—that she had been too pale since her husband died, and the color in her cheeks was an attractive look.

Mareah smiled at him. "Everyone wishes for both," she said. "I wanted a daughter ... "

The hope had ended, in the same way his had. Vonran suddenly remembered the first time he had seen Mareah. Judah had seemed proud of his new bride, but Vonran, looking at her, thought she was very young and a little unsure, a little afraid as she met Telnaria's dignitaries. She was still young, and sadder now, but not afraid anymore. She was an empress.

These were new thoughts, and before Vonran had begun to stir himself from them Mareah turned away. "I will leave you to your work, Regent." She left without waiting for a reply.

Vonran wondered if she was embarrassed.

He looked around the room, trying to pick up what he had been doing before Mareah arrived. His back was turned to the entranceway, but this time he heard the steps.

Vonran turned to the entranceway. Adon Kereth nodded to him as he walked in. "Yes, Colonel?" Vonran asked a little coolly. Apparently anyone could come wandering in. He would see to it that that changed after he and his family moved in.

"I heard you were here, Regent," the colonel said. "I wanted to speak with you."

Suspicion started into Vonran's mind. "Go ahead," he allowed.

Kereth's gaze flitted around the room and came to rest on Vonran again. "When you became regent," he began, "I thought the Emperor's Guard should be given the duty of protecting you. My superiors disagreed; they formed a new guard for you. But I asked that if you moved into the Palace, your protection would become the Guard's responsibility. General Ikron denied my request; he told me today that you did not want the Emperor's Guard to protect you. Why?"

"Why ... ?" Vonran prodded, wondering if he should be angry at Dheval's lack of discretion.

"Why have you rejected the Guard's protection? I assure you, this upstart guard of yours is no match for us."

Vonran didn't doubt it, and suddenly he had an impulse to tell Kereth so, to tell him the truth. Vonran glanced at Kereth, his sharp but honest face, and wondered if he should tell him what he had heard on the verandah. Maybe Kereth, at least, was not his enemy. Maybe the truth could bring them to some sort of understanding, and Vonran could trust Kereth with his safety.

For a long moment Vonran considered it. But his wisdom prevailed again, the wisdom that he had learned and that had guided him through many fights before this. Vonran looked at Kereth. "I prefer my own guard, Colonel. An independent one."

Kereth studied him for a long minute, as if deciding whether or not he would accept that. Finally he nodded, turned, and left.

CHAPTER

VI

* * * * * * * * * * * * * * * * *

THE day was clear and cool, and every once in a while a wind swept through the gardens. The flowers were dying, many of them brown and shriveled, and dead leaves crackled underfoot. Elymas Vonran stepped lightly, wondering if this was the last time they would go to the open gardens until spring. He was certainly through with it.

The Lady Mareah was with him. They had begun taking walks to escape the awkwardness of having to looking at each other, of talking. The walks continued for different reasons.

Mareah stopped and knelt beside a small myral bush. She passed her hands through its branches, its leaves. "This is a good one," she approved. "I always found it strange that in Telnaria they value only its looks and smell. Outside we use it for food."

The wind picked up again with strength, and Vonran stepped into it, shielding Mareah. "What kind?" he asked. He had come to enjoy this aspect of their discussions. He associated with all kinds of people professionally, but his personal life had always been filled with people like him—city born, city bred, city through and through. Mareah brought him into another culture.

"The leaves are usually dried and used as seasoning. Sometimes they're used fresh."

"I must try it sometime." Vonran offered his hand and helped Mareah to her feet. They walked along the path, looking at the plants on each side. “Have you been able to find good tutors for Alexander?” Vonran asked.

“Yes. Mostly tutors he had ... ” Mareah paused, her thoughts drifting back in time, back to her husband, “ ... had before. Chief Kinlol is still teaching him.”

“How is that going?”

“Just fine,” Mareah said lightly, glancing over at Vonran. “He really is all right.”

Vonran wondered if she meant Kinlol or Alexander. He let his gaze wander, to the trees beyond the path, and commented on something that had been on his mind: “Colten Shevyn has been elected premier of the Assembly.”

Mareah didn't know what that meant to him, didn't know that he wondered if the long rivalry would be resurrected, if Shevyn would now become a thorn in his side. She didn't respond, and Vonran soon thought she wasn't going to at all. Then Mareah turned to him and asked, “Is that bad for you?”

He blinked, startled. “What?”

She shook her head at his surprise. “My husband was the emperor for five years. I learned something about his work—your work now. Does it surprise you that I know to ask the question?”

“It did. I should have known better.”

Mareah dipped her head in acceptance of the admission. “And is it bad for you?”

“Colten Shevyn is a capable and intelligent man. We long worked in the Assembly—usually on opposite sides.”

“And now he is premier, and you are regent, and neither of you can rise any higher. Peace?”

Vonran smiled at her acuity—and her pluck. “Possibly. We will see. Now the Assembly has an elected premier instead of a standing one, and it returns to normal business. The Assembly continues on, the Council continues on, the courts—”

“And the regent,” Mareah added.

“That is a discrepancy, isn't it?” Vonran took a careful look at Mareah's expression. “Alexander will be emperor, Mareah. It will be on you before you turn around.”

CXXXIII

"I know," she sighed. "It isn't right, Elymas. He shouldn't have to shoulder the emperorship at seventeen. It's too heavy a burden for someone so young. I worry about him. He doesn't even have Judah to teach him before he becomes emperor."

Vonran nodded. "Boys need fathers."

"And girls need mothers."

"That's true," Vonran acknowledged.

Mareah stopped and turned to him. "So what do you do?"

He thought, but it wasn't a hard question. "The best I can. It's hard to parent alone. It's not impossible."

"It was hard enough with Judah. Without him ... "

"It's harder just because you can't talk to him," Vonran said, his own memories flooding into his mind. "Just because he isn't there with you at the end of the day. Just because ... you're now alone."

"If I replaced 'she' for 'he' ... "

Vonran nodded. "I was talking about myself. But it's true of you also, is it not?"

Mareah looked away. "Yes."

"It becomes easier, Mareah. There's no time, no day or hour, when suddenly it becomes better. But eventually you will realize that life has continued and will continue, and you can—maybe you even should—start living it again."

Mareah nodded to his words, but her eyes wandered away from him and grew distant, as she was carried away by memories. "For months I've been glad for every day that passed," she said at last, her voice soft. "I marked the time; I felt that after enough of it had passed—enough days went by—I'd wake up and be able to take up my life again. I haven't woken up—not yet—but time has begun to move again." She looked over at him. "I still feel married."

"So I would think," Vonran said. "But someday, Mareah, someday your heart will be healed enough for you to love again."

Mareah raised her eyes to his. "Someday. Not today."

Her words gently pushed him back, whether she meant them to or not. Vonran nodded his acceptance of the statement, and they walked on in silence.

They hadn't gone very far when they saw two men up ahead.

Not much further again and Vonran recognized them—Garin Dorjan and Theseus Declan.

When they reached each other, they stopped and Dorjan said, “I apologize, Elymas. We came looking for you, but no one told us you weren't alone.”

Declan bowed to Mareah. “Hail, Empress.”

Mareah slipped away from beside Vonran and nodded graciously to the men. “A fair evening to you, gentlemen. I must be on my way.”

“The same to you, Lady,” Dorjan responded, as he and Declan moved aside to allow Mareah to pass between them. It was not good manners to stand in the middle of a corridor and make an empress—or emperor—go around you.

Vonran watched her go and then turned his attention to his friends. Dorjan was grinning. “Sorry, Elymas.”

The apology being insincere, Vonran ignored it. “What brings you to the Palace?”

“Guess, old friend,” Dorjan said. “We have missed you in the Assembly. Though if we had known ... ” He gestured in the direction Mareah had gone. “She's attractive, but isn't she young for you?”

Vonran felt his posture stiffen. “The empress and I have been meeting since the month after I took office. It is part of my duty as regent.”

“A pleasant part,” Dorjan said.

Vonran couldn't argue that, so he changed the subject. “Come to my new home. We'll drink and talk. I want to hear what is going on in the Assembly.”

Dorjan glanced at Vonran as he fell into step beside him. “You heard about Shevyn.”

“Yes. I'm sorry it was him and not you, Garin.”

Dorjan shrugged good-naturedly. “I wanted it. He envied it. It's ironic, Elymas. The only reason he is premier is that you are regent, and he opposed the regency to the end.”

“You might say,” Declan put in, “he lost to his own gain.”

Vonran shot a glance at him, grinning. “You have a good

memory. For your age."

When they reached the guest wing, Vonran put in the code and led his friends into the foyer. They stopped and looked around. Vonran pointed to a room on the right. "I use that one as a lounge. If you would like a drink—"

Dorjan headed into the lounge and Vonran was about to follow, but Declan stayed him. "You and the empress seemed quite comfortable together," he said. "Have you spent much time together?"

He had Dorjan's suspicions, but not his humor. "We both become lonely," Vonran said frankly. "We give each other company."

"And God comfort you both," the old man said kindly.

Vonran expected nothing good from God, and the thought thrust itself up like a thorn of bitterness in his soul. But he kept it from his tongue and from his face. Vonran smiled and, placing a hand on Declan's shoulder, led him to join Dorjan.

Adon Kereth was hurrying down the corridor, going home after a day of work. He was on his way to the underground hangar where the vehicles were kept. As he passed a short hall that branched out from the corridor, he saw a guard, and it registered into his awareness that there was something odd about him.

An alarm rang in his head, telling him not to become entangled, to go home. Another, sterner thought—he was commander. He should see what was wrong.

The conflict lasted only a second, and Kereth slowed, giving his attention to the man to see what was odd about him. It was plain—his head was cocked, to some voice only he could hear. The earpiece transmitters weren't visible, but many people made them obvious anyway.

Kereth could catch no whisper of the message, but the man's expression made his heart beat faster. "Trouble, guardsman?" His voice came sharp, sharper than he meant it to.

The guard looked at him, surprised, but he didn't hesitate to answer his commanding officer: “A man is trying to enter the Command Center.” He gestured to the closed door at the end of the hall, sealed against the Palace's common areas. “He is arguing with the sentries.”

“Well, if he's arguing, he is not too dangerous. It's the ones who try to get in silently that we need to worry about.” But as he spoke Kereth glanced at the door. “They're still dealing with him?” Kereth asked the guard, looking back at him.

He nodded. “Yes, sir.”

“They should manhandle him out,” Kereth muttered. “Why don't they?” Probably some elite, some arrogant politician or official. That irritated Kereth. Even politicians and high officials had to obey the rules. Especially them, in Kereth's opinion, and he was not above dealing them a memorable lesson of their subjugation to the law and its enforcers.

As a matter of fact, he could enjoy it. Kereth strode to the door, palmed the open-pad, and went through to see two guards arguing with a man. A man dressed in a military uniform, a man whose face, as he glimpsed it between the guards, seemed familiar ...

Kereth clamped down on his first reaction, which was to call out the man's name, and approached the ruckus. He asked in his sternest tone, “Who is this malcontent?”

They turned to look at him. “A colonel,” one of the guards said. “He insists he knows you, but we couldn't get confirmation from your office. We denied him entry, but he is persistent.” The last word was said like an insult.

Timos Dappler glanced at him and turned to Kereth. “Well? Are you going to admit it?”

“Admit to knowing you? That's against my better judgment. Still ... ” Kereth nodded to the guards, and they returned to their sentry positions. He looked back at Dappler. “What do you want?”

“Is that any way to greet an old friend?”

“Tim, you come to me out of the blue for the first time in two years. I want to know why.”

“There's the old frankness I remember. Half the people always said it was rude; the other half agreed, but they admired your candor."

Kereth didn't have time. "I'm on my way home, Tim."

"I wanted to talk with you, Adon. You can spare me that, can't you?"

"Of course." Kereth took a breath. "Would you like to come home and have dinner with me and Susanne?"

"No, thanks. I wouldn't want to go without my wife. I just want to talk."

"My office, then?"

"That's fine."

Kereth led the way. They walked in silence, and Kereth glanced at Dappler but could read nothing on his face. The two had met years ago, at the Advanced Officers Training Course. It was almost as difficult to get in as it was to pass, and those who succeeded had a very beneficial mark on their records. Dappler had passed, ranked just behind Kereth. He had gone on to as fast-paced a career as Kereth, taking every hard and rewarding assignment that came his way. He had always shown every sign of being ambitious, except that he was not burdened. He and Kereth had never delegated each other to their pasts, nor had they ever incorporated each other into their present lives. They came together and parted again, as their lives crossed.

Kereth opened up his office and let Dappler in. "What's new?" Kereth asked, trying for a somewhat friendly way to get the conversation going.

"Oh, not much. Only that I'm going to take temporary command of the Triv Base. If I do well enough, I understand that it might become a permanent command." It was a fourth-tier general command, and for it to become permanent, Dappler would have to be awarded the rank.

A shard of Kereth's old dreams dug into his heart. Dappler would become a general. He, stuck for years more in the Emperor's Guard, never would. "Quite an advance," he said.

"Anything new in your life?" Dappler asked.

"Oh ... " Kereth hadn't told even his parents this news, but why not tell Dappler? His parents would never hear it from him.

"Susanne and I are adopting."

Dappler's eyebrows jumped up. "Adopting? As in a child?"

"No. A vork. I always wanted a sharp-toothed little rodent."

"Boy or girl?"

"In a vork, does it matter?"

"Oh, come off it. Are you adopting a son or a daughter?"

"Both. We haven't found a girl yet, but we've filed to adopt a boy."

"How old?"

"Nine."

"That's old for a child to begin to be raised. But then, you're old to begin raising a child. I guess it evens out."

Kereth shrugged. "We were planning to adopt a toddler. But Susanne ... she met the child in a hallway of the orphanage, and he won her heart."

"Women." Dappler was smiling.

"Well, that's my big news." Kereth raised an eyebrow, wondering if Dappler would get his hint and get on with it.

He did. "I have another question. Why did you decide to stay in command of the Emperor's Guard?"

It was not what Kereth had expected, and it made him uneasy. However blindly, it struck too near his alliance with Kinlol and the other Chiefs. "What sort of question is that?"

"Do you mean why do I ask it, or what right do I have to ask it?"

"Both."

"Well, the right to ask is mine—on the basis of all the years we've known each other, if you must have a reason. Whether or not you answer is your right. As for why I ask ... " Dappler shrugged. "I think you may have a reason worth hearing."

"That doesn't tell me much, Tim."

"You want me to lay it out, Adon? Fine. I heard that you requested a transfer to another command and then withdrew your request. I heard about Avvon's new guard taking up residence in the Palace. I remembered that you've commanded the Guard for four years."

Kereth stared at him, baffled. "What does all that tell you?"

"If I didn't know you, not much. But I do. I know that you are decisive, and once you make up your mind you don't change it—especially in front of your colleagues. I know that you would hate the interference with your command. I know that you are ambitious. You want to rise and you know how you can. You know that you've commanded the Guard long enough. From here on in, it can only hurt your career. Why do you stay?"

"I stay because I choose to serve the emperor by protecting him."

"Another colonel would do so as well."

"My service is mine to give," Kereth told him, letting his tone harden just a little. "I will give it as seems best to me."

Dappler nodded. "I know. I thought as much. Your sense of duty has always been stronger than your ambition. But why should your sense of duty bind you here, to the detriment—the destruction—of your ambition? What holds you here, Adon?"

Kereth looked at him, a whole new world of danger opening up before him. Could secrets be so easily detected?

When he didn't answer, Dappler asked, "Do you worry about Emperor Alexander?"

"By profession."

"Come, Adon. You always shot straight."

"Literally and metaphorically."

"Literally and metaphorically," Dappler acceded.

"You only say that because you want information from me."

"Don't evade the issue."

"What is the issue?"

"Whether you think we have reason to fear for the emperor."

Kereth rubbed his jaw and regarded his friend thoughtfully. Then he gave him part of the truth: "I do. I think he may face danger. To kill him is to end the Alheenan line, and to end the Alheenan line is to put the rule of the Empire up for grabs."

"No. The rule of the Empire is in Vonran's hands, not the child's."

"Those words and their implication are yours," Kereth said

coldly.

Dappler studied him for a long moment, and slowly nodded. “Yes, they are. And you? Do you think Emperor Alexander is in danger because of Regent Vonran?”

“Regent Vonran has done nothing.”

“He hasn't needed to yet.”

“Then that makes it a difficult question, doesn't it?”

Dappler looked at him carefully. “You've always been an honest man, Adon.”

“And I'm not being now?” His voice began to rise. “I think the emperor may face danger. I think Vonran may cause trouble. I don't know. What more do you want me to say?”

“I don't know. Maybe there is nothing more to be said. But ... ” Dappler ran out of words. He shrugged. “Just a hunch. Just because I know you. Just because ... I overheard a conversation between a lieutenant of mine and a young officer of yours. He said that Gerog Kinlol had paid you a visit. I don't know. It could be nothing. But when I have so many things—things that may or may not be connected, things that may or may not be big ... ”

He didn't finish the sentence, but he didn't have to. Kereth knew exactly what he was thinking; he would have thought the same. And it struck him that he could bring Dappler into the conspiracy, subvert the military that much more. But he didn't. He knew Dappler, but only as well as their sporadic meetings permitted. He had no reason to doubt him and no reason to trust him. It wouldn't be wise to reveal to him the conspiracy, the strategy that even now General Gaelin was carrying out in Regial. One word spoken to the wrong ear could wreck all.

And so Kereth only returned Dappler's gaze. He gave him nothing more.

Dappler drew himself to a military straightness, as though suddenly feeling challenged. “I am loyal to the emperor.”

“So am I. What question of it arises?”

Dappler sighed. “I can't force you to say what you will not. But I am loyal to the emperor, and if ever you need a man to fight for him, I will.”

“I know, Tim. I'll remember.” That promise, at least, Kereth could keep.

Dappler's expression was one of disappointment; he looked nearly sad. He nodded to Kereth. “A fair day to you, Adon. Give my regards to Susanne—and I give you both my best wishes for your children.”

“Thank you, Tim. My best wishes to you and all yours also.”

Dappler nodded again and was gone. Kereth's emotions dipped downward, and a soberness marked with dismay began to take root in him. He had just turned away an old friend to keep a secret, to keep faith with new and unlikely allies in this strangest of things—a loyal conspiracy.

And thinking of his unlikely allies ... Kereth reached for the comm panel, grumbling to himself about always having to insist on these meetings.

Trey Uman and his wife entered the reception room—late, and therefore relieved to find it still full. Uman scanned the room and saw Elymas Vonran standing half-way across it, talking with other guests.

Well, he wasn't the emperor, but he was the regent and their host, and for that they were obliged to go over and pay their respects. Not their homage, Uman reminded himself, not their homage. He and Annora made their way over, her hand slipped over his wrist.

Vonran turned to them as they approached him, and he smiled in greeting. “Good evening, Chief Uman.” He looked at Annora and bowed his head. “Lady.”

“Good evening, Regent Vonran.” Liberated by Vonran's gesture of respect to his wife, Uman bowed slightly. “Thank you for your invitation.”

Vonran nodded. “You notice many of your colleagues here.”

“Yes.” Uman looked around the large room. “All of them, in fact.”

Vonran's expression didn't waver. “Chief Kinlol sent his regrets.”

“Ah. Yes. He left Telnaria early in the week. But the rest of the Chiefs are here.”

“Yes, and I am gratified.”

As Vonran spoke, Uman saw someone in the corner of his eye, and he glanced over.

Colonel Kereth was there. When Uman looked at him, he stepped forward. “Excuse me, Chief Uman, Regent Vonran. Lady Uman.” Kereth looked at Uman. “I have a message for you, Chief Uman.”

A feeling of warning surged up in Uman. He turned to Vonran. “Pardon me, Regent.”

As Uman came up alongside him, Kereth turned and strode away. He weaved through the people to the outskirts of the gathering and then stopped and turned back to Uman. “I want you to tell Kinlol that I need to meet with him immediately.”

Surprise spiked through Uman, but he accepted it without comment. “Kinlol is out of Telnaria.”

“I know. I can't get a hold of him. But you can. Tell him for me.”

“He has business. He won't come back—”

“I won't wait.”

Uman guessed that he really wouldn't. “If the matter is so urgent, maybe I can help.”

“The matter is Kinlol.”

Uman looked at Kereth, the firm set of his mouth and how he stood, muscles taut and ready to spring. Uman's instincts—formed by years in politics—flamed up, telling him that whatever was wrong could not be neglected. “We'll talk. Outside.” Not waiting for Kereth's reaction, Uman walked away. He returned to Annora, now talking with another guest who had also come to greet their host.

They stopped and looked at him as he came up to them. “My apologies,” he said, “but I have business I must attend to. Don't wait for me; I will rejoin you as soon as I can.”

Annora nodded. Uman glanced at Vonran, who had an expression of gracious acceptance. Then he left the reception room. Outside, the corridor was empty. Wondering if he should have arranged this discussion in more detail, he began walking tentatively down the corridor.

Kereth materialized in the entrance of a hallway that branched away from the corridor. “I'm glad you came.”

Uman wasn't sure what to make of that. In others he might take it for a nicety, but, even as little as he knew him, he did not think Kereth was a man who indulged in niceties. Sarcasm, on the other hand ... “I said I would.”

Kereth nodded. “Come.” He headed down the hallway, and Uman followed. He had been a Chief for years, but this was an area of the Palace he was not familiar with. He knew the official rooms, the grand rooms. He didn't go to the others.

Kereth didn't go far. He led Uman into a plain room, with a table, chairs, a—dispenser? Uman stared at it, looking at the controls where the type of drink could be entered in. It looked like an old model, and likely a broken one.

“The servants take their breaks here,” Kereth said.

“We're near the kitchens.” Another place Uman didn't go.

Kereth nodded. “We can talk here for a few minutes without interruption. Many of the servants are off for the day; the rest will be busy with Vonran's dinner.”

Uman looked at Kereth. “What do you need?” he asked.

“I need to talk with Kinlol.”

“Why so urgently?”

Kereth looked at him and then looked away. “You're not the one my complaints are for.”

It was not the problem Uman had expected; a problem nonetheless. “Complaints?”

“Grievances might be a better word.” Kereth looked back at Uman. “I need to meet with Kinlol because I never do. I haven't been communicating with him—or you, or any of my so-called partners.”

Uman endeavored to explain. “The less we communicate the less likely we will be linked. The less likely we are linked the less likely Vonran will discover our efforts. The less likely he discovers our efforts the less likely he undermines them.”

“Would you run through that again?” Kereth asked, though

he did not look confused.

Uman suspected sarcasm again. “Don't you understand it?” he asked curtly.

“I understand it perfectly. I just want to see if you can say it all again. The less likely, the less likely ... ”

Uman sighed, exasperated. “It's a way to keep our secret.”

“I think that for Kinlol it's a way to keep me out.”

Uman looked at the colonel. “Is that the issue?”

“Yes. Ever since General Gaelin left Telnaria, my whole part in this alliance has been to be an option Kinlol can pick up ten years down the road. I signed up as an equal, or I thought I did.”

Uman shifted slightly with the uneasiness that began stirring in him. “And you did.”

“Really? What is Kinlol doing, Uman? Is it related to his duties as Chief—or as ringleader of the conspiracy?”

Uman knew, and something crumbled inside him. “Ringleader,” he told Kereth.

“What is he doing?”

“He is meeting with Silas Anezka.”

“Do you know why?”

“Yes.”

“Do you see what I mean?” Kereth asked. “If I were an equal, why is it that you know all these things and I don't? I didn't know Kinlol had left Telnaria on *our*”—it came out very sarcastically—“business. I didn't know he was meeting with Silas Anezka. I don't know why he is meeting with Silas Anezka. I have no idea who Silas Anezka is.”

“Kereth, I didn't know that Kinlol never told you. You'll have to bring it up with him.”

“I will.”

Uman didn't doubt it, but he was now afraid that Kinlol had pushed Kereth to the point of quitting the alliance altogether. And he did not particularly trust Kinlol's reconciliation skills. So he decided to try at some reconciliation himself. “I consider you an equal partner.”

Kereth fixed a measuring look on him. “Then tell me. Who is

Silas Anezka, and why is Kinlol meeting with him?"

"The answer for both is one and the same. Silas Anezka is the emperor's steward."

"Amerii was replaced?"

"No. Amerri is the steward of the emperor's estates. Anezka is the steward of ... other royal properties."

Kereth regarded him with open and obvious suspicion. "What does that mean?"

"It's a secret you may tell no one."

"You will tell me then?"

"Only because you've given your hand to protect the emperor and the royal house." That was a good way to put it—it made it sound as if Kereth had given his honor in joining the alliance. "The royal house, Colonel, has more wealth than what is in the royal vaults."

"In other words, wealth it doesn't officially have."

Uman nodded, mildly impressed by Kereth's quickness. "Exactly. These resources—I don't know what they are or where they are specifically, but I know they exist. I know there is, in all likelihood, another vault. Perhaps there are caches of it—money, supplies, weapons, jewels, valuables—all hidden against a time of need. What is certain is that much of the royal family's money has been hidden in business concerns—and so not only hidden, but invested. Silas Anezka is the steward of these investments, and those caches. He is, you might say, the most trusted man in the Empire. I know only that these resources exist and that Anezka is the steward of them; not even all the Chiefs know that. I doubt Kinlol knows much more. But Anezka is the secret steward of the emperor's secret wealth—the best kept secret in the Empire. For that alone I'd like to meet him."

Kereth stared at him, and Uman could almost see his mind whirling to process all the information. "And," he said at last, "Kinlol is meeting with Anezka to ... "

Uman nodded. "To gain his help—the royal reserves, the secret wealth—for our cause."

Kereth went a little pale. "All that money ... "

"It's there for crises, Colonel. I don't think Emperor Judah used it in all his reign. Likely Emperor Rikon never did, either."

"It must be a tremendous amount," Kereth muttered. Then he looked sharply at Uman, his voice sudden and knife-edged. "We don't have a crisis."

"Not yet."

Kereth's jaw was working. "I don't think Kinlol should get his hands on that money."

"Tell him."

"I will."

Uman nodded and stepped away. "I hope I helped you, Kereth. I need to get back."

Kereth took a breath and nodded. "Thank you, Uman."

"You're welcome." Uman withdrew and hurried to the dining hall. He was admitted and took his place by Annora at the table. He looked around at the other guests—leading men, powerful officials—and then at Vonran.

Vonran was at the head of the long table, playing the role of emperor to perfection.

Vonran poured the drinks, asking as he did so, "How did last night go?"

Dorjan shrugged as he took a seat by Vonran's desk. "As well as any event like it."

Declan remained standing and he took no drink. "The dinner went well, Elymas."

"Have you heard people talking?"

"Some."

"What do they say?"

"What they usually say after an emperor's dinner."

"Ah."

Dorjan sipped the vynas, gave it a critical look, and then turned a yet more critical look on Vonran. "What makes you into a nervous hostess, Elymas?"

"Nothing. I wanted to have an emperor's dinner—nothing

more, nothing less. I want to be sure it was taken as an emperor's dinner, nothing more, nothing less."

"You succeeded," Declan said. "And it was good to do it. All the leaders of the government sit down together only when the emperor is with them. It is good for them to sit down."

"In theory I am the acting emperor," Vonran said. "I don't know how far that will be accepted in practice."

"What do you want to do?"

"I want to replace a Chief."

Dorjan's gaze shot to him, but Declan seemed unaffected. "That is well within the emperor's powers. But Chiefs are to be respected. They are powerful, ambitious men—and competent men, as a rule. They are not to be taken lightly."

"Emperor Judah left a strong Council—with one exception."

Dorjan's eyes lit up with his guess. "Fionn Dheval!"

Vonran nodded. Dheval was a weak link; he had no especial competence, no real loyalty to Vonran. Any use he had had for Dheval evaporated after he sent Gawin Gaelin to Regial. "That's one issue I agree with Kinlol on. Dheval could easily be replaced with a better man."

"I found it curious that he sent a general like Gaelin to Regial," Declan commented.

"I told him to choose a prominent and skilled general," Vonran said, taking care not to look at Declan's face. "The work is extensive."

Dorjan laughed. "I don't know about skilled, but he could not have chosen a more prominent one."

"How long will Gaelin be away?"

This time Vonran did glance up at Declan. "I don't know. He hasn't even presented a plan for the defense of the border yet."

"Will he stay on for the whole work?"

Vonran began to grow impatient. "I don't know."

"To the original question"—Dorjan spoke a little more loudly than normal, as he did when bored with the turn the conversation had taken—"I think you should get rid of Dheval if you want to. But, by all means, don't alarm the rest of the Chiefs. If you want to change the Council, do it slowly. A Chief this year, a few years later another one, later ... "

"He is not here to stay," Declan broke in.

Vonran looked at him—surprised that he would interrupt, surprised that he would take such a reproving tone.

Declan turned to him. "Until you pass your duties to Alexander, you must discharge them as seems best to you. Just keep the Empire's good—and only the Empire's good—before you, and you will do well." Declan glanced towards the door. "I must be on my way."

Dorjan and Vonran watched him leave in silence. Vonran turned to his friend. "You struck a nerve."

"What did I say?"

"Something about replacing the Chiefs one by one."

"Are they submitting to you?"

"As far as I can see."

"Are you worried about where you are blind?"

Vonran nodded. "Kinlol does not oppose me to my face, but he has not given up his opposition. I don't know what he'll do, but he'll draw others into it if he can."

Dorjan gazed, sharp-eyed, at nothing for a moment, and then looked at Vonran. "Then he is breaking the law."

"What?"

"He is breaking the law," Dorjan repeated. "You are regent. If he is trying to undermine you, he is breaking the law."

Vonran frowned. "Not necessarily. Kinlol is hardly the first to engage in such maneuvering—"

"There's a line, Elymas, and it isn't that fine. I don't trust Kinlol to honor it."

Now that Vonran thought of it, neither did he. "There's nothing I can do, Garin."

Dorjan looked at him. "Not yet. But you are regent. Don't let anyone deny that. They oppose you? You must oppose them."

He had already planned to do that. But that what they were doing was illegal—that was a new thought. And not one without logic.

“That dinner last night,” Dorjan said. “There's one way it could have been better done.”

“What's that?”

“If it had had a hostess. Gives you a reason to get yourself a woman.”

What came into Vonran's mind was not an image of a new wife standing by his side, but Dianthe, her gray eyes sparkling with spirit and intelligence ...

He heard Dorjan sigh. “I'm sorry, Elymas. I only meant ... I never would have said it unless—I assumed you and the empress ... ”

Vonran shook his head. “We are ... ” But he didn't know what they were. He had begun the meetings to keep Kinlol's influence from dominating the royal family. He had found, unexpectedly, companionship. A woman whose sorrow matched his own, who understood his work, who knew his world ...

What were they?

Vonran was brought out of his reflection when Dorjan pushed away from the table. “I have a meeting, Elymas. I'm sorry if —if what I said was wrong.” He hurried out.

Vonran slowly turned back to his work, bringing his computer screen to life with a tap of his finger. Nothing had happened since Dorjan came in, but now his world seemed a little different.

It was late at night when Kinlol's ship docked in the hangar of the Tel Aubur Base. An aide who had traveled with him took the controls of a hovcar, and Kinlol sat in the back. After assuring himself that the sound-barrier between the driver's seat and the passengers' compartment was activated, he turned to the comm unit. He tapped out the activation code and checked for messages. One caught his attention, and he accessed it.

The screen morphed into Trey Uman's image. He was not grim, but there was no smile or even friendliness in his face. “An issue arose in your absence,” he said. “I gave the colonel your house's entrance code; he'll be waiting for you when you arrive.

Good luck."

Good luck? What was that supposed to mean? Good luck with the issue? Good luck with the colonel? Was the colonel the issue?

Kinlol replayed the message: *I gave the colonel your house's entrance code.* He had given Uman that code in case of an emergency, but this didn't seem like an emergency. They had waited until he returned, and *the colonel* would be there to meet him ...

Anger stirred in Kinlol. When the hovcar drew up to the front of his house, he disembarked and went to the door and entered his code. But his hand hesitated over the last number, and he glanced over his shoulder at the hovcar, passing through the gate. When it—and the aide—were gone into the dark city, he turned back to opening the door.

Kereth wasn't waiting at the door, and that relieved him. And then he had to wonder—where was he? Kinlol went to the security terminal, tucked away at the side of the foyer, to the left of the door. He summoned a diagram of the house, all life-presences marked. Aside from his own, one showed up—in the downstairs study.

Kinlol went there, his irritation surging. He struck at the open-pad and strode through the door.

Kereth was standing by the bookshelf, his back to Kinlol. At Kinlol's entrance he turned. He looked calm, but his expression was spiced with something Kinlol didn't quite comprehend.

Kinlol held his anger down, unwilling to let it have the upper hand. "I assume you and Uman have a reason for this."

"Of course. But why start with us? What about you? Did you manage to get your hands on the emperor's money?"

Kinlol's eyes narrowed. It was an offensive question—and he was enough a judge of men to know that it was intentional. "So you're unhappy." Then a realization burst into his mind. "Wait—who told you? Uman?"

Kereth nodded. So he and Uman had been getting together in Kinlol's absence. And Uman had not only been throwing secrets out, he had trapped Kinlol into a meeting with the irate colonel. "Is that why you came?"

"It's one of my reasons." Kereth sat—on Kinlol's chair, behind his desk, in his study. It rankled, but Kinlol held himself in check, lowering his eyes to keep his gaze on Kereth's face. "I guess it's part of a larger question."

"And what is that?" Kinlol didn't want to deal with the colonel's issues, but he couldn't ignore them. He should have guessed Kereth would be a demanding partner; he had a demanding enough personality.

"What are we doing?"

Again? "Don't you know?"

"What I want to know"—each word came hard, like the pounding of a hammer—"is if you do."

Again Kinlol fought down the urge to strike back. "I know very well what we are doing. We are protecting the emperor."

Kereth shook his head. "Do you understand what you're doing?"

Kinlol folded his arms across his chest. "Perfectly."

"Do you? You're leading a conspiracy against the regent, subverting the military, preparing for war ... and pillaging the royal coffers to do all this." Kereth looked at him carefully. "Do you understand that?"

Kinlol glowered at him. "I understand that I am defending the emperor. I understand that I am protecting the institutions our ancestors made from being destroyed. I understand that I am keeping our country from a usurper's grasp."

Kereth sighed. "So clearly cut. So simply done. You may believe it, but ... "

Kinlol had the impression he was trying to be kind, and it infuriated him. "Tell me what you think, Colonel. It won't hurt my feelings."

Kereth studied him. "I think this isn't nearly as simple as you assume. I think you're playing a dangerous game, and you don't know how dangerous. A few days ago an old friend—a man I haven't seen in two years—all but asked me if I was involved in a subversion against Vonran. His basis was a few facts picked from the grapevine and what he knew about me. Do you think we can keep this secret?

Do you know what Vonran will do to us if we don't?"

Kinlol raised his eyebrows. "What?"

Kereth lifted his eyes in exasperation at the question. "It isn't as if we're models of upright, law-abiding citizens! If Vonran discovers this conspiracy, he's going to have it known by every man, woman, and child in the Empire. You'll be thrown off the Council and maybe thrown in jail, I'll be court-martialed and lucky to get only a dishonorable discharge. It will mean disgrace for the both of us—and for Uman, and Gyas, and the general."

It struck Kinlol that Kereth was leaving out the most important result, and he said, "And no one will be able to fight for Alexander and the royal house."

"All right. All right. If that's what makes you concerned. We will be disgraced and ruined—and Alexander will lose his small, faithful band. Are you concerned now?"

Kinlol was finding that the fierceness he had noticed in Kereth—the fierceness he had respected, the fierceness he had expected to be directed against Vonran—was very grating when directed against himself. "I am concerned. More concerned than you, I might add. It has been me, after all, who has insisted on meeting rarely and secretly."

Kereth's expression changed, but not for the better. "Ah, yes. That. I had come to regard it as your way of cutting me out."

A thought began to raise its head, but Kinlol ignored it. "Preposterous."

"Really? When you refuse to meet with me—even if you are concerned about security, aren't you just as happy not to talk to me? You even initiate major policies without telling me. Like getting the code to the emperor's secret vault. Be honest, Kinlol—with both of us. You didn't want me to know. Security was only your excuse for not telling me."

It was the truth, and it flew straight through all his defenses. And he was silenced by it.

Kereth's tone turned quiet. "So now we have it. Kinlol, I joined under the assumption that I would be an equal, that you would deal true with me. Was I wrong?"

Kinlol thought it over—going back, remembering what he had done and why. "Colonel, I have always thought of myself as a true man. I wanted an ally in command of the Emperor's Guard. I wanted ... " And he could think of nothing more to add.

"An ally in command of the Emperor's Guard," Kereth finished for him. "But a new partner—an equal in the conspiracy—me always in your counsels—you never wanted that, did you?"

"I never considered it," Kinlol told him. "But weren't you with us when we decided on our two policies?"

"Yes. Now you and the Chiefs are carrying out the one, Gaelin is carrying out the other ... and I'm a backstop."

Kinlol looked at him but could read nothing from his face. "What do you want, Colonel?"

"I want to know the terms on which I'm a part of this alliance. I want to know how far I've been wrong."

"The terms were never established, Colonel. And for that ... " It was hard. "I am to blame. And for leaving you out of our counsels ... I apologize." The hardest words.

And, at them, some of the hardness faded from Kereth's expression. "So you will listen as I fire off my opinion on raiding the emperor's vaults."

"Go ahead."

"I don't think we have a right to the money. I think taking it is dangerous—in a certain way. We have to be careful, Kinlol. While we make sure Vonran does not usurp power, we must make sure we do not, either."

"Colonel, we may need the emperor's money for the emperor's sake. Even wars have to be funded."

"And well I know it. I'm a soldier, Kinlol, and a jaded old cynic. We have to pay money to have anything—even a war. But, Kinlol, there is no war."

Kinlol nodded. "And until there is, I will not spend a single lim out of the royal coffers. And by then, the emperor will be old enough to be brought into our counsels. Do you disapprove?"

Kereth seemed to be thinking it over, an odd mixture of relief and embarrassment in his face. "No, not if that's the way it will be done." He hesitated a moment. "Why did you meet with Anezka?"

"To find out the extent of the resources and how easily they could be turned to use. To see if Anezka would make them ready for use."

"Did you get what you wanted?"

"I made a start."

"Well, now that I understand that, it's time to make some other things clear also."

"Colonel," Kinlol said, "let's put the past aside. Instead of establishing the terms on which you entered, let's establish the terms on which you are now in. You should be an equal. You deserve to be an equal. So to a full partnership, to loyalty to our emperor, our cause, and each other ... " Kinlol stretched out his hand—open, palm up. A question. A promise. A request.

Kereth looked at his open hand and then up at his face. Then he clapped his hand over Kinlol's, and he gripped firmly and strongly as they made and sealed their covenant with a handshake.

And they were, uneasily, allies.

CHAPTER

VII

* * * * * * * * * * * * * * * *

AND so the year advanced. Telnaria settled into sameness; what was new became old, what was unknown became comfortable.

As the autumn passed, Vonran entered into a quiet, intense search for a new commander-in-chief. Aided by his disciplined, dedicated staff, he examined different candidates. He wanted a man who could manage the military and fight a war, a strategist and a bureaucratic infighter. He was not looking for charm or pleasantness; he wanted competence and reliability. He wanted a pragmatist who would not get snared in a web of sentimentality, a man of cold, hard, fearless thought. Too many men were romantics, even those who had no right to be, even the old fox Kinlol. Vonran frankly did not understand how he obtained—or retained—such a view of the emperors. Their flaws were well-known to Vonran. He read history and he lived it. Of the two emperors he had known, only one was a better man than usual; neither could outwit him.

Vonran found Zidon Adesh, a first-tier general in command of the armed forces in the Royal Sector. Vonran sent his chief of staff to see if the general was willing to be commander-in-chief; when the report came back that he was, Vonran interviewed him. And he knew for a fact: He had found his man.

So he dismissed Fionn Dheval. Dheval sat stone-faced after hearing Vonran's words, then said, "I should have resigned long ago." And he cut off the transmission.

Why not? Vonran had already taken from him all he could.

In Telnaria, not a word was spoken against Vonran. Dheval had gained neither the friendship of the powerful nor the favor of the public, and there was no one to object to his dismissal. In addition, the state of the Regial border had become a minor scandal since Gawin Gaelin had been sent to repair it. Only a disaster could justify sending a man like Gaelin to a place like Regial.

Vonran had been disturbed at the development—not because it harmed him, but because he had not guessed it. He didn't like surprises in any case, and it made him nearly angry when they came from his own actions. But the scandal of the Regial border worked to his benefit in the end. Dheval was blamed for it, and Vonran's way was all the clearer to get rid of him.

Zidon Adesh joined the Council in as non-emphatic a way as any Chief ever did. One week Fionn Dheval sat at the table; the next, Zidon Adesh. And when Vonran entered the Room of Counsel and they all stood for him, he saw Adesh among them, just as much a Chief as those appointed by an emperor. A rush of pleasure went through him, and for the first time he felt the Council of Chiefs beneath his hand.

That was the first month of winter. The second came, with bitter cold. The Assembly recessed until spring, and many of the wealthy left Telnaria for sun-warmed estates. Even several Chiefs took their jubilees. Wrapped in snow, deserted in its winter, Telnaria lay cold and quiet as the weeks passed.

And Mareah and Vonran met together more and more. Vonran had wanted it much earlier; once—even twice—a week was far too little. But even after he was sure she felt the same, he held back. They couldn't meet without the servants and the guards knowing; from them, rumors would go racing through Telnaria. *The regent and the empress are in love* would fly from mouth to mouth; they would say it throughout Telnaria and it would go into the Empire. Vonran didn't want it; Mareah dreaded it. So they held themselves back. In a reflective moment, Vonran wondered whether they feared the rumors because they didn't want others to think they were falling in love, or because they didn't want to think they were falling in love. He never pursued the answer. It was as it was.

But desire grew and chafed against restraint, and they began seeing each other more often. When winter took hold and Telnaria grew quiet, they met as often as they wished. They even began mixing their children, meeting in the guest wing or the royal residence.

Then Gawin Gaelin returned to Telnaria. Vonran's aides had set up a briefing for him, and Zidon Adesh attended also. Gaelin summarized the work he had done so far, his conclusions from studying the situation, and the plans he had drawn up.

At the end of the presentation, there was silence. Vonran looked at the holograph Gaelin had made, a map of Regial depicting the network of defense he proposed building there. It looked nothing if not thorough.

Adesh was looking at it also. Then he glanced down at his compad, which was currently displaying Gaelin's report. "You have proposed the construction of twenty-seven new planet-side bases and two space stations."

"Yes."

"Do you consider that necessary?"

"I have planned a competent defense of Regial. Nothing more, nothing less."

Adesh studied Gaelin, his cold eyes so steady they looked almost unblinking. It would have unnerved many men, but Vonran's keen eye could not detect even a hint of perturbation from Gaelin. Adesh gestured, taking in the holograph and his compad. "Are you aware of the cost of these projects?"

"Fully."

Vonran looked at Adesh. "Is it excessive?"

"The cost is."

It was the answer to a different question than he had asked. "And the defense?"

Adesh's eyes went to Gaelin before resting on Vonran. "The defense is reasonable—ideal, even. But the ideal is often unattainable. The cost would be enormous. Money doesn't flow like water from the treasury."

"To the contrary," Gaelin said. "It does. The question is—will you channel it down my tributary?"

"The military cannot sustain your projects. We have all the Empire to defend. Men, weapons, ships, equipment, bases, and space stations—do you think we can send you all this?"

"Yes," Gaelin answered. "Not in a day. Not in a year. But over time—yes. The Empire is prosperous and the Assembly is generous with the military. What I must know is—do I re-draw the plans, or implement them as the resources allow?"

Adesh glanced at Vonran. Vonran remained gazing at Gaelin. "Could you do that smoothly?"

"Of course."

"Then the best thing is to implement your plans. How long would it take?"

"Full speed, all resources provided without delay—two or three years. Otherwise, it depends how much we slow the process."

"The military will not construct the space stations simultaneously," Adesh said.

"Then five years at the least. Likely more."

Adesh nodded. "Unless you object, Regent, likely years more."

"Would that treat the matter with less urgency than it deserves?" Vonran asked.

"Not in my judgment."

Gaelin seemed to consider his answer more carefully. "There is no imminent threat, Regent. The border is not secure, but we don't know that anyone is planning to exploit that."

"In addition," Adesh put in, "moving quickly might spook the Vothnians into action of their own."

Vonran glanced between the men. He wanted Gaelin out building bases and stocking armories in the wilderness as long as possible, but he didn't want the Empire to be vulnerable. If, however, even Gaelin said there was no imminent threat ... "Very well," he said. "Proceed. Phase the implementation."

"How slowly?"

Vonran gestured to Adesh. "Work it out, and bring your

suggestions to me. Tell me what tributaries will run lower if the water flows to you, General Gaelin. That way I may judge where the money will be best spent."

Gaelin nodded. "Thank you, Regent Vonran."

Adesh's gaze was on the holograph floating above the table, in front of him and Vonran. "Well-defended." He glanced down at his compad. "Well-stocked. You will be ready to do battle with the Vothnians."

Gaelin barely smiled.

Vonran rose to his feet. "Dismissed, General. I will see you tonight."

"Yes," Gaelin said. "Thank you for honoring me with such a welcome."

There was still displeasure in Telnaria over Gawin Gaelin and his royal-blooded wife being sent to Regial. Vonran had decided to welcome them back with a banquet and dance, both to keep the displeasure directed towards Dheval and to soothe any suspicions that he felt any animosity towards the general. It would also give him an opportunity to host the powerful of Telnaria and act the role of emperor among them. He had thought these things over carefully before arranging the festivities and sending the invitations.

Vonran nodded to Gaelin's thanks. "Should I not be pleased, along with Telnaria, to welcome you back?"

Gaelin bowed slightly and, retrieving his compad from the table and his info chip from the holo-projector, left the room.

Vonran turned to Adesh, now standing also. "What do you think?"

"Of the defense? It will be good, once it is done. Of Gaelin? He will do well."

Vonran gave no sign of the quiet relief that budded in him. It was a danger that had occurred to him—Dheval's replacement might want to bring Gaelin back. No sign of such a desire from Adesh yet, and that was good. "So you would not recommend re-assigning him?"

"No, not unless you have something in mind that I don't know of. I see no place where he would be more useful than where he is now."

Vonran nodded, pleased that Adesh took no account of Telnaria's complaining. "Then let us leave him there, General."

It was a large room, and well-lit. The light-panels high above in the ceiling were so bright they could not be looked at. The hard floor—muraled in dark browns and coppers—glinted beneath the light. It was bare, without furniture except along the walls. It was the dance floor.

Elymas Vonran arrived there from the dining hall, his guests coming after him. Among the first to arrive were Gawin Gaelin and his wife. Layne was soon in a conversation with another couple, and Gaelin, though standing by, was clearly out of it. Vonran decided they could have a private enough conversation as the room filled in, and so he went over. When Gaelin turned to him, he opened with, "I hope you are enjoying the evening."

Gaelin allowed that he was.

Vonran glanced over at the open doors and the people coming in, selecting his words. "Do you feel you are gainfully occupied?"

"In Regial? Of course."

That sounded promising. Vonran needed to know where Gaelin was on the matter, whether he wanted to stay or would try to get back to Telnaria as soon as possible. Like probing Adesh, it was dangerous, but nothing was as dangerous as ignorance. "Then you intend to implement the plans yourself?"

"That was my intention—if you and General Adesh permit."

Was there a question in that statement? "We have no other plans." As Vonran spoke his gaze wandered—and was netted by Mareah, standing across from him. It had been only natural to invite her, and to greet her when she arrived. Aside from that, he had had no contact with her, but all evening he had to make an effort to keep his eyes from wandering to her. Now he caught himself again and let his gaze re-focus on Gaelin.

Before either man could speak, the master of the banquet

came up to them. “The guests are assembled, Regent. Would it please you to begin the dancing?”

Vonran hadn't danced with a woman since Dianthe died, but his standard refusal died unspoken as he remembered Mareah. “Tell the musicians to get ready,” he replied. “I'll be ready to begin in only a moment.” He walked to Mareah and bowed to her. “Will the empress do me the honor of opening the dance with me?”

Mareah looked surprised but not displeased, and the color rose in her cheeks. “If the Regent is gracious enough to ask, I will certainly accept.” Beneath the words was a playfulness only Vonran could hear, because their formality was a joke only he could understand.

He held out his hand and she placed hers in it. As they walked out to the middle of the room, she said in a very soft voice, “Everyone will talk.”

Vonran knew that. But for the first time he didn't care—or, perhaps, for the first time he realized he didn't. He whispered his reply, “And why should we care?”

Mareah didn't respond until they stopped in the room's center. Then she turned to him and looked up with a smile that told him that—in this, right now—they were together, and the world didn't matter. It was the smile that, years ago, had made the lonely heart of the emperor's only son ache with longing.

Vonran's eyes were still fixed on her when the music started flowing through the room, softly summoning. As the notes rose up, he began, leading Mareah into the dance.

And they were a fine sight, out alone on the dance floor. Silver was just beginning to thread through Vonran's dark hair, maturity was in his face, and strength was in his hands. Mareah danced with him, her beauty and vigor undimmed. All their movements were graceful, perfectly matched to the music—and each other.

Adon Kereth sat on his lounge floor, his back against the couch. Today he was dressed casually, in civilian clothes; his uniform—

stiff, immaculate, openly proclaiming rank and status—was in his bedroom. He was shoeless, and normal clothes felt soft and loose. It was less confining, which is not to say that he found it liberating.

A boy sat facing him—nine years old, dark-haired and light-eyed. His son. Between them was a small, sturdy piece of wood, a series of shallow holes dug out on each side, and a single one at each end. There was a pile of smooth, artificial pebbles, colored black and white.

"This," Kereth instructed the boy, "is an ancient game of strategy. An old game of strategy," he amended, wondering if Cormac knew what ancient meant, wondering if simplifying his language for him was bad or good. Or good to a degree and then it became bad, in which case the question was at what degree ...

He pulled himself out of it and went on. "The goal is to end with as many pebbles as possible. At the beginning of the game, the pebbles are in these holes along the side of the board." Kereth stopped to arrange the pebbles. He was spending an afternoon at home, teaching his son to play a game, trying to be a father, trying to have a normal life. Trying to gain something that could not be summarized and declared in a few bits of metal pinned to a piece of clothing.

"Now," he said, dropping the last pebble into its hole. "The two holes on the end—the one on your right is yours. The one on my right is mine. You are trying to get pebbles ... "

Susanne came into the room. "Someone's on the comm for you, Adon."

"Thanks. Be back in a minute, Cormac." Kereth stood and went to the comm unit. He checked its settings quickly—auditory only.

Kereth knew a very few people who only used auditory, and he made a guess that it was one of them in particular. He hit a key and said, "Colonel Kereth."

And Gerog Kinlol's voice proved his guess correct: "I'm glad to get a hold of you, Colonel. General Gaelin is back in Telnaria."

Kereth rolled his eyes. "Who doesn't know? What with Vonran's big shindig the other night ... "

"The point, Colonel, is that we should all meet together."

"Great idea. Give me the password and tell me what level of the Tower of Cyneric you want to meet in."

There was a slight pause, by which Kereth knew he had tried Kinlol's patience. "We will meet at Trey Uman's estate. I trust you know where that is?"

"I can find it."

"Very good."

"When?" Kereth asked quickly, suddenly worried that Kinlol was about to cut off.

"As soon as we can gather."

Kereth glanced towards the living room. "Give me a couple hours."

There was a pause. "Why?"

"I have something to do."

"Such as?"

The question could be considered impertinent, but Kereth merrily indulged it: "I have serious game-playing to do, man." He cut off, satisfied by the thought that that would leave Kinlol wondering—and possibly seething.

Less than three hours later, Kereth arrived at Trey Uman's house. To his surprise, Uman himself answered the door and led him to the patio where the Chiefs had once plotted to thwart the Assembly. There was a table there on the patio, and the others were sitting around it—Gawin Gaelin, Gerog Kinlol, and Kavin Gyas.

Uman took one empty seat. Kereth took the other. It placed him opposite Kinlol. Their eyes met, but neither man spoke. Kinlol looked around at the others. "We are all gathered. And glad," he added, turning to Gaelin, "to welcome the man who is at the locus of our plans."

Gaelin bowed his head. "But what of your own efforts?"

"Nothing to report," Kereth said.

"Isn't our political strategy in progress?" Gaelin looked at Kinlol as he spoke.

"So it is," Kinlol said. "And it goes on. It's a slow work."

"And boring," Kereth put in. "So how goes the subversion?"

"The military build-up is everything we could want. Vonran approved it all—the bases, the weapons, the men. We'll have a small army at our disposal before all is done."

"Our disposal?" Kereth repeated.

Gaelin glanced at him. "Yes, Colonel. You once said that if you have the officer, you have the men. I've considered that very carefully. I drew up a list of men I have known in the military—fine men I know would help the emperor at any cost. I am planning to gradually bring them into Regial until all the ranking officers in the army there subscribe to our cause."

"Do you trust that many officers enough to tell them our secret?" Uman asked.

"No. But I will appoint the ones I do, and I will let them staff their commands with men they trust. And eventually ... "

"Every consequential post in the armed forces in Regial will be manned by a soldier after our own hearts," Kereth finished.

Gaelin nodded. Kinlol asked him, "You're not telling these men everything, I hope?"

"Don't worry. I won't be too generous."

Kereth addressed Gaelin, but he was looking at Kinlol. "Be downright stingy, General. If you want to keep a secret, keep it close." Kinlol returned his look, seeming to evaluate whether he was being made fun of, which he wasn't. Not really.

Gaelin turned to Kereth. "You must have known many men in your career. Do you have any to recommend?"

Tim Dappler came to Kereth's mind. "I'll think about it and let you know."

"You are amassing resources most impressively, General," Uman said. "Or so I see from Adesh's requests for supplemental funds for the military."

"Not to mention his attempts to have money diverted to him from other departments," Gyas added. "Than Au'Rhinn is not happy."

"Adesh is blaming you," Uman said.

"He's right," Gaelin replied.

"So the commander-in-chief doesn't like your plans? Do you

think he suspects?" Kereth asked.

"No. He just doesn't like the cost."

"And Vonran?"

"Vonran ... " Gaelin shrugged. "I cannot guess. Whenever I meet him I can see him absorbing everything around him—absorbing it into some world of his own. He's a very intelligent man, but who can guess his mind or his heart?"

That made Kereth uncomfortable, for more than one reason. "It's dangerous to have an enemy you can't guess. And if we can guess him so little there might not be any danger, in which case we, my friends, are the prize idiots of the decade."

The silence that settled was slightly awkward. "Nonetheless," Gaelin picked up briskly, "he did ask me whether I intend to stay."

"I assume you said yes," Kinlol replied. "What did he say?"

"That he and Adesh have no other plans."

Kereth looked at Gaelin. "Have you increased the army intelligence units?"

Gaelin turned to him a little quickly, his brows coming together. "No. Do you think ... "

Kereth shrugged. "As long as we're building ourselves the core of a military, we might as well build the core of an intelligence agency."

There was a pause in the conversation. Uman spoke first. "It makes sense to me."

Kinlol nodded. "Well-thought of."

"Did you just compliment me?" Kereth asked.

Kinlol looked at him.

Gyas asked suddenly, "What do you think of Vonran's replacing Dheval?"

"A good move," Kinlol said, but with a begrudging note in his voice.

"Dheval had it coming," Uman agreed.

"But you don't think this could be part of a larger plot—remaking the Council?"

Uman looked at him and then Kinlol. He sat back. "Suddenly

I feel insecure about my job."

"Vonran's demonstrated he has the power," Kereth said agreeably.

"Whatever his plans," Gaelin said, "there's nothing we can do. And here's another complication we can do nothing about: Mareah Alheenan is falling in love with Vonran."

No one would deny it. "Does he love her?" Uman asked.

Gaelin sighed. "I think so."

Gawin Gaelin stood in the foyer of his Telnarian home, hesitant. After a few moments he walked on, guessing at which room they would be in.

He found them in the den, as they called the room that was more or less Layne's. He stepped into the room and smiled at Mareah, hoping he looked—well, pleasant. "I'm glad you made it over, Mareah."

She smiled back. "It's good to see both of you again."

Gaelin glanced at Layne. She met his eyes, a knowing look in hers. They had talked about this last night. Layne stood up. "I'm going to check on the children." As she left, Gaelin went over and sat on the other end of the couch Mareah was on.

"How did your meeting go?" Mareah asked.

"Meeting?"

"Layne told me you were meeting with Chief Kinlol and some other men you know."

"Yes. It went well." Gaelin cleared his throat and began, gingerly, to approach the subject. "How have things been going with you and Alexander?"

"We've been fine. Things have been getting better."

Gaelin's heart should have jumped at that, but it sank. He guessed the main reason for the improvement. "And you and ... " *Don't be such a coward, Gaelin. Just say it.* "You and Elymas Vonran?"

Her brow crinkled down. "What?"

"You and Elymas Vonran. You ... " *Say it,* General *Gaelin.*

"You two are in love."

Mareah's eyes went down and then away. "Can you tell?"

"It was in how he looked at you, Mareah, and how you accepted it. Women keep their distance from men who give them attention they don't want."

"All right." Mareah cleared her throat slightly. "What of it?" As she spoke, she looked him in the eye.

It was bold enough, but Gaelin caught a hint of uncertainty. "Mareah ... " He stopped to think over his words. "Mareah, you are my wife's sister-in-law, her only brother's wife. I have always tried to be a brother to you. What I'm doing now, Mareah, I do as a brother. I ask you to accept it as that."

She paused. "This isn't going to be good, is it?"

"No. I'm afraid it isn't."

Mareah looked away again. "What is it?"

"I think you need to be careful of Elymas Vonran. There are many layers to him, many depths in his soul. Don't assume you have understood him. Don't assume that, ten years from now, he will be a man you will want to be married to."

Mareah looked up at him, anger sparking in her gray eyes. "How can you say that? You don't know him."

"Mareah ... "

"I know you never wanted him to be regent, but telling me not to marry him on account of that ... "

"This isn't about that."

"No?" she challenged. "Aren't you still opposed to him?"

She had no idea. "I thought the regency was a bad idea six months ago, and I still think it's a bad idea today. But the point is not about the regency, or Vonran as regent. The point is what sort of man he is. What sort of husband he will be."

"Dianthe Vonran was a happy woman."

That startled him. He decided, after a moment, that it was a good point. He sidestepped it. "As far as I could see, yes. My concern is for you. Tell me, Mareah. Where does God fit into Vonran's life?"

Mareah was silenced by that. "We haven't talked much about

... Him."

"Is he a Christian?" When Mareah didn't answer, Gaelin gently pressed his point. "You can't marry an unbeliever. You know you can't. Your first allegiance is to God, and He said ... "

"I know what He said," Mareah interrupted. "You don't know that Elymas is an unbeliever."

Elymas. "No, Mareah." He kept his voice gentle. "And you don't know that he isn't."

Mareah didn't reply. She sat still, looking away from him, the happiness that had been in her face now gone.

Maybe he had persuaded her. Either way, his heart ached.

The Empire's New Year began on the first day of spring in Telnaria. It was a holiday celebrated throughout the Empire with a three-day festival. On the morning of the first day, the leaders of the Empire gathered in attendance of the emperor's proclamation of the festival of the New Year. He proclaimed it every year; the holiday was not established by an abiding law, but a repeated decree. If the reader seeks the fine distinction of this, there is none. No one thought the holiday would cease anymore than they thought the whole government would go truant of a spring afternoon and never return to its work. But it gave them a ceremony, and it gave the ceremony an illusion of consequence.

After the proclamation the military showed its paces—ostensibly for the emperor, and in effect for the entire nation. When the finest troops in the Empire had finished executing their drills, they stood at attention in front of the emperor for his inspection. The ceremony, the drills, the sharp soldiers, the powerful men, the ostentation of might and mirth—it was a tradition and a spectacle. Through such things nations are bound.

This New Year they carried on the tradition without any change. They didn't have an emperor, it was true. But they had a regent, and that was enough.

Vonran knew what was expected of him, and he was happy to oblige. The people wanted grandeur, and he would give it to them.

To that end, he dressed more finely than he had since he couldn't remember when. His silver tunic was made of *laera*—a sturdy material with colors of remarkable vibrancy. Over his other clothes he wore a dark, sleeveless robe.

That morning, as Vonran got ready, his mind went over the New Year's ceremony. It was always held at the Great Plaza, which spread in front of the towering Court of Justice—the edifice in which the nation's highest court rendered its verdicts. The Hall of Assembly was nearby, and the Palace was in the distance behind. A broad terrace had been built at the Court's front, with a flight of steps leading up to it. Both the steps and the terrace were made of near-marble, white with faint streaks of light gray.

For the New Year's ceremony, a throne was set up for the emperor at the center of the terrace. People were seated on each side of him—at a little distance. The Council of Chiefs, the judges who held forth in the building behind them, the premier, and two other men from the Assembly sat on the emperor's right. All lesser guests were positioned on the emperor's left.

Vonran had, at one time, sat on the left. As his power in the Assembly increased, he earned a position on the right. Now he would sit in the center. Vonran had often thought that if emperors were elected instead of born, he would have been one. And now he reflected on the fact that he had become one anyway. In everything but title, he was the emperor.

The child—who was not emperor in anything but title—would also be there, with his mother. The men and women who arranged the ceremony had treated this awkward situation delicately. It seemed wrong to leave the empress and the last heir of Alexander the Mighty out of the ceremony, but it was hard to fit them in. They couldn't shift mother and son to the side with the government leaders, and putting them by Vonran—well, that had its own problems. Too close, and they would be seated where the emperor's family usually was—which, with the regent in the emperor's place, would make an embarrassingly implicative image. Too far away, and they would risk taking the center—of the terrace, of attention—away from Vonran. They couldn't supersede Vonran or even be on par with him—he was, after all, playing the role of emperor.

In the end, the issue was settled by seating Mareah and Alexander near Vonran, but a little behind him so that they would be in the background. Vonran had learned of the arrangement the day before, and he accepted it as a good one. And then it occurred to him that next year they might be able to avoid the whole dilemma. If he and Mareah were married, there was no reason why they couldn't sit together ...

The thought came casually, but it struck him immediately afterward. The rest of the day his mind kept turning to marrying Mareah, and it occurred to him again as he dressed for the ceremony. But what he felt now was comfort with the idea that sparked a current of mixed excitement and pleasure. He had found a woman he wanted to marry.

He was ready for marriage again. He wanted a wife, a partner in his work, in his household, in his life. He had married late, and he had found those years of riding alone easy. The loneliness that gnawed some of his friends touched him only occasionally.

But this time he was finding it hard. And it wasn't only the obvious, practical reasons—though there were those. When Dianthe was alive, he could work and not worry about anything at home. Dianthe could manage the household and raise the children at least as well as he; possibly—though he never said so—better. Now he was the only parent, the sole authority in the household, and he knew that he didn't fulfill those duties as he ought. He took time away from his work, but not enough.

His girls needed a mother—not just for the kind of love a mother gave, but because they simply needed another parent. He had work to do—a country to run! He couldn't be regent and a full-time parent. By marrying Mareah, he would give his girls a mother—a good mother. He had seen how she was with Alexander—kind but firm, loving and wise. And Vonran knew she would do the same for his daughters. Zelrynn, Vera, Lydia, little Cala—they would have a mother again.

And for himself ... he would be free to do his work, but that was a small thing. He would have companionship, a partner in his life and everything he did, the physical and emotional satisfaction of a marital relationship. Mareah was not Dianthe; she was not her equal in wit or spirit. But she had intelligence enough; she was a beautiful woman, with a nature of sweetness seasoned with spice. He loved her. Not as he loved Dianthe. Dianthe had reached him in ways Mareah didn't, had sparked some deep place in his heart that no one else had ever found.

But that was all right. He didn't have the sort of love he had had with Dianthe, but he didn't think he would have it with any woman again. There were many women. There was only one Dianthe.

Vonran looked in the mirror, making sure nothing was amiss. Then he went over to the bed. He had draped his robe over the bedpost, and as his hand reached to take it, he considered another benefit of marriage: He would likely have another child, maybe a son this time. But in a way, wouldn't he have a son as soon as he married? By marrying Mareah, he would effectively adopt Alexander ...

The thought clapped on him like a thunderbolt. His hand froze, his fingers just beginning to twist around the fabric of his robe. If he married Mareah, he would become Alexander's stepfather. If he became Alexander's stepfather ...

It would ruin Kinlol. Isolating Gaelin by sending him to Regial was one thing; isolating Kinlol and his accomplices from Alexander—which Vonran could and would do from such a position—would ruin them. How could they make themselves Alexander's champions if he didn't accept them? And if Vonran had the teaching and raising of the child, why would he accept them? No. Alexander would listen to him, and if he heard Kinlol and the others at all, it would be as strangers' voices.

The thoughts kept coming, one on another, as Vonran's mind raced through the possibilities of it.

And it looked, to him, like complete victory over Kinlol and his cabal.

CLXXII

When Vonran arrived at the Great Plaza, he found people already gathering on the terrace. He disembarked from the hovcar and, trailed by the soldier-guards, climbed the broad, shallow steps. He began greeting the people, and when he came to Mareah, he said hello and then leaned forward to ask softly, "Can I come see you tonight?"

She looked quickly at him, and the expression on her face was—oddly conflicted. But she nodded.

Vonran hesitated a moment and then moved on. In a few minutes the ceremony began. Announced by a herald, Vonran stood and delivered his proclamation—a decree of the three-day New Year's festival. He then sat on the throne again and watched the military make a show of its exercises. And a strange mesmerism overtook him. He had seen it before—on a holoscreen, and in the most recent years in person. But he had never before seen them as the man who commanded them.

The soldiers reached the end, and they stood at attention, weapons displayed in their hands. Vonran slowly rose and began to make his way to them, but he stopped while still on the terrace, on the lip of the first step. He scanned the rows of uniformed soldiers before him—just an emblem of the awesome might of the Empire's military. He looked out farther, at the crowd that edged around the plaza—just an emblem of the Empire's teeming population.

So much strength, so much glory. The Empire.

And he was emperor.

In that moment, all of his past life withered small and insignificant behind him.

Kereth stood with Susanne and Cormac in the front of the crowd. He watched the soldiers perform their maneuvers, and when they finished he looked up at Vonran. The regent stood up and walked to the edge of the terrace, but then he stopped and his eyes roved over the Great Plaza.

Unease suddenly blossomed in Kereth, and as he gazed at Vonran he abruptly noticed his silver and black attire. And that robe ...

It was not unfashionable. It was not effeminate. It was, Kereth realized, strangely like the royal vestments. Far from identical: the royal vestments were sleeved and usually brightly-colored—scarlet, blue, indigo, gold. They were also looser. Vonran's robe was open, like the royal vestments, but the left side had been fastened at his waist while the right hung loose.

It was like and unlike the royal vestments, as Vonran was like and unlike an emperor.

The regent walked down the steps and inspected the troops. As Kereth watched him, he felt his muscles tighten. A recognition of something that was happening, a realization of something that had happened, a presentiment of things to come—he didn't know. He only felt it, and he was barely aware that he gently drew Susanne closer to himself, while his left hand came to rest protectively on Cormac's shoulder.

Mareah looked into the mirror, leaning against the bureau with both hands. Her intention was to check on her appearance, but she could barely see her reflection for the thoughts racing through her head. They had come again and again since her conversation with Gawin Gaelin, and never more furiously than now.

Elymas was coming. She didn't know what to say to him, didn't know what to do. Her convictions veered wildly—first her brother-in-law was right, then he was wrong, then she wondered helplessly how she could know at all. They had never talked about such things.

Well, that was a point in Gawin's favor, wasn't it? At least he had thought so. But he had never liked Elymas Vonran, had made trouble for him, and was still making trouble. He was biased against him; his whole perspective was colored with it ...

Not necessarily. And she herself could well be biased in the opposite direction. She had spent so many hours with Elymas, found so much comfort, was drawn to him, could feel that he was drawn to her and the thought made her heart beat faster ...

A bell-like ring sliced through the silence, and Mareah started badly. She calmed herself. It was only the intercomm; she knew that. Mareah's fingers searched out the button and pressed. “Yes?” she asked.

“Regent Vonran has arrived,” came the reply.

“Thank you,” Mareah acknowledged.

Now she had to go out to him. Mareah took a moment to collect herself and then went to the lounge where they always met when he came to the residence. The door's setting was locked on open, which gave Mareah no opportunity to hesitate before entering.

That, she told herself, was just as well. She lifted her head a little higher and strode on in without a break in her pace.

Elymas stood when she came in. He smiled that soft smile, and his eyes were lit with happiness. He was in a good mood. He had had a good day.

Mareah smiled back and sat on the couch. He moved to sit next to her. “Do you mind my coming?” he asked.

Mareah looked at him, startled. “Why do you ask?”

He shrugged—a lift of his shoulders, a tip of his head. “You didn't seem pleased when I asked you if I could come tonight.”

“Oh.” Mareah let her gaze flit away, pondering her response. “I ... have been troubled the last few days.”

She could sense Elymas sit forward; she felt his eyes on her. “What about?”

“Oh, it's ... I need to think it through a little more.” Mareah took strength from this postponement. “We can talk about it later.”

He studied her. “All right. If that's what you want.”

She nodded. “So”—she grasped for a change of subject —“did you have a special reason for coming?”

Elymas smiled. “You mean besides you?”

Mareah smiled genuinely for the first time that evening. “Yes, Elymas, besides me—as titanic as that must be for you.”

He smiled at her teasing. “As a matter of fact, Mareah, I did. Assuming you're glad to see me.”

“I am.” Mareah's curiosity was aroused. “What is it?”

To her surprise, he didn't answer. He looked at her for a

moment, and then away. “You know,” Elymas said, “for having spent years perfecting my skill with words, this should be easier. It's not even any easier than the last time I did it.”

Mareah looked at him, a sudden presentiment almost taking her breath away. “Yes?”

“I'll put it plainly, Mareah. I love you, and I would be very glad if you would be my wife. Will you marry me?”

The question. Mareah's first instinct was to say yes, but her worries of the past few days froze her. She suddenly realized she was looking at the woven carpet, and she forced herself to think. When she spoke, her voice was low and she didn't look up. “Elymas, before I answer that, I need to ask you something.”

A few heartbeats. “Go ahead.”

Mareah paused, forming the question. “What place will God have in our marriage?” She found the courage to look up as she spoke.

Elymas was gazing at her, his expression one of ... bemusement? Mareah couldn't tell if he was thinking over the question or her, and she returned his gaze. “Whatever place you want for Him,” he said at last.

Her heart sank. “But what about you? What place do you want for Him?”

Another pause. Elymas' steady gaze didn't waver, but the bemusement in his face deepened a little. He didn't look befuddled, or even remotely upset. But Mareah knew him—a man so contained, intelligent, and even-keeled that she had never seen him rattled by anything. If confusion was plain on his face—however mild it appeared—she guessed that he was flummoxed, at least as much as he could ever be. It made her heart sink a little more.

Elymas sat back on the couch. “I don't know, Mareah. To be honest ... ” He sighed softly. “Since Dianthe died, God and I have been a little distant.”

The words almost hurt to say. “So you don't know what place He should have in our marriage, because you don't know what place He has in your life?”

He thought a moment and nodded. “That sounds ...

accurate." Suddenly he leaned towards her again. "But that doesn't mean I oppose Him. Tell me what you want, Mareah. I will be accommodating."

Mareah sighed. "I don't want you to be accommodating, Elymas. I want you to have convictions. I want you to lead."

Elymas looked a little surprised. "So that's what you want in a husband? A man who will take a lead in ... religion?"

She nodded.

"I didn't know that, Mareah." He sat back and looked away.

Mareah's heart ached. "You had no way to know, Elymas. I never said so. Until Gawin brought it up, I hadn't even thought much about it."

He looked at her quickly, and there was sudden suspicion in his expression—a hardness she had never seen in his face before. "Gawin Gaelin brought you to this?"

"No, not exactly." Mareah sighed. "He advised me not to marry you because he didn't think we shared the same convictions."

The suspicion was gone; anger took its place. "Mareah, what right does Gaelin have to tell us we shouldn't marry? I want to marry you. I thought you wanted to marry me."

Mareah's emotions were rising, and she had a sudden urge to stand up and pace, as if it would release her agitation. "It's more than that. It's a question of what's right. I have to marry someone ... " she remembered the phrase, " ... in the Lord."

"Is that what Gaelin says?"

"That's what the Bible says."

Silence settled, and neither one looked at the other. Mareah found herself blinking away tears, trying to keep them back.

Elymas broke the silence. "And that's God's Word to you and you will not disobey. And I will not ask you to. But Mareah, I can't ape beliefs I don't have."

Mareah forced herself to speak softly. "Aping is not what I want, Elymas. What matters to me is what you really believe."

"I know. But the point is that as I am, you won't marry me. I can't change what I am. I could only pretend, and I won't do that. And so ... " He took a breath. "There can be no later, can there?"

Mareah shook her head; her throat was too tight to speak.

Elymas stood up. "Well, Mareah, it's ... " His voice faltered, but he recovered quickly. "I'm sorry. I wish we could have made it."

Mareah nodded, feeling the tears in her eyes. "I'm sorry," she whispered, her voice unsteady.

A pause, and then Elymas's soft voice: "Good-bye, Mareah."

But he didn't move. Mareah could sense that, and she looked up at Elymas. He stood before her, sorrow shimmering on the surface of his deep, dark eyes.

"Good-bye, Elymas," she mustered.

He continued looking down on her for a long minute, and she maintained her gaze up at him. At last he nodded, and it almost looked as if he was bowing his head to her. Then he turned away and walked out, without looking back.

He was gone, and so Mareah at last gave way to her emotions, and her tears.

Vonran stormed through the corridors of the Palace. Even though his guards were behind him, he couldn't put up a facade of calmness. He restrained himself a little, though, and as soon as he was in the guest wing and the doors had closed between him and the soldiers, he took a swing through empty air. It was then that he noticed he had clenched his right hand into a fist.

He felt that angry. He would like to hit something—or someone. Maybe a specific someone. Gaelin or Kinlol, maybe. Because it was his fault, too. Kinlol, Gaelin, Kereth—it was them. They had done this. They must have seen what he realized just today—that his marriage with Mareah would ruin their plans. So they sent Gaelin—because he was Mareah's brother-in-law—to her, to tell her the marriage would be bad, that he would not be the husband she needed, to manipulate her with religion.

God, again God. How much had he lost ...

The sudden sound of scampering and a girl's laugh startled him. Even in his rage Vonran knew he couldn't see his daughters in this mood. His anger would upset them, maybe even frighten them.

That thought spurred him. He turned to the nearest room—the long one he had made the lounge—and he went in. The doors of the broad entranceway had been locked on open, but there was a control pad by the door jamb. As soon as he entered, Vonran turned to it and closed and locked the doors. He turned around again, and then for the first time he saw Theseus Declan sitting on the couch.

Declan rose to his feet, concern taking over his features. "Elymas? What's wrong?"

Vonran didn't reply. His anger was still bubbling, and he didn't trust himself to act or speak. After a long minute he walked over to the easy chair and practically threw himself on it. A moment later Declan also sat.

For a little while they sat in silence. Declan was the first to speak. "I came to see you. Zelrynn told me you were gone, and so I came here to wait for you."

"I was seeing the empress," Vonran told him.

Declan didn't reply at once. "So you have a relationship with her."

Vonran laughed bitterly. "Not anymore." He stared across the room, at the picture that had been painted on the wall. A golden maize-field rippled by the wind ...

"I asked Mareah to marry me," he said suddenly. He didn't measure the wisdom of such a confidence; it was the hot emotion swelling in his chest that pushed the words out.

He could feel Declan's eyes on him, and he knew without looking that they were filled with compassion. Mareah's answer was obvious from his behavior, but Declan seemed to want it said anyway. "And she said no?"

Vonran's anger surged up. "Yes. But she didn't want to." He remembered how she wouldn't look at him, the tears she tried to keep back ...

He could feel the probing of Declan's eyes. "Then what forced her to, Elymas?" His voice was gentle, but he was trying to force his friend to face a brutal truth.

Vonran was not willing; he believed it.

"Elymas?" Declan prodded, and this time Vonran tried to

formulate an answer.

And gritted his teeth. "Gaelin," he said. "Gaelin told her she shouldn't marry me. He and ... " Vonran didn't say it. "She would have married me if not for Gaelin's interference."

Declan considered him. "Ah, Elymas. You know better. When you are not so angry and the hurt is not so fresh, you will accept it."

Vonran only looked at him. It must sound illogical, from his point of view. He didn't know how Kinlol and Gaelin were conspiring against him. They had foreseen destruction and shrewdly headed it off. And their method surprised Vonran, though he now wondered whether it should. He had expected any low political blow, but he hadn't expected a personal one.

Declan raised his eyebrows a little. "In time, Elymas. In time."

Vonran didn't think so.

Declan settled back in his chair, and he said nothing. Neither did Vonran. The two sat together, silence surrounding them.

And a memory came to life in Vonran's mind. It was the day of the accident, the day Dianthe had died. Friends had come over and, when it grew late, took the responsibility of putting the girls to bed. Vonran accepted their help and wandered aimlessly through his house until he was at the back door. He stepped out onto the verandah and could think of nothing else to do but sit down. And so he did. He settled down on the floor of the verandah, one knee raised and his elbow resting on it. Alone in the darkness, relieved for the moment of responsibility for his children, the paralysis of grief overtook him. He couldn't move, couldn't think, couldn't feel. Hot tears filled his eyes and touched his face, but the sensation was oddly distant—as if he was that lost, so far, far away that he was losing connection with his own body.

After some time—he had no notion of time—the door opened and someone came out. A voice said, softly, his name, and nothing else. Theseus Declan's voice.

Declan came and sat by him, and neither one said anything. But Vonran could feel compassion and reflected pain in Declan's silence, and his presence was like a steadying hand on his shoulder, an anchor against slipping into the black chasm that yawned at his feet ...

That was when he had lost Dianthe. Now he had lost Mareah. She had never been his as Dianthe had been his, he had never shared with her what he had shared with Dianthe, and he hadn't lost her to death. He had only lost her to—

Kinlol. Vonran's open hand clenched against the armrest. But the hot anger didn't return. It was cooling into enmity. He had taken this fight too lightly.

As anger turned to enmity, sadness turned to bitterness, and they hardened over his heart like a crust.

Revlan was a sad planet. Too far from its sun, it was as much like a neglected child as a planet could be. Its clayish, infertile soil lay desolately under the wearish light, looking for all the galaxy like it knew it would never receive warmth enough, and even if it did it probably wasn't capable of wrapping its sad world in greenery.

A large building—sturdy, serviceable, and ugly—rose amidst the scattered, sickly plants. Detritus of construction littered the ground around it. A passenger shuttle had landed on the outskirts of the area, and two uniformed men approached it.

The hatch lowered, and Gawin Gaelin descended, followed by his aide, a captain. The two who had come to meet him stood at attention, hands raised in a salute. Gaelin saluted in return and told them to stand at ease.

One of them stepped forward. His short brown hair was coarse-looking and shot through with gray, and his skin had known too much sun. But Gaelin knew that behind that weathered front, he was strong. "General," the man said, "we are honored by your visit and ready for your inspection."

"As am I. Lead on, Colonel."

He did. The colonel, accompanied by his silent aide-de-camp, gave Gaelin a tour of the construction site, providing a stream of pertinent information. They ended in a half-stocked armory, and only then did the colonel run out of words. He stopped, his eyes on the weapons, and then turned around to face the others. “As you can see, General, very much a work in progress.”

“Proceeding briskly. Well done.” Gaelin met the colonel's eyes. He was one of the men Gaelin had spoken to, one of the officers who had joined the cause. He didn't know about the conspiracy in Telnaria, but he knew full well for what purposes Gaelin was building up the military in Regial—and he was ready to do his part.

Gaelin's eyes traveled the half-stocked armory of the half-finished base. It was under the command of an ally and moving quickly to full functionality. It would be for Alexander.

So Gaelin's slow subversion took hold. He looked at the weapons, stored for war against the Vothnians—and Elymas Vonran.

Book II

Since the founding of the Empire

Year 698

Chapter

I

* * * * * * * * * * * * * * * * *

It was late afternoon and the sun was nothing short of brilliant, pouring its light into the Palace as it slipped into the western horizon. Broad windows permitted the light to golden a large office on the west side of the Palace. A huge desk—polished so that it reflected back the light—was at one end of the room. Between it and the door were expensive furnishings, arranged into a lounge circle. The decorations of the office were few, tasteful, and costly.

This was the office of the regent, for the past eight years. Two years into his term he had abandoned the emperor's office to select a new one. He said it suited him better.

Two men were in the office, Elymas Vonran and Garin Dorjan. Dorjan lounged in one of the armchairs, drink in one hand and compad in the other. He read off the facts and ad-libbed others, taking a pause every so often to swallow a mouthful of vynas.

Vonran stood at the window, listening. After Dorjan finished, he gazed out, narrow-eyed, at the sunset for a long minute. Then, slowly, he turned around. "After all our work, it's that close."

"Shevyn and that jackanapes Ziphernan have formed a powerful lobby."

"Yes," Vonran murmured. "I knew they could cause trouble." Nemin Ziphernan had ambitiously accrued power during his years in the Assembly. Colten Shevyn, long a force to be reckoned with, had recently finished three terms as premier. Only a year ago had he finally been ousted and Dorjan put in his place. It was not a moment too soon; Vonran only hoped it was soon enough.

Dorjan was silent a moment. “Theseus Declan is helping them, too.”

Vonran sighed softly. “I know.”

“Our threesome is broken, Elymas. I never thought I'd see the day when Theseus would take Shevyn's side against you.”

Vonran shrugged stiffly. “He never agreed with extending the regency.” And since Declan first discovered Vonran's support of the law, their friendship had cooled. Vonran pretended to everyone, even himself, that it hadn't left a dull ache in his heart.

Dorjan tapped the compad. “Will you meet with him?”

“I cannot convince him of anything.”

“Maybe not. But even if it doesn't help pass the Extension Act, it might help your friendship.”

“Ah, Garin ... ” Vonran shook his head.

“What, Elymas?”

“I don't think it would do any good, but for the sake of our friendship as it used to be ... ” Vonran shrugged. “I will if he will.”

Some of the tension left Dorjan's face. “Good.”

Vonran almost told him again that it wouldn't do any good, but he checked himself. “When are you going to bring the Extension Act to a vote?”

“As soon as we have all the support we can get. You've done very well, Elymas, and no one expects Alexander to do better. Everyone feels a little apprehensive at a seventeen-year-old taking the emperorship.”

Vonran laughed a little. “I know.” He had counted on it when he first proposed a law that would extend his regency five years. It came to be known as the Extension Act, and it was still exactly what Vonran wanted. It had been tricky, getting the law proposed in the Assembly while keeping it clean of his fingerprints. As always, he had managed.

Vonran glanced at Dorjan. “Tell me, Garin. Isn't that what makes this law so sensible? Won't everyone feel more secure when the boy is twenty-two? Will not the Empire be safer in my hands than his?"

"Of course, Elymas. No one questions that. But some think that the boy should rule regardless."

"So I've noticed. And some of them are even in the Assembly."

"Too many."

Admittedly, that was true. But Vonran was feeling strangely cheerful about their whole effort. He knew that Shevyn, Declan, and Ziphernan were the core of a formidable opposition. He knew that they had made a kind of back-channel alliance with Gerog Kinlol, who had finally learned a new trick and was treating delegates as friends instead of enemies. He knew all this.

But he knew other things, too. He had behind him ten years of prosperity and peace. Who wanted a change? Who wanted a boy emperor?

And he had ten years of preparation. Vonran had never forgotten where he had come from, and he hadn't let the delegates forget, either. He had maintained his network in the Assembly—a human network of friends, allies, and informants. He had taken strides to ensure that they always thought of him as one of their own who had made it into imperial power. The emperors and their officials had a long tradition of regarding delegates as nuisances or obstacles. Vonran did not have that luxury. Neither did he have the inclination, and at any rate it was not his style. He knew very well the desires and resentments of delegates, and he found he could satisfy them to a great extent without compromising his agenda. It had served not only his purposes at the time, but also this one. He had laid up ten years of good will.

Vonran had also dealt with the Kinlol conspiracy, as much as he could. Gawin Gaelin had remained in Regial all these years. As his children approached adulthood he sent them back into the Empire, living with friends and relatives while they completed their education, or took work, or found a spouse. Gaelin's eldest, Thaddaeus, had done all three.

Vonran had taken no direct action against Kinlol. He had allowed him to remain on the Council, judging it wiser not to remove him. But Vonran had found other opportunities to shape the Council. Two Chiefs—Javor Khiv and Than Au'Rhinn—had resigned, and two Vonran had dismissed. He had removed one, Gibeon Dishan, two years after Fionn Dheval. The Assembly—with Vonran's cooperation and approval—had crafted a new Articles of Interprovincial Commerce. Dishan's opposition was so fierce as to be borderline insubordination. Vonran made an example of him.

The second Chief he removed was Trey Uman. Vonran had noticed the association between Uman and Kinlol, and for years could think of no way to get Uman off the Council that was not self-damaging. Then a scandal erupted in the Office of the Treasury, with allegations of corruption smearing even Uman. Vonran doubted that Uman was guilty of any wrongdoing, but he knew a chance when he saw it. He asked for Uman's resignation.

His latest triumph was the dismissal of Adon Kereth. Vonran did not put an armed coup beyond Kinlol, and Kereth's command over the Emperor's Guard had increasingly disturbed him. But Kereth showed no intention of moving on, and the High Command showed no intention of making him. Vonran watched in amazement as Kereth stayed on year after year. He broached the subject a few times with Zidon Adesh. The third time the commander-in-chief asked, "Would you like me to have him replaced?"

Vonran conceded that he would, and Adesh never asked why. He did, however, get Kereth transferred to a regimental command. So, nine years into Vonran's regency, Kereth was finally out of the Palace.

Vonran surveyed the work of the past ten years—Gaelin exiled, Kereth removed, the Council re-shaped, the Assembly amicable, old alliances strong and new ones forged. And most of all: the Empire prosperous and secure. All this in his favor to have another five years.

Dorjan watched Vonran, lost in thought, and then he looked down at his compad. Slowly he raised his glass to his lips and drank.

Gerog Kinlol stood in a long, narrow hallway. It looked strangely musty and largely unused—as indeed it was, so far from the corridors and main rooms. There was a long, many-paned window in the wall, and Kinlol stood by it, against the wall. He was looking down at the floor, but his eyes weren't focused.

A sound roused Kinlol from his deep thought, and he looked in its direction. At one end of the hall, a young man had just entered. He walked forward without a word.

Kinlol had been waiting for him, but he didn't greet him, or go to meet him. He only waited, eyes on the floor, as the young man walked to him. He stopped a few feet away—close enough for a conversation, but a notable and respectful distance away.

Finally Kinlol raised his eyes. He saw, as always, Alheenan blood in the young man's features and dark hair. He was Thaddaeus Gaelin, cousin of Emperor Alexander, and the family resemblance was obvious to anyone.

Kinlol nodded to Thaddaeus. “Any word from your father?”

“He wants to know what goes on in the Assembly.”

Kinlol nodded again and turned away, leaving Thaddaeus to stand by as he mulled his answer. He knew in his heart that it wasn't right to treat the young man as he did, but even after two years he couldn't accept his intermediary role. He wasn't fooled by Gawin Gaelin's fine arguments about why it was a good idea. He knew the real reason Gaelin had made his son his proxy—he was grooming him for power. Kinlol disliked having to deal with Gaelin's young son rather than Gaelin himself, disliked even more the unilateral way in which Gaelin had made the arrangement. But he couldn't force Gaelin to communicate in a way he didn't want to, and he couldn't change his mind. Gaelin was advancing his son.

Kinlol wasn't pleased with his firsthand experience of the Gaelins' remarkable ability to pass ascendancy to the next generation. But Thaddaeus Gaelin was cautious, serious, and capable, and he had no grounds for complaint.

Finally Kinlol turned back to Thaddaeus. “Tell your father that our allies in the Assembly are working hard, but headway is difficult. The delegates are inclined towards Vonran. The premier is completely in his camp and riding hard for Vonran. Vonran himself is involved, though he is keeping his hand hidden."

"And what is your prognosis?"

"It's too close to know."

"Have you activated political support?"

"I have asked Trey Uman to begin probing the provincial officials."

Thaddaeus was silent a moment. "And if that fails, you are ready for our final option?"

Kinlol was growing tired of the questioning, and obstinacy crept in. "I am moving forward exactly as we planned."

"But we are ready?"

He was as respectful as he was persistent in pressing the point, and it irritated Kinlol even as he respected Thaddaeus for it. "Yes."

Thaddaeus nodded slowly. "My father will be satisfied. May I see the emperor now?"

Kinlol nodded curtly and, turning on his heel, began walking swiftly away. Thaddaeus followed him, and in a few minutes they arrived in one of the royal residence's studies. Alexander was waiting for them.

He was still a boy, not quite seventeen, but he was unusually serious and had shown a quickness of mind that had long pleased Kinlol. Thaddaeus bowed gravely to his cousin. He was seven years his cousin's elder—a grown, married man—but he knew what was due the royal blood. After all, Kinlol reflected, Thaddaeus had himself experienced what could be obtained through a good pedigree.

It was not a kind thought, and a tinge hypocritical. Kinlol made an effort to keep his expression clear of it.

Thaddaeus sat opposite Alexander and began relaying a report from Regial. Kinlol only half-listened. The province was securely in Gaelin's hands; if a problem had arisen beyond his ability to handle, Kinlol would have learned of it already.

A pinging sound jarred Kinlol out of his mental wandering, and he glanced over to see Alexander pressing a button on the intercomm. "Yes?"

Kinlol could faintly hear a voice: "Delegate Ziphernan requesting an audience, my lord."

"Send him in."

Kinlol didn't sit, but he circled around the furniture so that he stood to Alexander's right. Nemin Ziphernan came in. He was a tall man and young—in Kinlol's reckoning, at least—and had a dark, austere handsomeness.

Ziphernan bowed, as Thaddaeus had. "My lord," he said, "I have come on behalf of Colten Shevyn and the other delegates united to this cause. We have been considering how to defeat the Extension Act, and we have devised a new strategy."

"What is it?" Alexander asked, and Kinlol approved of his training.

"Rather than defeating the Act in a straight vote, we want to mire it in the committee process until it is too late."

Alexander hesitated a moment. "My birthday, you mean?"

Ziphernan nodded. "We will request the premier to direct the Act to the Committee for Revisions. There are enough delegates sympathetic to us there to hold the Act in the committee until time runs out." He paused. "It's how Vonran destroyed our resolution that would have affirmed the end of his regency."

Alexander glanced at Kinlol. "It is sound, my lord," Kinlol told him. "Once the Act is in the committee, it will remain there until the committee is done with it. If our support is as strong as Ziphernan says, they should succeed."

Thaddaeus spoke up. "The only issue is getting Dorjan to send it there."

"It's standard to have acts and resolutions submitted to the Committee for Revisions," Ziphernan replied. "What we ask is something very reasonable. Dorjan would have to guess our motives, which would take more thinking than I expect from him."

"He's not very clever?" Alexander asked.

"Clever?" Kinlol responded. "No, not in any conventional way. But he has an unusual and very valuable gift. He always manages to have the clever ones for his allies."

Elymas Vonran sat in an easy chair, compad in hand. His posture was relaxed as he read; it was the end of the day.

From his desk an alert sounded, and then a computer voice: *"Incoming transmission. Caller identified as Premier Garin Dorjan."*

Vonran lowered the compad, considering that. As the computer repeated its message, he pulled himself to his feet and went over. "Engage," he ordered, settling into the chair.

An image of Dorjan materialized over the desk. "Alexander's lobby has made their next move," he announced. "Or they will tomorrow."

Vonran smiled. News from the grapevine. "What is it?"

"Ziphernan wants the Extension Act submitted to the Committee for Revisions. Either they want to change it, or they're moving it towards a vote."

Vonran made a noncommittal sound, his gaze becoming unfocused as his mind went over the move. "How would they change the Act?"

He didn't look towards the transmission of Dorjan, but he heard his answer: "I don't know. It would have to be very crafty. But they could just be getting through with the formalities so they can have the vote. Maybe they think they have enough support now."

For a long moment Vonran, lost in thought, didn't answer. Then he snapped his attention back to Dorjan. "Have you sent the Act to the committee?"

"No, Elymas. The request hasn't even been made yet."

"Good, good. Deny it."

Dorjan stared at him. "Elymas, it's standard—"

"It's also fatal. How many laws have died in a committee? Deny the request. And then—" Vonran moved ahead, "—bring the Act up to a vote. Immediately."

"Immediately? We're not sure of our support."

"We can't let the Act go to committee. That's the cul-de-sac Ziphernan and Shevyn want to lure it down so they can ambush it. It's unacceptable. But you can't refuse to submit a law to the

Committee for Revisions and then do nothing with it. There's only one choice. Refuse the request and then call on the Assembly to vote on the Act."

Dorjan looked doubtful. "Are you sure that's what you want me to do?"

Vonran nodded. "Sure."

He shrugged. "All right. I'll do it, Elymas. If it loses we'll be done. No more hope."

"I know. If that is how it ends I will take all the blame."

"All right," Dorjan repeated. "I talked with Theseus. He'll be coming to the Palace in the morning."

Vonran could almost feel himself deflate. "Oh."

"Don't look like that, Elymas. He is your friend still. It will be fine. Maybe it will even make things better."

"I hope you're right."

"Tomorrow we will find out if I am right—and if you are. Good night, Elymas."

"Good night, Garin."

The image vanished with the transmission. Vonran leaned back, releasing his breath. Things were moving ahead quicker than he had planned, but he didn't mind. Alexander's birthday was in less than a month; they needed to move before the original act expired. It was fine. If only enough delegates would vote for the Extension Act ...

Ten years of peace and prosperity. A boy emperor. Would more than half the delegates take such a risk? It should be obvious to them all that he was the better man.

Vonran thought of Alexander and unconsciously smiled as he corrected himself: The only man.

"And so you see, Regent, that the tariffs have been beneficial to our economy, bolstering the industries of ... "

As the Chief of Commerce talked, Vonran looked at the charts projected over his desk, but he wasn't really thinking about them. He was thinking about the Assembly, which was about to decide the ruling of the Empire for the next five years, though most delegates were not aware of it. Bringing the Assembly to vote was a counter-punch to Ziphernan's strategy, and obviously could not be delivered until the first punch had been. But it was hard to wait.

Finally the Chief of Commerce finished. Vonran asked him a few questions and then dismissed the man and his aides. It was a good report, again. Now on to other matters.

And his heart dropped. The next item of business was to meet with Theseus Declan.

As if on cue, his intercomm came alive with his secretary's voice: "Delegate Declan is here for his appointment, Regent."

Vonran wanted to point out that he was just going to talk with the man, not give him a medical examination. Instead he ordered that Declan be sent in.

The door opened, and Declan came in. Vonran pushed away from his desk and went forward to meet him. "Good morning, Theseus," he greeted him—perhaps a little too cheerily.

Declan looked at him—not with hostility, but he was serious. "A fair day, Elymas," he said quietly. That was it.

Apparently the conversation was up to Vonran. He could handle that. "How are you this morning?"

"I am fine."

"How is your wife?"

"She is fine." Declan steadily—and quietly—gazed at him.

A small, sudden spike of irritation went through Vonran. "My daughters and I are fine, too," he said, turning away to go and sit down on the couch. "Zelrynn will be back from Sameeva today or tomorrow."

Declan came slowly over to the furniture set, but he didn't sit down. Vonran gazed up at him—leaning back, his arms resting on the top of the couch. The silence stretched on unbroken for a few minutes.

"So," Vonran said. "Do you want to shoot Garin, or will you leave the pleasure to me?"

Finally Declan did sit down. "He was only trying to help—both of us."

“Apparently mediation isn't his element.”

“He's not even here.”

“Showing more intelligence than either of us.”

“You think there is so little hope, Elymas?”

“Review the last ten minutes, Theseus. We said hello. After a pointless exchange, we stared at each other. The conversation starter was shooting Garin.”

Declan looked away, seeming to think. After a moment Vonran, against his better judgment, went on. “Speaking of Garin, I think we were supposed to talk.” Then he dove in. “About the Extension Act, in fact. He wanted us to work out our differences.” And then he went for broke. “But we already did talk, and we found that our differences are irreconcilable.” There. That was the truth, thrown out between them. Vonran watched Declan to see what he would do with it.

Declan kept his eyes away from Vonran. “We will never agree on the Extension Act. But we have had disagreements before. This is different. It disturbs me, because ... ” Declan sighed and finally looked at Vonran. “What you are doing is wrong. Surely you must know it.”

Vonran shook his head. “The Assembly passed an act to establish the regency. The Assembly may extend the regency. There is nothing immoral in that.”

“The emperorship belongs to Alexander. It is his birthright. After he reaches adulthood, who can deny it?”

“Alexander is a boy. He will be better off for having five more years. Just ask his mother. The Empire will be better off.”

“You will not. No one is ever better off, for doing wrong.”

Vonran didn't know what to do with that, and so he did his best to look as if the comment was not worth replying to.

Declan sighed again. He stretched out a grasping hand. “Elymas, you can't just take ... ”

“I am taking nothing. The Assembly is giving.”

Declan's expression hardened a little. “The honorable thing would be to refuse. But they would never even offer it if not for you, would they?”

Vonran felt his muscles stiffen. He heard the insult in Declan's comment and the accusation in his question. “And if I am regent for another five years—more than two decades of friendship will count for nothing for you?”

Declan hesitated. A pall of gentleness suddenly overtook his features. “Elymas, our friendship has meant a great deal to me. I have worked with you, I have known you, I have enjoyed your hospitality and offered mine in return. I knew your wife, I saw your daughters grow up. I even saw your heart broken. I have much to lose, and I hope I don't.”

“Then why are you making so much of this disagreement? Why is extending the regency the unforgivable sin, a shameful act to end our friendship?”

Declan seemed unable to answer. After a long moment he began, “Elymas ... ” A mechanical ping interrupted him, and he unclipped his carry-comm and brought it to his mouth. “Declan here.”

Vonran watched him, and though he couldn't make out the answer, he didn't need to. A presentiment was on him; he knew what Declan was hearing.

“I'll be right there,” Declan said slowly, and he lowered the comm, his eyes never leaving Vonran. “I'm going back to the Assembly now,” he said. “But you know why, don't you?”

For some reason, Vonran wasn't willing to give him less than the truth. “I do. Should my allies be too gamely to tell me news they hear?”

“You don't just know, Elymas.” Declan clipped his comm back to his belt with painstaking slowness. Then he looked back up at Vonran, and his old, pale blue eyes stabbed right through him. “It was your idea. Garin is bringing the Extension Act to a vote because ... you told him to.”

“Don't turn holy on me, Theseus. You and Shevyn and Ziphernan wanted the Act submitted to the Committee for Revisions because of sheer conniving. You know it as well as I do. I only matched you.”

“Yes, you did.” Declan's voice was quiet, but the gaze with

which he fixed Vonran was intense.

And under it, Vonran felt something shift inside him. *Don't stare at me like that, Theseus. Don't stare at me like you don't know me.* The plea hammered in his heart, but he gazed steadily back at Declan.

Finally Declan came to his feet, turned his back, and walked out.

Vonran, alone in the stillness that followed, felt that there had been some seismic shift, that something had changed terribly. He just wasn't sure what.

He put his face in his hands and rubbed his forehead. "You were wrong, Garin," he muttered. Horribly wrong. "Now it is my time. We will see if I am right."

The call found Nemin Ziphernan in a conversation with other delegates. The topic was a bill he didn't care about, but he was gauging how much his support was worth to its sponsors. One must give to get in this game.

Ziphernan felt his carry-comm vibrate—its silent mode of alerting him that he had a message. His hand went to it automatically, but he didn't draw it out. Then he noticed that the man he was talking to had made the same motion. Their eyes met, and both men took out their comms.

There was no caller, just a message. From the desk of the presiding officer ...

Ziphernan's heart beat faster, and he accessed the message. The words scrolled across the tiny screen. The premier had placed before the Assembly, for an immediate up or down vote, the ... Extension Act.

Ziphernan's hand tightened around the comm. The message began to roll through again, and he shut it off. Dorjan had called their trick—Dorjan or one of his more clever allies. Of course, Elymas Vonran was the most clever of all.

A delegate spoke. "They're putting the Extension Act up for a vote."

"Already?" another asked, his tone puzzled. "It hasn't even been to Revisions."

"I asked Dorjan to send it there this morning," Ziphernan said. "Apparently they consider it perfect."

The gathering was buzzing now with the message they had all received. Ziphernan got to his feet and headed out. As the door opened for him and he passed through, he yanked his comm free. But before his fingers could work the buttons, it pinged. "Ziphernan," he said into it.

Colten Shevyn's voice came back, terse as his own: "Where are you, Nemin?"

"I just came out of one of the west side meeting rooms."

There was a short pause on the other end. "We'll meet in the west cloakroom. I called Declan. He's coming back from the Palace."

Palace? Ziphernan lifted the comm to his lips. "I'll see you there." He clipped the comm to his belt and strode on. Soon he arrived in the cloakroom. He was the first, but Shevyn came in on his heels.

"How long till Declan gets here?" Ziphernan asked.

Shevyn passed his hand through his hair. "Hopefully not long. He's not far away, but he was talking to Vonran ... "

"Vonran?"

Shevyn shot him an impatient look. "What of it?"

Ziphernan shook his head. "Nothing." He had been leery of Shevyn's plans to ally with Declan in the beginning, but his fears had been groundless. Still, he would feel better if Vonran and Declan kept away from each other. They might remember they had been friends.

Shevyn paced. "Dorjan has placed a moratorium on all business until the Act has been voted on. I don't think he will approve an open-ended debate session, so we will not be able to filibuster."

"Maybe he will," Ziphernan said, "if Vonran doesn't tell him not to."

Shevyn frowned, a look of disapproval creasing his face. "Don't underestimate him, Nemin. He was a leader in the Assembly before you ever arrived."

Ziphernan's ire rose, but he didn't respond to the rebuke. "Well, why not override Dorjan?"

"Because we will not get two-thirds of the Assembly to override the premier and send the Act to Revisions—when we have not asked for a single revision. Since we will fail, it is best not to try."

Ziphernan thought and then shook his head. "Then what can we do to prevent the vote?"

"Nothing."

It burned, but Ziphernan had no arguments. "Then—"

The door opened, and both men turned to see Theseus Declan shuffle in. As he came up to them, Shevyn nodded in greeting. "Did it go well with you and Vonran?"

Declan shook his head, his eyes tired with sadness. "He is determined."

Ziphernan almost held his breath watching Declan, hoping he was not going to unleash another lament over how Elymas Vonran had left the straight and narrow path.

Shevyn took control of the conversation. "We have ruled out filibustering and overriding. The vote will go on today."

Declan nodded his assent, and Ziphernan said, "We should make a motion for a debate."

"It will be granted," Shevyn said. "And in oration, at least, we excel our opposition."

"I think Declan should be our advocate," Ziphernan said.

Declan raised his head to look at him, and Shevyn pressed his lips together thoughtfully. "That may be best. We all can speak, but if Declan will be our voice ... "

"I don't know that I want to," Declan said.

"Come, Theseus," said Shevyn encouragingly. "You know how the delegates respect you. You are almost the conscience of the Assembly. Speak and they will listen."

"Listen, but not follow."

Shevyn shot a look at Ziphernan, who got the message: Your turn. He stepped closer to Declan. "All the Assembly knows that you speak only for what is right, only for what is best for the Empire. There is nothing personal in your opposition."

Declan thought for a long minute, and then he sighed. "All right." And he left.

Ziphernan watched him go. "I don't know why he takes it so hard."

Shevyn sighed. "Elymas Vonran is his friend. He has been for a long time."

"He's argued against him before—with Vonran sitting there at the table." And it was one of the few times Ziphernan had seen Vonran show any humanity. He could still see Vonran watching Declan draw a line against him, his expression too still, something passing over his eyes that looked curiously like pain.

"It's not only that Declan finds himself fighting against Vonran. Do you know what it is to see a friend fall beneath himself?"

Ziphernan didn't answer. He only glanced away, adopting an expression as if he really did know. Ziphernan himself didn't blame Vonran; he was only doing what any man would do—except, perhaps, Declan. But Ziphernan kept that to himself. Too many of his allies seemed to really believe their own moralizing.

Shevyn pulled his comm free and went to work rallying their other supporters. Ziphernan watched him, too preoccupied to follow his example. He calculated that however Vonran might try to hang on to power—however he might, for a little while, succeed—he would soon be gone, and Alexander would reign for decades to come. If Ziphernan helped Alexander when he was vulnerable, he could expect rewards when he was in power. That was his reason for joining this fight on Alexander's side.

His first one, at least. His second was that he would deeply enjoy seeing Vonran defeated and stripped of the power he had enjoyed ten years. Ziphernan had come to resent him—Elymas Vonran with his burning eyes, his glacier coolness at every meeting, the fact that he had climbed so high with no more years than Ziphernan had—and without all the endless reminders and put-downs. He resented the reverence Vonran had earned, the respect that even his greatest enemies showed him. And he resented that he couldn't say, even to himself, that they were wrong. For Vonran was brilliant, one of those few people who was worth more than any computer. He reckoned the hardest and subtlest of all arithmetic—the arithmetic where the factors were human minds and hearts.

But that would not be enough, not to get him the prize he desired, not to keep the heady elixir he had savored ten years. Or so Ziphernan vowed to himself.

The debate lasted into the afternoon. Declan was in good form. Supported at turns by other delegates, he led the sally against the Extension Act. As the debate went on, hope slowly pushed up in Ziphernan's soul. He resisted it, but the small shoot of an emotion clung stubbornly on. The presiding officer declared cloture and initiated the vote, and Ziphernan still felt that bit of hope. He turned to his panel and cast his vote. His "nay" duly put in, he settled into his seat. And he waited.

Vonran had a live transmission of the gathered Assembly playing on his office's holo-projector. He muted the sound and kept to his work. He didn't care for the debate; all that mattered was the result. He knew, too, on whose side rhetorical mastery lay, and it was not his own.

Finally—it was a length of hours—a change in the image caught his attention. The view was now of the delegates seated in the galleries, and not a one of them was speaking.

They had gone to voting. Vonran stared at the image for a moment and then forced himself to turn back to his work.

It didn't last. Every few moments he looked up again. After a little while of this, he sighed in concession to his own weakness, turned on the sound, and returned to his work more easily now.

When it came, he heard it immediately. Vonran looked up, and the focus was now on the presiding officer. His expression was inscrutable as he spoke, his voice magnified to fill the Assembly: "By a vote of five hundred and thirteen to four hundred and six—

with eighty-one abstaining—"

He stopped, and Vonran's breath stopped with him. And waiting, eyes fixed, Vonran could hear his heart thudding softly in his ears.

The presiding officer raised his chin—and his eyebrows, too—as he gazed out at the delegates, his eyes passing some unknown judgment on them and the decision they had made. "The Extension Act," he announced, "has been passed."

Vonran could hear the rush of noise from the delegates—a cacophony of every reaction. But it was nothing to him. He pressed his clenched hand against his forehead, closed his eyes, and softly exhaled the breath that had been filling his throat.

"The Extension Act has been passed." The words struck like lightning—in the Assembly and in the Palace lounge. As an uproar began to rise, Kinlol reached for the control and cut off the transmission. And still the presiding officer's words lingered in the silent room.

"They failed," Thaddaeus Gaelin said.

"Yes," Kinlol agreed, reaching for the comm.

"Are you calling Trey Uman?" Alexander asked him.

"Yes, just as we planned."

Alexander looked doubtful. "How many of the provinces do you really think will declare for me?"

Thaddaeus answered before Kinlol could. "Uman fears not many. But we are certain of Regial. Once we have Regial, we will be ready if we lose all the others. Ready," he added, "for our final option."

It was late at night, and Vonran knew he ought to be either asleep or working. He did neither, and he felt no guilt. He was in a sanguine mood, settled comfortably in his study's easy chair. He contemplated his victory. He contemplated breaking the seal of a bottle of Charis cordial he had in the study.

The hour was late, and the house was silent. Vonran was

awake past the rest of his family, and the sound of the door opening jolted him to full alertness. He looked quickly—

And saw Zelrynn standing in the doorway, smiling at him.

The adrenaline vanished in the same rush it had appeared. Vonran smiled and stood up. He and Zelrynn met halfway with what, in the dignified restraint of their family, was an embrace. As they stepped apart, Zelrynn said, "I thought you might still be awake."

"You thought right, and I am glad you did." Vonran turned and led towards the couch. "How did you find Sameeva?"

"Interesting, mainly. None of it was dull."

"Did you make any friendships?"

"None that will last."

"I take it, then, that you met no young man ... "

She smiled and shook her head. "No, Father."

He waved the subject away with his hand. "Let it be. It is better to be single than unwisely married. And marriage is not the totality of life." They settled down on the couch, and Vonran turned a questioning gaze on his daughter. "I trust that you now know Sameeva, and understand Sameevans, much better?"

"Of course. I could tell you much more than you care to hear at this hour."

Vonran didn't doubt it. It had always seemed fitting to him that his firstborn was so much like him. It was immediately apparent in looks—Zelrynn had his eyes, his hair color, his complexion, his features re-cast into feminine mold. She was even tall. Later she had proved her likeness in mind also. He had cultivated that likeness, seeing to it that her intellect was trained and sharpened. He had taught her to think and how to think, and to collect knowledge wherever she went. Of course she was wiser about Sameeva now. "Someday you will have to tell me," Vonran said.

"How are my sisters?"

"Fine. You know Vera is still at the university. Lydia is still not sure she wants to follow, and I am allowing her time. Cala ... " He gestured the rest of the sentence.

Zelrynn smiled. "Little Cala. She is not so little anymore."

"She's only fourteen."

"And fast approaching twenty." Zelrynn looked at her father, and he could see both intensity and softness in her eyes.

"What is it?" Vonran asked.

"It just struck me, Father. In a few years all four of us will be gone and you ... "

He said the words she hesitated over: "I will be alone?" He shook his head. "That isn't to the point. Children grow up, and then they must make their own lives. What father would I be to hold you back?"

"I know you wouldn't. But no one should live forever in an empty house." Zelrynn shook her head. "There was a time when I would have been shocked to know I would someday say this, but why don't you marry again?"

"Because I had only one love in life."

There was sadness in Zelrynn's smile. "That would please me for my mother's sake, but for my father it concerns me." Then she spoke with sudden firmness. "Mother is in heaven, but you are still in this world. Seek happiness in it—how will it hurt her? She loved you; she would want it for you."

"It is not only a matter of whether I want another wife, but whether I can find one. You know I married late." And he had thought, once, that he could love another woman after Dianthe. He had ventured out of his solitude for Mareah Alheenan only to be driven back, gaining only grief. He turned back to other things, and in these he was not disappointed. "Now"—he mustered some authority into his voice—"worry on it no more. It's for parents to worry for their children, not children for their parents."

That was Vonran's way of sweeping the matter aside, and Zelrynn accepted it. "I heard about your victory in the Assembly. Congratulations."

"Thank you."

"Are you planning to train Alexander?"

"I think I will. The boy needs instruction on his duties. I could teach him."

"When will you begin?"

Vonran considered. "I could begin any time. He will be

inexperienced, but the longer the training, the more he will know. He should have two years at least; possibly more." He stopped, and wondered if he would be able to displace Kinlol as the boy's mentor, and what the upshot would be.

They heard the computer announce: "*Auditory message received from Chief Gerog Kinlol.*"

There was a pause. Vonran looked back at Zelrynn, who cocked her head—waiting for him to see what it was. Well, if she didn't mind, he would look.

Vonran got up, went over to his desk, and accessed the message. Kinlol's voice rose up: "I, Chief Kinlol, wish to speak to you, Regent Vonran, on behalf of Emperor Alexander and those who serve him. You have been victorious in the Assembly, but it has overreached its authority. The Ancient Code commands that the heir of Alexander the Mighty reign as emperor in his place. The Assembly cannot deny the emperorship to the man to whom the Ancient Code has given it.

"Therefore, we reject the Extension Act as immoral and lawless. We have asked the provinces to declare their allegiance to Emperor Alexander on his seventeenth birthday. So shall they prove obedience and fealty to their liege and the Ancient Code, the cornerstone of our government.

"I tell you this as a courtesy, Regent Vonran. Now you know."

The computer signaled the end of the message with a ping. Vonran breathed in deeply and exhaled as he leaned back in his chair. "The old fox."

Zelrynn had come to stand by the desk. "Doesn't it worry you, Father?"

"The law will stand, Zelrynn, no matter agitators like Kinlol."

"What if the provinces listen?"

"I trust they will not." Vonran glanced up and saw worry in his daughter's eyes. "You will see. In three and a half weeks, you will see."

CHAPTER

II

* * * * * * * * * * * * * * * * *

THE sound was much like ringing. It was low, insistent, and far too close to his head.

Adon Kereth jerked into consciousness. He lay tense but still in the darkness, orienting himself. He was at home, in bed, and he had woken up for ... the message.

Kereth pushed the covers off and quietly swung his legs to the floor. Beside him, Susanne shifted, and he murmured a wordless reassurance as he stood up. She didn't need to wake up yet.

Kereth left the bedroom, maneuvering cautiously in the darkness to the computer. He sat in front of it, intending to see if Kinlol had sent him the message. Instead he rubbed his eyes.

He could feel tiredness pressing against his eyes, and it made him feel old. He should be sharp, alert, on it, not ... trying to rub the tiredness out of his eyes. Sighing with some theater, Kereth accessed the comm center. Sure enough, Kinlol's message was waiting for him. “Here you go, Kereth,” he muttered to himself. It was the middle of the night and his emotions refused to be whipped up, but his heart began thudding a little faster as apprehension finally laid a hand on him.

The message was one line of text: “Only Regial remains faithful.”

Kinlol would put it that way. Kereth's heart sank as he absorbed that news, and he quietly put the computer back into sleeper mode and returned to the bedroom.

As he got back into the bed, Susanne asked, “What happened?”

“Only Regial declared for Alexander,” he answered.

“When do we leave?”

“Tomorrow, in the morning.”

“Should we wake the girls?”

“No. Let them sleep.” Kereth leaned against the bedboard.

When he stayed there, Susanne said, “Aren't you going to sleep?”

Kereth considered. He still felt a little tired, but he was alert now; his mind was beginning to turn. “I don't know,” he murmured. “I don't know if I can.”

After a moment Susanne sat up and leaned against him. He wrapped his arm around her and they sat together, silent in the darkness.

The day had barely dawned when Kereth arrived at his office. His aide-de-camp was waiting for him. The man began quickly as soon as Kereth entered, “Did you hear what happened, sir? Emperor Alexander—”

Kereth raised his hand to stop the words. “I know. Now, muster the regiment.”

The aide-de-camp's eyebrows went up. “All of them, sir?”

“Everyone who qualifies under the term 'regiment'. Muster them on the parade-grounds.”

He stared at him. “The parade-grounds.”

“Yes. They wouldn't all fit in my office.”

“Yes, sir.” The aide hurried out.

Kereth sat down in his chair and wondered if he should plan what to say or just speak from his heart. And he almost heard his father's voice—“It's all right to speak from the heart, as long as you check it with your brain first.”

Kereth smiled faintly. He leaned back in his chair, feeling thoughtful, even mellow. After a few minutes he got up and headed out to the parade-grounds. He normally did not have much use for speech-making, but this one he would enjoy.

The regiment—his regiment, his men—stood at attention on the parade-grounds. Kereth saluted and then ordered, “At ease.” He watched as they relaxed and then said, “As you all have heard by now, Emperor Alexander has rejected the regent's claim to rule in his place. But when he asked the provinces to reject it also, all of them refused except Regial. Only Regial has obeyed the emperor.

“And so, to Regial Emperor Alexander has gone with his loyalists. Now the regent rules in Telnaria, but the emperor rules in Regial. We can only serve one master, and so we must choose between the two.”

He paused, looking at the soldiers. Some of them gazed back impassively, but others were beginning to look nervous. Kereth went on, “I choose Emperor Alexander. I will serve the one I made an oath of loyalty to; I will serve the one the Ancient Code has made my ruler. That is my choice; you must make yours. I am leaving for Regial, to serve my emperor according to my vow. I will not command any of you to follow me, but I ask you to.”

Kereth surveyed the ranks, wondering how many—if any at all—would follow him to Regial. And he hoped with a pang that he would never fight against any of them.

An unexpected sadness raised its head, and Kereth looked at them soberly. “The lines are drawn. You are with Emperor Alexander or you are against him; you are with Regent Vonran or you are against him. There is no middle ground.” Kereth glanced at his aide-de-camp. He looked a little dazed, and it took him a moment to catch on, but then he turned towards the troops and barked, “Attention!”

They came sharply to attention and raised their hands in a salute. And Kereth, for the last time, saluted them.

Then he did a military about-face and marched off the field. And though he had planned from the beginning to march away if it came to this, a voice whispered in his ear that he was abandoning them. And maybe he was. But he had other loyalties also, and when they clashed he had to choose.

He had chosen ten years ago. And so he walked off the parade-grounds, off the base, into a new reality. He did it without doubt, without hesitation, without regret; only an uneasy premonition, as he drew a line and walked it.

The capital ship of the Empire—the ship of the emperor—streaked through hyperspace. It was called the *Glory of the Empire*, and as much as any ship could live up to such a name, it did.

It was actually the first time Alexander had been on it, and he would have enjoyed it more had it not been carrying him to an unknown future in Regial. He had felt a thrill—with something like fear in it, but it was not unpleasant—when they had boarded the *Glory* at midnight the day before. He had felt they were doing something secret and daring. There was something surreal and romantic in the journey through darkness, through a sleeping city, to the grand ship that had docked unused for a decade. Then he watched Telnaria grow small beneath them, had watched its lights grow faint and disappear at their midnight departure. In other words, it had been an adventure.

Then came reality. His only home was far behind, and he didn't know what was going to happen next. He thought about that, and he couldn't help a feeling of gloom. In truth—sitting alone in the emperor's viewing cabin, gazing at the blurred stars—he didn't really try.

He heard the door open and looked over to see his mother. She smiled at him. "Bored already, Alexander?"

"A little," he muttered, not willing to admit that he had nothing better to do than sit here and feel sorry for himself.

"Has Chief Kinlol talked to you today?"

"A little—this morning." Mareah Alheenan was always checking up on Kinlol, and Alexander sometimes wondered if she even liked him. It was only as he had grown older that he came to see the tension between the two. He didn't know what it came from—dislike, distrust, secret history, or a simple lack of comfort. He wondered if he would ever dare to satisfy his curiosity by asking.

Mareah sat by her son. “What did he say to you?”

Sometimes he wondered if Kinlol ever talked to her. Alexander shrugged. “Not much.”

Mareah watched the stars streaking past. She sighed, but Alexander didn't know what at.

They sat in silence. “Mother,” Alexander said at last, “what do you think will happen after we get to Regial?”

“I don't know, Alexander. You might ask Kinlol. But I think that the next move will be the regent's.”

He looked at her carefully. Her gaze was distant, her voice soft. “Kinlol says that no one will abide a divided Empire,” he ventured. “Do you think Vonran will try to stop us—with force?”

She didn't answer, or even move, for so long that Alexander decided she hadn't heard him. But then Mareah shook her head. “I hope not, Alexander.”

She always seemed wistful or sad when talking about the regent, and she never put him down. Alexander wondered if that was another story he would have to ask for. “Mother, do you think I will get the emperorship—like this?” She looked at him. “I mean ... ” He failed to find the words.

“No one knows the future,” Mareah said gently. “I can't reassure you about what's going to happen.”

Alexander looked away. “We didn't let it go. We fought him.”

She cocked her head. “Whom?”

“Vonran.”

He slammed his fist onto the desk. “What are they doing? What *are* they doing?”

Vonran's staff regarded him silently—and from as much distance as they could manage. It was a rare show of anger, and they were unnerved by it.

Garin Dorjan—who had the benefit of a superior position and more familiarity with Vonran's temper—shuffled forward. “Why don't you talk to them?” he suggested.

“Because Kinlol won't allow it!” Vonran paced away from them. He pressed his palms against the desk and leaned on it, trying to get a hold of his anger. He had thought Kinlol would have no choice but to accept the Assembly's and the provinces' decisions, but no. He was going to put Alexander on the throne in Regial, and then ...

Vonran didn't know. It was outside his calculations. He had never thought of such a scenario.

Dorjan bravely spoke again. “The prefect of Regial supports them, but the military has a strong presence there. It is under your command—”

“No.” Vonran laughed mirthlessly. “It is under Gaelin's.”

A pause. “He will not obey you?”

“I know he will not.” He saw it all now. All the military force Gaelin had mustered in Regial he had always intended to turn against Vonran. Kinlol would go to Regial, set up Alexander's government there, and wage war to regain the rest of the Empire. He would start a war—

And give Vonran a chance to crush them all. Yes, he could, and he would. He would crush them entirely and end their opposition once and for all.

Vonran turned to his chief of staff. “Call Zidon Adesh,” he said. “Tell him to leave whatever he is doing and come here.”

They had military might? So did he. They had strategy? So did he. They had cunning?

So did he.

Tokar was the seat of Regial's government. It was the name of both the capital city and the capital system, and Kinlol had never learned which had borrowed the name from the other. After leaving Telnaria they went to Tokar. It wasn't much compared to Telnaria, but it was the grandest city in Regial.

Alexander had called it a grubby town upon getting a full view of the factories. Kinlol did not mind such opinions, as long as they were discreetly expressed. He himself had no complaint against the city. Tokar served its purpose, though in a way that was decidedly without glory.

The prefect had given them a wing of his mansion, and a large lounge had become a sort of communal room for them. The room was in Regial style. There was a fireplace, whose stone hearth adjoined the dark wood floor. The windows were single-paned, the walls were white plaster, the furniture was wooden. A group had assembled in the room—Kinlol, Alexander, Mareah, Thaddaeus Gaelin and his wife, Lily, and Gawin and Layne Gaelin.

General Gaelin asked, "Has anyone heard from the colonel?"

Kinlol was still not missing him. "He will arrive any time." Then Kinlol shifted to a more interesting subject. "I am glad to see you have Regial in order."

Gaelin shrugged. "It is amazing, the sort of connections you can forge if you try. Regial's officials have been the boldest, merriest co-conspirators you can imagine. We have Regial as surely as we have the military."

"Speaking of which, I hear you have asked young men all over the Empire—and especially Regial—to volunteer in our army. I assume you have the training of these men arranged for."

Gaelin smiled. "Yes, the training—and the recruiting. I have sent a recruiting officer to at least one major city on every planet in Regial."

"You think this will end in bloodshed?" Mareah asked.

"There's possibility enough," Gaelin responded.

Mareah didn't respond to that, but she was not given much opportunity. The door opened, and in came none other than Colonel Adon Kereth.

Kereth's attention went to Alexander first. He walked up to him and bowed. "Here I am, ready to fight."

Kinlol saw the look Mareah gave him; perhaps Kereth did also. He turned to her. "Hail, Empress."

She nodded with the graciousness and authority of a monarch. "It is good to see you again, Colonel."

"Thank you." Kereth looked at Kinlol.

Kinlol gazed back. He hadn't seen the colonel in a year, but he didn't seem as if he had changed.

“I see,” Kereth said, “you got out from under Vonran's nose all right.”

No, he hadn't changed. “Of course.”

“He must be furious.”

“I imagine he is.” The thought didn't bother Kinlol.

“What has he done?” Kereth asked.

“Nothing yet. He has been trying to parlay with us.”

“And you don't want to talk with him?”

Kinlol shook his head. “Words are a weapon to him.”

“What isn't?” Kereth looked over at the general and then around the room. “After all these years, here we are gathered again. Now what do we do?”

Kinlol smiled enigmatically. “Nothing.”

The holograph was suspended over the table, showing Regial and where it bordered the rest of the Empire. Zidon Adesh indicated the border. “You can see the position of Gaelin's forces. Regial is strongly fortified—but only fortified.”

Vonran looked at him. “And what does that mean?”

“Simply, Regent, that his forces are in a defensive posture. We see nothing to indicate an attack.”

Vonran thought a moment and shook his head. “It's been ten days. I thought they would move immediately. Could they have cloaked ships—”

Adesh shook his head. “They are not attacking, Regent.”

His voice was not raised, but it had such finality that Vonran knew the statement brooked no argument. “All right. They are not attacking. What are they doing?”

“Nothing.”

Another thing he hadn't factored into his calculations.

“They are damaging even so,” Adesh said. “Colonel Kereth invited his regiment to follow him to Regial. A third of them did.”

Vonran raised his eyebrows with surprise. “A third?”

“I hear he gave a good speech. But others in the military

defected to Alexander also."

Anger stirred in him. "And you are letting this happen?"

"No. I issued orders to put an end to it. But you see, Regent, that given a choice between a reigning emperor and a reigning regent, many will choose the emperor."

Adesh was right, but Vonran was surprised he would speak so frankly to him. And he decided to be grateful. It made things clearer for him. So this was Kinlol's strategy—and as long as they were not attacking, Vonran could never justify ending their resistance through an attack of his own. It was a pity, really. That would be the easiest way.

And suddenly Vonran was surprised at himself, at his desire to end it all through war. When had that ever been a part of him? When had he ever been a man of violence? He had always used other means.

Vonran's intercom came alive: "The group from the Assembly is here, Regent."

"Send them in." Vonran looked at Adesh. "Thank you, General."

Adesh nodded and shut down the holograph. The door opened and the delegates came in. Vonran noted that Declan was not among them, nor Ziphernan. But Shevyn was—and, naturally, Garin Dorjan, the premier.

Adesh stepped away from the desk, the holo-projector in his hand. He nodded respectfully to the delegates and went out.

"Welcome," Vonran greeted them. "Please, be seated." Vonran led the way, sitting in an armchair. The delegates sat on the furniture around him. "Would you like a drink?" he asked.

No one accepted, and Vonran knew their business was serious. Well, if they weren't going to drink, they might as well cut to the chase. "What is the word from the Assembly?" Vonran asked.

"Hothnay of Teari will speak for us." Dorjan's voice was measured enough, but when his eyes met Vonran's he lifted his shoulders so marginally it was only the implication of a shrug.

Vonran understood. It was Dorjan's apologetic half-shrug, which he could not give with the other delegates in the room.

Whatever they were here to say, it was not in his favor. Vonran's eyes traveled to Hothnay. He raised his eyebrows questioningly.

"Regent Vonran, we speak on behalf of the Assembly—and all those the Assembly represents. We wish you to know that we—the Assembly and the provinces—find the current situation unacceptable." Hothnay paused, looking at Vonran as if he expected an immediate comeback—perhaps some yelling.

Vonran looked at him with all the passivity he could pour into his gaze, and it seemed to get to Hothnay. He went on, a little hurriedly, "The Empire is not divided. The provinces are unwilling to lose Regial. And they do not like Emperor Alexander's departure. The Empire has not rejected its emperor. The people—the Assembly—are disturbed that he has left us to rule somewhere else. It looks as if he has gone into exile. That is intolerable."

Vonran looked at Hothnay and then over at the other delegates. They were tense, ready to stand their ground against him. Shevyn was in fighting mode—Vonran could recognize it easily by now—and Dorjan, Dorjan was silent, trying to be a noncombatant. He didn't want to fight against his own side, or against his friend.

Vonran allowed the silence to grow as his eyes went over them all. He brought his gaze back to Hothnay and gave his answer: "I agree completely."

Hothnay's expression wavered, and he looked almost lost. Vonran went on, "We must bring Emperor Alexander back. I have tried to speak with him, but neither he nor his advisors will hear me. But perhaps you will have greater success."

Vonran ended; the delegates only stared on. He waited patiently; it would come to them presently.

It was Dorjan who said it. "You want the Assembly to pass a resolution petitioning Alexander to return?"

"Yes. If we are agreed that that is what we want."

"We are," Hothnay said.

"Do you really think Emperor Alexander will come meekly back because we ask him?" Shevyn asked. "He rejected the Assembly's decree that the regency would extend another five years. Why would he submit to our petition that he obey that very decree?"

"You underestimate your power as the representatives of the people," Vonran said mildly. "But in any case, I do not expect him to come back to an unchanged situation. Despite the rights and authority the law has given me, I will make concessions to him in order to persuade him to return. But, as I said, he will not hear me."

The delegates thought—and, again, it came to them. "Then any resolution," Hothnay said, "must really be a petition that he parlay with you to establish the terms of his return."

Vonran affected consideration and then nodded. "Yes."

The delegates looked at each other—except for Shevyn, who regarded Vonran with open suspicion. Their rivalry was so old and so well-established that there was no longer any pretense about it. "So," Shevyn said, "you share our conviction that it is bad for Alexander to be in Regial?"

Vonran sensed a trap, but he answered the question. "Bad? The word I would use, Shevyn, is dangerous. It threatens to divide the Empire. If we are not careful, it may come even to war. That is why we must resolve the situation as quickly as possible."

"Then you will go to great lengths to end this," Shevyn said. "Perhaps you will even go so far as to abdicate."

Vonran kept the rebellion in his soul from showing on his face. "I will do what is necessary to uphold the law and the peace."

Shevyn probably intended to take apart that answer. Dorjan spoke before he could. "It is a bold and feckless thing, flouting the Assembly's law and going to Regial."

It was an implicit criticism of Alexander, and Vonran's first impulse was to give implicit agreement. Then he had his second impulse, and that one he followed. "To be sure, it is. But do not pass judgment on Emperor Alexander."

"You already have, Regent," Shevyn told him curtly.

"I have not. Defying the Assembly and flouting the law is feckless, but I would not be quick to blame Alexander." They all looked at him, and Vonran motioned with his hand as if trying to put the point delicately. "He is very young. His advisors have been raising him since his father's death ... " Vonran trailed off and lifted his shoulders in a slight shrug.

The delegates understood the allegation, and they looked at each other. It was terribly probable. Alexander was only seventeen. He never would have done this—he never would have thought of it —on his own.

Vonran hoped they would believe it. He knew Kinlol was behind this, too—and where he lost against Alexander he could win against Kinlol.

It was Dorjan who spoke again. "Then, when we ask Alexander to parlay with the regent, we must ask that it be the emperor himself."

Shevyn turned to him. "We are doing that?"

"Isn't it the least we can do?"

"It is that," Hothnay said.

Shevyn looked as if he would have liked to disagree, but it was getting awkward already. Vonran looked at Hothnay. "Is that the Assembly's entire message?"

"Yes."

"Well, then, gentlemen ... " Vonran stood up. "We must stay in contact to coordinate our efforts. I will give my chief of staff orders to ensure that we do."

The delegates stood up and took their leave. Shevyn, before he turned to go, gave Vonran a look that told him he knew he was up to his tricks. Dorjan came up to Vonran and shook his hand, and he leaned forward to say low, "I admire you."

Within moments all the delegates were gone. Vonran flexed his hands, smiled to himself. He was back in his element.

Kereth slumped on the bench, staring out at the prefect's hunting grounds. In Telnaria they had gardens.

He heard footsteps behind him, but he didn't turn. Nor did he turn when he heard Thaddaeus Gaelin's voice: "Chief Kinlol is wondering where you are."

"So?"

Thaddaeus didn't respond to that, and after a few moments Kereth looked at him. He didn't look much like his father. He took after his mother—dark hair and Alheenan features. He was only a few years older than Cormac—and at that thought Kereth's heart constricted. Cormac was supposed to follow them to Regial, but there was no sign of him yet. Kereth wouldn't be at rest until there was.

Kereth motioned for Thaddaeus to stand in front of him. "You know," he remarked, "I have been away for more than a year. How is Kinlol handling your messenger role?"

A pause. "I think it irritates him sometimes."

"I guessed as much. Don't let it bother you, Thaddaeus. I irritate him, too. And after I left—why, you just took over for me." Kereth looked at Thaddaeus, and he did not seem encouraged. So Kereth raised his forefinger and clarified, "Just because Kinlol is irritated, it doesn't mean anything against you. Don't let it bother you." This was said not so much as advice but as a command. "Now, what does Kinlol want with me?"

Thaddaeus took a moment to remember. "He wants to 'take counsel', as he puts it."

"Why?"

Thaddaeus looked as if maybe he wasn't supposed to know, or wasn't supposed to tell. "The Assembly has passed a resolution requesting that Emperor Alexander return to Telnaria—or at least parlay with Vonran to establish the terms of his return."

"Hmm." Kereth considered that a moment—and then, shaking his head, he got up. "I suppose I am going to have to talk about all this."

"Yes, sir."

Off Kereth went, and Thaddaeus followed behind him. He found Kinlol, Gaelin, and Alexander in the lounge.

Kereth dropped into an armchair. He sensed Thaddaeus coming to stand straight and stiff to his right. It didn't cause him to correct his own posture. Kereth looked over at the other three. "So, do you want to parlay with Vonran?"

"No," Kinlol answered.

"Will you parlay?"

"Maybe," Gaelin said.

"Vonran will not offer anything satisfactory," Kinlol said.

"Probably not," Kereth said. "But he might—depending on what pressure the Assembly is putting on him. But even if he doesn't—it doesn't matter. We have public favor; we can't risk losing it."

Gaelin nodded. "And we will lose it if we do not even appear to be open to reconciliation."

"I don't like it," Kinlol said. "Who knows what Vonran is up to? He's cunning; he never does anything without power."

"We don't have to give him anything he asks for," Kereth pointed out.

"He knows that," Kinlol snapped.

Kereth looked at him, surprised by his ferocity. "What else can we do? We can't stay sulking in Regial while Vonran is trying to bring Alexander back. We have to at least hear him."

"He doesn't want to be heard! He is plotting something, and we will be walking right into it!"

"So what?" Kereth leaned forward, raising his voice, "We have no choice!"

Kinlol leaned forward—

"Gentlemen." At least Gaelin still sounded calm. "We have heard both your points of view. It is for Alexander to decide."

They looked at him. The boy had a trapped look on his face, but—to Kereth's surprise—he was gaming. "We would risk a ... trap?"

Kinlol nodded with dour certitude. Gaelin joined in, "Quite possibly."

Their attention turned to Kereth, and he muttered, "Vonran is crafty."

Alexander looked at the general. "What do you recommend?"

"That you parlay with Vonran. I don't know what we will lose by meeting with him, but I know what we will lose if we don't."

"What about the Assembly's other request?"

Kereth's eyebrows went up. "Other?"

Kinlol shot an irritated look at him. Gaelin answered, "They want Alexander himself to be present at the negotiations."

“That's reasonable. He is the emperor. But the terms of the parlay have yet to be negotiated.” Kereth looked at Kinlol, hoping he got the point—Alexander could be there, but they couldn't allow Vonran to exploit his inexperience.

“I say the same,” Gaelin concurred.

“I would not advise you to parlay with Vonran,” Kinlol said, “but if you do, you should be present.”

Alexander had that look again. He glanced at Kinlol and then at his other advisors. Kereth met his eyes and held them, as if he could give him strength through his gaze. After a long moment Alexander spoke, “We will parlay with Vonran.”

His voice was anything but confident, and he had the expression of a hunted rabbit, but he had made the decision. It was good.

Kinlol was finding that nothing had changed between him and Kereth. His admiration and irritation were as strong as ever. At their past meeting his irritation had been in high gear, as Kereth sauntered in, took the chair as if he were king of the place, and started the conversation without preamble. Kinlol didn't even get a chance to explain what the situation was. And Kereth had sat in that insolent slouch—until he straightened in order to more aggressively press his point.

Alexander followed Kereth's advice—though it comforted Kinlol somewhat that it was Gaelin's advice, too. Kinlol waited until Kereth left before he turned to the boy. “I will arrange the parlay. With your permission, I will try to set the time seven or ten days from now.”

“Why?”

“To increase the pressure on Vonran. It will weaken his position when he comes to the table.”

Alexander nodded—Kinlol never expected disagreement from him—but when Kinlol's eyes went to Gaelin, he found him looking at him. Gaelin raised his eyebrows.

Kinlol gazed back impassively, wondering what that look

was for. “Gaelin, are we ready for an attack on Regial?”

“The preparations proceed. But how ready can we be?” Gaelin looked at Alexander. “With your permission?”

The boy nodded. Gaelin stood up and left—followed by the diffident and, to this point, forgotten Thaddaeus.

Zidon Adesh presented himself in front of Vonran's desk. “Your orders, Regent?”

Vonran looked up at Adesh. “You come so quickly to the point, Adesh.”

Adesh stood silent.

“Adesh,” Vonran said, “Alexander has agreed to parlay with me. I will try to bring an end to this diplomatically. But even if I fail, an end must still come. It is bad to have two leaders rivaling for control, but there is no worse evil than a civil war.”

Adesh stood considering—Vonran didn't know what. He was an intelligent man. He knew what Vonran was saying. “You want battle preparations.”

It was a statement, and Vonran did not answer it.

“The first thing is to have a battle plan. What are your directives?”

Vonran had given that some thought. “Your first directive is not to harm a hair on Emperor Alexander's head. He must be treated at all times with respect. See that your men adhere to this. The second directive is to inflict minimal destruction. If we must use force to make these people submit to the law, we will. But use no more than is necessary—and no less.” Vonran held Adesh's eyes a moment, to impress on him what he was saying. Adesh gazed back, utterly unfazed.

Vonran went on, “The people will not tolerate a long campaign. Neither will I. Any military action must be effective and short-lived. The revolt must be destroyed swiftly and decisively.”

Adesh studied him. “Will you leave the execution of these orders to me, Regent? Will you trust my judgment?”

It was a request not only for freedom but for deference.

Vonran looked at him. "You are the general, Adesh. I will not manage the battle. You may direct it according to your discretion—but whether you do it well will be decided at my discretion."

"So be it. How long do I have?"

"A few days. Kinlol is using delaying tactics in arranging the parlay. But as soon as we are ready for the parlay, we must be ready for an attack also."

"It will be done, Regent."

CHAPTER

* * * * * * * * * * * * * * * * *

ALEXANDER walked into the monitoring room of the Mela Base, and it felt like an escape. After spending all afternoon with Kinlol and the general—being lectured by them, instructed by them and, most embarrassing, dressed by them—he was finally free to go. He put some distance between him and the still on-going preparations for the parlay, making his way to the monitoring room.

Colonel Kereth was busy in there, along with some other officers. He was standing by a sort of table. It was white, and the light glinted off it like a kind of metal. A panel was installed on the edge of the table, and Kereth was working on it.

Alexander walked over and stood next to him, glancing over at the small screen. He was bored enough to feel a passing interest.

Kereth took a quick look at him. "Sharp," he commented.

Alexander glanced down at his clothes. "It's the third outfit they made me try on."

"Kinlol is always fastidious."

"But why does my appearance matter so much?"

"Appearances don't matter, Alexander. But they are important."

Alexander tried to work that out so that it wasn't a contradiction. "Why?"

"Because people who don't realize that appearances don't matter judge by them."

"Oh." Alexander watched the colonel hit keys. "What are you doing?"

"Making sure everything is in order."

"For what?"

Kereth didn't reply. Alexander, who knew his answers often came in actions rather than words, watched him. In a couple moments, a holograph suddenly sprang to life over the table. And Alexander recognized what it was showing: the room where he had already spent too much of his day. He could see the table—straight at the ends but curving at the sides—where they would sit down to parlay, the blindingly white walls, the tannish carpet with its brown weave ...

And people. Kinlol was there, talking by the table with a subordinate of his, whatever his name was, and General Gaelin talking to Thaddaeus.

The realism was remarkable. It was the view a giant would get if he were to lift the roof and look down into the room. After a moment Alexander reached towards the curving table. His fingers passed through, and he felt only a slight tingling from reaching into the holograph. It was strange that something that looked so real could be so unsubstantial.

"Is it a recording," Alexander asked, "or a live transmission?"

Kereth nodded. "It's a live transmission. This is exactly what is happening in that room right now. While you parlay, I—or another security officer—will be watching from here."

"Do you get sound?"

Kereth hit something, and then they could hear a faint buzz of voices from the holograph. "Of course I could turn it up," Kereth said, who instead turned it off. "But you will be listening. We are security. We will be watching."

"Is that why it's so precise, so ... ?"

"So like being there? Yes, Alexander. This is as close as we get to being in there while staying here."

Alexander looked at the holograph and then around the room with renewed interest. "What about the rest of this?"

Kereth stepped away from the table, motioning to the right side of the room. “That is where we monitor the inside of the room. On those monitors there our people can get close-ups of everyone and everything inside the room. Right next to them we will be having a security officer monitoring the readings from the sensors.”

“The sensors?”

“Yes. The whole room is strung with sensors programmed to sense everything from communications signals to metal alloys to gases and chemicals. The people at those consoles will be tracking Vonran and everyone in his party for as long as they are here. And next we have people monitoring outside the room. We will be keeping watch over all the room's entrances and exits—clear out to hyperspace.”

Alexander wondered if he should feel nervous or reassured that they were keeping an escape route clear. He looked around the room and noticed a console set apart from the others. No one was at it, but the computer screen was lit. “What's that for?” he asked, gesturing.

The colonel looked over and smiled. “That is for your cousin.”

“Thaddaeus? When did he start in work like this?”

“Today. You see, it was decided that the only people who should be at the table for our side are you, General Gaelin, Chief Kinlol, and the prefect. So Gawin Gaelin offered me the services of his son during the parlay. I found a use for him.”

“What will he be doing?”

“That requires a little explanation. Gaelin has put the entire military on alert for an attack. They have centralized the system so that all threats will be processed and reported through the same channel. In fact, right here in this base the military has a monitoring room of their own. Like we have done here, they have networked all the computers to a main operating system. I have established an interlink between that system and that computer over there.”

Alexander tried to make sure he was understanding. “So you are having Thaddaeus monitor the military monitoring threats?”

“Yes.”

"Why?"

"Because I am a curious man, Alexander."

Alexander looked at him. A woman sitting at one of the consoles spoke up. "Colonel, Chief Kinlol wants to know if the emperor is with you."

"Tell him yes, then ask him why."

The woman turned back and obeyed. Then she reported, "Regent Vonran has arrived. He is in a capital ship, and he has been accompanied by two warships and three frigates."

Someone whistled, and Kereth muttered, "If I didn't know better I would think he came for a battle instead of a parlay."

"Maybe it's his idea of an intimidation tactic," a lieutenant suggested.

"Or his idea of a grand entrance," Kereth replied. He turned to Alexander. "Chief Kinlol has requested your presence in the conference room."

Alexander nodded, trying to hold back the anxiety flooding into him. "I should go then."

When they had negotiated the terms for the parlay, they had agreed on the border planet of Armanas for the location. Kinlol had then set it up on the base Mela, which was an orbiting station around the planet.

Apparently they didn't want him to come planet-side. Vonran, sitting in the captain's chair on the bridge of his capital ship, thought about that as Armanas filled the viewport. The emperor's ship, *Glory of the Empire*, was also in orbit around the planet.

The comm officer spoke up. "Mela has hailed us. They welcome us to the parlay, and bid you come on board."

"Send an acknowledgment." And then to no one in particular: "Is my shuttle ready?"

"Yes, Regent," the second officer replied.

"Good." Vonran stood up. "Tell the delegates we have arrived and send them down to the shuttle."

Vonran headed down to the hangar. He had agreed to come

accompanied by his security detail, one aide, and a delegation from the Assembly. The delegation had been requested, independently, by both Kinlol and Shevyn. Vonran had acceded, and he found it to his interests—provided the right delegates were chosen.

They were. Partisans for him in the recent controversy were obviously out of the question—and it was easy to make partisans for Shevyn and Ziphernan out of the question, too. That left the moderates, the nonpartisan, middle-of-the-road, no-conviction moderates. If Shevyn or Ziphernan or even Declan were at the table, Vonran might have trouble. But the moderates would be at the table, and he would find them more malleable.

It was a short journey from the ship to the station, and they were met by the base's commander and a few of his officers. He escorted them to a room, and as they entered, he announced, "The Regent and his party, my lord."

As the commander stepped aside, Vonran got a full view of the room, and he almost blinked. His first impression was of light—light from the panels, shining off ungarnished white walls. His next was of an oddly shaped table and people behind it.

Vonran moved forward, paying no attention as the commander—and, per the terms of the parlay, Vonran's security detail—left the room. He came up to the table and bowed his head to Alexander. "Hail, Emperor Alexander."

Alexander looked at him—was it with nervousness?

Vonran glanced over at Kinlol, Gaelin, and the prefect of Regial. To them he spared only a nod. Then he took his seat—the center seat on his side of the table.

Everyone else followed his lead, and as soon as they were all seated Vonran began. "I believe we should begin this parlay with a statement of what we, by agreement, are here to decide. By the desire of the people and by the request of the Assembly, we are here to return Emperor Alexander to Telnaria."

Vonran looked at Alexander. "You have made your displeasure with the Extension Act clear. Why do you desire so much to reign now?"

Alexander hesitated only a moment. "It is not only a desire

to reign now. I have no certainty that I will reign at all—if the Assembly keeps denying my right to."

It was not too bad. A little rehearsed, maybe, but not too bad. "The Assembly will not deny you again."

"Why not? I have as much right now as I ever will."

That was better. "I will speak frankly. You were denied the emperorship because the Assembly feared you were not ready to assume it."

"You could make that argument again and again."

"If nothing changes—yes. But the situation will not remain the same. I will train you in your duties—as your father would have, had he lived. That way, when you assume the emperorship five years from now, you will be prepared."

"We heard nothing of this from you," Kinlol said.

Vonran supposed he had shown restraint to stay out of the discussion so long. "I apologize for not making it clear to you." He wasn't sorry at all, but he had to concede on the little things since he wasn't going to concede on the big things. "I did not think it time to speak of such things yet. I thought that two or three years from now I would train Emperor Alexander as emperors train their sons." Vonran looked back to Alexander. "But if you desire it, I can begin your training as soon as you return to Telnaria. Five years of instruction and no one will question your fitness."

"Is that all you are offering?" Kinlol demanded.

"What more do you want? A resolution from the Assembly confirming the end of the regency? Interim powers? My pledge?"

"You miss the point, Regent." There was an edge to Kinlol's voice. "We want all the powers of the emperorship returned to the true heir."

Vonran knew that. "They will be, Chief Kinlol. In five years, after he has been prepared. You know he has received no right training."

Kinlol stiffened a little. Vonran had expected him to take it that way. "You know what the Ancient Code says."

"And you know what the Assembly says."

"Which is the higher authority?"

That was a good riposte. "The Assembly has not taken the emperorship away." Vonran turned to Alexander—a less formidable opponent. "You will take the emperorship, Emperor Alexander—and very soon. The Assembly has given you five years to prepare—to grow older, to train, to take a wife if you can. I will teach you and then step aside."

Alexander looked at him. "How can I be sure?"

Now this was going in the right direction. "What pledge do you want? Set the standard. I cannot promise a resolution from the Assembly—but I will do what I can." Vonran kept his attention on Alexander, excluding Kinlol and the others from his focus.

He seemed uncertain, and glanced over at his advisors. Vonran drove home his appeal. "The people want you to return to Telnaria. The Assembly has petitioned you to come back, bide the years in preparation, and take the emperorship." The Assembly had never declared it wanted Alexander to submit to the Extension Act, but Vonran didn't fear correction from the delegates now at the table.

Alexander looked over at them. They didn't disagree—and that was as good as agreement.

Vonran could see the yielding rise in Alexander's eyes, and so it was very inconvenient that Kinlol broke into the silence, "It is not good enough. You are still regent."

"I wasn't asking you," Vonran said coldly. "You are not the one wanted to return to Telnaria." He looked back at Alexander. "I make my appeal to you—not only I, but also the Assembly and your people. Return to Telnaria. The emperorship will indeed be yours.

"What else will you do? Secede with Regial from the Empire? Will you take an army and try to force the rest of the provinces to submit to you? Do you want war?"

"No," Alexander said. "No one wants war."

"So all would say." Vonran cut a glance at Kinlol. "But some find it to their purposes."

Alexander looked defensive. "I don't want war."

Vonran slowly nodded. "I know you don't. So I am telling you: return to Telnaria and receive the emperorship peaceably, in the time set by the Assembly."

Alexander wavered. Vonran could see it. Then he looked over at Kinlol, who shook his head almost imperceptibly. Looking back at Vonran—and not quite looking him in the eye—Alexander said, "As Chief Kinlol said, it is not good enough."

Vonran glanced at them. "Your advisors do you a disservice, Emperor Alexander."

Alexander didn't respond.

So he had failed. "Under what conditions will you do as the Assembly has asked?"

This time Alexander did meet his eye. "None."

"I see." And he saw that the parlay would not get him what he wanted. "If you will not return, then there is no point in discussing it." Vonran stood up and bowed slightly to Alexander. "May you find good counsel—and good counselors." With that final shot, Vonran turned and strode out. The delegates hurried along behind him; his guards, joining him as he left the room, kept pace. It was a tense and silent walk down to the shuttle, and once they had boarded everyone sat—except Vonran. He stood throughout the trip back to his ship.

The parlay had failed. That he knew. What made his mind race was what to do next. He had turned his carry-comm off—yet another condition of the parlay—and now he reached his hand to where it hung on his belt and turned it on again.

And he didn't use it, not yet. He felt it—the weight of so small an object—as he went through his alternatives. And when he stepped onto the bridge, the decision was upon him.

That weight pressed on him, too. Vonran walked over to his captain's chair, acting as if he were unaware of the eyes of the bridge crew on him. The hum of activity had been suspended; there was strange silence on the bridge.

The captain spoke first. "Orders, sir?"

"We're leaving, Captain."

A respectful pause. "Where, sir?"

And there was the question. Vonran ignored it as he unclipped his comm and tuned it to the special frequency. It had been set up—the whole complicated communications link had been set up

—so that he, and he alone, could send this message, and no one could detect it.

The parlay had failed; here was his second plan, the plan he had carefully drawn up. Vonran grasped the comm to raise it to his mouth—

And his hand didn't move. He told himself, again, that this was what he had already decided to do, all he could do—

Except abdicate. Yes, he could do that. He would sacrifice his regency—he would sacrifice the five more years he had worked for, the five years he still hungered after—but it would put an end to the conflict. And it wouldn't be humiliating. The whole Empire would praise him, Declan would treat him like a friend again, Kinlol would have to admit he had done a good thing.

And then, without the regency, he would do ... what? Be what? He was ten years and a lifetime gone from the Assembly, his years in Traelys were so far away they almost belonged to another man, and his family was slipping from him one by one—Dianthe to death, his daughters to adulthood and their own lives.

He would walk away from the regency to an empty life, to a sunset in the mid-afternoon. He could taste the years like dust in his mouth.

He tasted them as he lifted the comm and spoke into it, "Adesh—carry on."

That was all that was needed. He turned off his comm and turned to the captain. "Take us to Hyatha."

Colonel Kereth watched as the image of Vonran left the room, disappearing off the table. "That's that," he muttered. Then he called over his shoulder, "Track them as they leave."

Someone acknowledged, but he didn't turn. After a pause he turned on the holograph's sound, and he heard General Gaelin's faint voice: "I thought you were going to ask him to abdicate."

Kinlol began answering him, but after a moment's consideration Kereth turned the sound off again. He knew by watching alone how the parlay had ended. He didn't need to hear the post-action chatter.

"Sir, the regent's party has left Mela. They're shuttling to the *Anand.* We're in the clear."

"Let's not close up just yet," Kereth said.

"Yes, sir."

Kereth ignored the looks the security officers threw each other. He leaned against the holograph-table and waited. Shortly, someone reported, "Vonran has entered hyperspace with all his ships."

They waited. Kereth bided his time.

When a few more minutes passed and nothing happened, he finally accepted that it was over. "All right," he said. "Let's pack it in."

Thaddaeus Gaelin spoke up. "Colonel Kereth, I finally have some action here. There's a report of an anomaly from a military transport in the Nomu system."

Kereth walked over to Thaddaeus' console. "What kind of an anomaly?"

"Someone on the ship reported seeing a darkening over the sun's surface. There are some readings from the ship's sensor logs—the bottom line is that there was no change in the sun to explain the darkening."

There was a brief silence. "What does that mean?" a man asked. "I mean, what is the significance of it to us?"

Kereth leaned forward, gazing at the image of the Nomu system on Thaddaeus' screen and ignoring the talk behind him. No change in the sun—so the darkness would have to be something else, cast by something else ...

"Thaddaeus, do they have an image of this darkening?"

"No. It lasted only five seconds, passing across the margent of the sun and then vanishing."

Vanishing into space. Kereth brought his hand down, clapping it against the console. "Call out a red alert. We're under attack."

They looked at him like he was crazy.

Kereth looked back, with all the forcefulness a fierce spirit and a quarter century of military authority had given him. “Now,” he ordered. “Make sure they start bringing the outer shield to full power.”

A major turned back to his console to obey. Kereth looked back at Thaddaeus. “When did all this take place?”

“Approximately seven minutes ago.”

“And how far is it from here to Nomu, as a ship can go in hyperspace?”

“I would estimate around twenty minutes, sir.”

“That doesn't leave us much time. I need to speak to your father.”

“Colonel,” Thaddaeus said, with calmness and immovability, “what is going on?”

“How do we explain the alert?” another asked.

Kereth was working his comm, and he didn't bother to answer. “Ven?” he asked. When he received a response, he ordered, “Get the ship ready to fly. I'll be down soon.”

He looked up to find everyone staring at him. Then—feeling himself deeply patient—he explained, “The sun wasn't darkened at all. Its light was blocked by something our observer couldn't see.” Kereth stopped there, to let them work it out themselves.

Thaddaeus got it first. “A cloaked ship.”

Kereth nodded. “You got it.” He turned and headed out. The corridors were now filled with hurrying—and confused—people, and Kereth quickly made his way through them to the room of the parlay. When he walked in, he found Gaelin, Kinlol, and Alexander still there. Kinlol and Gaelin were in urgent conversation with a few men who had come, doubtless, on account of the alert.

When Kinlol saw Kereth, he broke away from the others and pointed to him as he said, “Maybe you can explain this!”

That gained Kereth everyone's attention. He strode up to the group before responding, “Vonran is attacking.”

“Where are his ships?”

“In hyperspace. A cloaked ship was seen against Nomu's sun. Now that system isn't far from here. The force will be here soon. We have to evacuate.”

Gaelin's brow furrowed and Kereth could see he took the report seriously, but Kinlol's expression was a pungent mixture of suspicion and scorn. "How do you see a cloaked ship? How do you know it is Vonran's warship attacking us? How do you know that it is part of a force of ships?"

Kereth made his voice hard and edged. "By the shadow it casts when it gets too near a sun. Because no ship is cloaked except for infiltration and attack, and only Vonran would do either to Regial. Because he would not attack with only one ship."

Kereth didn't wait to see if Kinlol would accept that. He turned to Gaelin. "I suggest you muster our own forces. I am going to take the emperor to the auxiliary site."

Gaelin nodded. "Go quickly."

Kereth turned to Kinlol. "You may go where you please unless the emperor commands otherwise, but I suggest that you come with us."

"I will," Kinlol said.

And then the sound of an alarm filled the room—and, indeed, the whole base.

"What does that mean?" Kinlol asked, as grimness overtook Kereth and Gaelin's expressions.

"The enemy has attacked," Kereth answered as Gaelin began working his comm.

In a moment he looked back up at them. "Five warships, five cruisers, and seven frigates have come out of hyperspace."

"I'm flattered," Kereth said, who sounded surprised.

"What?" Kinlol asked.

"It's a lot more firepower than they need to take the base. But the point—can we get Alexander past it?"

"We'll evacuate the entire base to Tokar," Gaelin said. "I'll order the fleet to coalesce around the planet and its system. We'll fight there."

"Is that strategy sound?"

"It's sound enough. They won't suspect its real purpose."

"You've fooled even us, Gaelin," Kereth reminded, almost chidingly.

"Alexander will evacuate when the rest of us do—but to the auxiliary site. Vonran will chase us to Tokar, and he'll never suspect that Alexander has escaped him entirely."

Kereth, if he thought about it, could poke a hundred holes in that plan.

He didn't have time to think about it. He didn't have time for anything. He nodded. "All right. I'll take Alexander down to the ship and wait for your word." Kereth turned—and nearly walked into Thaddaeus Gaelin.

Thaddaeus stepped aside, moving to stand by his father. "Wait, Kereth," Gaelin called, and then turned to his son. "Go with them, Thaddaeus."

Thaddaeus looked unmoved by the command. "Why?"

"Because that is how you will best serve the emperor."

Kereth waited for Thaddaeus to begin walking towards him—and Thaddaeus, for the first time he could remember, argued with his father's command. "I don't want to. Lily is in Tokar."

Gaelin looked at his son, and there was such gentleness and such hardness in his face something twisted in Kereth's gut. Gaelin laid his hand on his son's shoulder and looked straight at him, into his eyes.

Thaddaeus looked back.

Gaelin spoke softly, "I know, son."

For one long moment they gazed at each other. Then Thaddaeus turned away, and without a word or look behind him joined Kereth and followed him out of the room.

Kereth led the way down to their transport, and though the base was filled with the sounds of a place under attack, his thoughts kept flying to Susanne, and Cormac, and the young man walking so quietly behind him.

Zidon Adesh watched the battle. It was going well; both the *Glory* and Mela were isolated from each other, mired in the fire of the ships that swarmed around them, pressing ever closer in.

But precisely three things bothered him. The first was that

Mela's outer shields had already been brought to full strength when he had opened fire on it about five seconds after coming out of hyperspace. That meant they had been expecting this attack. That was the reason for the second thing that bothered him—the lifelessness of their defense. All they were doing was returning fire. It made him wonder what they were putting their creativity into. And finally: Why hadn't reinforcements come yet to Mela? It was a short hyperspace jump.

Adesh watched the rebels weaken beneath the attack, and silently readied himself for whatever they had up their sleeve.

Kereth had gotten himself a seat up front, right behind the pilots. Alexander and Kinlol and Thaddaeus were in a cabin aft, but he wanted to direct the mission as much as he could—and what he couldn't direct at least he would be able to see.

No one spoke or even moved. They could hear the sound of the station being assaulted, and every once in a while they could even feel it—when Mela shook and shuddered under the barrage.

They had an open channel to the base's commander, who was overseeing the defense of Mela, and suddenly his voice filled it: "Colonel Kereth?"

"Here," Kereth replied.

"It's nearly time. Be ready for my signal."

"We'll be waiting," Kereth replied. And his soul turned to the thought of the battle about to begin, and in one word he tried to express it as best he could: "Godspeed."

The young lieutenant half-turned to his superiors as he reported, "Three warships have just come out of hyperspace. They're not yet in firing range, but they've begun moving."

Adesh didn't need to look up from the tactical display to know that the captain was reaching for his comm panel. "No, Captain," he said.

"Sir, I'm going to divert—"

"Don't divert anyone yet. They can't do us any harm where

they are, can they?"

"No, sir."

Adesh knew he was confused, but he didn't explain himself yet. He looked at Mela as it was portrayed on his display and then looked out the viewport at the battle. And he waited for their next move.

The pilot held his hand over his instruments. Moments stretched by, and then a voice came over their comm: "Mela to all ships: Go, go, go."

His hand swooped in, the ship lifted off the floor and shot out the hangar even as its huge doors yawned open.

The sudden outpouring of fire was so startling some on the bridge jumped at it.

Even Adesh blinked—a wholly unnecessary reflex, because the viewport had already darkened. For a moment everyone just looked, adjusting to Mela's sudden offensive.

Then the lieutenant spoke again, suddenly urgently: "Sir, the enemy warships are moving in fast."

"Turn around the *Hawk* and the *Ares* to face them. Everyone else, attention on Mela."

The officers looked towards it. Their ships were beginning to press in again, though very slowly because of the steady stream of lasers and torpedoes. Then a junior officer pointed to something by the station, behind the fire. "Look!"

And, straining, they could see small ships racing into space.

Kereth thought they were going to make it. No one targeted them as they flew out of the hangar, and they banked away from the battle, accelerating towards hyperspace.

And then a frigate appeared in their path. The pilot veered to its left, trying to maintain their straight line to hyperspace, but it was not allowed to be. Another frigate closed in on them there, and their ship shot up in a steep climb. Kereth felt the explosion of a detonating torpedo at their rear, and he began to feel appreciation for the pilots' skill.

And then he almost had a heart attack, as they nearly crashed into the cruiser bearing down on them. A wild swerve saved their lives, and the pilot translated that into the beginning of an angling spiral.

Lasers found them, and the ship shuddered even as it curved. Kereth clasped the sides of the seat and began praying with his eyes wide open.

“Move us forward,” Adesh ordered. “Take up the assault on Mela. Order all other ships except the *Avenger* to target the escaping shuttles.”

“Some of them are frigates, sir,” the lieutenant pointed out.

Adesh didn't answer. It was not relevant to his orders.

Those nearest the fleeing ships had already moved in on them, and now another three broke off the frontal attack on Mela and joined them. Adesh's ship, with the *Avenger*, pounded the station—now again weakening.

The comm officer spoke: “Sir, the *Ares* reports that one of the enemy ships has escaped the engagement and is heading towards us.”

Adesh looked away from Mela.

They had given up trying to make it into hyperspace. Now they were just trying to stay alive.

Kereth had avoided piloting during his military career, and his churning stomach confirmed his wisdom in the matter. He kept his jaw clenched and kept on looking out the viewport, though he saw nothing more than a spinning kaleidoscope of space, stars, ships, and explosions—all streaked by the occasional burning laser-ray. And even as it flew, their ship rocked and shivered—though how much from the hits it took and how much from the paces it was being put through Kereth couldn't tell.

He was no pilot, but he doubted they could survive much more.

"Sir," a junior officer reported, "the enemy ship is joining the battle with the *Glory*. It is firing on the cruiser we have there—" He stopped, making a kind of choking sound. "The cruiser is dead in space. The enemy is turning on our warship—"

There was a pause, and then the captain's voice: "The *Glory* is breaking away. It's making a line towards hyperspace."

"Order all frigates and cruisers not engaged with a warship to break way from their engagements. Divert two cruisers to take up the assault on Mela, and have the rest converge on the *Glory*. Bring us in after them."

Adesh's ship abandoned Mela, passing around it to target the *Glory*. The smaller ships reached it first and dogged it, but the *Glory* didn't pause to return fire. It strained ahead of them, accelerating into hyperspace just as Adesh's ship opened fire.

It brought a sudden moment of stillness. "They've escaped," the captain said.

"Sir," a lieutenant reported, "the *Avenger* reports that it is receiving no more resistance from Mela. However, some of the small transports escaped into hyperspace—"

Even as he spoke, the captain gestured towards the viewport and said, "Look, the other ship flees also."

Adesh didn't bother to debate whether stopping it would be wise. He knew they would not be able to, and they only watched as that enemy, too, winked into hyperspace.

"The *Ares* and the *Hawk* report—"

"That the enemy warships retreated," Adesh finished. "I guessed as much. They have fulfilled their objective." He didn't add, *And defeated ours.* He didn't need to.

"Captain, convey an order to the *Avenger*. I am giving them the task of securing and holding Mela and its people until further orders. All other ships are to begin the cleanup. Now, open a secure channel to General Telai. I'll take it in my flag room." Adesh turned and strode off the bridge. He settled behind his desk just as an image of Telai materialized.

"I assume the battle is over," he said.

Adesh nodded. "We failed. Most of the rebels escaped us—and, it appears, all of the important ones. Have you heard anything from Intelligence?"

"I have. Rebel ships are mustering around Tokar."

"Did they begin before the attack?"

"Shortly after."

"The *Glory* escaped us. It probably went there—along with the other ships."

Telai lifted an eyebrow. "The head of the serpent."

"Yes. But to strike now would be ... injudicious."

Telai didn't disagree. This was good military sense.

Adesh reviewed his options one last time. "Deploy the fleet, Telai," he ordered. "Be sure that every rebel commander is offered a chance to surrender; if he refuses, engage him. After he is conquered, move on. We will take Regial ship by ship and base by base."

Telai nodded, his face as serious as the war he was about to begin. "I hear and obey. Today the conquest of Regial begins."

Chapter

IV

* * * * * * * * * * * * * * * * *

Alexander had never seen an uglier planet. The surfaces of most planets were a swirl of blue and green, but this planet, though it had a great deal of water, had little greenery. The ground was a sickish dark tan, sometimes mottled with other colors, marked by bare rocks that jutted out of the dirt. The snow-covered poles seemed unusually vast, and the light was oddly weak.

This was Revlan, his new home. Alexander had a sinking feeling as he looked away from the planet skimming beneath them to Chief Kinlol. "I don't see the auxiliary site," he said.

"It is here," Kinlol replied.

Alexander looked past him to Thaddaeus. He didn't appear to have heard.

Alexander looked out again. Apparently no one was going to give him answers about this auxiliary site. He felt annoyed about that —and about having to go to Revlan in the first place. Every time he moved it was several steps down the ladder—from Telnaria to Tokar, from Tokar to Mela, from Mela to Revlan. Kinlol's advice had taken him to each one.

Alexander fidgeted a little underneath the thought. It felt unfair, but it was true, wasn't it? He had gone to Tokar on Kinlol's advice, to Mela, and Revlan ... No, Revlan—the auxiliary site—that had been Kereth's idea. Kereth had come in and announced he was going to take him here, and invited Kinlol to go along.

But what else could Kereth—and Kinlol—have done? Vonran had attacked. Because Alexander wouldn't come back to Telnaria, because Kinlol told him not to.

Beneath them the landscape changed; a huge canyon yawned open. Alexander noted it with passing interest. That interest increased when he realized that the ship was banking down. The canyon grew larger and larger, and then they were inside it.

Alexander felt his heart in his throat as the ship weaved past walls of sheer rock and jagged outcroppings. They bore down on a dark opening in the canyon wall, and the next moment they had left sunlight behind. Then the ship came to a halt, hovering in the air.

Alexander shifted impatiently, wondering what was going on and wishing that he was in the front. After a long minute, he heard the sound of something shifting or moving. Alexander looked, but he could see nothing clearly in the half-darkness outside the ship.

And then they were moving again. Slowly the ship moved forward, and within moments they had passed into something—a tunnel, Alexander guessed—far darker than the cave. That thought revived his nervousness. He fought it down as much as he could.

He didn't know how long they traveled through the tunnel. All at once it ended, and they were in a dimly lit cavern. Alexander could feel the ship sweeping in to land, and he muttered, "Finally."

The ship settled down on the ground, and the three were standing when the door drew open and Kereth half-leaned into the room. "We're here. Let's go out. The general is waiting for us."

"General?" Alexander asked as the colonel disappeared from the doorway.

"The commander of the site, I presume," Kinlol answered.

They stiffly made their way aft and found the hatch already open. Alexander felt the coolness of the place roll over him as soon as he stepped onto the ramp. He saw Kereth and the two pilots talking with a lean man in a general's uniform. His short hair was mostly white, though it still had some distinct brown in it, and his face was weathered with the sun and years.

As Alexander approached, they turned to him. The general bowed. "Welcome to your auxiliary site, my emperor. I am honored to host you, but I regret the circumstances."

Alexander nodded to him—he wasn't sure what to say—and Thaddaeus and Kinlol came up behind him. "What news from Tokar?" Thaddaeus asked—the first time he had spoken since they left Mela.

The general looked sober. "Come inside. I'll tell you, and then show you your quarters."

In a few minutes he had led them to an office—Alexander assumed it was his own—with a tactical display mounted on the wall. It was showing a map of Regial, marked by red and green dots. The green dots were centered around Tokar and its system, though some were scattered over all the screen—except where the red predominated.

"After the battle at Mela," the general said, "the Fourth Fleet, with support from the Third, invaded Regial. They have conquered the Nomu system, the Quan system, and the Phira system. They're pressing hard to Tokar, taking or destroying everything in their path. They are stalled by resistance right now, but it won't last. They have superior numbers, and they have time on their side."

Kereth studied the display. "It's too early to tell, but they seem to be encircling Tokar—attacking the systems around them."

The red dots had gone to the left and right of the green mass, rather than straight at it. Alexander looked at them, then at Kereth.

It was the general who answered. "I think they are. The strategy is simple—they're going to cut Tokar off from all outside support and then move in on it. They'll take it ship by ship, planet by planet—until they reach the seat of Regial's government."

And all of a sudden Alexander remembered that his mother was there. He stared at the display, and no one spoke. There didn't seem to be anything to say.

The general stirred himself. "I'll show you your quarters. You've had a long trip from Armanas."

Alexander followed him out, hanging at the back of the group. As they made their way through the passages of the underground base, he gathered his courage and walked up to the colonel. He kept his voice low, half-ashamed to be asking but unable not to. "What about my mother?"

Kereth had to lean over to hear him, and as he drew back he gave him a look of compassion. "She is in no danger."

"But when Vonran gets to Tokar?"

"He has no reason to harm her." Then Kereth sighed. "I know. A lot of people get hurt in wars whom no one has any reason to harm. But don't worry. It will do neither you nor her any good. For now, everything is fine. Hold on to that."

It wasn't much good. Alexander didn't say so; he didn't say anything more.

Behind them, Thaddaeus walked in silence, turning over their conversation in his mind.

Zidon Adesh had been about to retire when the summons came: he was to report to Regent Vonran—in person.

Adesh could only guess why. It may have been done for the benefit of the press—because these things always reached the press—but Adesh doubted Vonran had made the demand for the sake of public relations alone. It struck him that it could be for his sake—an assertion of dominance. This would make sense in the all too likely scenario that Vonran was angry with him.

Vonran was on Hyatha, staying in a prefect's summer home. Adesh slept on the journey there. Then, when they arrived, he carefully dressed and groomed to a truly military level of spit and polish.

The summer home was nestled high on a forested mountain—the tallest and wildest in a range of tall, wild mountains. A servant met him at the landing pad and led him to a second-story summer room. Adesh stepped in and found a hall—a long, narrow room, whose right wall was—floor to ceiling, end to end—made entirely of glastel.

Vonran stood by the clear wall, talking with an aide of his. There were other people in the room—all courtiers, by the look of it. They did not call themselves courtiers, and if someone else did they doubtless would have been filled with honest indignation, and would have rattled off official positions and duties. But Adesh saw a group of people hanging obsequiously on a man of power, and he called them courtiers.

He crossed that hall, coming to stand in front of Vonran. Vonran ignored his presence, although he was the only one. Adesh could feel the attention of the room pressing on him as the regent completed his business with his aide.

Then Vonran turned to him, and his expression was unrevealing enough. But a light glimmered in his eyes and disappeared, and by an instinct Adesh recognized danger.

Vonran didn't speak to him even yet. His eyes flickered to his courtiers and he ordered, "Leave us. I must speak to the general alone."

Within moments the room emptied. They heard the click of the door sliding into place and then Vonran spoke. "You may explain to me why I shouldn't immediately relieve you of duty and have you drummed out of the military."

So he was angry. "Why should you, Regent?" Adesh asked, gentling his tone to a lack of all emphasis and emotion.

Vonran's eyes flashed. "I will ask the questions, not answer them. You will answer me."

Well, if he wanted to be that way about it. "You shouldn't relieve me, Regent, because I have done my duty well."

"If you honestly believe that, I must reassess my opinion of your intelligence. You invaded Regial. You attacked planets throughout the province. The Assembly is up in arms. The public is in shock. Half the Empire's military is fighting itself in Regial. Casualties are mounting and the war has just begun." Now Vonran's voice began to rise. "Do you realize what you have done? To the Empire? To me?"

"I obeyed your orders, Regent."

"I ordered a swift, decisive military operation to end the revolt. I never commanded a war; I never authorized it."

"Forgive my contradicting you, Regent, but you did authorize it. You ordered a military attack against the rebels. You opened up this war with that order."

Vonran seemed to grow taller in his anger as he drew himself erect. The flashing in his eyes was turning to fire. "You know very well I ordered a single, decisive operation."

"You also gave me an objective—destroy the rebellion. The operation failed, but I still had an objective to achieve. And I will achieve it."

"You didn't consult me before expanding to a war."

The regent, Adesh had noticed, was shrewd about all forms of power except military. "Regent, you passed that threshold when you ordered the first attack. Once you have resorted to force, you must continue until you win. You must destroy the enemy—even if they refuse to be vanquished on the first try. The attack failed. If I had done nothing, what would you have me do now?"

That was the first thing he said that actually got through. Vonran hesitated, and then he came back much faster than Adesh expected. "And why," he asked icily, "did you decide to destroy all of Regial instead of Kinlol and his lackeys?"

"Regent, the attack on Mela failed. Alexander and his advisors escaped in the *Glory of the Empire*. After the battle I received word that warships were mustering around Tokar, and I guessed that the *Glory* had gone there also. Telemetry from an intelligence probe confirmed that guess a few hours later. But even knowing that the leadership had gone to Tokar, I had not the strength to attack yet. A powerful force was already gathering, and I could expect reinforcements to arrive at my back from all Regial.

"So I ordered General Telai to deploy the fleet. We will attack Tokar and destroy the revolt, but first we must cut them off from all outside support."

There was still a stern set to Vonran's mouth, but now his eyes were thoughtful. "And how did the first attack fail, General?"

"Somehow the rebels received advanced warning of our attack. The station had already raised its outer shields, which bought them time. They devised a strategy to escape the trap, and they implemented it well."

"Is there a traitor in our ranks?"

"Perhaps, but not necessarily. They may have detected the

cloaked force as it was lying in wait in the Nomu system. There's no telling."

The regent's anger was fading fast, but he didn't let up yet. "Your failure to win a quick victory has cost me dearly. Two Chiefs have resigned from the Council—a rare rebuke, Adesh, and not one I enjoy receiving."

"I heard. And they are both the last of the Chiefs Emperor Judah appointed, are they not?"

Adesh knew, from the way Vonran looked at him, that he understood what he was saying—that Vonran could now remake the Council in his own image, with all the Chiefs his own. But Vonran didn't respond to the point. Instead he went on, "The Assembly will have my head."

"I don't think they're capable, Regent Vonran. What can the Assembly do to the emperor?"

Vonran looked disgusted by such ignorance. "More than you know, Adesh."

"I know they are restricted by the Powers in War law."

"I haven't declared the nation to be in a state of war."

"I know. But they have noticed already." And Adesh immediately questioned his wisdom in taking a sardonic tone when he was—however temporarily—out of favor.

Vonran didn't react. He seemed to be preoccupied with something else. Then his eyes re-focused on Adesh. "And how long do you think it will be before you finish the job?"

"I can't say. Subduing the rest of Regial should be only a matter of days—but the bulk of their strength is concentrated in Tokar. That will be the difficult part."

Vonran nodded, and again seemed distracted. "And you are giving them opportunity to surrender? Your troops and officers know to respect the life and person of Emperor Alexander?"

"Yes."

"This may be salvageable." He sounded as if he were speaking half to himself.

"The rebels will be dealt with," Adesh said.

Vonran looked at him. "You have only the rebels to deal

with. I have the entire nation," he reminded him, a little curtly. "Now go. Deal with them. I will deal with the country."

Adesh bowed.

Gerog Kinlol was at work in his room, reading off his computer screen. A *ding-ding* sounded, and he responded, "Enter."

Colonel Kereth did, and *how* he did. He didn't so much walk as barge into the room and over to Kinlol's desk. "Have you seen that speech Vonran gave about what happened?"

"Yes." Kinlol didn't look away from the words on the screen.

Kereth leaned over him, tapping out commands into the computer. "It's in the base's data system," he said. "I need to access—ah."

Something appeared on the screen, and as Kereth resumed working Kinlol calmly stated, "I said I have seen it."

"I heard you. It's quite the piece of work. I watched with an enormous amount of admiration and repulsion—which is an interesting experience in and of itself. Here."

As Kereth spoke, he hit a final key and the recording of Vonran's speech began in the middle: " ... the preparations the emperor's advisors made are now obvious. They led the emperor to Regial, they delayed the parlay and then refused to negotiate terms for Emperor Alexander's return. Now they have turned against the military those regiments they illicitly control ... "

Kereth hit a key and the recording froze, then disappeared. "That's only where he dropped the subtlety. Throughout the speech he made it very plain that it's *all our fault*!" Kereth threw out his arms to further illustrate his point. "The Empire is a victim, he's a victim, Alexander is a victim. It's all the fault of those nefarious villains, that sinister, shadowy crew—the emperor's advisors! You know who you are!"

Kinlol looked at the colonel, not trying very hard to keep his disdain off his face. "Very good, Colonel. You have proven yourself. After the war you may become a commentator on the press nets."

"Very good, Chief Kinlol," Kereth replied, his voice a

parody of the tone Kinlol had just taken. "You succeeded in making fairly clever sarcasm. You have proven you may someday have a fully developed sense of humor. Perhaps after the war.

"But now to my point. That speech was just the roll-out of a new public relations campaign. That propaganda is being disseminated all through the media. Those delegates who were at the parlay are on the news, saying that yes, Vonran did offer compromises; yes, Alexander refused to return no matter what he offered; and yes, it was on your advice."

Kinlol looked at him. Kereth looked back and spoke with deliberation, "We are losing the public."

Kinlol held his eyes, then looked back at the computer. "What concerns me is that we are losing the war. And my counsel has failed me."

He said it so calmly, with so little emotion, that it took Kereth two seconds to realize what he had just said. "Whoa," he commented, and glanced around for a chair. There was none. "Don't lose faith on me now, Kinlol. The time for doubts will come later, after we're out of this hole."

"Any ideas for a course of action?"

Again Kereth looked for a chair. It didn't quite fit, holding this conversation and not being able to look Kinlol in the eye. "They say the first thing to do when you find yourself in a hole is to stop digging." Kinlol looked at him. "It means, my friend, that when you have a problem the first thing to do is nothing wrong." Kereth went to Kinlol's right and sat down on the bed, finally bringing them to a reasonably similar eye level.

"What are we doing wrong that we should stop?"

"Or what might we do wrong, that we should avoid?" Kereth countered. "What might we do at all? Think."

"I have been." Kinlol said nothing more—and that was also, Kereth gathered, what he had thought of.

After a moment Kereth shook his head. "All right. Re-formulate the question. What is our objective? To put Alexander on the throne. What stands in our way? Vonran. Why have we been unable to defeat him? Because he is stronger than us. How is he stronger?"

When Kereth stopped there, Kinlol motioned. "Go on."

"I answered the last few questions. You answer that one."

"He has outwitted us," Kinlol said plainly. It was a little painful to say, though not nearly as painful as it had been to realize. "He knows what he wants, and he pursues it with cunning and subtlety."

"That's part of it, I grant you. But not all. He has brawn as well as brains. It's true that if he were a fool or a weakling we would have won by now. But if he did not have the government and military behind him we would have won, too. So our objective must be this: to sap Vonran's strength and increase our own."

"I wish I knew what Gaelin was planning to do with our military."

"He'll be able to do nothing more than defend, and even in that he will eventually fail—if Vonran's fortitude doesn't fail him first."

"I think we can be confident it won't," Kinlol muttered.

"We can. As things stand, Gaelin is accomplishing one thing for us: He is giving us freedom to act. First because Vonran doesn't know even to look for us, and second because Gaelin is taking up a significant amount of Vonran's time and resources. We must decide what to do with that freedom."

Kinlol was about to reply when Kereth's comm pinged. Kereth unhooked it from his belt. "Colonel Kereth," he answered.

Kinlol could hear the response: "This is General Lyos. We have a visitor—a small military frigate. I don't know the officer, but he has the codes. I would like you or Chief Kinlol to meet him with me."

Kereth looked over at Kinlol. "Certainly. In fact, you may get us both. At the landing zone?"

"At the landing zone," Lyos confirmed. "And as soon as you can. The ship is being directed there as we speak."

"We'll be there shortly, General," Kereth promised. "Kereth out." He stood up. "Are you coming?"

"Certainly."

They arrived at the landing zone just as the ship was circling to land. General Lyos was there, flanked by a few soldiers—infantry soldiers, Kereth realized, functioning as bodyguards. Apparently they weren't quite trusting yet.

Kinlol took up a position near the general while Kereth stood a little in front of them all. For a moment everything was still, and then the hatch opened and a ramp extended from the ship. A young man dressed in a military uniform appeared in the open hatch, walked down the ramp ...

And joy and amazement seemed to stop Kereth's breathing. It certainly turned his head. "Cormac!" he called, and before he knew what he was doing he ran to his son and threw his arms around him.

Cormac returned the hug awkwardly. "Dad," he said, keeping his voice down, "I'm on duty."

Kereth released his son, stepping back to look at him. All in one piece, walking on his own power with no bandages. Finally he looked back at Cormac's face. "Well, Cormac, I'd normally leave the hugging to your mother, but she isn't here, so I have to step in for her."

"Where is she?"

Kereth regretted his answer. "Tokar. With your sisters." As Kereth spoke he noticed a man coming out of the ship. He took a second glance and began shaking his head. "Tim Dappler," he said. "Is there anyone else in there I know? My cousin Titus, perhaps?"

"*General* Dappler, Colonel," Dappler corrected. "And no, there is no one else. Only my pilot and I." Dappler nodded towards Cormac.

Lyos stepped forward. "How do you know of this place, General?"

"That's part of a long story I have to tell all of you."

Lyos nodded and turned, leading them into the base.

Thaddaeus Gaelin stood just inside. He stepped forward, placing himself barely—but definitely—in Lyos' way. "May I join you, General?"

Lyos looked at him. "And why would you want to, Gaelin?"

"My father sent me here to help the emperor. I think I will be of help."

For a long moment Lyos gazed at him. Then he slowly nodded. Thaddaeus joined in the procession. They arrived at Lyos' conference room and took their places around the table.

Lyos turned to Dappler. "Now, why did you come here and how do you know of it?"

Dappler glanced at him, then around the table. "I guess I can take it that General Gaelin never told any of you the arrangement he made with me. About two years ago he came to me and said that he was preparing to take the throne from Vonran militarily, should the regent refuse to step down. He asked if I would be willing to lend my aid. I said I was, and he had an assignment for me—a plan he wanted me to execute.

"The plan was this: If war became necessary, he would ask young men all over the Empire to volunteer to fight for their emperor. He wanted me to plan for their training—and oversee it, if things went that far.

"As you all know, things did. Gaelin issued his call, and I came to Regial to turn his band of recruits into an army. Five days ago, the day of the parlay, I was in the Nomu system. The recruiters had finished their work there, and all the recruits had been gathered into transports to be taken to the planet we had chosen for training. I had the same destination, and I was planning to make the trip with them. But before we left I heard two things. The first was that Adesh's forces had attacked Mela. The second was that Gaelin had ordered our forces to muster at Tokar to defend the emperor against Vonran's attack.

"Now, you must think a moment about the situation I was in. I had, under my command, transports full of recruits—most of them boys, green as spring—and the middle-class ships that had been assigned to escort them. I couldn't join the fighting with that.

"But avoiding the fighting wasn't easy, either. Adesh's full-scale invasion and his obvious intention to take every piece of Regial made that clear. To make a long story short—and to get to the point—I kept my recruits safe from Adesh by hiding them, and I hid them in the best place available—the Vaaris Cluster."

Everyone at the table stiffened, and at that moment no one paid attention to anything but Dappler. "You did that without killing anyone?" asked Lyos.

"We were very careful."

"You can only stay in the Cluster so long," Kereth told Dappler.

"I know. That's why I came here."

"Yes," Lyos said. "Here. How do you know about the auxiliary site?"

"General Gaelin told me," Dappler said simply.

"Yes," Kereth muttered. "I'm starting to wish he had told us a few things."

There was a moment of silence. Thaddaeus Gaelin looked from face to face, with an intentness Kinlol did not understand.

Kereth broke the silence. "We had all better think on this." He nodded to Dappler, and there was a glimmer in his eyes Kinlol did not trust at all. "You have given us a lot to think about."

Zidon Adesh stood straight and tall on the bridge, looking out the viewport. He saw his ships in formation, and across from them the enemy warships.

It was only a sliver of the picture he saw in his mind. He saw the whole system of Tokar thick with Gaelin's forces. Ships stood sentry in orbit around planets, and ringing around the system, facing outward, the rest of his ships were arrayed in staggered formation. And he saw the Fourth and Third fleets facing them, converging on every side.

It would be a terrible battle, but also the last. With this, all of Regial would be taken, the revolt utterly crushed.

Adesh turned towards his captain and nodded. The captain signaled the comm officer, and after a moment the officer said, "The channel is open, sir."

Adesh nodded to him and said, "All ships, this is General Adesh. Engage."

As he spoke he glanced towards the viewport. His ships

began to shift in their formation, re-ordering themselves as they angled towards Gaelin's forces and drove at them.

The foremost ship hit black space, and fire blossomed in its hull. Burnt and twisted wreckage fell away from the ship, and still the flames crept along its exterior. The ship drifted to starboard—and explosions tore that side, too.

Adesh twisted to the comm officer. "Open the channel again immediately!"

A few heartbeats, and then: "The channel is—"

"Adesh to all ships: Abort the attack. I repeat, abort the attack and fall back!" He signaled to the comm officer, who cut off. "Now," Adesh said, "find out if any other ships hit mines."

It was a quiet few moments, and then the officer reported, "Three more ships are reported damaged by mine explosions."

Adesh nodded grimly. "Cloaked space mines—probably all around Tokar, between our ships and theirs." Another problem to be addressed, another problem to be overcome.

Another problem to be explained to a certain impatient regent.

Thaddaeus Gaelin stood outside Colonel Kereth's quarters, and he felt a little apprehension creeping up his neck. He pressed his fingers against the open-pad, and after a moment the door opened and he stepped inside.

The quarters they had been given were all the same—small, dark rooms with a bed, a closet, a computer, and a food dispenser. Kereth sat at the computer, so absorbed in his work that it took him a couple minutes to look up. "Something on your mind?" he asked, looking at the screen again.

"Yes." As Thaddaeus walked up to Kereth he glanced at the screen and saw the heading of the document he was reading: "Irregular: The Military Strategy of—"

Then his gaze was back on Kereth, who was now looking at him. "I was wondering if General Gaelin had ever told you that there is a military ship depot in the Vaaris Cluster."

Kereth's eyebrows had begun to tilt up when he called his father General Gaelin. Now they jumped onto his forehead. "No, he didn't. I gather he told you, though."

"Yes, he did."

"Who else did he tell?"

Thaddaeus had spent a long morning figuring that out. "Aside from those who were involved in the construction—none that I know of. I spoke to General Dappler. They didn't find it—perhaps because they didn't go in far enough, but perhaps they passed it by. Sensors aren't worth much in the Cluster."

"I know. Tell me about this depot."

"You know how my father had this underground base built as an auxiliary site. Around two years ago he decided to build another secret facility, a smaller one, in the Vaaris Cluster. Partly as a refuge, but also to modify the one flaw in the Revlan site—its disadvantage as a launching site. The facility is mostly a depot. It has a capacity of a class-B fighting force. It is crude relative to this facility; I would call it functional, nothing more."

Kereth looked at him carefully. "Have you been there?"

"Only once. On my last visit to Regial before the war started my father took me there and showed it to me."

"I didn't know your father had so many secrets."

"He has his reasons. Everything—Revlan, the depot, Dappler's program, all the officers who joined us—they're all just parts of the whole. My father tried to keep the parts from knowing the whole."

"But he knew the whole."

"Of course. Someone must."

"Of course. But now he is in Tokar, and we are on Revlan, and for the time being never the twain will meet."

And here was his opening. "He deposited all his knowledge somewhere in case something like this happened."

"Where?"

"Me."

Kereth didn't look nearly as surprised by that revelation as Thaddaeus expected him to. He twisted his finger in the air.

"Meaning you know everything?"

"Yes. He told me everything he did. I knew all his plans. When I came from Telnaria to visit my family, he took me with him on his rounds through Regial and showed me what he had built and was building. No one ever suspected—not even you or Chief Kinlol."

Kereth turned his head away, and slowly he nodded to himself. "So that is why he sent you with us."

His words hit a sore spot, and Thaddaeus muttered without really deciding to, "One of the reasons."

Kereth spoke gently. "My wife is in Tokar, too, and so are my daughters. And Alexander's mother is there. She's the only immediate family he has. Your father will do everything he can to keep them safe."

Thaddaeus knew that, and it hadn't stopped his worrying, especially at night. But he only nodded politely.

But Kereth, perhaps, knew what he didn't say. His eyes were steady on Thaddaeus and full of compassion.

It made Thaddaeus uncomfortable, and he straightened his posture, bringing his arm behind his back. "That's all I had to tell you."

"And I thank you. It's a useful asset." Kereth's eyes traveled to the computer screen. "A very useful asset."

"The space mine, as a tactic and a weapon, has been much neglected by military strategists and scholars. The reasons are self-evident—difficulty in effective use, precise positioning, et cetera. Still and all, better use can and should be made ... "

"What are you reading?"

At the question Adesh lowered his compad and looked at Elymas Vonran. "A strategy paper written by a young major on the use of space mines. A little pedantic, don't you think? But the major went a long way. He married the emperor's daughter and became a very respected general."

"What is the relevance?"

“The relevance is that this is Gaelin's writing on the tactic he is now using against us in Regial. Unfortunately, if he follows his own advice—including on how to keep cloaked space mines from being detected and disabled—we have quite a challenge.”

“And what are you planning to do?”

“Draw up a battle strategy that will take the mines into account.”

“In other words—an even bloodier battle.”

“If there were another solution, Regent, I would rejoice to do it.”

“And there isn't? General, the Assembly is enraged, and the Empire is alarmed. And that is because all the Emprians who have died are only the beginning if you have your way.”

“Aside from surrendering, what option is there but to fight?”

Vonran gave him a vaguely superior look—the look he gave obtuse people who had worn out his patience. “You want to break the rebels, but the only way you can think of is militarily. Break them economically. The military itself will crumble.”

It was an intriguing idea, but the question remained ... “How can that be done?”

“Fortunately for us, Adesh, Tokar is the system in Regial most vulnerable to such an attack. It's known as the gateway to the Empire. Nearly all of Regial's imports and exports pass through Tokar. Its economy has come to rely heavily on such traffic. In fact, I imagine there are people there feeling the loss of business right now.”

“Because of the blockade,” Adesh said, beginning to get the hang of it.

“Yes. Do you know how many planets there are in that system?”

“Eight. Three are inhabited. Terraforming was begun on another two planets, but abandoned decades, maybe centuries ago.”

Vonran nodded. “So you have three planets suffering the elimination of a large part of the economy, and at the same time having to support a small army. Think of the requirements for Gaelin's fleet of ships alone. Tokar will crack under the burden eventually. Our job is to make sure they stay under it."

"A siege, in other words. You want to besiege Tokar and starve them out."

"Yes. They have already locked themselves in. We need only station ourselves outside the door."

"It would cost a great deal of money."

"Better to spend money than lives."

"I can't argue with that. But what about the time? Tokar might hold out for years."

Vonran waved his hand. "We will see. If things change we can adjust the strategy. In any case we won't merely wait. Surely there are ways you can nibble at their strength aside from all-out war. Think about it. You'll come up with something."

"Then that is our strategy?"

"It is."

"If I may speak openly, I think the people will still be uneasy."

"The more astute ones, perhaps. But they will be relieved that there is no fighting, and humans can get used to anything. If nothing happens, it will fade to the back of their minds. The rebels will give in to us eventually—and without a bloody defeat."

"Let us hope so, Regent."

"Let us do it, General," Vonran corrected him. "Return to Tokar and keep me appraised. I am going back to the city, so this will be the last time we speak face to face for a while."

"What city?"

Vonran's expression indicated he thought that an unnecessary question. "Telnaria."

They sat at the table—Tim Dappler, General Lyos, Gerog Kinlol, Emperor Alexander, and Thaddaeus Gaelin. Adon Kereth had the floor.

"No one will argue with me," he began, "if I say that our current strategy needs adjusting. But I would like to go a step further. I think our strategy needs replacing. The Assembly has proven weak in opposing Vonran, and what of our military Adesh hasn't destroyed is pinned down in Tokar. By the actions of his fleet Adesh appears to have exchanged attacking Tokar for laying siege to it. We have some men, some resources, but nothing compared to what Elymas Vonran has.

"My point is this: We can't challenge him in a conventional war. But we are ideally situated for guerrilla warfare. The recruits will be our soldiers. There are enough of them to maintain constant operations against Vonran. We have ships, weapons, and intelligence sources. We have a sympathetic populace to hide and help us. We have a launching site for attacks and a hiding place for our ships in the Vaaris Cluster. We have this base. We have targets throughout Regial—the forces besieging Tokar and the supply route back to the Empire. And there are loyal and brave Emprians outside Regial; we can set up cells within the Empire and work against Vonran there, too. In sum, we will cause Vonran no end of trouble until we are a swarm of hornets driving him from the throne."

Some of his audience looked at the table; others looked at each other, seeking a judgment on Kereth's words. Dappler spoke. "If the recruits are going to be our irregulars, I'm going to have to change their training program."

The attention of the table turned to him, and Kereth answered, "Yes, but bear in mind we want them to be the emperor's soldiers, loyal to the Empire and honorable. We must teach them to fight like irregulars, to be commandos—but also to be soldiers. I'll not create a band of rag-tag, lawless fighting men."

"To be sure," Lyos said. "And you must create an officer's program, to find, train, and commission worthy men among the recruits."

"So all the military men agree," Kinlol said.

They turned to him. "You don't?" Kereth asked.

Kinlol regarded him coolly. "I haven't decided. I don't make rushed judgments."

Kereth folded his arms and returned Kinlol's look. "Go on."

"We may be able to wage guerrilla warfare, but what will it accomplish? Can it really bring us to victory?"

"Don't underestimate guerrilla warfare as a strategy," Lyos said. "Governments have been overthrown by it before. The material damage is only part of the warfare; the rest is demoralizing the enemy and corroding his will and support among the people. Our goal is to overthrow Vonran, not conquer the Empire."

Thaddaeus spoke up. "I support the strategy. What other alternative do we have?"

Kereth looked at Alexander. "Do you approve of this strategy?"

He glanced at Kinlol, then looked at Kereth. "We don't have any other, and it has the support of most of my advisors. Yes, I approve."

"I assume I will be bringing the recruits here for training," Dappler said.

"Yes," Kereth said. "And I think their training should be as lengthy as is needed. When our offensive is launched it must be professional and robust from the beginning. Even so it will take some time before our attacks begin taking a toll on Vonran."

Thaddaeus lifted his hands in front of him and pressed them together. "And of course," he added, "when we begin attacking, Vonran will begin hunting us."

A sober silence stole over the table. After a few moments Alexander stated, "Colonel Kereth, I appoint you to oversee the implementation of this strategy. And since that means these generals here will have to report to you, I also promote you to general."

Kereth turned to him—looking, for the first time Alexander could remember, stunned. Then he slowly smiled and bowed. "I accept this command with gratitude, my lord. I will serve you to the best of my ability."

Kinlol looked at Alexander, and nodded slowly in approval of his old pupil.

Telnaria was quiet at Vonran's return. He could feel it in the very silence of the Palace's halls as he walked through them. People drew away as he approached, fell silent and stared. They had always made way for him, they had always grown quiet and watched. But now it all seemed to be a little more.

The delegates were already waiting for him in his office. They stood when he entered, and Vonran greeted them and motioned to them to sit again. He also sat down, taking a moment to survey the delegates. Declan, Shevyn, Dorjan, and Ziphernan were all there. Vonran had directed that the delegates be offered drinks after being brought into his office, and about three-fourths of them had accepted. Not Declan, but he had never drunk much.

Vonran let his gaze slide past Declan, not looking into his eyes or even his face. His eyes came to rest on Dorjan. "Does the Assembly have any words for me, Premier?" he asked.

"We have questions, Regent," Dorjan answered, and Vonran couldn't tell if he agreed with their questioning or only represented it. "We wonder why it was necessary to attack Emperor Alexander and his loyalists."

Vonran spoke coolly. "Because they were in rebellion and could not be brought peacefully to submit."

"Rebellion against you?" Shevyn asked. "Submission to you?"

"No, Shevyn. To the law—the Assembly's law." Vonran's gaze swept to the other delegates. "I sent the delegates who accompanied me back to the Assembly to report what had happened. Did you not hear from them that Emperor Alexander refused to accept any offers I had made him or would make him?"

"Indeed we heard it." Ziphernan made that concession, but he looked at Vonran boldly, as if in open judgment of him and everything he had to say.

Vonran controlled his irritation and his voice. "Then you will know that the only way I could end their rebellion was by force."

"No." Declan's voice was so quiet it was almost hard to hear, but he looked straight at Vonran as he spoke. "You could have abdicated."

There, it had been finally put to his face. He took it as a challenge and rose to it. "And to whom would I have been abdicating? To Alexander—or Kinlol and Gaelin?"

"You think they exercise such power?" Ziphernan asked.

"I do. And if I tell you that it was Kinlol and Gaelin who seized control of Regial and the military there, will any one of you disagree? And if I tell you that it was by their prompting and not his own will that Alexander went there and would not come back—who will disagree?"

No one would. And Vonran took control, ending that topic and opening a new one. "Now I have declared the nation to be at war, but I hope that no more Emprians will die. I have ordered General Adesh to withhold from attacking Tokar. He will remain outside Tokar with his forces, and in due time it will be plain to Gaelin and Kinlol that they have no hope of victory. When they surrender, the war will come to a bloodless end. Emperor Alexander's advisors—who have manipulated him in the vulnerability of his youth and fatherlessness—will lose all their power. And Emperor Alexander will return to Telnaria to receive his Empire in the proper time and way."

Again the delegates didn't contradict him. But instead of feeling his usual pleasure of victory, Vonran was struck by a new thought: strange, that even the delegates seemed subdued.

Dorjan stood up. "The Assembly will advise you as to our thoughts."

Everyone else stood up also, and as the delegates began to leave, Declan came up to Vonran.

Vonran stiffened a little, waiting for a lecture, a rebuke, a piercing look from pale blue eyes ...

Declan smiled—and though it was kind enough, it was not quite the smile he usually gave Vonran. "I heard that Zelrynn and Lydia both left this morning. Now Calanthra is the last pretty little sparrow in your nest."

"Yes," Vonran acknowledged stiffly. Three of his daughters had left, the last would soon, and then he would be alone. And what had that to do with Declan?

"Will you be available to meet later?"

And then he would receive the lecture, the rebuke, the urging to be a good man and abdicate to Alexander. Vonran looked at

Declan and slowly shook his head. "No."

They were in one of the Hall's common rooms, and it was filled with delegates. The men who had gone to see Elymas Vonran had returned with their report, and the delegates had seized it with an intense and morbid interest.

Ziphernan was in the thick of the excited delegates, sitting at one of the small tables, quietly nursing a tall glass of maple-brew. When he had listened to the bevy of voices for a long while, he spoke up. "I suppose repealing the Extension Act is not allowed."

"Don't boast, Ziphernan," a man answered. "We know you were right."

"I don't mean to boast. I wonder what we are going to do now."

The man pulled a chair out and sat opposite Ziphernan, eyeing him warily. "Do? What can we do?"

Ziphernan kept his voice just loud enough that everyone who wanted could hear. "Are we not the Assembly? A creative use of our powers could unseat Vonran yet."

"What powers?"

Ziphernan—and all the delegates who had been clustering around his conversation—turned to the voice. Colten Shevyn—recent premier, leader of the Tremain delegation, old enemy of Elymas Vonran—stood by the bar, his back to it as he gazed at them.

"We have the power of passing acts and resolutions."

"There is no act we can pass that will unseat an emperor—and while an emperor has to listen to us, he does not have to obey."

"Doesn't the Assembly watch over the people's purse? We could cut off funding for Vonran's little adventure in Regial."

"He has declared the nation to be at war, and for that war he can spend all the money he pleases."

"I know that." Ziphernan was surprised at Shevyn's opposition; he had expected help from him first of all. "We can challenge his declaration, can we not?"

"We can, but it will not succeed. If the military is engaged at all it will not succeed." Shevyn paused, raking an assessing gaze over Ziphernan. "You underestimate the emperor's strength—especially in a time of war."

Ziphernan looked at him carefully. "You keep speaking of the emperor, but Vonran is not one."

Shevyn looked at him with deadly calm. "Yes, he is."

Ziphernan looked around and saw that none of the delegates were going to contradict Shevyn. "And so you have all given up." Anger began to boil up inside him. "You are not going to do anything!"

"Neither are you," Shevyn informed him. "You will yet learn the limits of the Assembly, young friend."

Something inside Ziphernan prickled at the misnomer. "So Elymas Vonran has won."

Shevyn nodded, and there was something in his dark eyes Ziphernan had never seen before and could not understand. "He always wins."

It was a strange landscape. The land rolled as far as the eye could see, sometimes swelling up into small hills, never quite flat. There was almost no living thing growing from the earth, but though it had the barrenness of a desert it did not have the heat. The soil was strange—hard, half-dry, thick, clotted clay. The small hills were grainier than the ground, buffeted and worn down by the wind.

Adon Kereth took in the sight as he disembarked from the shuttle, and he thought to himself that he would never again call Susanne's home desolate. Tugging at his thick jacket, he headed over to the simple, dark brown buildings that rose bizarrely in that barren place.

Tim Dappler stood outside with a handful of officers coming and going around him. He was watching a group of recruits run the course he had marked for them.

Kereth walked towards him, and he was within a few paces when Dappler turned around and, seeing him, came to attention.

"At ease," Kereth said.

"Are you here on inspection, General Kereth?"

Kereth nodded, and a warm feeling shot through him at the title. "I'm taking a look at things. I see you have the beginning of a base camp." He nodded towards the buildings. "And this is exercise?"

"Informal exercise. We haven't completed the training grounds, but I thought some athletics would be a start."

Kereth looked over at the recruits. He saw one man—one boy? He looked young—running ahead of the others. He kept his advantage and, to Kereth's surprise, increased it. He reached one of Revlan's hills and ascended it with a nimbleness that set off an unexpected spark of envy in Kereth. He crested the top, skidded and leaped his way down, and shot off on level ground. And then Kereth noticed how lightly he ran. By instinct or training his feet and legs were bent to take the least amount of impact—and cause the least amount of sound.

Kereth turned back to Dappler. "The one in the lead—he has the makings of a good commando. Fast and quiet, very stealthy."

Dappler looked over and nodded. "I've been keeping my eye on that one. Do you know how we learned of Vonran's attack because one of his ships got too close to a sun for a moment?"

"Yes."

"He was the one who saw that on board a transport and reported it."

"Observant too, then. Any leadership qualities?"

"I'm not sure yet. I do plan to have him tested for the officer's program, if that's what makes you ask. He has had some responsibility. He listed 'miner' as his occupation for the past three years."

"Does he look older up close?"

"He's young, but apparently old enough. Have you ever heard of the Nomu mines?"

"I know of them." Kereth cleared his throat. "When will you begin formal training?"

"Three days, sir."

It felt a little strange to hear Dappler call him that. Kereth glanced over at him, wondered if he should ask another military question or bring up what had been bothering him ever since Dappler arrived. He looked around, saw they were alone, and chose the second. “I'm glad that you made it into our conspiracy, Tim.”

Dappler showed deep interest in his compad for a moment, then lowered it and looked at Kereth. “You were part of it from the very beginning, weren't you? All those years ago in your office in the Palace, this is what you wouldn't tell me.”

Kereth sighed. “Yes. Ever since you arrived, I've thought about that meeting. I'm sorry I couldn't tell you, Tim.”

“You did what you had to.”

“I'm sorry all the same.”

Dappler nodded and then met his eyes. A slight smile creased his face, and he shook his head. “Back to business, General?”

Kereth grinned. “Of course. I became a general, Tim, and I still have to work.”

“Should have been promoted in peacetime.”

Kereth looked over at the recruits. “The foot soldiers of our war. Our irregulars. Little did they know what they were getting into.”

“When do any of us?”

For a moment Kereth was struck by the truth of that. He looked at the desolation of Revlan, sky and bare ground stretching out beyond every horizon, and he said a prayer for the years ahead.

Book III

Since the founding of the Empire

Year 701

CHAPTER

I

* * * * * * * * * * * * * * * *

"DOES Chief Kinlol know about this?"

Adon Kereth looked over at Thaddaeus Gaelin and shook his head. "No. And why should he? I'm entirely within the authority the emperor gave me."

"Maybe, but when he finds what you're planning for a mere commando, he will not be happy with you."

"He won't find out what I'm planning. He'll find out what I've done. And I will have you remember that D'John Ryanson is no 'mere commando'. He is the best commando we have, and the finest officer that Dappler trained. He is, in a word, the cream of his crop."

"Yes, but what crop?"

"Meaning?"

Thaddaeus looked frustrated. "Recruits!"

Kereth glanced at him and looked away. Outside of his father's shadow, taking a place among Alexander's highest advisors, Thaddaeus had grown in self-confidence—or at least in boldness. And Kereth approved of such changes in anyone. But sometimes Thaddaeus showed the easy, cultured superiority of elites. "And I will have you remember that all our success is owed to recruits who became soldiers, commandos, and spies."

And that success had been considerable, given their circumstances. It was nearly eight months after Vonran began the siege of Tokar before they launched their first operation. Now, more than two years later, they had harmed and harassed Vonran out of much of his advantage. And they had thoroughly exhausted the people's tolerance for the war. All the while, they had escaped detection. Not bad at all.

Kereth strode down the corridors of the Revlan base, Thaddaeus following along behind him and matching his strides. They came at last to the overhead observatory of the shooting range. Kereth walked up to the parapet and looked down, searching the range.

He found him. “There.” He pointed, and Thaddaeus gave a casual glance downward. He was obviously unimpressed with the sight of the soldier practicing his marksmanship, but Kereth watched closely. He followed the bright bolts from the soldier's gun to their targets and took in a breath in appreciation. “A fine shot,” he said. “Almost as good as I am.” He turned to Thaddaeus. “Go down and bring him up.”

Thaddaeus looked still unsure of this venture, but he went without a word. Kereth backed away from the parapet so that Ryanson wouldn't know he had been watching him, and he stood erect.

He heard the sound of boots on metal stairs behind him, but he didn't turn. After a moment Ryanson and Thaddaeus came into his sight. Thaddaeus abandoned Ryanson, coming to stand a little to Kereth's right, and Ryanson presented himself military-style.

Kereth returned the salute. “At ease,” he commanded. He had met Ryanson already, and not by mistake. Tim Dappler had kept an eye on him, and so had Kereth. Now he looked Ryanson over critically. A year or so older than Cormac, Ryanson was still young. He was ruddy, with dark hair and dark eyes. His dark green uniform was clean and straightened, his boots were polished, and his sidearm was holstered in plain view. Kereth could just see the defining lines of muscles through his sleeves. Ryanson stood with proper respect, but not awe.

Handsome, but not pretty. Neat, but not dandified. Confident, but respectful. Cheerful and friendly—but an expert commando and a deadly marksman.

Yes, he would do fine.

"Captain Ryanson," Kereth began, "I have asked you here to discuss your next mission with you."

Ryanson looked at him and then glanced over at Thaddaeus. And when he looked back at Kereth, all he said was, "Yes, sir."

Elymas Vonran took out two glasses—crystal, delicately crafted. He poured each half full of dark vynas, and then he took the cups. Turning to Garin Dorjan, he offered him one and then sat down on the couch, taking a sip.

Dorjan sat across from him. "What's wrong, Elymas? You look tired."

"So do you."

Dorjan shook his head ruefully. "It's the bad news, Elymas. It keeps coming, and the war goes on." He deliberated a moment, then said, "I'm not seeking re-election. I'm going to step down after my term is finished."

"Why?"

"Because it's not fun anymore. You're gone from the Assembly, busy with matters of war and peace, and Declan is in Carsyt. Even Shevyn isn't what he used to be. He used to be a much more sporting enemy, and Ziphernan is gone altogether. I don't suppose you ever found out where he went?"

Vonran shrugged. "Not for certain."

"The word is that he defected to Alexander."

"I know. That's what my intelligence officers consider most probable. But no one can confirm it." Ziphernan had disappeared more than two years earlier, and Intelligence still couldn't tell Vonran for certain where he was. They had conducted a thorough investigation, even taking in Ziphernan's wife in order to question her. She claimed complete ignorance, and if some in Intelligence had their doubts, Vonran didn't. He could easily believe that Ziphernan had abandoned his wife without a word of explanation. The scum.

"So, Elymas." Dorjan's voice was exaggeratedly casual. "When did you last see Theseus?"

"I don't know." But it was a lie. Vonran did know the last time he had seen Declan—right after coming back to Telnaria from Hyatha. He hadn't even gone to the farewell party they had held after he resigned.

Dorjan watched him carefully. "I want to speak frankly to you, Elymas, as one friend to another."

Conversations that began like that were always unpleasant, but Vonran answered, "Go ahead."

"Elymas, you have to end this war. For two years Alexander's forces have been attacking, and the people have grown weary of news of battle and death. How many soldiers have died? It presses on them. And they are growing nervous. They are nervous because the rebels have expanded their attacks outside of Regial, and because of the Treason Statutes. You may need such laws to stop traitors and spies, but it makes the people afraid. They are anxious about being misunderstood—or having an enemy settle a grudge—and then being investigated or questioned. You must end the war and lift the War Powers. The Empire will not endure much more."

"I know, Garin."

Dorjan still looked at him anxiously. "It must be done now, Elymas. The Assembly is murmuring and the people are becoming mutinous. Many think—many say privately—that you should abdicate to Alexander."

"Is that what you think?"

"I think you should end the war. However you do it makes no difference to me."

"I know, Garin," Vonran repeated.

"What are you going to do?"

Vonran looked at him—the only real friend he had. "I have called my war council together. Something will change. I promise you, I will not let the status quo remain."

"Will you abdicate?"

Never. Vonran cocked his head, looking at Dorjan, and then he drank from his cup. "We will see."

Aside from Vonran there were five men at the table—Chief of Intelligence Elad Zephon, Zidon Adesh, General Telai the commander of the forces in the field, the Chief Counselor, and the Chief of Justice.

This was his war council, and they were all in trouble.

Vonran opened the meeting. "I am sure you all know of the rebels' recent attack on a supply convoy journeying to Regial. It was a success paralleled only by all the other successes they have had over the past two years." Vonran let that sink in, then concluded, "Gentlemen, the fight against the rebels is a disgrace."

At this rebuke they were silent. Then Adesh rapped his knuckles against the table. "If I may, Regent, the military is fighting them wherever they can be found. The difficulty is in finding them."

"In other words, Adesh, it is not your fault. But whose fault is it, then?"

"As you would tell us, Regent, placing blame is secondary. But we must pinpoint the problem, and the problem we are having is in intelligence. The rebels know what we are going to do and where and when we are going to do it. It allows them to prepare. It allows them to win. They choose the time and place of our confrontations—while we cannot. We haven't yet been able to chase the fox to his hole."

"I know we haven't been able to find the rebel bases," Zephon answered. "But that is because we haven't been able to find a traitor. Everyone in the insurgency is there by a deliberate choice, made in support for Alexander."

"The issue, Zephon," Vonran told him, "is not only that we don't know their movements. It's that we can't even keep them from knowing ours."

"For that, there are many people in the government—and the military, and the public—who are sympathetic to Alexander. Like all successful insurgencies, this one has a populace that helps them."

"That is one of our primary problems," Adesh said. "Traitors and spies on every hand."

"The Treason Statutes are in full effect," the Chief of Justice, Gamaliel, told him. "We are already doing all we can."

Adesh looked at him with cold-eyed scorn. "All you can?"

The other man wavered under the response. "All that the law permits."

"Then the law does not permit enough—if it is the law and not craven counsel that inhibits us from dealing with filthy quislings."

The Chief began to grow angry. "We have punished many people and questioned many more."

"But the people," Adesh answered, "still are not afraid to help Alexander."

"Is that our business now? Making the people afraid?"

"Our business is winning, or so I thought."

Vonran looked at Adesh and appreciated the clarity. "If you have a new policy to propose, Chief Adesh, put it into writing and circulate it among the Council. Now we must face the issue—how to adjust our strategy."

"I had intended," Zephon said, "to wait to see if the plan bore fruit before telling you, but Intelligence has been trying to discover the rebels' hiding place. An agent of ours has managed to infiltrate their network, but he has no idea yet where their base is."

"And their leadership?"

Zephon shook his head. "Unknown. We are sure that General Gaelin is in Tokar, and we believe that Adon Kereth is leading the insurgency. General Kereth, they call him. But we still have no certain word on where Chief Kinlol and Alexander are. If Kereth could escape Mela, so could they."

"And Alexander probably did," Vonran said.

"Most likely," Zephon agreed.

"Which makes it all the more imperative that we find their hiding place. But even then they would have a strong hold-out." Vonran turned to Telai and Adesh. "How goes the siege?"

"Tokar will soon break," Adesh answered. "Within a year Gaelin's forces will fail."

Telai glanced at his commander-in-chief and then at the regent. "That is our most conservative estimate. We think it more likely to be a matter of weeks—months at most. Tokar is in an economic depression and has been for a year at least. Soon they will no longer be able to maintain their strength against us, even if they want to. But we have another concern."

"What is that?"

"That Gaelin's forces will melt away and join the guerrilla warfare against us. If that happens, our victory will be hollow."

"The solution, General, is simple. Do not allow his forces to melt away. Destroy them—and destroy him. Devastate the opposition in Tokar so that it is eliminated forever."

"We may have to break the siege, then, rather than waiting for them to fall," Adesh said. "If Gaelin is planning to turn his regular army into an irregular one, we must act preemptively so that he cannot carry out his plans."

"Develop a strategy," Vonran ordered him. "Keep me appraised of your progress." He turned to Zephon. "And it is on you, Chief Zephon, to discover the rebels' hiding place."

Zephon bowed his head. "I hear and obey, my lord."

They were just another two men hurrying through the crowded streets of the city. No one watching the passersby would have picked them out. Treason is a notable distinction, but often an invisible one.

Adon Kereth saw the tavern and wove his way to it through the people. He had enough confidence in D'John Ryanson's abilities to know for sure he was following.

Within minutes they were inside, looking around the tavern. Kereth glanced over at D'John and saw just a hint of leeriness in his face before he smoothed it away. Kereth swept a casual gaze over the room, looking for the source of D'John's unease. He saw nothing but a tavern, the musicians, the customers, the bar, the drinks ...

Kereth guessed, and he resisted taking another glance at D'John. He must have had a moral upbringing—and some allegiance to those morals, if after two years of war a drinking establishment made him uneasy.

Kereth led the way to a small table against the wall. He took his seat and glanced at the menu installed on the left end of the table, against the wall. As he selected a Takari ale—a mild drink—he asked D'John, "What do you want?"

"Nothing, thanks."

Kereth entered the order and settled back in his chair. Their contact for this meeting was to approach them, and that meant they had nothing to do for the moment but wait.

After a few moments D'John spoke. "Are you sure you want me to do all the talking?"

Kereth nodded. "From beginning to end. This is our fifth contact; you should know what to do."

He gave him a dubious look and complied, "Yes, sir."

A young woman came up to the table, carrying a tray with a tall glass of ale and a cup of water. She set the ale before Kereth, the water before D'John, and asked, "Are you gentlemen on your way to Traelys?"

A little surprised, Kereth looked at her and then over at D'John.

He answered her, "No, we just came from there."

"Where did you start from?"

"Telnaria."

"Where are you going now?"

"Sikor. Do you know the best way to go by?"

"Go north until you reach a small town, then turn east down the road. You should reach the city three hundred miles down. You will see beech trees at the edge."

D'John nodded to her. "Thank you."

"You're welcome." She walked away from them.

The two men looked at each other. Kereth wanted to remark on the cleverness of this contact, but he decided to keep the observation for safer territory. They lingered in the tavern long enough for Kereth to finish his ale, and he was careful not to hurry through. Then he paid the bill and they were off.

Following their instructions, they went north down the city's main street until they came into a residential district. They turned onto the first avenue that ran to the east, and three houses down they stopped. The house had gables white as beech trees.

Kereth didn't move. He waited for D'John to take the lead, and after a moment he did. He went up the steps of the house and pressed the caller's pad. In a moment the door opened, and D'John said to the man who stood there, "We came from Telnaria to Traelys, and now we are going to Sikor. We were told this is the way to go by."

The man looked at D'John, then Kereth. Then he nodded. "Come in."

They followed him inside, to a room with nine people in it. D'John stopped, facing them, and Kereth took a position behind him. And D'John began, introducing himself as a representative of Emperor Alexander and doing the work of establishing another cell.

It was the middle of the morning by the time of Revlan's base. Everyone would be awake and about their work. Kereth—having survived seven secret rendezvous with co-conspirators in enemy territory—would now have to face Kinlol. He knew that the Chief would have gotten curious about his absence, and in four questions get the whole truth of the matter from Thaddaeus.

Kereth stood up. "Captain?"

D'John, in the pilot's seat, looked back at him. "Yes, sir?"

"You will have the day free, except for writing your report and being debriefed on your next mission—and one other thing." Kereth jerked his head towards the hatch. "Come on."

When they reached the far end of the hangar, they found Thaddaeus Gaelin standing there. "A fair day to you, General Kereth. And to you, Captain," he added, turning to D'John. The Gaelins may have been elitists, but they were well-bred elitists.

"Likewise," Kereth returned. "Have you seen the emperor?"

"Not since this morning's consultation. Chief Kinlol is wanting to see you," Thaddaeus added, and Kereth could tell he knew why. Thaddaeus had begun as the official intermediary between his father and Kinlol, and he had become the unofficial intermediary between Kinlol and Kereth. Both men had taken to telling him their plans and activities, knowing that in a short time the other would question Thaddaeus and hear everything. Kinlol and Kereth understood the arrangement, and Thaddaeus understood it, too. If he objected to being a messenger between Alexander's most powerful advisors, he never showed it.

"I'll speak with him soon enough. Come, Captain." Kereth went through the hangar's doors, with D'John following and Thaddaeus joining. He went to the north side of the Revlan base where they had established the royal province. The area was closed off to most people on the base, without explanation, and there Alexander and Kinlol spent most of their time.

Kereth made his way to what could loosely be called the emperor's office, and he was admitted by the guard. Going inside, he found Alexander sitting at his desk with Kinlol standing behind him. Both of them had turned all their attention to Kereth and his small procession. Kinlol watched with disapproval; Alexander with interest.

Kereth presented himself in front of the desk, bowing to Alexander. "My lord, I have come to present to you Captain D'John Ryanson. He is the most skilled of all your commandos and the most outstanding of all your officers commissioned since the war began. With your permission, my lord, I will make him your spokesman to our covert cells within the Empire and Regial."

Kinlol rewarded Kereth with a look of veiled irritation, and Kereth knew him well enough to hear the unspoken promise: *Wait until I get you outside the emperor's presence.*

But Alexander studied D'John with increased interest, and he motioned him to come forward. D'John did—and, following Kereth's example, he bowed and greeted Alexander, "My lord."

Kereth studied D'John's expression and caught a hint of vague uncertainty. For a long moment Alexander gazed at D'John, and then he said, "I will consider your recommendation, General. In fact, I will interview him. Right now." And he made an imperial gesture—doubtless learned from Kinlol—dismissing everyone else.

The three—Thaddaeus, Kinlol, and Kereth—promptly left the room. Outside, Kinlol turned on Kereth. "You did not wait for my recommendation before presenting Ryanson to the emperor."

"I didn't need to, Kinlol. I already knew it. You are opposed."

Thaddaeus—showing the discretion that would take him far—chose this time to leave, going away from them down the corridor.

"You oppose the idea," Kereth went on. "I support it. The emperor will decide."

"General ... " Kinlol glanced at the guard, and then turned and began walking in the opposite direction Thaddaeus had gone. After they had put a little distance between them and the guard, Kinlol said, "General, we cannot make the boy our representative."

"Not to be querulous, but he would be Alexander's representative, not ours."

"You *are* being querulous. You know what I mean. That boy cannot represent us—the emperor, our entire cause—to all our operatives."

" 'That boy' has led men into combat, he has fought and killed. No one who has taken responsibility for the lives of his friends and the deaths of his enemies should be called a boy."

"Then he is a man unqualified to be our representative. Do you know the responsibility of being the emperor's ambassador?"

"I do. It will make him a leader to our underground movement. It is good for them to have a leader in the real, and not only in the abstract."

"I won't argue that point. But if they must have a leader, why not Thaddaeus?"

"We don't need a Telnarian elitist for every important task. D'John is more than qualified. He is young, well-spoken, and good-looking. He is an officer, a warrior, and a leader. Because he is unknown to Vonran's government—and because of his training—he will be able to carry on covert work much more safely than you or me or even Thaddaeus. And if he is caught—well, at least Emperor Alexander will not have lost one of his chief officials."

Kinlol stared at him. "That's cold."

"That's war."

"And how old is your officer, warrior, leader?"

Kereth was a little reluctant to admit it. "Twenty-three."

"Twenty-three?" Kinlol echoed.

Kereth didn't answer. He knew well enough.

"So you would have this task put in the hands of a twenty-three-year-old."

"You would have had the emperorship put in the hands of a seventeen-year-old."

"That's a different matter entirely."

"Is it? Kinlol, I remember your arguments in favor of putting a seventeen-year-old on the throne, and I am not above throwing every one in your face."

Kinlol looked at him carefully. "I suppose I can agree—if he will be fine."

"He will be fine. He will be perfect."

Kinlol shrugged, but it looked stiff. "Very well. I will not advise the emperor to reject your proposal. I will only caution him as to its liabilities. And if turns out badly—it will be on your head."

"What a gracious agreement."

"It's agreement, and that's enough."

Kereth held up a hand. "All right. I never said I wouldn't take it. I take all agreements, no matter how ungracious."

Kinlol looked at Kereth like he wasn't quite sure what to do with that remark—or him.

Alexander fiddled with the keys of his compad, pretending to work. His mind kept returning to D'John Ryanson, standing stiffly in front of him in his army fatigues, a sidearm strapped to his thigh.

He envied him. That surprised Alexander, but he couldn't deny it. He had approved General Kereth's plan for Ryanson, and the captain had left for his first mission—and an important one, at that. Alexander could wish that their places were switched just for the next few days, that he was the one on a mission and Ryanson was desk-bound.

Alexander idly accessed a file, skimmed over its words without thinking about them. He could hear Kereth and Kinlol's voices coming from behind him. They didn't always argue, but somehow even their discussions sounded like arguments.

Kereth had taken the floor from Kinlol: “There is no question that Gaelin cannot hold out much longer. Tokar will fall soon. Vonran is ready to pounce. We can't let him have his way with them.”

“How can we stop him? We still can't challenge Vonran in conventional warfare, and you have thought of no irregular operations that can turn the tide of the battle.”

“What about Arkin? What good can we get from Sameeva?”

“Be pleased to remember that we don't even have a treaty with King Arkin.”

“And why not? After spending nine months sipping fine wine with Arkin and his court lackeys, Ziphernan should have something to give us.”

“Like Arkin's army?”

“That would be nice.”

Alexander tuned them out again. This was a running argument between the two—Nemin Ziphernan and his efforts at securing a treaty of mutual aid with Arkin, king of Sameeva. Kereth was impatient with Ziphernan's progress, and Kinlol—perhaps out of sheer habit—took the opposing viewpoint. Alexander had often wondered how the two ended up on the same side.

What brought his attention back to them again was the sound of the door opening. He looked up to see Kinlol leaving and Kereth following, and he called, “General!”

Kereth turned back to him. “Yes, my lord?”

“There's something I want to discuss with you.”

Kereth returned obediently, drawing a seat opposite to Alexander. “What is it?”

Alexander looked down again, trying to formulate his thoughts. “I am wondering if perhaps I should go out.”

“Out?”

“On a mission.”

“You mean as a commando or a spokesman to the underground? Like D'John Ryanson?”

“Yes. Like that. Perhaps if the soldiers knew that I fought

with them ... ”

Kereth looked at him, his eyes disturbingly keen. “You are young,” he pronounced, “and you are bored. You want to be where the action is. You want to fight—like D'John Ryanson. But you are not D'John Ryanson. He is a common man, and his life is his own. He can use it and gamble it as he pleases. You are the emperor; you must live for your people, and you must not gamble your life. If you die, the house of Alheenan will die with you, and the Empire will be given over to anarchy. The people will be left to the mercy of whoever manages to seize power. Most likely it would be Vonran—and we have seen what kind of ruler he is. You must remain where you are safe; you cannot put the people at risk.”

Alexander found himself looking at his compad again, wanting to rebel and finding no grounds to do it on.

“Do you remember when you and I played chess?”

Alexander looked up at Kereth, a little surprised at the question. “That was a long time ago,” he murmured.

“Do you remember how the first rule was to always protect your king, because if you lost him you lost the game?”

For some reason that stung. “The king was essential. He was also useless.”

“No, Alexander. He is the only indispensable player on the board—and therefore is protected at all costs. You have your place, Alexander, and your duty. No station is without its disadvantages.”

Alexander nodded dully, in unwilling acceptance.

Kereth stood up. “It is hard sometimes. But remember that every station has its advantages, too, and not least yours. Wait until you really are emperor.”

Zelrynn Vonran riffled through the pages and then pushed the book aside. She glanced up at the clock. Even for her father this was late.

She stood up and began pacing through the private library. After her father came back from the debacle in Regial, he moved out of the Palace's guest wing and took over the Royal Family's residence. It had disturbed her at the time, and even after three years she still wasn't used to it. She never felt at home in the royal residence; in these rooms she felt like a stranger, almost an intruder.

Taking one last look at the clock, Zelrynn shook her head and left the room. She had hoped to see her father tonight, but if he intended to spend all hours of the night in his office, she would just go to bed. Cala already had.

As Zelrynn stepped lightly through the corridor, walking along one wall, she heard voices ahead. Curious, and a little apprehensive, she moved forward cautiously. The corridor made a ninety-degree turn, but just as she came to it the words coming from beyond became distinct.

"Gamaliel's counsel is weak. He has no stomach to deal harshly, even with traitors. They are destroying us, and the old coward equivocates and frets."

The voice was familiar, and after a moment Zelrynn placed it: Zidon Adesh. What was he doing—

"I know you think that way." That was her father's voice, calm and controlled. "And again I say: If you have a new policy to recommend, formulate it and submit it for review."

There was a pause, and then Adesh answered, "I have heard of two soldiers convicted in a court-martial for treason. With your permission, I will deal with them as traitors should be dealt with. Only two men, Regent. An ... experiment, if you will, to see the effectiveness of my technique."

Adesh's words sent a chill tingling up Zelrynn's spine, and she knew that whatever Adesh planned to do—whatever punishment he would not name—was something terrible. She waited, heart pounding faster, for her father to break his silence and forbid Adesh to carry out his plan.

After a long moment he answered. "Very well."

Zelrynn stepped away, and after a moment of indecision went back to the library. She found herself standing by the long table again, picking up the same book she had just put down. She saw the words printed on the page, and she heard the words her father and Adesh had just spoken. An experiment ...

The conversation turned furiously through her mind, but

something interrupted her thoughts and she looked up, startled.

Her father was standing in the doorway, looking at her. And though she hadn't seen him in months, she made no move to close the distance between them. Zelrynn found herself studying her father's face. Was it her imagination, or was the set of his mouth harder than it had been?

"I'm surprised you're still awake," he said. "It's very late."

"No later for me than it is for you."

He smiled a little. "Such is the peril of teaching your children logic. I am defeated."

The smile, and the comment, eased the tension that had tightened its grip around her. This was like the father she knew. "At least you taught me well." Zelrynn deliberately turned shut the book, and she said, "I am going to the Library of Tinath in a few days. I will do research for the university there. But in the meantime, I am thinking about taking a holiday. Why don't you and Cala come with me?"

"Cala can go if she wants, but"—she knew the words before he said them—"I have work to do."

"When was the last time you had a holiday, Father? It would do you good to rest, to get away from Telnaria. It will clear your perspective."

"My perspective is fine."

After hearing him acquiesce to Adesh, Zelrynn knew that wasn't true. "It would do you good."

"Now you sound like your mother. I can't leave, Zelrynn. I have important work."

He always had important work. "I understand. Are things worse in Regial?"

"Hopefully, Zelrynn, they will soon be getting better."

CHAPTER

II

* * * * * * * * * * * * * * * * *

THE house was large and splendidly lit. The light spilled from the house onto the lawn, and even from the street D'John Ryanson could hear the sound of music and voices.

He stared at the house and slowly took in a breath. He had stopped his hired hovcar a full two miles from his destination, not wanting to give anyone that knowledge. General Kereth had assured him that this was as reliable an arrangement as any, that other agents had carried it off before with no trouble. He still worried, and he was hiding his trail as thoroughly as possible.

No hesitancy, he thought. *Act. Act like you belong.* D'John strode up to the property, stepping on the multi-stoned pathway that led up to the house. He walked up the steps and stopped at the open doorway, turning to the doorman who had been eyeing him since he entered the grounds. "Naphtali Malik," he said.

The doorman consulted a compad, then stepped aside. "You may go in."

"Thank you." D'John walked into the house, and into a world he had never known.

It looked like a palace to his inexperienced eye, a gleaming hall which opened into music-filled rooms. And it teemed with people, their very appearances proclaiming wealth and sophistication.

D'John was dressed just as finely as they were. When he had

first put on the clothes he had felt silly. Now he felt like a hypocrite whose masquerade was obvious to the world. These people brought a feeling of terrible awkwardness on him, and the thought rang through his mind: *You're not in Nomu anymore.*

Remembering his mission—and so, to some extent, forgetting himself—he gathered his confidence and strode in. He made his way through the crowd, and to his relief no one took any notice of him. Halfway through the hall he finally saw a face he recognized, if only from pictures.

Trey Uman, once Chief of the Treasury, a conspirator against Vonran to this day. D'John approached him, and when Uman's attention turned to him, he gave the recognition phrase: "I just got in from Armanas."

"And I'm glad that you did, Naphtali. I am pleased to welcome you to my home on such a gala occasion."

"It's positively glittering."

Uman smiled and placed his hand on D'John's shoulder, guiding him away. "How is the weather in Armanas?" he asked, keeping his voice low so that D'John could hear him beneath the noise of the crowd.

"Still stormy, but with signs that it may clear up."

Uman nodded. "Come, Naphtali. There is someone I wanted to introduce to you. He is close to your age, young friend."

D'John followed Uman as he led him into one of the rooms leading off from the hall. His heart was beating faster, but not only because Uman was taking him to meet the insurgency's contact from Telnaria. This strange, glamorous world was nearly blinding him with its brilliance.

In a short time D'John could tell whom Uman was taking him to meet—a man, noticeably older than himself but still young, pale-skinned and golden-headed. When they reached him, Uman said, "Kile, this is the man from Armanas I wanted you to meet—Naphtali Malik. Naphtali, this is Kile Metan."

Metan regarded him coldly. "As in the Metan family—you have heard of our corporate empire."

Metan's voice gave the lie to his words, and D'John knew

that Metan didn't really think he had heard of his family. D'John could tell that this man belonged to the world he was in—and that Metan knew, or had guessed, that D'John didn't. And it raised his hackles, so that he replied, "You must be very proud of your ancestors."

Metan's expression flickered. Uman spoke. "I will leave you two to pursue your business together."

D'John caught the underlying command, and he turned to Metan as Uman walked away. Metan nodded for him to follow and then strode briskly away. In a short time they were in a small side-room, comfortably furnished as a sitting area. As the door closed behind them, Metan turned to D'John. "You are Emperor Alexander's representative?"

"You are the Telnarian contact?"

His tone was a little haughty. "Self-evidently."

D'John controlled himself and, as Trey Uman had told him, pursued business. "I was told that some prominent men of Telnaria and Traelys were joining league against Vonran. The emperor sent me to liaison with that league, and they apparently sent you. What do you have to tell the emperor and his commanders?"

"You may tell Emperor Alexander that we support his claim against Vonran, and we wish to see him take the throne as quickly as possible. To that end we offer our services. I have been sent with a list of all the men in our alliance—the only such list in existence."

"We have protected greater secrets."

Metan looked at D'John as if he disdained his confidence, but he reached to his belt and, after his fingers worked for a moment, drew out an info chip.

Metan watched D'John after he took it, and he asked, "What do you plan to do?"

"Emperor Alexander and his commanders will decide how to use your services—after we establish your trustworthiness."

Metan looked personally offended. "Are you impugning our integrity?"

D'John looked at him. "No." Deciding that that statement should be enough to close the matter, he moved on. "Do you have anything else you want me to report to Emperor Alexander?"

"No."

"Then I will say good-bye." Without waiting for a reply, D'John left the room. General Kereth had decided to make contact with the Traelys-Telnaria league through Trey Uman, at an enormous social gathering. He had told D'John that the party would last so long, and have so many guests, that no one would notice him coming and going. With that assurance D'John left immediately.

He had been given some information about Trey Uman and his involvement in the fight against Vonran, and it was enough to put him on his guard. Nemin Ziphernan had joined the insurgency through Uman, and shortly afterward Vonran's Intelligence had put him under surveillance. Uman remained in contact with Kereth, but largely inactive. Largely; not completely. Apparently Vonran had no proof against him. If he had, Uman would have been taken by Intelligence already. But however elusive Uman had proved to be to Vonran, D'John was still a little nervous at meeting with a man under suspicion at his own house—even if he threw the social event of the month to cover that fact.

D'John walked through the neighborhood, retracing the two miles he had walked earlier. He came into the business district and made his way to the alley where he had stashed a change of clothes earlier in the day. A trash incinerator was at the end of the alley, taller than D'John and nearly as wide as the alley.

D'John cautiously slid his hand into the narrow gap between the incinerator and the building next to it. Though it had been turned off hours earlier it was still warm.

His hand caught hold of the bundle, and he pulled it out. Then, standing, he tossed the bundle over the incinerator. That committed him. As quietly as possible, he climbed up the incinerator and jumped onto the ground behind it. There was a small area between the incinerator and the alley wall, and D'John quickly changed his clothes in the darkness.

Again clothed normally, he went back the way he had come, throwing over the clothing and then climbing over himself. He turned his wristlight on long enough to wrap his fancy clothes in the bundle-cloth and toss it into the incinerator. When it was turned on the next day, it would destroy the evidence of how he had been dressed and where he had gone.

Going on from there, D'John hired a hovcar to take him to the spaceport where he had docked his ship. There was little traffic in the port at this hour, and he went directly to the man on duty. The man glanced up at him, with an interest that raised a feeling of uneasiness in D'John. “How may I help you?” he asked.

“I want to un-dock my ship.”

“Name?”

“Malik, Naphtali.”

The man looked at him keenly, and a light sprang up in his eyes. Then, a little too casually: “You may go ahead, sir.” He slipped his hand beneath the counter, and D'John tensed, waiting for him to draw out a weapon. But he drew his hand back, and it was empty.

D'John nodded. “Thank you.” He walked a few paces away, alarms going off furiously in his mind. Then he turned back. “Is the cafe still open?”

“The cafe is open twenty-four hours a day.”

“Great.” D'John strode across the lobby, into a corridor branching away from it. Then—relieved to be out of the clerk's sight, relieved he hadn't shot at him as he walked away—he began looking for an escape. There were men waiting for him somewhere in this port, and he had to get out.

He walked down the corridor, his eyes combing every part of it. He saw a door with a word written on the wall above it—EMPLOYEES.

D'John slowed, looking at the door, looking at its sign. It was interesting, when he thought of it, how such a simple instruction could keep everyone—all the ordinary, decent people—from even thinking of entering ...

He was through the door in moments, barely pausing to palm the open-pad. Of course the door wasn't locked. Who would go into the employees-only section of a business?

D'John found himself in another hallway, with rooms without doors leading off from it. He sauntered down the hallway as if he belonged, eyes taking in everything. If they thought he was heading to the cafe it might throw them off, but not for long. When he arrived at neither his ship nor the cafe they would start looking for him. And he had no idea of their set-up, how many men there were—

Again the hallway opened up, but not to a room. It was a short hallway, with a double-wide door at the end and not a single other door.

That looked like an exit. Hoping, D'John went down the hall, palmed the open-pad, and watched as the door opened up to darkness. D'John stepped outside, and as the door closed behind him he hurried forward—

His legs connected with something hard, and he fell flat on his face. Muttering wordlessly—and very unhappily—D'John pushed himself to a sitting position and rubbed his shins. He would have some fine bruises the next day.

D'John didn't move, waiting while his eyes adjusted to the light. He could make out quite a few dark shapes in the pale moonlight—some large, some small. He was outside, but where *was* he?

It didn't matter. He was leaving. D'John got to his feet and cautiously—and quickly as he dared—got moving. After going a little while he figured out where he was: a junkyard of spare parts.

He picked his way past the clutter, coming at last to a wall. He quickly climbed up, balanced on the top for an instant, and then jumped over.

He landed on solid ground, and his first reaction was relief, for he had not looked before he leaped. The next instant that was wiped away, as the sound of an alarm filled the air—and he knew that he had triggered it.

D'John crossed the street, staying close against the next building as he ran swiftly and silently away.

It had been a long night. D'John had spent it on the move—looking for a way out, a place to hide, anything. Twice he had come within earshot of his pursuers, and even now he was sure they were nearby.

And now it was daylight. D'John's wanderings had taken him to an assemblage of stately buildings rising in the middle of huge, rolling, green lawns.

Ilemor University, the most prestigious institute of learning in the Empire. D'John took in the place with dismay, but he joined the stream of people and let it carry him into one of the buildings. He paused briefly in the wide corridor, selected a door at random in the space of two seconds, and strode through it with great purpose.

He found himself in a lecture hall, and the lecture seemed about to begin. D'John chose a seat as far back as he could while not setting himself apart from the other students. D'John looked towards the front of the hall, and he saw a man about his own age fiddling with something on a high, narrow desk.

At first he assumed it was another student. After a long moment he realized it was the professor.

A huge holograph appeared above the desk—an old map. The professor stepped back and, still looking at the holograph, began to speak. "Today's lecture is about the Calution uprisings. To understand these events we must understand the political and social climate they occurred in. The situation was complex, formed by the preceding era of turmoil and societal metastasis ... "

D'John resisted the urge to lean forward and thump his head against the table. It had been a long night; it promised to be a long morning, too.

By sheer will D'John remained in an upright position, eyes focused on the professor as if he cared about the Calution uprisings. The professor didn't turn away from the holograph. He stood with his back to his students, talking steadily, clearly, and without inflection.

And as D'John watched he noticed something even stranger: He found the lecture interesting.

When the professor finished, the students collected their compads and headed out. D'John went in the opposite direction. There was one long, narrow aisle leading down to the front, and D'John went down it. He came within feet of the professor as he gathered his things, calculating his position to be directly in the professor's line of vision. The professor took no notice of him.

D'John cleared his throat. No reaction. Finally he spoke. “Professor, I arrived late at the university this term. This is your first lecture I heard.” D'John paused, trying to tell if the man took this statement at face value. Because he didn't even glance in D'John's direction, it was impossible to know. “I would like to be able to hear your earlier lectures.” Again he got no reaction, and he wondered if he was speaking to a deaf man. But the notion had to be dismissed. There was no reason for such a condition to go uncured. D'John tried one last time: “Do you have recordings I could hear?”

Finally the professor looked at him. “No. But I have transcriptions. Follow.”

D'John did, puzzled by him but hopeful that he was being taken to his office.

He was. Once they were in the room, the professor went immediately to his desk without a word to D'John. As he began digging through a drawer, D'John looked around the room.

There was nothing to see. The only items in the room were a desk, chairs, and cabinets. The walls were completely bare—no pictures, no diplomas, no decorations of any kind.

“Do you have a compad?”

The question brought D'John's attention back to his host, who was sitting with compad in hand, ready to make a data transfer.

“No.”

The professor looked at him, then at his compad. And he held it out to D'John.

D'John stepped forward and accepted it, watching the professor as he bent down over his desk, burrowing into some sort of work.

D'John looked at him, weighing his newly acquired compad in his hand while weighing his options in his mind. He had wanted to lay low in Ilemor for a good part of the day—perhaps all of it, and then continue by night. With luck they would search past him, but if they did come to Ilemor he was much more likely to escape them in a private room than a public one. He wanted to linger at Ilemor, and it would be nice to do it in this office as long as possible.

“Professor,” D'John began, and when the professor looked

up D'John realized he had nothing to say. He looked at the professor and noticed that his skin was white—not like someone who was naturally light but like someone who didn't get enough sun. The first comment that came into D'John's mind was: *You're a strange bird.* He went with his second thought. “I don't believe you're much older than I am. How did you become a professor at a university like this at your age?”

D'John expected it to be a sensitive point. He didn't get even a flicker of response. “My acumen is superior to that of the vast majority of the population.”

There was no hint of pride or even pleasure, and so the statement didn't sound arrogant. In fact, it almost sounded dull. “Ah. I see. Well, I would like to say that, as interesting and informative as your lecture was, it missed the point. The people didn't revolt because of the Belis reforms—at least not directly. They revolted because they were hungry. The only thing the reforms had to do with it was contributing to the depression in the region.”

For the first time the professor really looked at him. “My lectures are based on a thesis I wrote specifically to get a professorship at this university. I defended it against tenured professors, and I won.” D'John braced himself for the slap-down. “Explain your theory.”

“Ah ... ” This was exactly the response D'John had wanted, and it caught him flat-footed. “What makes normal citizens rebel ... ”

D'John was interrupted by the ping of a comm, and the professor pressed something on his desk. “Yes?”

“Professor Anderliy? This is Administrator Braxen.”

D'John frowned at the woman's voice. Despite her clear, smooth tone, she sounded shaken. He quietly walked forward, closing the distance between him and the desk.

“Yes?” the professor—Anderliy—asked again.

“Intelligence agents are making an inquiry.”

D'John's hand slipped beneath his clothing and wrapped around his sidearm. He leaned his body forward slightly as Braxen went on, “They are looking for a fugitive, and they think he may be here. Is anyone with you in your office?”

With his left hand D'John swooped across the desk and pressed mute. With his right he pulled out his sidearm and trained it on Anderliy.

Anderliy looked up at him, and at the blaster.

"The answer," D'John told him, "is no." He hit mute again and waited, weapon ready.

Anderliy leaned forward and answered, "No."

D'John again muted their end as Braxen answered, "Well, good. Be wary of people you don't know."

"Sage advice," D'John said, experiencing irony. "Ask her if the inquiry will cause any disruption."

Anderliy obeyed. "Will they be disruptive?"

From the pause on the other end, D'John guessed the term had been badly chosen. Braxen answered cautiously, "The authorities will be here as long as they deem necessary. They may need to make a thorough search."

Translation: They might be here for a while, and they will probably get in the way. D'John nodded to Anderliy, who answered, "Thank you."

D'John swiped at the controls, cutting off. "Now, stand in front of me."

Looking at him intently, Anderliy stood up and circled around the desk. D'John watched him carefully, following his hands.

When Anderliy stood in front of him, he relaxed a little. "You have a vehicle around here?"

"Yes."

"Where?"

"In the underground hangar."

"Good. Well, I need a ride out of here, and you're it. Take me to your vehicle, and don't get clever. If you are tempted to try anything, remember that I am armed and I have nothing to lose. I'm running from certain death, and that does not make a man chary."

Anderliy just looked at him, with something that looked strangely like curiosity. D'John had sparked no other emotion.

D'John stared at him, and nearly told him he was strange again. Instead he told him, "Now march. Not too fast, not too slow, and I'll be right behind you."

Anderliy obeyed, and soon they were in the corridors of Ilemor University. D'John was alert to everything around him—his whole environment and all the people around him, including Anderliy. For all his hard words, he wasn't willing to shoot him if he tried to escape, and he could only hope that Anderliy didn't know that.

It felt like a long way down to the hangar. Finally they made it, and then they were at Anderliy's vehicle—a hovcar, and a rather unimpressive one. D'John stood by as Anderliy opened the hovcar and then ordered him, "Get in."

He did, and D'John followed. He turned around so that he had Anderliy in view and then drew out his blaster. "Close it." D'John watched while he obeyed and then said, "All right, front seat. You're driving. Take us out of here."

As Anderliy took the driver's seat, D'John sat in the second row, at the opposite end of the hovcar. He had a clear view of Anderliy and the controls, and he sat quietly as Anderliy took them out of the hangar. No one stopped them as they left the building, and that was a relief. No one stopped them as they left the grounds. The university receded out of view, and time began moving forward again.

D'John exhaled unconsciously and shook his head.

"Where?"

D'John jerked his head sharply to look at Anderliy. "What?"

"Where?" Anderliy repeated.

"Where do you live?"

"On the university grounds."

"Why?"

"Why not?"

D'John could tell him, but it wasn't worth it. "Never mind." That was one option ended. The only other agent for Alexander that D'John knew of in the city was Trey Uman, and he couldn't go to him. And he knew of no cells at all in the nearby cities.

So he was on his own. "I need to get off the planet."

"Spaceport, then?"

D'John almost felt irritated with him. “No. They'll be watching every spaceport within three hundred miles of here.” Every spaceport they knew of, at any rate. “Take me to the seedy part of town, to a tavern where all the low-lifes get together.”

“I don't know where that is.”

D'John looked at Anderliy. “I guess that was a stupid thing to say. Get a map.”

Anderliy worked on that, and D'John moved up to the front passenger seat. He watched the screen in the control board, and after a moment a map of the city came up. It didn't take long.

D'John indicated the place to Anderliy, saying, “We can expect to find a lot of people of low character who pursue illegal activities there.”

Anderliy glanced at it. “You're hiring a smuggler to ferry you off the planet.”

“Yes.” D'John looked at him and felt guilt souring in his stomach. “I'm going to let you go after I find a way off the planet. I don't plan to hurt you.” There was silence for a few minutes. And then D'John went on, “And in case I don't get a chance to later, I want to say I'm sorry. I'm sorry for threatening you, for hijacking your hovcar, for taking you captive, and for ruining your day.”

Anderliy was silent for a moment. “You're an insurgent, aren't you?”

“Yes. I fight for Alexander.”

“Then take me with you.”

“What?”

“I want to join the insurgency.”

“Why?”

“As a professor of socio-political history and theory, I know that Emperor Alexander is the lawful ruler and Elymas Vonran is a usurper.”

“And you want to do something about it?”

Anderliy took a glance at him. “Yes.”

D'John stared—and believed him. “My name is D'John Ryanson. What is yours?”

“Zachariah Anderliy.”

"What do you want me to call you?"

"I don't care."

"What do your parents call you?"

"Zachariah."

At least they liked it. "What about your friends?"

"I never found out."

Which was an indirect way of saying he never had any. "And you don't care what I call you?"

"No."

"All right. Zach." D'John suddenly became aware of the weight of the blaster in his hand, and he looked down at it. It would be appropriate to put it away. Appropriate, but not wise. True, he thought Zach—as he had nicknamed his unlikely recruit—was sincere. True, he thought that Zach was incapable of overpowering him whether he was armed or unarmed. He thought so, but he wasn't sure. D'John was in a dangerous business, and if he wanted to live he couldn't take chances. Even now holstering his sidearm would be a small leap of faith.

D'John took a small leap of faith.

Adon Kereth sat on a shipping crate, studying diagrams on his compad, even though it depressed him.

An agent of theirs in the military had sent these diagrams—all of them blueprints of Adesh's vaunted new superships. The diagrams had come with the information that Adesh was preparing to send the superships on their maiden voyage—to Tokar. It was another piece of intelligence pointing to an imminent attack on Tokar.

Their experts had examined the diagrams and found nothing to exploit. Kereth was studying to determine if the new ships would bring a palpable advantage to Adesh. If his military judgment was worth anything, they would.

Kereth laid the compad down on the crate and glanced around the hangar. He didn't know why he would rather be in a large, deserted, badly lit hangar that smelled of lubricants than his quarters. But he did, and so he sat disconsolately on a shipping crate instead of disconsolately on his bed.

He always missed Susanne, but sometimes he ached for her all through, body and soul. Tonight the ache burned with desperation. He thought about Adesh attacking Tokar, and he was afraid for her and for his daughters. And he remembered that Alexander's mother was there, and Thaddaeus' mother, wife, and two of his sisters. It would seem that if men were going to fight in wars, the least that could be given them was that they leave their women behind in safety. Adesh could attack Tokar at any time, and Kereth still had not thought of a way to save the day.

Please, God, he prayed silently. *Please.*

And then he remembered another thing he had to worry about. Intelligence had swooped into Trey Uman's city the very night he had met with D'John Ryanson. Uman had gone unmolested, but no one had heard of D'John since that night. If he had been caught, he could be dead at this very moment. Or perhaps in the hands of interrogators. And Vonran's government, in its desperation to crack the insurgency, had come to overlook excesses.

If anything happened to the boy, he would feel terrible—not only for D'John but also for his parents, two people he knew nothing about except that they would feel the same about their son as he felt about his.

Kereth sighed to himself. He looked around the hangar, and feeling assured that he was alone, he bowed his head and began to pray.

When he heard the sound of the hangar doors lumbering open a few minutes later, it felt like an intrusion. He tried to ignore the incoming ship all through its entrance and landing. Only when he heard its hatch release did he reluctantly open his eyes and raise his head.

He looked towards the newly docked ship, and he saw D'John Ryanson stepping out, followed by a stranger.

Relief flooded him. Kereth rose and walked over. When D'John—turning from securing the hatch—saw him, he came to attention.

"At ease," Kereth commanded. "You are past your return

date."

"Yes, sir," D'John acknowledged without guilt or shame. "I have a long debriefing for you."

"I'll take it immediately. Who is this?"

D'John glanced at the man he had brought with him. "Zach Anderliy, new recruit. Part of my story."

Anderliy. Somehow Kereth had heard that name connected to something important. He gazed at Anderliy a long moment, and it didn't come to him. He glanced back at D'John. "Come to my office, both of you. I want to hear all about it."

He turned and led the way. At his office door Kereth entered the code.

And frowned when the doors opened to a fully lit room. Kereth strode in—to see Kinlol sitting at his desk.

Kereth folded his arms across his chest and instinctively asked, "Isn't it past your bedtime?"

Kinlol gave him a look of indifference for that remark. "I wanted a word with you." He glanced at Anderliy and D'John. "Privately."

Kereth turned to them. "We will need a minute."

"Yes, sir." D'John headed out, Anderliy followed, and the door closed.

Kereth looked at Kinlol. "What?"

"A half hour ago we got a communications package from Ziphernan. Finally we have substantial gains."

"Marvelous. Do we have troops?"

"No. But if all goes well, we may. They have proposed terms for a treaty. I think they are reasonable. I want to advise the emperor on it in the morning consultation."

"And you want me to advise the emperor, too. I'll be ready. Anything else?"

"Yes." Kinlol nodded at the door Anderliy and D'John had just gone out of. "Do you know who he was?"

"Yes. D'John Ryanson," Kereth answered, just to be difficult. Kinlol gave him a look, and Kereth said, "Zach Anderliy."

"The moniker must be new. I never heard it before."

Kereth stared at him. “You mean you know him?”

“I know of him—as Zachariah Anderliy.”

“The name Anderliy sounded familiar to me, but not Zachariah.”

“And the names Philip and Anice Anderliy?”

Kereth thought—and this time it came to him. “They're physicists—famous physicists. They have done work for the government and the military—even under Vonran. In fact, they were employed in the supership project. And Zachariah Anderliy ... ”

Kinlol nodded and finished, “Is their son.”

D'John stepped out of General Kereth's office with relief. It had taken longer than he expected, but it was over. Nothing stood between him and his bed now.

Except, of course, the last duty Kereth had given him: finding quarters for Zach. Revlan was always crowded, and at his rank (none) he would have to share. That made the decision easy.

D'John turned to look at Zach, who was slowly stumbling his way towards him. He was rubbing his eyes vigorously and probably could not see anything. “Hey, Zach. Don't walk into a wall.”

Zach lowered his hands and looked at him. Then he went back to rubbing his eyes.

“Come on, Zach.” Trusting Zach to follow, D'John strode ahead. Living quarters were in another part of the base altogether, and D'John hurried through. When he finally arrived, he ushered Zach into the room and explained, “As General Kereth told you, you will have to have a roommate. And it will be me. Top bunk is mine.”

D'John sat in the room's only chair and began tugging his boots off. Zach sat on his bunk and, pushing up his eyelid, pried something small and clear from his eye.

D'John stopped halfway through his left boot to watch Zach go through the process with his other eye. “What's that?” he asked.

“Eye lenses.”

“What for?”

“I'm nearsighted.”

“If you don't mind my asking, why didn't you have that corrected?”

“My parents tried. But the doctors' equipment was damaged. The laser's modulating controls were faulty.”

D'John winced and shook his head.

“They repaired most of the damage in later operations. But my nearsightedness is permanent.” Zach rubbed his eyes again.

And D'John guessed, “And your eyes hurt.”

“Sometimes.”

D'John watched as Zach slipped his lenses beneath the bunk and drew a small bottle out of his pocket. He dripped a little liquid into each eye and closed them.

D'John began working on his boots again, asking, “You have any siblings?”

“No.”

“Oh.” It was much the same tone D'John would have used to say, 'I'm sorry to hear that.' “I have seven. Five brothers, two sisters. All my brothers are older than me, and all my sisters are younger.”

Silence. D'John tried again. “I'm surprised at how much time General Kereth took with us—especially you. You may not know this, but he took an unusual interest in you. I wonder if he has any plans.” Or, D'John also wondered, any suspicions.

Zach shrugged and, pulling back the covers, got into bed.

D'John stood up, shoving the boots aside with his foot. Zach Anderliy wasn't the first man he had recruited, but there was something different about him. Apparently Kereth thought so, too.

The last thought D'John had, as he went to sleep, was what would all come of it.

Chief Kinlol, General Kereth, and Thaddaeus Gaelin had arrived for the morning consultation, and their behavior was strange. Thaddaeus kept looking at Kereth and Kinlol. Kinlol seemed immensely satisfied with something; Kereth cut looks of irritated concern at him.

Alexander began by asking, “What do we have this

morning?"

"We received a message from Nemin Ziphernan late last night," Kereth answered. "He finally has something for us. Kinlol will tell you about it."

"King Arkin is ready to sign a treaty with us. It will be a treaty of friendship, of mutual aid without conditions. It is an ideal treaty. They have added only one term we did not propose."

Kereth watched Kinlol with a fierce you're-avoiding-the-point look on his face. Alexander looked at him, and knew that the term, whatever else it was, was not good. "What is that?"

"Arkin wants you to betroth yourself to marry his daughter."

Alexander blinked. "What?"

"Go on." Kereth's voice brought Alexander's gaze to him. He still had that fierce look. "Tell him the catch."

"You mean that wasn't it?"

"It gets worse," Kereth replied. "Go on, Kinlol. Tell."

Kinlol gave him one of his own looks—his vexed-but-I'll-deal-with-you-later look. Kereth got it a lot. "King Arkin's daughter is thirteen years old."

"What?"

"Before you reject it out of hand," Kereth said, "there are a few things you should consider."

"Is Kinlol going to tell me?" Alexander demanded—with an acidity he immediately regretted.

Kereth was not stung. He gave Alexander a look of amusement—and Alexander didn't know whether he liked or disliked it. "No. I will tell you at least one. First—because it occurs to me first—you should know that you will not marry for at least another five years. The age of majority in Sameeva is eighteen, and you will not marry the girl until she is an adult. The power to decide when you do marry will be Arkin's. It will be a term of the betrothal that the marriage will be set at his discretion. It's fitting, but it leaves you with no certainty as to when you will marry."

"And you must understand," Kinlol said, "the nature of this betrothal. Betrothal is a promise to marry—morally binding, perhaps even socially binding. But it is not legally binding. A man should not break his betrothal, but he is free to—as free as he is to walk down the street. That will not be the case here. Here it will be a term of an international treaty. In other words, you will be in a legal contract to marry King Arkin's daughter. As a matter of law you will have to marry her someday—and you must live like it."

In other words: no dalliances. Alexander looked at Kereth and Kinlol—and then, as an afterthought, at Thaddaeus, who appeared to have developed a fixation with his wedding band. "Enter into negotiations. See if they will accept anything else."

"They won't." Kereth's voice was respectful, but it allowed no argument. "We have spent months negotiating this treaty. This is what Arkin wants. He will not accept anything else. There is nothing we can give that has equal value—or that compensates him for what he gives us."

Alexander looked at him in disbelief. "Nothing?"

"We're in a weak position for negotiating."

Kinlol nodded. "We do not have anything to give him but promises for the future. In the meantime, opposing Vonran could cost him his kingdom. We are asking him to risk everything. He has the right to expect a reward. This is a substantial one. By arranging a marriage between you and his daughter, he is ensuring that he will not be treated only as a friend but as a relative. And the next emperor will be half-Sameevan. His mother will be from Sameeva, and through that prism he will see the entire country. When he deals with the king of Sameeva, he will be dealing with someone whose blood runs through his veins. We have promised friendship and good will to Arkin and his people. He means to secure it."

"And if I do not betroth myself to his daughter ... "

"You will have no treaty," Kinlol said. "What Arkin is asking is reasonable."

"Reasonable?" Alexander's tone was one of austere, almost haughty disbelief—the tone in which Kinlol had taught him to express his incredulity.

"When you consider what he is risking, and what you are receiving, and how much you need it ... "

"I know your advice then." Alexander looked at his other

advisors. “What is yours?”

Thaddaeus coughed slightly. He didn't want to be involved.

“It isn't a simple question,” Kereth said. “It affects all your life. On the one hand, marriage is full of risk. It can make or ruin a life. If you marry badly, you will pay the price for years. But in this case, if you do not marry you may not have any years at all. If we lose this war Vonran will kill every man sitting at this table. We need all the help Arkin can give us and more. This treaty may be the difference between victory and defeat, and you will only get it by betrothing yourself to Arkin's daughter.”

“In other words—if I marry her I may have an unhappy life. If I do not marry her—I may die.”

“That puts it very well, Alexander.”

Alexander tried the concept in his mind—marrying the girl. And it did not fare well. “She is seven years younger than me.”

“That is about the difference between your father and mother,” Kereth pointed out.

Alexander looked at him. He hadn't remembered that. “My father was never forced to marry a stranger after waiting five years to do it.”

“Your father was never in a fight for his throne and his life.”

That was what it all came back to—what, maybe, it all came down to. Alexander hoped it wasn't, but as he looked at his advisors, he could find no reason for that hope.

“That went as well as it could have,” Kereth pronounced, as soon as they were out of Alexander's office.

“Better than I expected,” Kinlol answered.

“Why?”

“Because you argued on my side.”

“Don't be surprised. It happens once every year.”

“Do you think he will do it?” Thaddaeus asked.

“What choice does he have?” Kereth answered. He glanced at Kinlol. “I interviewed both D'John Ryanson and Zachariah Anderliy last night. Then I did some research into Anderliy's background. Everything indicates that his defection is sincere."

"I don't doubt it," Kinlol answered. "Zachariah Anderliy has a brilliant mind, but he will never be anything but a scholar."

"Who is Zachariah Anderliy?" asked Thaddaeus.

"A recruit Captain Ryanson brought back with him," Kinlol said. "He is also the only child of the Empire's most prominent physicists—and probably is more intelligent than either of them."

"Yes," Kereth said. "But what good does it do us? If he were in his parents' field we could find a use for him. But what use do we have for a professor of government?"

"None—for the moment."

"And Tokar?"

Kereth looked at Thaddaeus—and read his own emotions in his eyes. "I don't know. If Alexander agrees to marry Arkin's daughter we may be able to negotiate some military assistance, but there is no guarantee. I have racked my brains for a way out and have come up with nothing. So I have decided to seek help from our commanders—and whatever resident experts we have, including Anderliy. I will brief them and see if they have any saving strategy."

"It's a good idea, General, but aren't briefings usually given by subordinates to superiors?"

"Yes."

"Are you concerned about the image of briefing your inferiors?"

"The thought occurred to me. That is why I was going to ask you to do it."

Thaddaeus' expression didn't flicker. "Of course. When and where?"

D'John noticed them in one of the back corridors. Three commandos he knew, forming a half-ring around a scholar he knew. The commandos' expressions were ugly with jeering.

Zach literally had his back against the wall, and doubtless that was true in a metaphorical sense also. D'John went over. He knew a hazing when he saw one.

"Lem!" he shouted.

Lem turned to him. "You're just in time, Ryanson. Join the fun."

D'John crossed his arms over his chest and bore a hard-eyed gaze down on Lem. "Get out of here."

"Is this your sense of humor?"

"Is this your courage? Get out."

"What are you, the guardian angel of maladjusted scholars? Why do you care?"

"It's enough for you that I do." D'John glowered at Lem until he shook his head and glanced at his followers.

"Come on. There'll be no fun with him around."

D'John watched them until they were gone, and then he turned to Zach. "Sorry about that. Hazing is not one of the nobler things the military breeds."

"And the military is not the only thing that breeds it," returned Zach calmly. "I wanted to speak with you about that briefing we received."

"Sure. Come on." D'John led Zach to a small planning room. After the door was closed and they were seated at the table, he said, "Go ahead."

"Gaelin said that there was no weakness in the superships that could be exploited. That conclusion is wrong."

D'John looked at him curiously. "And how do you know that?"

"I know everything about the superships."

"How?"

"My parents designed the crucial components."

"Your parents designed the superships—for *Vonran*?"

Zach didn't blink. "He was the one who authorized the research."

"Okay." D'John drew the word out. Zach had repeated his question more than answered it, but he decided to move on. "What is this weakness, and how did the scientists who examined the diagrams miss it?"

"I can only guess, but they were probably focusing on a

direct attack on the reactor and the other main systems. The weakness lies in the transmitters."

"All right. Start from the beginning, and take it slow."

"The superships are advanced in shields, weapons systems, and mobility beyond any other warship. The design of all these things is superior, but what truly makes it work is the reactor. If you equipped a normal warship with these systems it would fail, because its energy source would be insufficient to sustain them."

"All right. What about the transmitters?"

"There are two kinds of transmitters—those that are conduits of energy and those that transmit data. I'm talking about the former. My parents brought energy transmitters to a new level of development. The transmitters in the superships can carry levels of energy that would destroy normal transmitters. Therein lies its weakness."

"How so?"

"All computers can be destroyed by a surge of energy if it is high enough. The level necessary to do such damage is unattainable in normal ships because the transmitters would be destroyed while trying to carry the energy. But the transmitters in the superships could transmit the energy."

"So, if I grasp what you're saying, the superships have the weakness of being capable of frying themselves."

"That's a rough approximation."

"But it's true."

"Yes."

D'John looked at Zach, evaluating this information. "Your parents must have known. They must have put in fail-safes."

Zach affirmed that with a nod. "They programmed the transmitters to shut down if they received an uncontrolled surge of energy. That can be circumvented. They also programmed the transmitters to shut down if they received a certain level of energy." Then Zach's expression changed, and oddly enough, he looked embarrassed. "That doesn't need to be circumvented."

"Why not?"

"Because the level is set too high. If you hit a narrow

window, you can still send a destructive energy charge through the ship's computer systems."

D'John frowned. "Why did your parents set it too high? They didn't—they didn't leave the ships open to sabotage on purpose, did they?"

"No. They set the level as low as they could. If they made the transmitters any more sensitive, they would have run the risk of computer systems shutting down in the middle of battle."

"So it's a bug they didn't work out before building the superships."

"They expected to correct it in a few years. In the meantime, they attempted to hide the defect."

And if not for Zach, they would have succeeded. For a moment D'John studied Zach, trying to determine what emotion he felt at destroying his parents' work. He saw no emotion at all.

D'John looked away, bringing himself back to business. "Are you sure that, if you were at the right control panel, you could destroy a supership?"

"Yes."

D'John envisioned it. "And then those three ships would be floating dead in space in the middle of a battle."

"For a short time."

D'John's head jerked towards Zach. "A short time?"

"They would then combust."

"How?"

"The reactor. It is decentralized from the main computer systems, but that would insulate it from complete failure only for a time. The coolant system would eventually fail."

"And then the reactor would overheat and explode." D'John's mind churned. "Adesh will be relying on those ships. If we destroy them—better yet, if we destroy them before the battle is joined, the explosions will damage other ships, too. And if we then attack in the middle of the chaos ... " It almost overwhelmed him to think about.

D'John stood up. "Thanks, Zach. I need to talk to General Kereth." He left the small room and went through the corridors. At this late hour they were mostly deserted, and he had nearly reached

Kereth's office before he saw another soul.

He gave the other man a glance, intending to pass him by, and then he recognized him. D'John stopped a few feet in front of Emperor Alexander, feeling instantly awkward. He bowed to him and tried at a greeting. “A fair evening, my lord.” Then he made to pass him by.

Alexander held up a hand. “Wait a moment, Ryanson. What business do you have here?”

D'John wanted to ask him that same question, but he didn't dare. “I have something to report to General Kereth, something having to do with Tokar.”

“What is it?”

“I think we have a way to sabotage the superships.”

“Ah.” Alexander gazed at him, and there was something in his eyes that D'John didn't understand. “Are you married, Ryanson?”

“No, my lord.”

“Do you know a girl you would like to marry?”

D'John looked at Alexander with bewilderment, but he answered the question. “No. It's a time of war, and I've put romance aside until it's over.”

“I see.” Alexander hesitated a long moment, finally saying, “I gather you wouldn't marry a girl you didn't know.”

D'John resisted the urge to stare at the emperor as if he were an attraction at a side-show. “Barring extraordinary circumstances, no.”

Alexander's expression turned thoughtful, and strangely serious. After a few moments he made a dismissive gesture and said, “You may go, Ryanson.”

“Thank you. I mean, as you command.” D'John made good his retreat.

Alexander walked a few steps down the corridor and then glanced over his shoulder at D'John Ryanson as he vanished around the corner. On the other side was Kereth's office.

For the past ten minutes Alexander had been wandering

around this part of the base, debating whether to go in and talk with Kereth about betrothing himself to Arkin's daughter. He needed a father to talk to, and Adon Kereth was the closest thing he had to one. The closest thing he had, and yet not close at all. He had no father—and tonight, as he wanted one, the old ache roused itself in his heart.

Alexander looked back in the direction of Kereth's office—and the direction D'John had gone. That settled the question for him. It was time to go back—and make his decision alone.

CHAPTER

III

* * * * * * * * * * * * * * * *

THE room was so brightly lit, and the table was so well-polished, that it glimmered.

Alexander noted that, but acted as if he didn't. He let his eyes slide past the wood to the large sheet of paper lying in the center of the table. Beside it was a long stylus, before it the table's only chair. His chair.

Alexander moved to take it, trying hard to keep his swirling emotions invisible to those watching him. He seated himself in front of the paper—the treaty—and ran his eyes down the calligraphed words. At their end King Arkin's signature sprawled—and next to it an empty space beckoned his hand.

Alexander glanced up at the witnesses. There were seven, as the law stipulated. Arkin's special envoy, Stephan Simon Haladith, and his two companions represented the Sameevans. For his side, Gerog Kinlol, Nemin Ziphernan, Thaddaeus Gaelin, and General Kereth stood.

They were the crucial part of the ceremony. It was like a wedding. He could sign the treaty alone and a man could say a marriage vow alone, but it only counted if there were people to hear and know. All promises had to be made to someone.

Alexander's eyes sought out the term that mandated his marriage to Arkin's daughter—Acsah. He had found out her name. With his signature, in one moment, he would make her his promised bride.

Time itself seemed to slow as he reached for the stylus. He checked the point, pressed it against the paper, and drew it across. It left his name in its wake.

Alexander dropped the stylus onto the table, looking up at the witnesses. “We are now bound in a treaty of sworn friendship.”

Kereth nodded. “And now that that is so, let us discuss the sending of troops.”

“Of course.” Haladith turned to Alexander and bowed. “We are honored, my lord.”

“As am I,” Alexander answered, but it was only reflex. As Kereth began to engage Haladith, he glanced back down at the treaty. To keep his life, he'd taken a bride. To gain his throne, he'd acquired a wife.

Alexander looked at the negotiating men, but he felt no concern. It was a sure thing, getting troops from Arkin to help them defeat Vonran at Tokar. A small part of him was detached enough, cold enough to observe with irony that getting a wife, troops, and victory was not bad for one treaty.

Elymas Vonran looked down the table at Adesh. The commander-in-chief was staring at his compad, but Vonran wasn't at all sure he was reading it.

Vonran glanced up as Elad Zephon approached the table. Noticing Vonran's gaze, he bowed to him and then took his place.

Zephon was the last. Now everyone was gathered. Vonran looked at Adesh. “Begin,” he ordered.

Adesh stood up. “My lord, my colleagues,” he said. “I am pleased to tell you that we are ready to end Tokar. As you know, I have sent the superships on ahead ... ”

Vonran stopped listening. He knew Adesh's plan; he had approved it. This was the briefing of the Council. Adesh would leave immediately afterward to go to Tokar and oversee the attack. The conquering of Tokar would be a great blow to the insurgency, but not, Vonran feared, a fatal one. As long as Alexander lived there would be someone fighting for him. As long as Alexander lived there would be no peace.

Vonran looked at the holograph suspended above the table. It was a map of Tokar and the space surrounding it, and Adesh motioned to it as he spoke. Alexander could be in Tokar, he supposed. But he didn't believe it. Adon Kereth had gone in the opposite direction from Gawin Gaelin, and Vonran couldn't believe he'd gone alone. He thought Alexander was hiding with Kereth, not entrenched with Gaelin. The rebels would guard their gold.

Vonran's eyes traveled to the stars surrounding Tokar. Somewhere among them Alexander was hidden. He had to find him —and end him.

Movement brought Vonran's attention back to Adesh. He had turned away from the holograph and stood facing the table. “The rebels will fight,” he said, “but they will fail. The strategy is well-laid, and we are far stronger than they. We will go and defeat them.”

Vonran nodded in lofty approval. “The fates smile on you.”

It was as august an assembly as Kereth had ever spoken to. The emperor was there, with Kinlol, Thaddaeus, and their chief commanders. D'John Ryanson, the appointed head of their commando operation, was there along with Zach Anderliy. Stephan Simon Haladith and a few other important Sameevans completed the picture.

Kereth took his place in front of the mounted tactical display. “As you know,” he said, “our purpose is to save Tokar and turn the battle into a strategic defeat of Vonran. The first element of our strategy is targeting Adesh's superships.”

Kereth pressed a button on his remote, and an image of the ship appeared on the screen. “This is the supership—a powerful and advanced warship. Tokar is its first opportunity to show its colors. The strength the superships will provide to Adesh is considerable.

“It is a strength we will use against him. These ships have doubtless factored heavily into Adesh's calculations. We will destroy them. Zach Anderliy has provided us with the method of sabotage—

namely, a powerful energy surge capable of disabling the ships' computer systems entirely. We will send a commando team aboard each ship to sabotage it. Because the precise level of energy we need is unknown—and because the margin of error is very small—Anderliy will be on one of these teams. When he determines the answer, it will be sent to the other teams.

"Within a short time the reactors aboard the superships will overheat and combust. The explosions will do considerable damage—and wreak considerable havoc—to Adesh's forces. During the first moments of their confusion, we will begin our conventional offensive. The Sameevan task force, together with that of Emperor Alexander, will attack Vonran's forces. With the attack sprung, we will broadcast a message to General Gaelin. He will rally his own troops and join the battle. The enemy will be caught in our pincer."

Kereth stopped there, surveying the faces of his audience. He saw no doubt, or fear. Only grimness, and in it determination.

He nodded briefly to them, his companions of war. "God go with you all."

Zach Anderliy kept wondering how he got himself into this. When he volunteered to help Alexander, he thought they would take as service the only thing he had ever done—analysis, study, an endless learning, knowing, understanding. He never thought they would put him on a ship with false markings, a false transponder code, three commandos, and tell him to infiltrate and destroy a warship. It was bone-shaking.

He was on a cargo shuttle, and only the commandos who were serving as pilots had seats. He and D'John were in the cargo hold, sitting on the floor in between huge shipping crates. Zach felt a clinging anxiety crawling over him, never strong and never leaving. It was wholly new, and wholly unpleasant.

He glanced over at D'John. The other sat with his back against the wall, his right arm casually draped over his raised knees. In his right hand he grasped a blaster.

D'John stared off into nothing, his expression that of a man lulled by daydreams or physical ease. Zach stared at him, at his relaxation.

He looked too long. D'John glanced over at him and met his eyes. Zach immediately looked down.

D'John's voice followed him. “How are you doing?”

“Fine,” Zach responded, without thinking about the question.

He felt D'John's eyes on him. Then D'John spoke again. “When we get back, I'll speak to General Kereth about getting into contact with your parents.”

That brought Zach's gaze up. “Why?”

“To let them know you're all right. They must be suffering right now.”

Zach shook his head. “They aren't.”

“Come on, Zach. You disappeared. For all they know you could be dead. Don't you know what even the thought would do to them?”

“They're fine.” Even if they thought he might be dead, even if he really did die. As long as they had each other, they would be fine. Together they were complete—so inexorably complete that there was a way, and a place, in which their union excluded everyone else. Zach had always stood outside that inner room. There were times when he felt like he was another one of their experiments—what would happen if they combined their genes. He thought they were pleased with the results.

“They care more than you think.”

Zach looked sharply at D'John. “What?”

“Your parents. They care more than you think.”

Zach stayed silent, reflecting on the fact that D'John didn't know his parents and therefore had no facts on which to base that conclusion.

D'John shook his head. “They're parents, Zach. They care. Don't you know anything about parents?”

Apparently not. Zach settled back against the wall and tried to find some topic to fill his mind. He didn't like what the conversation—or the upcoming operation—was stirring in him.

D'John's voice again: “Got the pre-battle jitters yet?”

Zach looked at him. "Yes," he said mildly.

"If it's any encouragement, you're at the worst part."

"How so?"

D'John fiddled with his blaster. "You are thinking about the battle, about dying and pain. You're afraid. But when you are actually in battle, you won't have time for it."

Zach watched him twirl the blaster between his fingers, and he wondered if he would ever be able to act like that on the eve of battle. He decided the answer was no. "You seem fine."

"I do all right." D'John looked at him. "No one dies until God takes them. Unless you're called you can't go, and if you are called you can't stay. When God decides it's time for me to die, nothing will be able to save me. If He decides it isn't time—nothing can kill me. It's not in my hands, and it's not in their hands. So I don't worry."

Zach looked away and wondered if this was fatalism or faith, peace or despair. He had never heard anything like it.

He felt a change in their movement, but he couldn't tell what it was. He glanced at D'John and found him looking up at the ceiling. "What?" Zach asked—whispering, for no reason he knew.

"We're slowing down. Soon we'll be docking."

And then de-boarding. Zach's heart began to climb into his throat.

In a few moments he felt the ship settle on the ground. D'John stood to his feet, holstering his sidearm. "The hatch will be released in a minute, Zach."

Zach stood up, feeling every muscle tense. The double-wide hatch opened, and there stood their pilots—the rest of their team.

"Follow me," D'John muttered.

Zach nodded. They had worked out what he would do as they made their way to the engine room—he would follow D'John.

D'John shared a look with one of the pilots as he walked forward. He jumped onto the deck and strode right.

Zach followed, struggling both to keep up and look casual. Their ship was tucked in among dozens, perhaps hundreds of others, and D'John led him through the aisles formed by the docked ships. In a few minutes they broke out of them.

Zach got his first view of the open hangar, and he nearly stopped. The sheer size of it ...

His objective came crashing back to him, and he whipped his head in D'John's direction. He was heading straight for the hangar doors, and he wasn't far away.

Zach picked his pace up. He noticed sentries standing at the doors, combat rifles across their chests. D'John looked all right, and Zach gathered his courage and followed.

Nothing happened, and they were in the corridor. Zach finally came alongside D'John, and they passed unnoticed through the corridor until they came to the lifts. Zach had never liked lifts. They had always discomfited him, being in such close quarters with people in a place he could not leave. Now he simply stood behind D'John and tried to look bored.

The ride down took a while. They continually stopped to allow people on and off, and all of them had the air of impending battle. It drove up Zach's anxiety, until finally they were delivered to their destination.

A shorter walk down a narrower corridor led them to the doors of the engine room—and its two sentries. Unlike the men at the hangar, these were hawk-eyed and focused right on the two infiltrators.

"This area is restricted," one of the guards told them.

"We have orders." As D'John spoke, his fingers drew out an infocard, about an inch long and a centimeter wide.

The guard took it and pushed it into a slot in his compad. Zach's eyes fastened on it. D'John had assured him that they had expert forgers, with excellent intelligence on which to base their work.

Though, of course, it was always possible that the government had made changes they were not yet aware of. If that happened, the orders would be exposed as fraudulent, and in the usual course of things, they would be arrested, interrogated, and summarily shot. But the usual course of things would be disrupted, because if they were exposed, D'John would have no other choice except to open fire on the guards and storm the engine room.

All that was on Zach's mind as the stone-faced guard processed the infocard. It seemed to take a long time.

Finally he looked up. Sliding out the infocard, he handed it back to D'John. “You may enter.”

D'John took the infocard and passed between the guards without a word.

The room was dominated by three banks of computers. One officer stood among them, pacing as his gaze passed over the seated men and women. D'John went to him and asked, “Are you the supervisor here?”

“Yes.”

“I am here to requisition a station, according to my orders.” Again D'John produced the card, and again Zach went through having it confirmed.

After he had processed it, the supervisor gave back the card and walked away from them. He went to a station and spoke to the light-haired woman seated there. She got up and left.

D'John walked over and waved Zach to the seat. Zach settled in front of the screen. For a moment he only looked at it. Then, as he focused on his task, his brain began to click away. He prowled through the computer system, thoughts of danger fading fast into the back of his mind.

D'John stood sentry, hand over his holstered blaster. He had nothing to do but wait, and it was getting under his skin.

Zach worked away at the computer. D'John, when he glanced at the screen, saw nothing readily intelligible to him. Usually he looked out, resisting the urge to glance behind his shoulder.

And he thought about the timing of it all. The other commando teams should be getting in place even as he waited, and D'John knew what might happen if they took too long in getting the information to them. Every moment increased the danger of exposure. Exposure meant death for the commandos, and for many others besides. Possibly—if they failed to destroy the superships—

even defeat.

General Kereth was coming, too, with the entire task force. They had begun their hyperspace journey hours ago, aiming to arrive shortly after the superships went bang. If the commandos took too long or failed, the consequences to their strategy could be catastrophic.

And there was nothing D'John could do about it. It was Zach's game now, and D'John wasn't fit even to be a spectator. So he stood, and thought, and imagined failure and defeat. As the minutes went by sweat began to collect beneath his collar.

D'John felt someone's eyes on him, and he looked over to see the supervising officer watching them. Their eyes met, and then turned away. D'John's gaze went back to the far end of the room, and their time spent tarrying in that room felt even longer.

A drop of sweat slipped, and D'John felt it trickle down his back.

Then he heard a light tapping and looked down to see Zach holding his hand over his compad. “Done,” he said, softly.

D'John picked up the compad and looked over the file Zach had created. All the information was entered. D'John encrypted the file and transmitted it to the two addresses he had committed to memory. Then he deleted it.

Zach looked at him expectantly, but D'John held back a moment. The other commandos had just gotten the information. They should be moving in, and their strikes were supposed to be as simultaneous as possible.

D'John let a few short moments go by, and he filled them with silent prayer. Then he met Zach's gaze. “Do it,” he ordered.

Zach did it. Then he stood up, pushing away from the station.

They had accomplished their mission. This supership was minutes away from destruction, and the other commando teams were equipped with the knowledge they needed to destroy the other two.

Now they only had to get out alive. “Come on,” D'John murmured to Zach, as he turned away and made for safety.

"Sixty seconds until re-entry into real space."

The navigation officer's words entered the silence and hung there. No one answered him.

General Adon Kereth stood on the bridge, his right hand behind his back. He didn't move as he gazed steadily at the viewport. The moment of truth was upon them. Their strategy, their calculations, their actions were about to be shown as good or bad, sufficient or wanting.

The seconds passed away, and then a tremor passed through the ship. The stars' blurred lines vanished; they were out of hyperspace.

Adesh's armada filled the viewport, and it looked as if the battle had started without them. Damaged ships held their positions; wreck and debris floated.

The relief that shot through Kereth was so great he had to keep his posture from drooping. "Comm," he said, "send the hail to General Gaelin. Captain?" Kereth turned to the captain, who was bending over his display.

"All ships are out of hyperspace and reporting, sir."

"Then send them all this message." Kereth jerked his head towards the viewport. "Engage."

They had been receiving telemetry from Tokar since Adesh arrived. They had a first-class view of the panicked evacuation from the superships, then the ships crumbling in fire, torn apart by explosions within.

Then Alexander's fleet materialized—a larger and more formidable force than anyone had expected he could have. Then the battle was joined, and Gawin Gaelin broke the siege of Tokar, sallying out against his besiegers.

The battle raged, and with slowly growing horror the distant watchers accepted that the tide of battle was not going to turn again. And then it was over, and Adesh's fleet had been scattered, retreating from Tokar in disarray.

Vonran saw it all. When the conclusion became plain, there was no reason to go on watching. Yet he did, and none of those with him dared to move or even speak.

Finally he stood up, and everyone came quickly to their feet. “Get me reports,” he ordered. “I want to know what we lost. I want to know where we stand.” And he strode out of the room.

He went to his private study and there threw himself into an armchair. He rubbed his face, agitation boiling inside him.

He had lost. When everything was aligned in his favor, he lost—again. What was against him that this kept happening?

Vonran sat contemplating, trying to find something, anything. Any idea, any cunning that could save him.

The comm pinged, and Vonran glanced towards it with irritation. Everyone knew the disaster they had just suffered. Anyone who would disturb him was either brave or stupid.

After a moment he got up. He would see.

Kereth made his way through the throng—soldiers, officers, tactical support crews, technicians, men and women. They had all turned out to celebrate victory. The grim, giant hangar of the *Turbulent* was hardly the ideal place, but the celebrants didn't seem aware of it.

Kereth scanned the faces of the crowd as he pushed through. He was looking for one in particular, and if he didn't find him soon he would just have to leave.

Kereth spotted him and moved in that direction. “Ryanson!”

D'John Ryanson turned at his voice and came to attention.

“At ease,” Kereth said as he came up to him. “I see the success of your mission, Ryanson.”

D'John raised his voice to be heard above the crowd. “It was the perfect mission, sir. In and out, no trouble.”

“You've pulled off many such missions, Ryanson. You have made yourself a valuable asset to the emperor, as I hope you will continue to be.”

“I certainly plan to, sir.”

“General!”

At Thaddaeus' voice they turned to see him several paces away. He had a look of some urgency on his face. Kereth was late.

Kereth turned back to D'John. "I plan for it also. Enjoy the celebration." Kereth took a small black box and put it into D'John's hand. Then he turned and hurried towards Thaddaeus, leaving D'John to find his major's bars.

Kereth joined Thaddaeus, and they walked through the people without speaking to each other. When they arrived at the lifts, Kinlol was waiting for them—standing against the wall. The three went into a lift, and as soon as the door closed out the noise Kinlol said, "We're late."

"My father said he was arriving at the dignitaries' hangar twenty minutes ago," Thaddaeus confirmed.

"Little harm will be done by making him wait a few minutes," Kereth answered. "I had someone to meet tonight."

"Whom?" Kinlol asked.

"Major Ryanson."

"Major—" Kinlol stopped. "You delayed us to promote him?"

"To tell him of his promotion."

"Why couldn't it wait?"

"This is a night for good news."

The rest of the ride passed in silence. The lift stopped, and as they stepped out Thaddaeus said, "He's waiting in a council room. I had the guards direct him there."

"Go ahead, Thaddaeus. We will follow." Kereth held back as Thaddaeus went on.

Kinlol stayed, but not cheerfully. "Why, Kereth?"

"He hasn't seen his father in three years. Give them a moment." Kereth let a few moments pass and then led the way to the council room. They came around a corner and found Thaddaeus and Gawin Gaelin standing in the corridor, a door directly behind them.

Gaelin looked past Thaddaeus at them. "There have been times," he said, "when I was not sure I would see any of you alive again. Now we meet in victory." His eyes rested on Kereth. "I hear they call you General now."

"The emperor commissioned me to lead the fight against Vonran."

"You have done well," praised Gaelin. "As have you, my son," he added, turning back to Thaddaeus. "I am proud." Gaelin allowed that comment to hang for a moment, then said, "You, and the emperor, and the general left me with a great trust. I rejoice to say that I have been faithful." He stepped away from the door, the expression on his face suggesting joy. "Go in."

Premonition seized Kereth, and he went forward. Gawin Gaelin removed himself from the way. Thaddaeus beat him through the door.

Kereth barely entered the room before he heard her voice: "Adon!"

He turned to Susanne, already running towards him. In a moment she was in his arms. They held each other tightly, and Kereth rubbed his cheek against her hair. "Thank God," he said. "Thank God."

Zidon Adesh had been mustering the remnants of his armada at Hyatha when the summons came. He was to go to Telnaria and report to the regent immediately. Adesh obeyed. It would have been cowardly to run.

He took his personal frigate and made a straight journey to Telnaria. At the Palace he was sent to the upper floor; the regent was waiting for him in his study.

When Adesh entered the study, he saw the regent sitting behind his desk. Adesh approached, but he did not even consider the visitor's chair. Standing before Vonran he said, "Reporting as you commanded, my lord."

Vonran looked at him, and Adesh saw no anger in his face. There was a strange levity in his eyes—and that chilled Adesh more than any amount of fire. "You're back from the battlefield." His voice was as undisturbed as his expression. "How did it go?"

Adesh didn't know why Vonran would ask that question, but he had no doubt he had a well-considered reason. "It was catastrophic," Adesh answered.

"That's a very good word, Adesh. Only it is too weak. What word would not understate the disaster of Tokar I don't know."

Adesh watched Vonran uneasily. In so many men these irrelevancies would have inspired his contempt, but no hint of that colored his emotions. An image rose in his mind—a cat with gleaming eyes.

"And all our well-laid plans go awry once again. As they have for years, ever since that attack on Mela. Would you not agree, Adesh?"

This was more to the point—and Adesh read his own condemnation in it. He expected no mercy for this failure, but punishment—dismissal, humiliation, penalties, perhaps even death. But whatever it was, he would go without so much as one weak word, one weak twitch of a muscle. Adesh straightened his back even more, and said, "What is your will, Regent?"

Vonran regarded Adesh a moment. "To change the Empire for all history. I've received word from Elad Zephon. Alexander is in an underground base on Revlan. His other redoubt is in the Vaaris Cluster. Both must be completely annihilated."

"Are you giving the assignment to me?" Adesh asked, just to be sure.

"Yes. Concerning our defeat, Adesh, there are two factors. The rebels received help from the Sameevans. Intelligence reports confirm that, even though their ships at the battle were unmarked. But even more importantly, they had intelligence that enabled them to sabotage the superships. That will not happen to this operation."

"What are your instructions?"

"To deceive the rebels, we will have to deceive our own side. Devise a plan and prepare your fleet, but tell the crews they are attacking Armanas—or some such place. Make it plausible, and reveal the truth to as few as possible. Most should not discover their true destination until they are there."

Adesh's mind ran with the possibilities. "I will have the information widely and quietly disseminated. The rebels will hear of it and make counter-preparations. That will divert their resources and keep them out of mischief until we strike." He nodded. "This has potential."

"I'm glad you think so," Vonran said dryly. "Our purpose is to end this conflict once and for all by killing Alexander. I have been patient with you, Adesh, but my patience has its limit. I will not tolerate another failure."

"If I fail you again, I will willingly face any penalty—including the executioner." Adesh didn't say the words lightly, and he knew by Vonran's face that he didn't accept them lightly.

"Then don't fail me. It would be a pity to lose a man who faces death so bravely."

"And I would find it rather a pity to die. I will take this command, my lord, and I will not bring about your downfall or mine."

"So be it. And once you succeed and the Empire is in my hands for all my days—perhaps we will then punish Sameeva for its presumption."

Adesh took satisfaction in the thought. "I imagine we will."

Chapter

IV

* * * * * * * * * * * * * * * * *

Adon Kereth fiddled with the remote, adjusting the image on the tactical display. When it shifted to his satisfaction, he turned back to the table. He had assembled Alexander's war council—now including both D'John Ryanson and Zach Anderliy. They were expanding their war against Vonran; Kereth judged it time to expand other things as well.

Kereth began, addressing them: "As you know, we have spent the last two weeks consolidating our hold on Regial. Elymas Vonran responded, but showed a lack of initiative that caught our attention nearly from the beginning. As the days passed, we began to receive reports of secret troop movements and preparations. It was very vague in the beginning, but eventually we managed to piece together a picture of what Vonran is doing.

"Adesh has been mustering an attack fleet, but we have it on good authority that he intends to divide it and attack two places simultaneously. One operative told us that Adesh has been assembling special ground-assault troops. These are men trained in penetrating and capturing planet-side bases. Another operative has told us that Adesh is also assembling troops skilled in taking floating installations—space stations, orbiting stations, space platforms. One of these, and a planet, are Adesh's targets. Now, the golden question is—which floating installation and which planet? That we have had a great deal of trouble ascertaining, but we think we have discovered the answer.

"First, the code-name for this operation is Gateway. From instructions given to the commanding officers it is plain that their task is to capture and hold a strategic point, through which other troops and ships will pass. In other words, the purpose of Operation Gateway is to secure a vantage point from which to launch other attacks. As the name indicates, this will be Vonran and Adesh's gateway.

"To find the location of this 'gateway' we used the process of elimination. We have concluded that the twin strategic points"—Kereth turned to the display—"are the planet Jearim and space station Nylo 3. As you can see, Nylo 3 is located alongside the border of the Kelim province and along the border of Vothnia. Jearim is the border planet nearest it. Taking these would indeed give Vonran a gateway into Regial. On one side would be Kelim, which is under Vonran's control. Far more significantly, their right flank would be the border of Far Vothnia. That would leave them open to attack on only two sides."

Kereth turned back to look at his audience. "Defending Jearim and Nylo 3 is now the focus of our efforts. We are diverting resources to the area even now. Our defense strategy is still being revised; the paper you were given has only the rough concept." Kereth stopped.

After a long minute D'John spoke. "Has the emperor approved?"

"Yes. He has given us leave to go ahead." The consultations with Alexander continued, though now over a great distance. He had wanted to join them, but Kereth, Kinlol, and Gaelin had persuaded him otherwise. They all agreed it was better that he remain in the safety of Revlan.

D'John looked hard at the display. "Are you certain Jearim and Nylo 3 are the places Adesh is planning to attack?"

Kereth looked at him, a little surprised at the question. "As certain as I can be without Adesh confiding in me. Do you think the assumption wrong?"

"It's very reasonable. There's just something about it ... " He trailed off and shrugged, looking down at the table. "Just a funny way of pursuing victory."

Kereth wasn't sure what to do with that. He changed the subject. "Unfortunately, Vonran still has superior firepower. But we are hoping that provinces will begin seceding from his government to join ours. Nemin Ziphernan has been on a tour through the provinces, having discussions of that nature with sympathetic prefects."

Kinlol nodded. "And he is sure to bring at least some of them in."

"We have a chance," Thaddaeus said. "After three years, we really have a chance."

D'John nodded, and muttered, "We also have a civil war."

Zelrynn Vonran sat alone in her cabin. She gazed at the streaked stars. They were near Telnaria; the space cruiser would not be in hyperspace much longer.

She was returning to the Palace to see her father. She had to speak with him, to find out what he was thinking and feeling and what he intended to do. She had her guesses, but she had to know. If she was wrong, she would be happy. If she was right, she knew what she had to do.

Zelrynn looked away from the stars, a sudden tightness in her throat. She swallowed, trying to ease it away. She couldn't allow emotions to color her judgment; she couldn't display them in front of her father.

The ship came out of hyperspace, and Zelrynn could see the planet beneath her. It grew larger and larger, and then the cruiser entered its atmosphere. They docked in Telnaria's largest spaceport, and from there Zelrynn hired a hovcar to take her to the Palace.

It was late evening as Zelrynn arrived, and that was all for the best. Her father was most likely to be available this time of day. She made her way to his study, pressing her fingers against the open-pad. In a moment the door opened and she went in, forcing her lips to curve into a smile.

Elymas Vonran looked up and smiled at his daughter. “I'm glad to see you got in, Zelrynn.” He stopped, looking at her. “I was going to say good evening—but perhaps it isn't.”

“What do you mean?”

“You look so serious.”

She should have known he would see it, forced smile or no. “I am serious,” she answered. “My country is on the verge of an all-out civil war.”

“Ah, so that is what troubles you.”

“Does it not trouble you?”

“As a matter of fact, Zelrynn, no. We may be on the verge, but it will never come to that.”

Zelrynn felt compelled to ask the question, although she was half-afraid of the answer. “How could there be no fighting? Will you abdicate to Alexander?”

Her father considered the question for a long moment. “No. I have another solution.”

“What is it?”

“You know, Zelrynn, there are things I cannot discuss.”

Zelrynn looked away from him, considering what to say next. Her heart was sinking already, with a deep dread that the solution was peace made with Alexander's blood. “Father, you should.”

Vonran repeated the word: “Should?”

“Abdicate to Alexander,” Zelrynn finished. “He is the emperor. The throne is his, not yours.”

“As the Ancient Code decrees,” he said, with a tone and look in his eye that gleamed with gentle mockery. “Your school-day jargon is with you still.”

“School-day jargon? You are not calling the Ancient Code that?”

“No. But romantic notions about the Alheenan dynasty are just that—jargon. There is no truth in it.”

Zelrynn wondered what, in her father's mind, that had to do with it. “Be that as it may, Father, the emperorship belongs to the house of Alheenan.”

"For as long as it endures. The house of Alheenan has been on the decline for generations. Alexander is the last heir. The Alheenan dynasty dies with him."

The words created a horrible tingling, and Zelrynn said, "Father ... "

He took no notice of her. "And it was time for it long ago. They will perish and their hegemony will perish with them, and the Empire will be free. We have been loaded down with their dead weight for too many years—too many centuries. The sun is rising on our history again. From now onward, emperors will be rule by merit —not by blood."

"That's murder," Zelrynn almost gasped. Murder and treachery, stealing the throne he himself had made empty.

He looked at her, an oddly impatient expression on his face. "Killing an enemy in war is not murder."

Zelrynn stared at her father, and suddenly felt as if she had never seen him before. "You are not the father who raised me," she told him. "My mother loved a good man. She would not have known you."

Those were her first words he really heard. Her father's face went still, and he looked at her long and carefully. He stood up and quietly went around his desk.

Zelrynn held her ground as he crossed the floor—kept her chin lifted and her gaze fastened on him. But she could not quell the small prickle of fear that pierced her.

He stopped in front of her—looming over her, as he always had, though not until this moment had it felt threatening. Then he reached out his hand and touched her cheek, and she was surprised at how light his fingers felt. And he spoke, his voice soft but very clear. "Hold your head high, Zelrynn. You are my daughter." Then he stepped around her and walked straight on, out of the room.

Zelrynn waited until the door closed, and then she turned and looked at it. She waited a few minutes to be certain he was well away, and then she followed him out. She had accomplished her mission, and now her course was clear. She had settled her mind, no matter how her emotions turned.

Kavin Gyas had resigned from the Council of Chiefs in protest of the regent's first resort to violence. Now he lived out his quiet retirement in a secluded house on a mountain slope. It was just four hundred miles from the city where his friend Trey Uman had settled.

Zelrynn came to his home uninvited. She gave her name to Gyas' servant and waited for him to announce her. She didn't know what Gyas would make of such forwardness, or of Elymas Vonran's daughter, but she had to speak with him.

The servant returned and led her into a golden-colored lounge. Kavin Gyas rose when she entered. "This is most unexpected, Lady Vonran," he said.

"For you, it doubtless is. And why waste time and words? You want to know why I, a daughter of Regent Vonran, would come to you. It is because I hope you will help me. Trey Uman is an old and close friend of yours, is he not?"

Gyas regarded her warily. "Yes, he is."

"No doubt you are aware of his extracurricular activities—the ones that have earned him the attention of Intelligence."

"I don't follow all the pastimes of my friends—or of Intelligence."

"I will not ask you to admit it, but we both know what he does. Now, here is the point of my visit. I want to meet with Emperor Alexander. I am asking you to ask Trey Uman to arrange it."

Gyas looked startled, and then even less at ease with her. "And why would you want to meet with Alexander?"

"So I can put the Empire into his hands."

Gyas stared at her with mingled surprise and suspicion. "You would betray your own father?"

The word dug deep into Zelrynn's heart. "No. I would save my country—and him."

Gyas looked at her long and searchingly. "Very well," he said at last. "I will speak with my friend. Where will you be?"

"I am going to the Library of Tinath. I will wait to hear from you—or Alexander's operatives—there. I advise Chief Uman not to contact me at all."

"So be it."

D'John had conducted quite a few briefings in his day, but none before the lead generals of the military. Gawin Gaelin, Adon Kereth, Thaddaeus, and Chief Kinlol were his audience. General Kereth had given him the task of developing the strategy for repelling Adesh's ground invasion, and now he had to present it. And he couldn't help it: He suffered from stage fright.

He began: "We don't know whether Adesh intends to infiltrate the command bases before the space attack, or launch a frontal assault after it. So I have designed this strategy to defend against both ... " D'John laid it all out, and when he reached the end, he waited for their verdict.

General Kereth glanced over at Kinlol and gave him a distinctly smug look. General Gaelin nodded. "It will do," he said. "We will implement it. What is your next assignment?"

"None that I know of, sir."

"Well, there's one that you don't know of, Ryanson," said Kereth. "I was planning to send you away just after this briefing." He glanced around the table. "Just an hour ago we received our first communique from Trey Uman since Ryanson's mission there. He has a contact for us. He says it is of the highest priority and rates our best agent. That's you, Ryanson. It's a contact mission and nothing more. Take one other man and be back in three days, if you can."

"Yes, sir. Where am I going?"

"The Library of Tinath."

D'John wasn't sure what planet that was on, but he could look it up later. "How will I know the contact?"

"Call on the eagle."

"Call on the eagle?" D'John repeated.

"My reaction exactly, Ryanson. I looked up a diagram of the Library. One of the guest lodges is called the Eyrie. Your contact will be there."

"Is there anything else I should know, sir?"

“Nothing that you haven't already learned.”

D'John nodded. “It seems straightforward enough.”

“Yes. And that, Ryanson, is when you should keep your eyes open widest.”

The Library of Tinath had been built on the heights of the Tinath mountain range. The Library was on the other side of the world from the city Telnaria, and far north, near the pole. It was a frigid place, high in snow and low in oxygen. The builders had had to expend great effort in only making Tinath livable. D'John, viewing their work, was left to conclude that they wanted isolation. The only other explanation was that they were insane.

He and another commando, a captain called Lang, arrived at Tinath late in the evening. They sought out the guest lodge called Eyrie. For a moment they stood in front of it. D'John glanced around the makeshift neighborhood of lodges. No one in sight, for what it was worth. He looked at Lang. “Well, let's meet the eagle.” He pressed the call-pad and waited.

After a few minutes the door opened. A beautiful woman stood in the doorway, looking at them.

D'John overcame his surprise—a beautiful woman was not his typical contact—and said, “We were told to call on the eagle.”

He saw recognition of the code-phrase in her eyes. She nodded and stepped aside.

D'John and Lang accepted the invitation, coming into the lodge. When the door had closed behind them, D'John asked, “Why did you want to see us?”

She turned to him. “What I have to tell you must be said to the emperor himself.”

Now there was something no contact had ever told him. “I'm afraid that's not our policy.”

“I know.”

As D'John looked at her, suddenly she was familiar to him. There was something about her facial structure, the darkness of her hair and eyes against the paleness of her skin ... “Vonran,” he said, before thinking.

She smiled. “Yes.”

“Yes?” D'John prompted, drawing out the word.

“I am Zelrynn Vonran. Elymas Vonran is my father.”

The word sprang into D'John's mind—*trap*. He shot a look at Lang, who had the same thought written all over his face.

“Don't be afraid. It's no trap. But I must see Emperor Alexander.”

D'John looked at her, trying to read anything in her eyes. “About what?”

“If I told you, you wouldn't need to bring me to Alexander to find out.”

D'John was certain she was not going to tell him anything. He glanced at Lang, who muttered, “Your call, Major.”

They had traveled back to Revlan—Gawin Gaelin, Thaddaeus, Kereth, and Kinlol himself. Nemin Ziphernan had returned from the Empire, and they were there to hear his report to the emperor.

It was a glowing one. After recounting his travels and talks with all the prefects, Ziphernan concluded, “I have absolute assurance that as soon as we give the word, six provinces will come over to us. Kavin Gyas is certain that he, together with Trey Uman, can bring their province in. We have reason to believe that once these six come over, another five will follow. That will give us twelve provinces, without fighting, within days.”

“Vonran will still control the majority of the country,” Kereth pointed out. “And it will be more than double ours.”

“It will start with that many, General,” Ziphernan answered. “It won't end with that many. The people are thoroughly tired of Vonran. Many of them are afraid. And their leaders fear Vonran. They fear his ruthlessness and his power-lust. They will come to us if they think we can win.”

“I doubt all of them will come. And Vonran wouldn't let the provinces simply desert him. If some of the provinces secede and others show signs of doing the same, he will send in the military, disband their legislatures, and depose their prefects."

"All true, Kereth," Kinlol said. "We will still have to fight. But we will be able to win. That is the crucial thing."

Kereth raised his hand. "I am only warning you all. The war is not dying down. We have not won yet—and we will not win easily. It will be hard. Millions of Emprians will die."

That grim thought filled the air, and Kinlol decided he didn't want to dwell on it. "We have to decide when to have the provinces declare themselves. If it is done soon enough, perhaps it will preclude Vonran's attack on Jearim and Nylo."

They heard a ping, then a mechanized voice: "General Kereth?"

Kereth keyed his comm. "Kereth here."

"Major Ryanson is on base. He wants to report to you immediately."

Kinlol stated the obvious. "He will have to wait."

"No," Alexander said unexpectedly. "No. Bring him in. Let's hear his report."

Kereth relayed the order into his comm: "Send him to me immediately."

Ziphernan asked, "What is the major reporting?"

"He went to Tinath to meet a contact—a high-priority contact," Kereth said. "Uman arranged it."

Kinlol looked at Kereth. "Should he not have gone back to Tokar? Why would he come here?"

"We'll find out soon enough."

This prediction was shortly followed by the door opening, and D'John Ryanson came in. Kinlol noticed Ziphernan focus a discreet but evaluating gaze at the young officer.

Ryanson bowed to Alexander. "My lord." He turned to Kereth. "Sir."

"What happened, Ryanson?" Kereth asked.

"I met the contact at Tinath and brought her back."

"What does she have for us?"

"I don't know, sir. She wouldn't tell me. She will only speak to the emperor. So I brought her here."

That was beyond Kinlol's tolerance. "We do not allow contacts to see the emperor at their demand."

"I understand, Chief Kinlol," Ryanson said, turning to him. "But we have never had a contact like this before."

Kinlol despised claims like that. "And how do you know that?"

"Because, Chief Kinlol, Vonran has only four daughters, and if one of them had defected before, I would have heard about it."

Kinlol didn't know what expression was on his face, but it must have been satisfying to Ryanson. Kinlol could see the unsuppressed amusement in his eyes—and, though it was slight, his smile.

Saucy pup. Before Kinlol could think of something to swipe that look off his face, Alexander spoke. "Bring her in, Ryanson. I want to hear what she has to tell me."

Ryanson marched out. "This should be interesting," Kereth said.

"I hope it is profitable," Kinlol replied.

Kereth cocked his head at him, but before they could go further, the door opened again, and Ryanson led in a young woman.

Good breeding overtook the men, and they came to their feet —all except Alexander. As emperor he lived under rules of courtesy all his own.

Kinlol assessed her—and knew her. Zelrynn, Vonran's firstborn, long said to take after her father. She approached Alexander and curtsied. "My emperor," she hailed him.

Alexander studied her. "You wanted to speak with me. Why?"

"Because I want to make a bargain with you."

Alexander answered coolly. "What can you give me, and what do you want?"

"For the first question—I can give you the key to your throne. You are preparing to fight a civil war in which millions will die—but you need remove only one man."

"Your father."

If Zelrynn felt any shame at the point—either for what he did or what she was doing—she didn't show it. "Yes. Take him, and you have the throne. I can get you into the Palace. I trust, once there, you can complete the work."

"So that is what you offer. What do you want?"

Zelrynn hesitated a moment, and her expression and her voice softened a little. "By his actions, my father has forfeited to you both his life and his freedom. I want both. I would buy my father's life and freedom with your throne. That is my bargain."

There was a long moment of silence. "I have heard you," Alexander said at last. He looked at Ryanson. "Major, call in the guard."

Ryanson obeyed. He stepped out of the room and returned in a moment behind the guard.

"Sergeant," Alexander said, "I want you to provide this woman with quarters and see to it that she has everything she needs."

The sergeant bowed, and he and Zelrynn left the room. Ryanson looked at Alexander. "Am I dismissed, my lord?"

"No." Alexander flicked his hand at an empty chair. "Sit down."

For one moment Ryanson stood still in awkward surprise. Then he joined the men at the table.

Alexander made eye contact with Ryanson and asked, "What do you think of her method of handing over her father? Is it enough?"

"What is the objective? I mean, after we capture Vonran, I assume we then force him to abdicate. Will we do that in the Palace, or will we have to take him somewhere else? Is the operation an extraction?"

Alexander glanced at his other advisors. "What do you think?"

"My advice, lord," Kereth said, "is no—do not leave the Palace. It will lend credibility to his abdication if it takes place in the Palace."

No one disagreed with that, and Alexander turned back to D'John. "No extraction. Is it feasible?"

"Zelrynn Vonran is on the inside; I believe she can get us in.

From there ... yes, we can capture Vonran. There will be dangers, some of them significant—but yes, it's feasible."

"I'll defer to your judgment on that, Major," Ziphernan said. "But is it the best strategy for winning? We have whole provinces ready to come over."

"What can we lose?" Kinlol meant it as a rhetorical question.

D'John didn't take it as one. His expression shifted, and he said, "With all due respect, sir, the life of every man who goes."

The rebuke hit home, and for a long moment complete silence reigned. Then Gaelin began speaking. "I don't fear a trap. I believe Zelrynn's motivations. But what of the price? It's not only that justice demands Vonran's death. Can we be certain of ending this war without it? What if, after we set him free, he incites his followers once again? What if they disregard his abdication and fight for him? What of Zidon Adesh?"

The other men traded uneasy glances all across the table.

Zelrynn paced, as much as she could. The room they gave her was pathetically small.

She knew that what she was doing was right. Alexander was the rightful emperor; it was only just that he take power back from her father. Beyond question she was serving the good of her country. Millions of her people would be spared from death—and millions more from griefs of every kind. It was even for the good of her father. She was protecting him from imprisonment and death. She was saving him from adding more and more sins to his account, from bringing Alexander's shed blood onto his head. His lust for power was destroying everything good in him. That deadly cup heated his blood and turned his head, and it was high time to take it from his hand.

Zelrynn kept these things cycling through her mind, and it didn't help, at least not enough. Right thing or not, doing it kept her heart in turmoil. But she could hold back her emotions, hold them down while she worked with all her energy and ability. It was another thing she had learned from her father, another thing he had taught her.

The door drew open, and a soldier stood there. "Ma'am," he said, "I have been ordered to take you to Emperor Alexander."

"Then let us go." Zelrynn went with the soldier, and they retraced the way back to where she had first talked with Alexander. It occurred to her, as she looked at the drab, utilitarian base, that her father would give a great deal to know about it. Then he would destroy it, fully intending to leave Alexander dead.

Soon she again stood before Alexander. His advisors were seated all around him—and Zelrynn was a little surprised to notice that the young commando who had brought her here, Major Ryanson, was one of them.

"Lady Vonran," Alexander said, "we are curious about your motivations. Why are you handing your father over to us?"

"To save him—and my country."

"So you love both. Which do you love more?"

It was a strange question, but Zelrynn couldn't afford to pick and choose which questions she answered. "I would say my father."

"That's natural. But you know that all loves must give way to right and wrong."

Zelrynn nodded as apprehension sent heat tingling through her. "I know."

"Then, even if we refused to protect your father, shouldn't you still hand him over—for the good of the country?"

Zelrynn stared at him, and what was horrible was that she knew he was right. She couldn't allow innocents to die for the sake of a guilty man—even if he was her father.

But that didn't mean she would give in without a fight. "I insist, Emperor Alexander," she answered.

He looked at her for a long moment. "Some people say," he said at last, "that your father murdered mine."

Unexpected compassion flooded her. "He didn't. He wouldn't have, not then. Whatever he is now ... " Zelrynn couldn't finish the sentence.

Alexander didn't speak. Nor did anyone else. Zelrynn held out, hoping to call their bluff before they called hers.

A few long minutes passed. Then Alexander said, "I accept your bargain." He looked around at his advisors. "You are all witnesses. You will honor this pact with the Lady Vonran."

"Of course, my lord," Kereth answered for them all.

Alexander looked back at Zelrynn. "Major Ryanson will work with you to determine what you can do to hand your father over."

"I will do what is necessary, my lord," she answered. "But it must be decided swiftly. I must return to Telnaria as quickly as possible."

"I am putting this whole operation under orders to be carried out as soon as possible. Major Ryanson, as the finest commando serving me, this mission is assigned to you. You will choose the best men we have and devise the strategy. Because of the import of the mission, I am putting you under the direct supervision of General Kereth. He will review your work and have the final say. General Gaelin, you are to devote yourself to defending our territory. Ziphernan—continue to develop the secession strategy."

"My lord," Kereth said, "I think it would be best if I went on this operation."

"Why?"

"So that I can deal with Vonran."

"It may be a good idea," Kinlol put in.

Alexander glanced at him, then Kereth. "You have my permission."

"Thank you."

Alexander had ordered his subordinates to be quick. They outdid his highest expectation. Not twenty-four hours after receiving the assignment, they reported they were ready to go. Alexander ordered them to present their plans.

They gathered around him in his office—Kinlol, Kereth, and D'John. Gawin and Thaddaeus Gaelin had already left Revlan to oversee the defense of Regial's border.

Kereth gave the briefing. "Unfortunately," he began, "I have had no time to prepare viewing material. So you'll have to use your imaginations. Now, you know there are limestone caves beneath Telnaria. In one of these caves is a secret tunnel that leads up to the Palace."

"Do you mean," Kinlol said, a look of some suspicion on his face, "that there is an underground entrance to the Palace?"

"Exactly."

"I never heard of it. How is it that you know something I don't?"

"As for this particular case, Kinlol, Emperor Judah told me. When I had been the commander of the Emperor's Guard for three years, he told me of a secret escape route from the Palace. The royals had kept it strictly for and to themselves, but he wanted me to assure its functionality. I was ordered to do it alone and to keep this secret to the end of my days. I gave the emperor my word, made sure the royal escape route was still viable, and forgot about it for years."

"I hope," Kinlol said, "that you didn't forget we had a secret way into the Palace until Zelrynn jogged your memory."

"As a matter of fact, Kinlol, I didn't. We can't use the route without someone already inside. It was made to be an escape route, Kinlol. It is an exit, not an entrance. The door can only be opened from the inside."

"Surely there is a way to force it open."

"Surely there is, and surely the door was built that if anyone tried, the Emperor's Guard would be alerted immediately. That is why we need Zelrynn. She will let us in. The entrance is located in one of the underground storage rooms. There is a lift nearby that leads directly up to the royal residence. We will arrive late at night, and so Vonran should be there."

Kinlol shook his head. "I still think it would be better to kill him."

"We couldn't do that with honor," Alexander answered. "Is that all, General?"

"Yes, my lord."

"When will you leave?"

"An hour, unless you say otherwise."

"I don't." Now to let fall his surprise. "I have one addition to your plan. I am coming."

There was a shocked pause. "I would advise against it, my lord," Kinlol said. "Very strongly."

"I know, Kinlol. And I know you'll say the same, Kereth. But I have stayed behind while others went into danger long enough. This time I will go, depose Vonran, and take my place on the throne. All the Empire will hear that I am in command in the Palace." And it was time he defied all his advisors; it was time he declared his independence.

"Consider carefully, Alexander," Kereth cautioned. "If you are lost, so is our whole cause."

"And yet ... " The voice, unexpectedly, was D'John's, and he looked up at the men. "Think of the difference between the emperor claiming the throne from the Palace, and claiming it from a secret base in Regial."

Kinlol took a patronizing tone. "The risk is great."

D'John maintained a respectful demeanor. "There's a time for great risk."

"In my judgment ... "

Alexander interrupted Kinlol, gently but firmly. "It is my judgment that decides the question. And I am going."

Kereth and Kinlol looked at each other. Kereth looked at Alexander, and a strange expression that seemed to carry both sadness and happiness slowly came over his face. "You are the emperor," he said at last. "What can we say?"

Kinlol's face was unreadable. He took a look at Alexander, a look at Kereth, and then his eyes went back to Alexander. "Then I am coming, too," he declared.

Alexander looked at him, surprised. "Why?"

"Let's be brutally frank, Kinlol," Kereth said. "What can you contribute that gives you a reason to put your life at risk?"

"I have served the emperors, the house of Alheenan, all my life. If this mission ends in disaster, then the emperors, the heirs of Alexander the Mighty, and the Empire of my fathers will end with it. I will meet the same fate they do."

Alexander had felt much frustration, much annoyance with his old counselor over the past few years. He had yearned for a chance to rebel. Suddenly he was so moved by the old man's loyalty that it nearly staggered him.

Kereth looked at Kinlol intently, wonderment alight in his eyes. “All the years I have known you, Chief Kinlol, you have talked like a politic man—sometimes wise, sometimes only political. This is the first time I have heard you talk like a man who charges the breach for love of his country.”

And no one could miss the approval, or the respect, in the general's voice.

Afternoon faded over Telnaria. Elymas Vonran stood at the window, watching the sun turn west. It was something to do.

He heard the door open, but he didn't turn around. Then he heard Zidon Adesh's voice: “Forgive my tardiness, my lord. A matter came up that I had to deal with immediately.”

Vonran waited.

“My lord, I have come to report that our preparations are complete.”

Vonran turned to him. “Everything is in place?”

“Everything. We await only your command.”

“Then I give it to you. Go, and do not come back until you can report that Alexander is dead.”

“As you command.” Adesh bowed and left.

Vonran turned back to the window, considering. It would be more than a day before Adesh opened his attack on Revlan and Vaaris, and hours after that before anyone knew the outcome. He had all that time to wait.

Vonran left his office and went up to his residence. He had just come in when he heard Cala call to him, “Father?”

“Yes, Cala.”

She came out from the lounge. “Zelrynn called this afternoon. She's coming here tomorrow.”

“Ah.” Vonran kept his surprise from showing to his

daughter. After their last conversation, he hadn't expected Zelrynn to come back for a very long time. "Did she say why?"

"No."

Vonran evaded the curious look she gave him for the question. "You'll enjoy seeing your sister again." Then he noticed her clothes. "What are you dressed for?"

"The dinner-party. I was leaving just now. You said I could go a few days ago. Do you remember?"

He didn't, but perhaps that was due to being distracted at the time. He had been distracted a lot lately. Vonran looked at his daughter and said abruptly, "You look just like your mother."

Cala remembered little—maybe nothing—about her mother, but she knew he was praising her, and she smiled shyly.

The smile brought back more memories of Dianthe. Vonran leaned down and kissed Cala lightly on the forehead. "Go ahead," he said. "Enjoy yourself." And maybe there would be a young man there who would fall in love with her as he had with Dianthe, and she, too, would fly his nest. She was seventeen, and for the first time Vonran fully realized that she had grown up. He couldn't stop the sadness that brought.

Cala smiled at him, said her good-bye, and hurried out. Vonran had come home to eat dinner, but now he wasn't really hungry. He went to his bedroom. On the end table by his bed he kept a picture of Dianthe—her eyes sparkling, her mouth curved in a half-smile that spoke of hidden knowledge, and hidden laughter. She had always seemed to carry both with her.

Vonran picked up the picture and looked at it. Then, sudden and unwelcome, he heard his daughter's voice: *My mother loved a good man. She would not have known you.*

He slammed the picture onto the table and turned away. It wasn't true. Zelrynn didn't understand. They would always know each other. They had shared love, life, themselves. Nothing could wipe that out.

The conviction brought no warmth with it. Maybe it brought tiredness; he felt nothing else. Slowly Vonran turned back. He gently lifted the picture, regretting his rough handling. He looked at the image of his wife, and the weight and number of his years without her crushed down on him.

"Our little Calanthra," he said aloud, feeling love and sadness. "All grown up."

CHAPTER

V

* * * * * * * * * * * * * * * * *

THE journey through the limestone caves had been long and strange. Now at last they found themselves at the end.

D'John glanced at his companions as they gathered at the dead end of a rocky passageway. There were only two other commandos; the rest of the company were the three most important men in the insurgency, and D'John still experienced surreality over that. The artificial light was strange and uneven in these underground places, and everyone looked strange in it.

General Kereth knelt by the cave's wall. D'John took out his comm, but looked at the general, unsure what he was doing. "Should I send the alert to Zelrynn, General?" he asked.

"Go ahead."

D'John sent the alert. Zelrynn wasn't far away. At least, she wasn't supposed to be.

A sudden grating sound filled the chamber, and D'John turned to see a section of the wall pulling forward. It swung around, with surprising speed, and one of D'John's men had to jump clear. He looked quite displeased.

D'John stepped closer to the opening, shining his wristlight at it. The room within appeared to be hardly wider than its door and only a few paces deep. D'John's light caught on something metallic, and he focused on it. After a moment he understood what it was: a ladder, built into the rock face.

Again the feeling of incongruity slammed him. He glanced at Kereth. “So we have to climb up to it. How far?”

“Far enough to start climbing now.”

“I thought as much. I'll take point; Lang, you follow behind. Then will come General Kereth, then Chief Kinlol, then the emperor. Makis, you bring up the rear.” D'John turned off his wristlight and, going forward, took hold of the ladder's rungs. He climbed up it by feel, hearing the others follow. The noise grew louder as each person joined, until the tunnel echoed with the sounds.

So they ascended in the dark.

Zidon Adesh stood on the bridge of his ship, staring out the viewport. He saw the strange, streaked lights of hyperspace collapse, and they were in real space again. A planet hung before them, far from its sun, remote in remote space.

Revlan, the harbor of their long-elusive enemies. Adesh's hand clenched.

One of the young officers began talking urgently: “There is a frigate to starboard, near the planet. It's accelerating away from us.”

“Capture it if you can,” Adesh said. “Destroy it if you must.” He waited as they carried out his orders. Once this small nuisance was taken care of they could move in on the planet. He had waited three years for this; he could wait a few minutes more.

Zelrynn had thought it would be a good night for Cala to be away from home. Her first step in accomplishing that was arranging an evening with her, Cala, and Vera and her husband. After dinner, before they set out for the theater, Zelrynn took Vera aside.

“I want to ask a favor of you,” she said. “After the play I am returning to the Palace. I want you to make sure Cala goes home with you.”

Vera brushed her dark hair back. “Why?”

“I'll tell you tomorrow; I can't tell you tonight. Trust me, Vera.”

Vera put her hands on her hips. “What is going to happen at

the Palace tonight?"

Zelrynn gazed at her sister a long moment before answering, "Trust me."

The two sisters stood staring at each other until finally Vera turned away. "All right."

Zelrynn smiled. "Thank you."

That night Zelrynn returned to the Palace alone. She slipped out of the theater before the play was over, leaving Cala in the hands of her sister and brother-in-law. It was getting late, but it was still before the chosen time.

Zelrynn, guessing where her father would be, went to his study. She would have preferred to go straight to her room, but she knew what she had to do. The door drew open for her, and she went in to see her father seated at his desk—his work in front of him, a long-stemmed glass by his hand. He glanced up at her, then back down at his work. "Did you enjoy your evening?"

"Yes. Father, I should tell you that Cala isn't here. She's spending the night at Vera's house."

He nodded, and Zelrynn turned around to leave.

"Zelrynn."

At his voice she turned back. "Yes?"

"Where are you going?"

"To my bedroom."

"I know it's late, Zelrynn, but you never minded the occasional late night. Why don't we talk for a while?"

Over her life he had extended that invitation to her many times, and she had never refused it—until today. "I'm sorry, Father, not tonight." Then she hurried out so she would not have to see her father's face.

In her bedroom she hardly knew what to do with herself. She paced, she sat, she tried to read. Finally her comm pinged. Zelrynn hastily took it out, reading the one-line message just to be sure. Then she left her room.

Zelrynn made her way to the lift in darkness. The last thing she wanted was to meet her father on her way down. The lift bore her down to the storage rooms that housed the personal possessions of the house of Alheenan. Clothes, jewelry, furniture, all manner of artwork—there was such wealth there, stored and forgotten by people who had never been poor enough to learn its value.

Zelrynn went into a room near the lift. Near the far wall was a clear space—a patch of bare floor. A tallish end table stood close by. It had one drawer, which Zelrynn opened. She slipped her hand into it, feeling along the roof of the drawer. Finally her fingers slid across the catch. She pressed on it, then took her hand out and stepped aside. She was not entirely sure what was going to happen next.

After a moment she felt a faint tremor through the floor beneath her feet. Zelrynn backed away a few paces and watched.

She didn't have to wait long. A large square of the floor sank down and then slid away. She was now staring down a dark, well-cut hole.

And nothing happened. Zelrynn stood back, seeing nothing, hearing nothing. After a while she heard faint sounds coming from the passage. Gradually they became louder, and Zelrynn knew that people were coming up the tunnel.

Then—it took long enough—a man emerged. For one moment—standing with only his head and shoulders above the pristine floor—he looked comical. Zelrynn had to restrain her smile as D'John Ryanson climbed into the room. "Glad to see you, Major," she said, and meant it. For some reason she was glad that they had not sent complete strangers.

He nodded to her. "Glad to get here." He stood to the side of the opening. Another commando—she recognized him, too—followed him out. Then General Kereth came, and after him Gerog Kinlol.

He, the first of all of them, looked worse for the journey, and Ryanson helped him as he came up. Zelrynn looked at the Chief in surprise. Then the next man caught her eye—Alexander himself. Zelrynn was still trying to understand that when a sixth man, one she did not recognize, came up.

"That's all of us, Zelrynn," Ryanson said.

Zelrynn went over to the table and searched out the catch

once again. The segment of floor rose back into place, and she marveled at how flawless it looked.

"Where is your father?" Ryanson asked.

"As of an hour or so ago, in his study."

Ryanson nodded and glanced at Alexander. "I don't suppose ... "

"What?"

"Never mind. Show us the way."

Zelrynn turned and led the way to the lift. They went up in silence, and Zelrynn noticed that the one she had never seen before, Makis, kept gripping his sidearm. It brought on sudden fear.

The seven of them had no sooner gotten out of the lift when Ryanson said, "All right, everyone. Hold it." He looked up and down the corridor. It turned sharply at each end. "Where is the study?"

Zelrynn pointed to the corridor that branched out on their right. "Go down that until you reach the first corridor that opens up on your right. The first door on the left will be it."

"All right. Makis, go left. Stand your ground at the beginning of this corridor. If you encounter any trouble, contact me immediately."

"What is wrong, Major?" Alexander asked.

"Your presence—no disrespect intended. General Kereth, if you would stand sentry opposite Makis at the other end of this corridor ... "

"Certainly, Major," the general answered, and Zelrynn couldn't tell if there was irony in his voice or not. "But first, I would be interested in hearing your plan."

"I am going to take Lang, go to the regent's study, and seize him. The rest of you will remain here. At the first sign of trouble, get into the lift and leave the Palace. Head into the caves immediately. Don't wait. Lang and I will stay behind and cover your escape if we can. They will never need to know how we got in here or that the emperor came to the Palace. Understood?"

"Yes, sir," Kereth answered.

Ryanson looked at him. "You know, General, it's not very sporting to mock a man who can't answer you for fear of a court-martial."

"I'm not mocking, Major."

Ryanson stared at him a moment, then turned away. "Come on, Lang." The two men left, disappearing down the corridor.

Zelrynn looked around her. At each end of the corridor an armed man stood guard. Near the middle, she stood by the lift with Emperor Alexander and Chief Kinlol. And two commandos were now making their way to her father's study. It wouldn't take them long to reach it. Then—she could picture them readying themselves by the door a moment, bursting through, grabbing her father ...

She didn't want to imagine her father at that moment. The minutes crept past in unbroken silence. Alexander and Kinlol began shifting, glancing at each other and down the corridor. Makis and Kereth maintained their concentration.

Kereth suddenly stepped back, and Lang walked into the corridor. Zelrynn looked at him, surprised that she hadn't heard even one footstep.

Lang spoke in a soft voice, "The major says to come to the study, as quietly as you can."

Zelrynn thought that a little strange—and she could tell, by the way General Kereth frowned, that he did also. They all grouped together, as if sensing danger in their soft-spoken summons, and made the short journey to the study.

Zelrynn steeled herself as she walked into the study. Her gaze flitted around, ready to face her father ...

She looked sharply at D'John Ryanson, standing behind her father's desk. "Where is he?"

"My question exactly."

Her heart sank. "He wasn't here?"

The major shook his head. "No. We don't have him."

"Perhaps," said Kereth, "he went to bed."

Perhaps. Perhaps not. Zelrynn crossed over to the desk, reaching over to work the comm. "Captain?" she asked.

"Yes?" The man's voice came through the comm.

"This is Zelrynn Vonran. I just came into my father's study and found it empty. Is my father here?"

"He is in the Palace, milady."

"What about the residence?"

There was a pause. "He is not in the residence, milady. He passed a few guards not long ago. You will probably find him in his office."

"Thank you." Zelrynn cut off.

D'John gestured to everything laid out on the desk. "He's been working." He lifted a half-full glass. "And drinking."

Kereth looked at it. "What and how much?"

Zelrynn was offended at the implication. "You don't need to wonder. He is completely sober."

"Drunkenness is a sin, I hear," Kinlol said.

The sarcasm stung her, and she snapped back, "He always stays in control of himself, if you need an explanation to believe me."

Alexander cut into the conversation. "Does he usually go to his office to work at this time of night?"

Zelrynn looked at him, calming down. "No. I have never known him to do it before."

"I hope nothing's afoot," Kereth murmured.

"I hope he gets back soon," Lang said.

"Who said we're going to wait?" Kinlol asked.

"We can't go down after him. What does it hurt us to wait?"

Ryanson spoke suddenly: "That can't be good."

Everyone turned to look at him. He was looking at a holo-projector in his hand. Ryanson glanced up at them and then held out the projector. He activated it, and an image sprang up—the planet Revlan.

A shocked pause followed, broken by Ryanson: "Personally, I can think of only one reason Elymas Vonran would have to be interested in a planet like Revlan."

Adesh stood staring out the viewport, gradually becoming more and more impatient. "Captain?" he asked at length.

"We have a report, sir." The man must have been relieved.

"The frigate and our new prisoners have been brought on board."

Adesh opened his mouth to give the command—

"One of the prisoners is of special interest, sir," the captain went on. "Nemin Ziphernan."

The command died unspoken. Adesh considered, and slowly turned away from the captain. "Captain, give orders to the entire task-force. I want them to cloak and move in around the planet, but no one should attack until I give the order. And have Ziphernan brought here."

Adesh kept his back turned to the rest of the bridge until he heard two men approaching him, and a voice said, "Here he is, General."

Adesh turned around, and a slow, satisfied smile creased his face. He looked Ziphernan over and then glanced at the soldier. "Come, now. There's no reason to bind him. He's our guest here today—to the annihilation of Revlan."

Ziphernan looked at Adesh, cold pride in his eyes. It irked Adesh, and he dug in again, hopefully this time closer to home. "The regent will be pleased when I report to him. He will be glad to have his hands on you. Or perhaps," he continued, "I should call him the emperor. He will be before the night is through."

Ziphernan looked at him with scorn. "When the night is through, Vonran will not be the emperor. He won't even be the regent."

"Don't boast like a hero or a fool, Ziphernan. You are no hero. Are you a fool?"

"You will see."

Adesh was beginning to find the younger man's confidence disturbing. "Alexander will soon be dead," he said, probing. "Revlan cannot withstand us. It will be completely destroyed."

"I imagine it will be." And Ziphernan did not look bothered at all.

That bothered Adesh immensely. All of a sudden, he felt himself on the verge of another disaster—a plan flawlessly laid, skillfully executed, and one thing gone wrong, one fatal thing. "Follow me," he ordered Ziphernan. He went into his flag room, adjacent to the bridge, and pointed to the conference table. "Sit."

Ziphernan took a seat and raised his eyebrows at Adesh. "And what turn did the conversation take that it needs to be taken behind closed doors?"

"If you want to keep information to yourself, Ziphernan, keep it to yourself. Don't gloat over me with it. Why doesn't Revlan's destruction concern you? What is going to happen to Vonran tonight?"

Ziphernan looked at Adesh a long minute and then glanced away. He wasn't going to answer.

At least, he wasn't planning on it.

Vonran walked along the verandah, the wind cold against his face. He hadn't realized the year had gotten so old.

He had come out hoping to clear his head. He had been restless, ill at ease all day, but over the past hour it had become worse. Neither the walk nor the cold, fresh air was able to drive away his uneasiness.

Vonran glanced up at the moon, large, pale, and cold. Its light was the only light he had to see by. He could have walked in less. As Vonran looked at it, he thought of Zelrynn, and he sighed and walked on. When he first heard she was coming to the Palace he thought it meant she had not rejected him, but now he realized he was wrong. Zelrynn had barely said hello and good-bye to him before taking Cala and going out to spend the evening with Vera. When she came back, he asked her to come talk with him. He had no subject on his mind, just a desire to know that he still had his daughter. And she said no and went to bed.

So now he knew: She had come back to see her sisters. She didn't even want to see him. He had lost her, just as he had lost Declan's friendship. Zelrynn had spoken to him the way Declan had looked at him—like a stranger, and not one they wanted to know.

The wind seemed to carry Zelrynn's words to him: *You are not the father who raised me.*

My mother loved a good man.

She would not have known you.

That was how she denied him, how she made him a stranger to her—and a stranger to Dianthe, the only woman who loved him and received his love in return.

Vonran looked ahead, and suddenly this walk seemed familiar to him—the night-darkened walk on the verandah, between the pillars and the alcoves. Long ago he used to take walks through the Palace for no good reason. But one useful thing had come of it—he had learned of Kinlol's conspiracy against him. It was on this very verandah, in one of these alcoves—

Vonran stopped, looking at the alcove ahead of him. His eyes carefully traced its intricately carved lintels. Could it have been this very alcove? Could this have been where he stood in the shadows, listening to his enemies plot against him?

He had never had peace in his life since that moment. That sudden knowledge startled him; he had never realized it before. But it was true, unquestionably true. The conspiracy he had discovered had become one of the central facts of his existence. His mind had revolved endlessly around it. For more than a decade it had lain—usually secretly—beneath so many actions and words. Everything he did was informed by it—and all at once the ceaseless calculating, machinating, and fighting felt like a burden.

For a while Vonran stood still. He remembered that even now Adesh was killing Alexander, and so ending Vonran's struggle with him. Standing in the dark, in the wind, he tried to comfort himself with that thought.

Adesh drew out the bottle, considered the words stenciled on its surface. “A strong berry wine,” he said. “Too sweet for you? Too potent?”

“Are you a wine savant?” Ziphernan asked.

“I'm not even a wine dilettante. But I am an appreciative drinker. Will you join me?”

“Certainly. It is dull to drink alone.”

“You're practically the Good Samaritan, Ziphernan.” Adesh

poured out the wine and brought Ziphernan's cup to him. He settled in his own chair and watched Ziphernan take a drink. “Tell me, Nemin Ziphernan,” he said. “Are you a good man?”

Ziphernan laughed. “What is a good man, Adesh? A man who follows whatever dusty moral conventions are currently held up by society?”

“I am glad.”

Ziphernan looked at him. “Of what?”

“Of your answer. A good man would not betray his master or turn on his colleagues. A good man would rather be dead than a traitor. But you are not a good man.”

“Are you presuming that I will betray Alexander?”

“Of course you will—if the price is right. You never fooled me, Ziphernan. I know you. I know what you are. You hide it from most people—but I see it.”

Ziphernan leaned forward. All merriment had vanished from his face; he looked almost dangerous. “What do you see?”

“That you care about nothing but yourself. You have no morals, no principles, no ideals. You don't love your nation or fear God or care about honor. Everything you do, you do for yourself. You only helped Alexander because Alexander can help you more than Elymas Vonran. But if Elymas Vonran can help you more than Alexander, you will help him.”

“You talk boldly, Adesh.”

“I talk truly. Now tell me. What do you think Alexander will give you?”

“He will make me Chief of State.”

“Is that the most you hope for?”

“I see the premiership as a possibility.”

“Ah. Well, then, I can beat Alexander's payment. I can promise you both those things—and the possibility of the emperorship.”

“What do you mean?”

“Not any disloyalty to Vonran. That you must put out of your mind altogether. But the man will not live forever. When he dies, the throne will be empty. I know what he plans—he plans to eliminate the dynasty. Emperors will henceforth be elected."

"To life-long terms?"

"I can't speak to that, except to guarantee that his term will be life-long."

"Of course."

Adesh could tell by Ziphernan's expression that he was thinking, and thinking hard. He waited.

Ziphernan abruptly stood up and turned away. "I know all the counsels of Alexander," he said. "I know all his plans. At this moment I know where he and his chief men are."

Anticipation began to grow hot within Adesh, but he held his silence.

Ziphernan turned back. "So we must act swiftly."

Adesh stood up. "Say on."

Ziphernan paused, eyeing Adesh carefully. "We are now in league?"

"We are in league," Adesh assured him. "I will pay your price—Chief of State and a chance at the emperorship. But first you must pay me mine: Where is Alexander?"

"At the Palace."

"The Palace? Then the regent—"

Ziphernan nodded. "I would talk to the commander of the Palace Guard immediately."

Vonran stepped out of the lift, into the darkness. He went forward.

He turned into a corridor, and three paces down something set his skin tingling. He glanced behind him, opened his mouth to activate the lights—

Sudden movement came from behind him, and a strong arm locked across his chest. He began to struggle—and then he heard the distinct sound of a blaster's safety catch being disengaged, right next to his face. He went still.

"That's right," his assailant said, and stepped back, loosening his grip. A horrible chill swept through Vonran, raising his hair on end, as he waited for the assassin to fire.

The man's voice broke through his tension: "All right. Start walking, towards your study."

Vonran obeyed. By the time they arrived at his study his heartbeat had slowed down only a little. He paused in front of the door, feeling that his doom lay just beyond it, and then he hardened himself against fear and walked in.

The room was fully lit, and that surprised him, though not for any rational reason. It surprised him even more to see Alexander sitting at his desk, Adon Kereth and Chief Kinlol standing behind him. Vonran's astonishment, for one moment, swept away everything else. So it was out of curiosity, plain and simple, that he glanced behind him at his waylayer. A young man, with a military look to him.

"Come forward," Alexander commanded.

Vonran did so, his gaze moving between Alexander and Kereth and Kinlol. It seemed a strange dream—a nightmare, in fact—to find them all in his home when they were supposed to be under Zidon Adesh's attack.

Alexander nodded to the young man. "Thank you, Major." Then he looked at Vonran. "I will keep this straightforward, Regent. You are being removed from your position. Whether by death or by abdication is your choice. Major Ryanson here will provide for the first option. Chief Kinlol has prepared for the second. Chief?"

Kinlol looked at Vonran, gloating in his eyes. "I have drawn up the papers for your abdication. You need only confirm them with your voice imprint, and I will issue the declaration to the government and all the Empire. Then we will ask you to broadcast a short message announcing your abdication and ordering your troops to stand down. That will do it."

"We realize it sticks in your throat," Kereth said. "But you have a good motivation. You die otherwise."

"And if I do it?"

"You live."

In a small way that was the truth; in the way that mattered, it was a lie. Vonran knew that after he had served their purpose in yielding power they would try him for treason. It would be a self-righteous charade of a trial, with a foregone verdict and a foregone sentence. His choices were between immediate and delayed execution.

Apparently impatient with his silence, Alexander spoke again. “Death or abdication, Vonran. Make your choice.”

Vonran looked at him, saw his certainty as to which he would choose, and resented it. “I choose,” he answered, “death.”

The looks that overtook the three men's faces were almost satisfying. “I didn't think even you loved power that much,” Alexander commented.

“More than life,” Kereth said. “Even more than your children.”

Vonran despised the sentimental play. “What do you care for them? You have my choice.” Again fear began to twist in Vonran; again he tried to ignore it.

Kereth's expression changed; the hardness seemed smoothed away. “You may not believe me, Regent,” he said, in a quieter voice. “But I do care. For your sake and for their sake, let go. You've fought too long, and if you don't back down now, you will lose everything.”

Vonran didn't try to hide his contempt. He showed it plainly, digging into it. It made him feel stronger. “I don't believe you, Colonel. I am not a fool; I don't believe your false compassion—or your false mercy.”

Kereth's eyes narrowed, and then realization lightened his face. Alexander looked bemused, and vaguely disturbed. Kinlol gazed steadily and angrily at Vonran, but there was something hollow about his anger, as if he were not really regretful.

Vonran looked over at the major, Ryanson. Ryanson had his blaster out and ready, but there was a look of deep unease on his face, and he glanced at something on the other side of the room. Vonran followed his gaze and saw his daughter. Zelrynn stood there watching, her face very pale. He started, looking at her, and in that moment regretted that she had heard everything he said.

The ping of a comm pierced through the heaviness that filled the room. Then a man's voice came over the comm: “Regent Vonran, this is Colonel Dilv. We have received a report that there will be an attempt on your life tonight. I have put the Guard on high alert, and I am sending men up to your residence. Please respond, Regent."

Ryanson turned towards Vonran, gesturing with his blaster. He opened his mouth and then shut it again, shaking his head.

Dilv continued: "Whether you respond or not, I am sending the men to you immediately."

Ryanson leaned over quickly, sweeping his hand over the control panel. "You're too late, Colonel. Keep your men away; we have the regent, and you don't want to make us do anything rash." Ryanson turned the blaster in his hand, bringing its handle down over the control panel. He straightened and looked at the other men. "That will buy us a few minutes. I hope you're all quick thinkers."

They stared at him.

Colonel Dilv watched his men—heavily armed and darkly dressed—assemble in the corridor. He saw motion in the corner of his eye and turned to see a man hurrying to him. "Report, Major?" he demanded.

The major stopped, took a look at the gathering soldiers, and turned to Dilv. "Everything is in place, sir. I have snipers positioned outside, and I have men stationed at all the entrances to the residence."

"Good."

The major glanced at the men, then down the corridor. "Are they nearly done unsealing the doors, sir?"

"I believe so."

He was silent a moment, conflict evident on his face. Then he spoke. "If you don't mind, could you explain this entrance to me?"

"Explain?" Dilv prodded.

"How do you know of it and why does no one else?" he clarified. He had been serving under Dilv for a couple years.

Dilv let a few moments of silence go by and then gave his answer. "Years ago, Jansen, when I was a young officer, I served in the Emperor's Guard. I discovered an old stairwell leading up to the Royal Family's residence. It was long disused and mostly forgotten. When my commander at the time learned of it, he had it sealed and covered at both ends. By his order it was eliminated from all the records."

Jansen looked uneasy. "Are you sure the intruders don't know of it?"

"How could they?"

"Colonel, you could still provoke them into killing the regent."

"I know. That's why I'm leading the men up. I am leaving you in command down here."

"Yes, sir."

A lieutenant came up to them, stopping at a respectful distance. "Sir?"

"Yes?"

"The doors are unsealed."

"Thank you." Dilv walked away from the lieutenant and Jansen. He stood in front of the black-clad soldiers, and they went silent, turning their gazes to him. "We are ready to go in," Dilv told them. "I don't need to remind you how difficult this mission is, or how important. A man's life has been put in our safe-keeping, and this mission will determine whether or not we fail." Dilv gave that the moment of solemnity it deserved. Then he commanded, "Move out."

They turned down the corridor, reaching a scene of minor destruction. A section of the wall had been torn out; the door had been cut out and put to the side. Dilv approached the opening and peered up into the darkness. Then he motioned to his men and entered.

The old stairwell was thick with strange smells, and Dilv was surprised at the broadness of the steps. He made a quiet and careful way up them, and cautiously eased himself through the crude opening at the stairs' head. He moved to the right and stood silent. He heard nothing in the room or from the corridor beyond. So he lifted his combat rifle and activated its mounted light.

It illuminated a man standing in the middle of the room. Dilv jerked his weapon upward, focusing on the man's chest, right at his heart. But he didn't fire, and in a moment he realized why: The man was showing no signs of a threat. Dilv's light shown off his raised hand—empty, palm outward. It was the gesture of parley.

"Colonel Dilv?" the figure asked.

The voice stirred a long and deeply slumbering memory in Dilv. "I am. Who are you?"

"I wish you joy of your advancement," the man went on. "Last we met, you were a captain."

Those words awakened the memory further. Dilv lifted his rifle, shining the light on the man's face. He blinked hard, and recognition hit Dilv like a hammer. "Colonel Kereth?"

"General Kereth. I have advanced, too." Kereth turned his head, getting the light out of his eyes. "I thought you would remember this entrance, Dilv. You didn't disappoint me."

"Yes," Dilv said, automatically. His mind was reeling. "You—"

"I am one of the men you came hunting for. I still serve Alexander, like you and I once did together. Who do you serve now?"

Dilv lowered his rifle a little. "I serve my country. I do my duty where I have been placed. I don't pick sides when the great ones bicker."

"You said something like that to me, long ago. When this whole ordeal started, you said that the great ones would have to sort it out."

Dilv was surprised at the man's memory. "I did."

"And you believe it still?"

Dilv found himself feeling defensive, and it irked him. "Of course." He gripped his rifle, holding it at the ready.

Kereth must have noticed, but he didn't show any response. "Then take your own counsel. Let the great ones sort it out."

"What do you mean?" Dilv let his suspicion be heard in his voice.

"If you don't mind turning on a light, I will explain it to you. I will explain everything."

Vonran sat at one end of the room, flanked by a guard on either side. He had been relegated there by his captors, who had then clustered around the desk talking urgently. Zelrynn was among them, and that puzzled and disturbed him.

The debate became heated, and eventually Adon Kereth left the room. Vonran watched him go and then looked back at the others. They carried on their discussion. And he had nothing to do but lean back in his chair and contemplate the bizarre situation he was in—a history-changing crisis, in which he was present only as an observer, and a limited one at that.

Finally there was movement again. The major and Zelrynn moved away from the desk, crossing the room to him. Ryanson looked at the soldiers and ordered, "Guard the emperor." They obediently left, and Ryanson took up a guarding position to Vonran's right.

Alexander had said that Ryanson would provide for his execution, and that gave Vonran an uneasy feeling as he saw the major standing there. He glanced over at Zelrynn. "What's on your mind?" he asked, keeping his voice soft, nearly gentle.

"How urgent it is that you abdicate."

He should have guessed. "I see."

"Father, is it true what General Kereth said—that you care for power more than your children or your life?"

"No, Zelrynn. I would never put you beneath that."

"Then why are you going to die for it?"

"Even if they don't kill me tonight, they'll kill me soon enough. The only question is whether they convict me of treason before executing me for it."

Zelrynn stood silent a moment. "Father, you don't understand. They are not going to kill you if you abdicate. They gave me their word."

"And you believe them?"

"They are honorable men."

"You're naive, Zelrynn. They won't let me live. Kinlol is too shrewd for that, and Kereth thinks I deserve it. I am not going to be made a fool by trusting them; I'm not going to give into them or make it easier. I would rather die in defiance than meekly step aside, and then be publicly tried, condemned, and killed."

Zelrynn thought about that. "Perhaps I was wrong," she said at length. "Perhaps it isn't power you are clinging to, but pride."

She was reminding him more and more of Declan, and he didn't like it. He turned his head away from her, looking to his left.

There were no chairs or couches near him, and so Zelrynn knelt on the floor in front of him. She tried to meet his eye, but he wouldn't look at her. This conversation was hard enough without that. "These men are telling the truth," Zelrynn told him. "They haven't lied to you or me. If you abdicate, they'll give you your life. If you refuse, they'll take it. You must believe it."

When he didn't answer, she went on. "What about Cala? What about Vera and Lydia? Don't leave me here to comfort my sisters. Don't leave us as orphans. None of us wants to lose you."

Zelrynn's words added to the burden he had been carrying these last few days, and he thought he felt it split a hairline crack in his heart.

Zelrynn wasn't done. Her voice was edged with emotion as she said, "I fear for my own pain. I fear for my sisters. But most of all I fear for you. I fear for your life. I fear far more for your soul. Are you ready to meet God?"

The door opened, and Zelrynn quickly stood up. Vonran looked, and he saw Kereth come in, Colonel Dilv right behind him. Kereth went in front of the desk, where Alexander still held court, and bowed. "My lord, this is Colonel Dilv, the commander of the Emperor's Guard. He has come to witness the transfer of power."

Alexander looked at Dilv, who bowed. "Very good, Colonel. Welcome."

"Thank you, my lord."

Kereth walked over to Vonran. "Regent, everything is prepared for your abdication. Even the Emperor's Guard is ready to assume protection of Emperor Alexander. It is time to end this war—without one more drop of blood being shed."

And by the way Kereth looked at him, Vonran knew Kereth understood what he had thought—that he would be executed. His first instinct—not to trust—flamed up, but it had no strength. All he really felt was the burden of the years—his loss, in one way or another, of friend, daughter, and wife, the ceaseless fighting and calculating, the fatigue and heartache.

For the first time in years, he felt himself yielding.

Chapter

VI

* * * * * * * * * * * * * * * * *

Adesh paced the floor up and down. He didn't mind the fighting and he didn't mind the planning; it was the waiting that always dug beneath his skin. Ziphernan sat calmly at the table, slowly drinking down his wine.

The door drew open, and the captain burst through. "General—"

Adesh looked at him with irritation. "I ordered that no one was to enter."

"I know, sir. But you must see this." The captain hurried to the mounted tactical display and began working its control panel. After a moment, its screen transmogrified to the image of Elymas Vonran. His voice carried through the room: " ... before the Empire to announce to you my abdication."

Adesh cut a glance at Ziphernan, a horrible feeling shooting through him. Vonran's voice went on: "I hereby yield to Emperor Alexander and renounce all claim to authority and obedience. Tonight, as I step down from the regency, I take up, again, the station of private citizen, and I bid you all farewell." For a moment he looked somber and proud, and then the image vanished.

"To the point," Ziphernan muttered.

Adesh looked at the captain. "This was a live broadcast?"

He nodded. "And just before it, all our channels were filled with the written announcement of his abdication. I contacted the other ships, and it was the same with them—"

He was almost breathless with the shock of it all, but Adesh didn't share his surprise in the least. He knew exactly what had happened. It was over. He was over.

All at once the screen shifted again, and this time it was Alexander who appeared. "My people, this day I have assumed my father's throne, as the Ancient Code decrees for the descendants of Alexander the Mighty. I have taken command of all the armies that have been warring in our nation. Their enmity is now ended as they are united under the same banner.

"With the end of the war, I announce the suspension of the War Powers Act. Within seven days it will be completely rescinded throughout the Empire. When those days are over, I will send my officials to all the provinces to ensure that the prefects have repealed the Treason Statutes. As for the military, the generals will re-order it for a time of peace. Many men will be released from service and sent home.

"There are those who have acted to keep me from my throne and therefore are open to the charge of treason. But this is a time for reunion and peace, not recrimination and bloodshed. I am declaring amnesty for all who will swear allegiance to me. Only the few highest men—who led those placed under their command to unfaithfulness—will be held accountable."

The captain watched with rapt attention, but Ziphernan and Adesh looked at each other with concealed anxiety.

Alexander watched as the technicians took their equipment and left. He couldn't yet believe that he was emperor.

Dilv came to attention. "My lord, I request on behalf of my men that you come down and receive their fealty in the Judgment Hall. That has long been the tradition."

Alexander didn't really have to think about it. "Of course, Colonel. Open the Judgment Hall. I will be down momentarily."

Dilv bowed and left. Alexander looked around—and his eyes landed on Elymas Vonran. He was standing to the side, his face so unrevealing it captured Alexander's attention. He gazed at the man he had just displaced and tried to imagine what, behind his mask, he was feeling. Alexander glanced at D'John Ryanson. "Major, I want you to take your men and set up a guard around Vonran. Allow him some freedom, but keep him under watch until he is sent to his new location."

"I would prefer," Vonran said, "a cell without rats, if that can be arranged."

"Set your mind easy," Kereth answered. "Neither death nor imprisonment awaits you."

"Yes," said Kinlol. "The worse you will suffer is banishment to some obscure corner of the Empire."

Vonran looked at him coldly. "You always were a fool at the last, Kinlol."

"It is not by *my* will."

Alexander broke into the conversation: "You deserve to be punished, Vonran. I'm not sparing you for your own sake. Your daughter helped me get the throne, and she asked in return your life and your freedom. I promised her I would give her both, and I will keep my word. You are a thief and a murderer, but you have been protected ... " Alexander looked over at Zelrynn, bringing the attention of the room to her, and he finished, " ... because you did one thing right."

Alexander turned to Kereth and Kinlol. "Let us go." The three left the study and went through the Palace to the Judgment Hall. It had been closed thirteen years before, at Emperor Judah Zebulun's death. Now it was opened for his son. The ornate doors were flung open, and the men passed into the hall.

The men and officers of the Emperor's Guard were already gathered, and they stood at attention as Alexander passed by. He went to the raised dias across the front of the room. Just before the carved and gilded steps he stopped and looked at the throne. It was large, high-backed and with broad armrests. Alexander was acutely aware, at that moment, that no one had sat on that seat for thirteen years, that the last man to sit there had been his father. And his heart was smote again with melancholy longing for the man he barely remembered, the father he had lost before he ever knew.

Alexander walked up the five steps and sat on the throne. All the men in the room—the soldiers, the officers, General Kereth, and Chief Kinlol—knelt before him.

He was emperor.

Zelrynn approached the door to her father's room. She wasn't going to sleep with this between them.

Major Ryanson stood at the door. When she told him she wanted to speak with her father, he gave her a sympathetic look and relayed her request. Zelrynn stood by, a little anxious for the answer, until the major opened the door and stepped aside.

Zelrynn walked in and saw her father standing across the room, his back to her as he gazed out the window. Zelrynn resolutely walked forward but stopped a few paces short of him. He could hear her from here. It was close enough. Zelrynn glanced at the window and saw rain running down it. "It's raining, I see."

He didn't answer, apparently not in the mood for small talk. Well, neither was she. Zelrynn went on, "Alexander and his advisors will be wanting you to leave Telnaria soon. They will not want you living in Traelys, either." There they were—the only two places he had lived since he left his home city. For that city he had never shown even a hint of nostalgia. "Carsytt is probably not too conspicuous, though. You will be able to live near Theseus Declan. If you have any other ideas ... "

He gave no response, and that was Zelrynn's only item of business. She moved to what was really on her mind. "Alexander told you the truth, Father. When I saw that you were determined to get the emperorship by any means necessary, I went to him and offered my help. I told him I would hand you over to him, and in return I demanded that he spare your life and give you your freedom. We made the bargain, and I fulfilled it. So did he."

Zelrynn watched her father, but he didn't even move. Agitation began to creep beneath her skin, and she said, "I'm sorry I had to do it, but I'm not sorry that I did. It was the right thing. You always told me that those who couldn't think for themselves were the worst kind of cripples. You taught me—Mother taught me—that some things are right and some things are wrong. The right things must be done and the wrong things must not be. I thought about everything that was happening, I decided what the right thing was, and I did it." Zelrynn stopped herself. She could have gone on—she wanted to go on—justifying to him what she had done. She wanted to ask him not to fault her for it. But she controlled the impulse. Too many words, too much emotion, and arguments turn to prattle. She heard that thought in her own voice; she realized that they were her father's words.

Zelrynn stared at her father, helpless in the face of his stone impassivity. She glanced behind her at the door and then looked back at her father. She had only one thing left to say. "I know I handed you over to Alexander. I know I engineered your defeat. I know what you lost because of me. I want you to know that, for all that, you are still my father, and nothing can change that. I love you, and I honor you, even if my conscience calls me to a different path." Zelrynn waited, and when the reception to her words was the same as ever, she turned and walked towards the door. But when she reached it she looked back. The strangeness of her father's stillness made her turn again.

She crossed the whole floor this time, coming close enough to him to see his face. And when she did, it stopped her where she stood.

He stood unmoving, gazing out the dark, rain-streaked window, and in complete silence Elymas Vonran was weeping.

Adesh had gotten rid of his captain quickly enough, and then he stood with his back to Ziphernan, facing the wall. His mind ranged over what had happened, and finally he put a thought into words: "I believe I feel sorry for him."

"Don't tell me you've been wasting your thoughts on Vonran," answered Ziphernan. "And if you must get lachrymose, do it over yourself. It might make you productive."

Adesh turned to him. "You are in as bad a position as I am. Worse, in fact. I was never on their side."

"If you're threatening me, come out and say it. I don't have time for verbal plays."

"I am not a charitable man, Ziphernan. I would find a certain satisfaction in you falling with me. But I would find much more in both of us escaping together."

"Now that is a productive thought. As of now, my position with Alexander is intact, because no one but you knows of my betrayal."

Adesh nodded to the fact—and where it was leading. "You save my neck and I'll save yours."

"That is what I call an offer that can't be refused."

Two days had passed for Alexander in a whirl. Kinlol advised him to consolidate his hold on power and then have the coronation, and he did. He advised him to receive all the elite and powerful of Telnaria, accepting their congratulations and homage. Alexander did. Kinlol advised him to order the troops to stand down, and he did.

Then followed an intense debate in Alexander's inner circle as to what to do with Vonran's highest officials. Nemin Ziphernan, hurrying from Regial, argued eloquently that they should be stripped of rank and otherwise treated with mercy. Kereth and Kinlol wanted the worse offenders stripped of their pensions also. Alexander acquiesced.

Evening came on the second day of his reign, and he was tired of acquiescing. Alexander went into the study he had appropriated from Vonran and found his two chief advisors there. Kinlol was still busy and in good spirits. Kereth was relaxed, lounging back in his chair with his feet propped up on the desk. Showing how good his mood was, Kinlol was not even giving Kereth's upraised feet irritated glances.

Alexander walked up to the desk and pulled the chair out. Kereth swung his feet to the ground, and Alexander wanted to tell him not to bother. He had looked comfortable, and his attitude was by far the most superior. But Alexander said nothing. He knew the general; he was not the type of man to prop his feet up on the emperor's desk as he sat at it—not even if he had had a hand in raising the emperor.

Kinlol waited until Alexander was settled at the desk before beginning, “My lord, there is the vital issue of—”

Alexander turned to Kereth and interrupted, “What happened to Major Ryanson?”

Kereth's eyes went from Kinlol to Alexander, and he raised his eyebrows—and Alexander felt fully reproved for his rudeness. “He is returning to Regial, along with Lang and Makis.”

“The other two can go, but I want Major Ryanson to remain here. In fact, I want to see him tonight.”

“I'll arrange it.”

Then—already penitent—Alexander turned back to Kinlol. “What were you saying, Chief?”

“I was bringing up the matter of your Council of Chiefs. With all of Vonran's high officials dismissed, you will have to fill every position.”

Alexander grudgingly turned to business. “I had planned to make you Chief of Justice, General Gaelin commander-in-chief, and Nemin Ziphernan Chief of State. I have no ideas for the rest.”

“You know that many of the Empire's wealthy men pledged their help to you a little while ago. I think you should reward them by making one of their own Chief of Intelligence—or Chief of Commerce, if it suits you.”

Kinlol had taught him long ago about the political uses of the Council of Chiefs. “Very well. Bring me some recommendations.” Alexander paused, and then threw out an idea that just occurred to him. “What about Zach Anderliy?”

“What do you have in mind for him?”

“Chief Counselor.”

Kinlol considered it. “He clerked under Gamaliel before becoming a professor at Ilemor. He was known for being able to ingest large amounts of information in short amounts of time, and then summing it up brilliantly. And he is, in terms of raw intellect, one of the most impressive men in the Empire."

"Because of his upbringing," Kereth said, "he has unusual knowledge—and unusual connections. But, as we have seen, it can come in very useful."

Alexander was startled at how accepting they were of the proposal—and vaguely disappointed. "Then start an inquiry. Find out if he is willing." Alexander glanced at Kereth. "What about you?"

"Me?"

"Do you want to be a Chief? Chief of the Provinces, maybe?"

Kereth seemed to find the idea amusing. "It's a generous offer, and the chance to be on the Council and annoy Kinlol for years on end is appealing. But no. I think I will pass on the opportunity."

"You want to remain a general?" Alexander asked. Whatever post Kereth wanted, he would see that he got it.

"As a matter of fact ... " Kereth glanced between them. "I think I will resign my commission."

Alexander stared. "What?"

"I've been in the military for more than thirty years. I've earned my pension."

"I never thought you were in it for the pension, General."

"No. No, I haven't been. But I have been general, I have been through a war, through exile, through battle, and finally through victory. What's left after that? To spend my time wrangling appropriations for my pet projects? No. I'm ready to move on."

Alexander looked at the general, fascinated. "To what?"

"Civilian, entrepreneur, businessman. Landowner. And more children."

"Does your wife know all this?" Kinlol asked.

"Not yct, but she will be entirely happy. I know my wife, Kinlol. She is arriving with our children in the morning. Now that the war is over, we will discuss our plans, and her first proposal will be to adopt again. But I am going to beat her to it. I am going to ask her what she feels about adopting a baby or two."

He seemed happy, but Alexander felt sadness creeping in.

Kereth was moving on—from him. He fell silent.

Kereth stood up. "By your leave, my lord, I will see to your orders regarding Major Ryanson and then retire."

Alexander nodded, and the general left. Kinlol stood also. "With your permission, I will leave, too. I will have more recommendations for the Council tomorrow."

Then he was also gone. Alexander stood up and circled around the desk. Leaning against its front, he crossed his arms and looked around the room. It was not very appealing to him. Perhaps he should have it re-done.

Alexander gazed at the room, his thoughts roving until they were interrupted by the door's chime. "Enter," he commanded.

The door opened, and D'John Ryanson came in. He approached Alexander and stood at attention. "Reporting as ordered, my lord."

The formality was dismaying. Everyone came to him bowing and saluting. That was not without enjoyment, but it created distance between himself and others that he sometimes regretted. "At ease, Major. I hear you're being sent back to Regial."

"The operation is completed. I have no reason to stay."

"I know. Are you going back home, now that the war is over?"

"My plan right now is to stay in the military."

"I see." Alexander evaluated the major. "I think I would like to have you in my service—my close service."

D'John looked slightly perplexed—and slightly concerned—by that formulation. "It is my honor to serve the emperor, but what use could you have for me ... close?"

Alexander tried to think of an answer for that—and an idea blazed into his mind. He looked at D'John and spoke as if he had always known: "Chief of the Provinces."

He looked dubious. "Chief of the Provinces?"

Yes, and wouldn't that annoy Kinlol? Alexander nodded affirmatively. "You have already acted as my representative to the underground. Now you will be my representative to the prefects, and their representative to me. You will have to live in Telnaria, of course, but the position requires you to travel to every province in the Empire."

"My lord, will the prefects accept a man with my ... qualifications?"

"Major Ryanson, you will be going to them in my authority, not yours. If they reject the man I send to them, they reject me."

"I am honored that you think I deserve such a post, but I'm not qualified. I don't feel prepared."

Alexander was surprised at his resistance. "Major, you wouldn't start before some study and instruction. As for the men who are older, who have been in government longer—they may have more experience, but how many of them sided with me against Vonran?" Alexander watched that sink in, and then he went on, "Only a few. It was men like you who rallied to me—the volunteers, the fighting men. You have proven yourself beyond any of them. You have been my representative, you have advised me, you have been crucial to victories from Tokar to this last operation. You're the only one I have really talked to. You are the one I will reward—for yourself and for them all. Why shouldn't I give you power and a position ahead of men who were less faithful to me?"

That was, Alexander could tell, an effective argument. D'John stood indecisively, and then asked, "Do you mind if I think it over?"

"Of course not. You are free to think it over and decide as you will. I desire you to serve me in this way, but I will not compel you."

"Thank you. May I go?"

"You may."

D'John bowed and left, and Alexander began pacing the room, enlivened over the prospect of D'John Ryanson as a Chief. He wanted him on the Council, and the fact that Kinlol would object strongly made it all the better. His decisions were his own, and he was pleased to make one free of his advisors' consent, free even of their counsel. He was tired of receiving all his options from them. He was ready to strike out in independence.

CCCLXXIII

D'John wandered through the Palace grounds, singing softly to himself. It was an old song, of mining beneath the mountain of Kaldarez.

His mind was on his home. He had been so eager to leave it, so eager to fly, and he still didn't want to go back. After all he had done and seen, how could he go back? He hadn't been happy with being a miner when he had never been anything else. How could he be content in it now?

Though he had never seriously considered going back to Nomu, he had apprehensions about staying in the military. He had joined to fight a war, had worked and risen in a highly unorthodox way, and he wasn't sure he would like being in a conventional military establishment. But, he had reasoned, what else would he do?

Now the emperor had given him an alternative: Chief of the Provinces. And he wasn't sure what to think of it.

D'John stopped singing. He glanced around him. It was a clear night; the stars glinted above him—but smaller by far than the stars he had grown up under. He didn't mind living in this strange city, didn't mind being the emperor's representative. But a worry stuck in his mind—that he was getting into something he didn't fully understand, that he was biting off more than he could chew.

So it would be a challenge. Was it a challenge he was afraid to face?

As D'John turned that question over, seeking the line between wisdom and cowardice, he thought of Alexander's words to him: *I desire you to serve me in this way.* That had been the truth. He had been surprised by how the emperor had urged the position on him. Why did he want D'John so badly? Was he really that eager to reward the common men who fought for him?

There was no way for D'John to know, and he wondered how much it mattered. The emperor had asked for his service, and his reasons were his own. D'John thought of the demand on him. He thought of the place he had grown up; his imagination spooled out visions of a staid military career and the Council of Chiefs.

The unknown future summoned up his spirit of daring, and he slipped towards a decision.

Alexander had just finished dressing when his bedroom's intercom came alive: “My emperor, General Gaelin and his company are here and begging an audience.”

“Send them in.” Alexander stopped at the mirror to adjust his collar, and then he headed towards the lounge that had been designated a receiving room. It was cheery at this hour in the morning, filled with light from the broad eastern windows. Alexander arrived before his visitors. He wandered over and peered out the windows until he heard noise behind him.

Alexander turned to see Gawin Gaelin and his wife Layne. Thaddaeus and Lily entered behind them, and after them—

Alexander stopped, seeing his mother. Then he went to her, bypassing the others. She was smiling, but when he got close Alexander saw that there were tears in her eyes. She hugged him, and Alexander returned the embrace. She held on, and Alexander endured it as long as he could before whispering severely, “Mother.”

She laughed as she stepped back. “There are things you can't deny a mother when she hasn't seen her son in three years. And besides, Alexander, we're among family.”

Alexander glanced around him. Technically that was true, even if he often forgot to think of them that way.

When his eyes reached Gawin Gaelin, the general bowed deeply. “Hail, Emperor.”

He was hailing not only Alexander but his own victory, and Alexander smiled at his joy. “Welcome, General. Are you ready to give up your command in Regial?”

“Ready—but you know I go wherever my service to you requires.”

“You have been long at a hard post, General. But now I have a new place for you—the Council of Chiefs.”

Gaelin's pleasure shone through his expression. “I am honored—and pleased—to accept.”

Alexander wondered why it hadn't been so easy with D'John Ryanson. He turned to his aunt. “It's good to see you again, Aunt Layne.”

She smiled. “And it's good to see you. I am glad to see you take the throne. Nearly twenty years ago my father died; all too soon afterward, my brother died, too. Now you have taken your place at last.” Layne looked towards her sister-in-law, and Mareah smiled at her. They shared a look that was nearly conspiratorial, and Alexander suddenly wondered if his aunt had had an unseen role all along, spurring her husband in his efforts on Alexander's behalf.

Alexander glanced among his family members, and his gaze landed on Thaddaeus. “Are you returning to Telnaria?” he asked.

“Yes.”

“What will you do?”

Thaddaeus' pleasant expression turned, in an instant, a little stiff. “I don't know. It hasn't been decided yet.” His gaze went to his father and quickly came back, but not before Alexander saw a strange edge flit in and out of his eyes.

These family gatherings were more enlightening than he had ever imagined. Alexander took up his responsibility as host and asked, “Have you eaten breakfast yet?”

They hadn't, and the six sat down together and ate. Afterwards the Gaelins left to begin the work of establishing their lives in Telnaria, and Mareah and Alexander were alone. Alexander pushed his glass back and forth on the table for a minute, then brought himself to ask, “Mother, did you hear that I'm engaged?”

“I did.”

That was all. “It's an unusual engagement.”

“Yes, I know. I'm sorry you have to wait so long for her.”

“Mother, do you think I did the right thing?”

“Do you mean right for you or right for her?”

“Both.”

Mareah gazed at him intently, and he became increasingly uncomfortable. “Kinlol urged me to accept,” he said—whether to defend himself or fill in the silence, he wasn't sure. Then, remembering how his mother had always acted about Kinlol, he added, “General Kereth thought I should also.”

“He is a good man,” Mareah said slowly. “And Kinlol is wise as a serpent.”

“Then you approve?”

“I understand. I am surprised, Alexander, that you would ask me.”

“Why?”

“In the first place, because it is too late to be considering the decision. You have given your word. In the second—I thought you had turned from the words of your mother to the counsel of men years ago.”

“Marriage is a—well, it's personal. You are the only person who thinks of me without thinking of the emperor. You're the only one who separates me from the Empire.”

“I'm your mother.” She appeared to think for a long minute. “Since you want to hear, this is what I have to say: Turn your focus to what you will do, not what you have done. If you love her and are good to her, you will do the right thing for her. If she loves you in return, you will have done the right thing for yourself.”

“I can't control that.”

“No, you can't.”

Alexander leaned back, his mind focusing on that truth. After a long moment Mareah spoke again. “Is Elymas Vonran still in Telnaria?”

“No. He and his daughters left for Carsyt. He's going to live in the home of Theseus Declan. Declan is loyal; he will tell us if Vonran starts making mischief again.”

Mareah gazed off. “Mother?” Alexander asked. She looked at him, and he ventured, “Do you have any reason for asking about him? Any story I've never heard?”

She cocked her head, regarding him. “I guess it does no harm to tell you. I nearly married him once.”

Alexander looked at her, appalled. “Mother!”

“He was a different man ten years ago. And you have never thought fairly about him.”

“He—”

Mareah held up her hand, and Alexander fell silent. "I know what he did," she said quietly. "Did you ever care what he was—a gifted man, a loving father, a lonely widower? Kinlol and Kereth had the training of your mind, and they taught you from the beginning to view him as a menace. It is a short trip from seeing a man as a danger to seeing him as an enemy. And you all made it."

A rather unpleasant feeling spread through him at her words. "But, Mother, you let them."

"I know, and I regretted it many times. But I never knew what else to do. I couldn't cosset you for seventeen years and then thrust you into the emperorship. You needed Kinlol's training; you needed Kereth's teaching. You are my son, but you belonged to the Empire, too, and I couldn't save you."

"Save me? From the emperorship? I was born to this."

Mareah looked at him. "Yes. You're right. You were born to be emperor, and to be emperor is a great thing." She smiled at him—but it was a sad smile. "You have become everything you were brought up to be—an emperor, and a man."

Alexander smiled in return, and wished he could take the sadness out of her eyes.

Before he left Telnaria, Vonran spoke to only one person besides his daughters. Garin Dorjan had been unhappy, his words full of regret for lost things. "When you were the premier of the Assembly," he said, "when Theseus was still there, when we were friends and allies and Shevyn was there fighting against us—those were the best days, weren't they?"

Vonran had agreed with him, but he didn't tell him, as they parted, that Dorjan's regret could never match his own.

He took Cala with him. Zelrynn came along, too; she said she wanted to see Theseus Declan. Vonran guessed that she also wanted an opportunity for them to prove to each other that there were no hard feelings.

Declan lived by the sea. He had built a large gray house on the shore. When they arrived Declan was out—but expected, they were told, to return shortly. The girls went to get settled in their rooms. Vonran began to, but soon he was wandering through the house. He and Dianthe used to take the girls and visit Declan here. He walked through the rooms, remembering them as he went. It was architecture to suit Declan—full of open spaces and light streaming through windows. Passing through broad corridors, he came to the back of the house. Vonran let himself out.

Vonran, standing on the verandah, could hear the water pounding on the shore. He breathed in the salty air and stared down at the beach. The waves assaulted the shore, never quite reaching the rocks that rose up out of the sand. They always glistened, by sunlight or moonlight, from the sea-spray. The white and yellow sea-flowers grew up among the rocks. Vonran remembered those flowers. He used to stand guard over his daughters as they clambered over the slippery rocks, picking flowers for their mother. They had a strange scent, salty as the sea.

The memories were still vivid, and the flowers and rocks could have been the same as those he stood by so many years before. His years as regent had rushed by, and his memories of them were blurred in the whirl. But of those slower, older days images and sounds and smells came back to him, fresh and clear.

Vonran blinked quickly, and not from the wind on his face. For a long time he stood fixed, gazing at the sea and the cloud-mottled sky stretched over it. They went on as far as he could see.

He heard a soft sound behind, a door opening and someone quietly stepping out. There was a brief lull, and then faint footsteps crossed over to him. A hand laid gently on his shoulder.

For a long moment Vonran stood, the hand resting lightly on his shoulder. At last he spoke. "There is no redemption."

The hand lifted, and Vonran slowly turned to face Theseus Declan. He searched the blue eyes for any hint of reproach, and to his surprise there was nothing but tenderness. "You are wrong there, Elymas," he said, his voice so gentle it competed with the ocean. "There is redemption, and you are closer than you have ever been."

After all he'd done? "How?" he asked.

"Because for the first time you know you need it."

Vonran looked back at the sea, endlessly sweeping and receding. Then he looked out, beyond the froth and crashing of the waves, and saw the tranquility of the far sea.

Peace. Eternity. He was ready to learn. He was ready to turn away from the world and find out.

He was ready, after fourteen years, to sweep away the ruins and the sand, and find the rock.

The coronation of an emperor was always accompanied by festivities throughout the Empire. All Telnaria turned out to celebrate, and the city teemed with sojourners to the emperor's coronation. That was why, the night before, Kereth arranged a smaller celebration. He invited only those who had been closely involved in the fight for Alexander, along with their families. Kavin Gyas and Trey Uman were at the top of his list, and they arrived with their wives and various descendants. Zach Anderliy had come to Telnaria to take his seat on the Council, and Kereth persuaded him that coming was a good idea. Then—on an impulse that was at least in part morbid interest—he invited Phillip and Anice Anderliy.

That night Kereth and Susanne danced until they were almost breathless. Then they retired to the refreshment table. Kereth had given Susanne her drink and was just about to pour his own when she nudged him. "Look."

He turned. "What—"

"Kinlol."

Kereth's eyes found him. He was sitting alone against the wall. "He's been sitting like that all night," Susanne said.

"You've been watching him?"

"You've been watching Zach Anderliy."

"That's different. I talked him into coming. I feel a little responsible."

"Well, he's all right now. But look at Kinlol. He ought to be happy, but he isn't acting like it. I think he needs a friend to talk with him."

"That's a good idea. Do you know where we can find one?"

"Now, Adon."

"What makes him my friend?"

"Thirteen years in the trenches."

"You're good." Kereth glanced over. "I suppose I ought to." He filled up the cup in his hand and made his way over to Kinlol. Kereth settled on an armless chair by Kinlol and raised his glass.

Kinlol's eyes took in the gesture of victory, and did not so much as flicker in reaction. "Where have you been today?"

"Family—and this."

Kinlol gestured across the room. "Do you see that?"

Kereth looked and saw D'John Ryanson and Zach Anderliy having what appeared to be a friendly and largely one-sided conversation. "It's a good thing," he said.

Kinlol's brow furrowed. "What do you mean?"

The question threw Kereth off. He had talked with D'John earlier and learned that his family wasn't able to come, and he had seen his regret. As for Zach, his parents did come, and created a minor spectacle. They were used to their fame, and all evening long they spoke to whoever came to them, standing so close to each other it was a declaration of their relationship. Everyone gravitated towards them—except their son. He gravitated to the wall and watched the goings-on, thinking and day-dreaming the night away. It had been painful for Kereth to see, and he had been relieved and even grateful when D'John began keeping Zach company. He had a feeling that his kindness would benefit them both in the end.

It was all too much to say. Kereth turned his head slightly in Kinlol's direction, knowing he was waiting for him to speak. "What do you mean?" he asked.

Kinlol looked over at the young men and sighed. "He has put boys on the Council. Now they will be my peers, equal in rank and status."

Kereth laughed out loud. "That's it? Tomorrow is Alexander's coronation; Vonran is in exile. The house of Alheenan is restored to the emperorship and you are restored to the Council—and you are feeling sorry for yourself because there are young men on the Council. Cheer up. Why ruin a joyful occasion with self-pity?"

Kinlol looked at him sourly, and Kereth found it motivation to go on. “You found Anderliy tolerable. At least you didn't protest. You protested Ryanson to the emperor, didn't you?”

Kinlol nodded. “Alexander told me that if age was the issue, it should be remembered that he is years younger than Ryanson.”

Kereth laughed. “Sound familiar?” He looked at Kinlol, perceived his unhappiness, and said, “Come now. You never thought Alexander would ignore his own generation—that he would surround himself exclusively with men as old as his father?”

Kinlol looked irritated with the lack of sympathy. “You are still the man you were when I recruited you. You are still a hard-edged fighting man, insolent and maladroit.”

“And you,” Kereth returned, “are a sour old curmudgeon.”

For a few minutes they sat in companionable silence. Kinlol broke it. “All the same, we did well together,” he said, his tone thoughtful.

Kereth's eyes combed the room—Alexander speaking to Trey Uman with poise and command, Thaddaeus dancing with Lily, Gawin Gaelin talking to Kavin Gyas, Mareah, Layne and Susanne clustered together. And he saw his own children, Zach, D'John, Nemin Ziphernan—everyone had come. Kereth looked back at Kinlol. “We won, didn't we?”

The End

ALSO FROM SALT CHRISTIAN PRESS:

SALT MAGAZINE

You'll get compelling discussion of relevant and sometimes controversial topics, uplifting and encouraging articles, practical advice, and witty, humorous attempts at self-promotion. Topics include Christian marriage, parenting, courtship, education, homeschooling, politics, and inspiration.

Get 12 issues of the best magazine this side of Kansas Expressway for only $24 (No Shipping Charge).

THE CHRISTIAN FAMILY: In the world, but not of it

Encouragement and short essays on the topics most relevant to the Christian family, as well as moving, inspirational, personal, and sometimes humorous essays on wife & motherhood, the near death of a daughter, a son's graduation, new babies, losing socks, and family 'vacations'. Lisa Barthuly of "The Old Schoolhouse" writes, "I love the honesty in the essays, and the insight and wisdom the McDermotts share. This book will make you laugh, make you cry and make you THINK. It covers many controversial issues. . .and points to God's Word for answers. . . Is an easy read. You will want to read it cover to cover! This is a MUST read for the Christian Family, my very highest recommendation!" Costs $14.99 plus shipping.

THE TRUTH ABOUT SEX:

THE MYSTERY OF THE COVENANT – TILL DEATH DO US PART

Beautifully written by author Terri Cooney, this booklet reveals the spiritual basis for the physical relationship between man and woman that should, when understood, give married couples a sense of awe and Christian singles greater motivation to remain pure. Great for married couples or anyone looking to marry. Only $1.99 plus shipping.

*Shipping $2.50 per order no matter how many items ordered!

SALT Christian Press, 2131 W. Republic Rd. #177, Springfield, MO 65807. saltchristianpress.com.